YOU CAN SAVE ME

CARNIVAL OF MYSTERIES

BOOK TWO

R.L. MERRILL

CELIE BAY PUBLICATIONS LLC

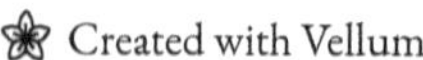 Created with Vellum

YOU CAN SAVE ME: CARNIVAL OF MYSTERIES (BOOK TWO)

Blurb:

Folk rock singer Dane Donovan vanished from a desolate highway rest area in 1979. Forty years later, he's found hitch-hiking in the California desert on a cold winter's night. He hasn't aged a day, but the road map of scars he wears tells a chilling tale.

Veteran detective Walter Muse took over Dane's missing persons case twenty years ago, but his haunting connection to Dane Donovan goes back to a peculiar run-in as a child with The Troubadour and his Talking Board at a traveling carnival. He receives a late-night call with Dane's whereabouts and races to Laurel Canyon to see for himself whether Dane is real —or a ghost meant to taunt Walter and his somewhat precarious hold on his sanity. Walter's carefully honed detective instincts are thrown out the window, however, when his obsession with the case develops into an undeniable attraction to the mysterious singer.

Dane is on a mission to stop a new killer hell-bent on picking up where Dane's kidnapper left off, and Walter is determined to protect him, no matter the personal and psychological cost. They'll have to rely on new friends and trusted colleagues—as well as the power of a mystical spirit board—to stop the killing, and have a chance at a real future together.

ONE

D^{ane}

December 2019

You can get lost
*   You can be found*
*   You can exist underground*

You can bring joy
*   You can cause pain*
*   You can start your life all over again*

You can do magic
*   You can stop evil*

You can run like mad from the devil

But you can't change your soul
You can't change your fate
And you can't escape from the mess you create

Only you can know
What I see
Only you can save me

On a dark desert highway somewhere in California, I walked alone on the dusty shoulder with a borrowed acoustic guitar strapped to my back and my sole possession tucked under my arm in a brown paper bag. I shivered as though evil was breathing down my neck, when in reality, I was the one in pursuit. The sky had a purplish hue with some storm clouds off to the north but directly above me, the stars flickered in a surreal dance.

I walked with purpose, and it was a very important one.

I'm the only one who can stop him.

I passed a sign that said Highway 58 to Mojave, and I pulled my salvaged coat tighter around my scrawny self. The ground was warm beneath my tattered boots, but the air bit into my skin like an icy monster gnashing its teeth, hungry.

I turned to look behind me and spotted headlights coming my way. It had been at least an hour since another car had passed. I stuck out my thumb, hoping they'd stop. The boots I wore were also borrowed, as were my clothes and hat. I chose them because they were the only ones in the carnival storage that were the right size and fit.

I had only one memory from before I'd started working

with the traveling carnival, and it was awful enough to make your blood run cold.

The lights hurt my eyes, and my energy flagged, but I kept my thumb out. I had something important to do, and if this car didn't slow down, I'd keep going until the next one came. Someone had to stop. How else did people get anywhere if not for thumb power?

The headlights grew nearer and were impossibly bright. I had to cover my eyes briefly as I was nearly blinded. I heard the crunch of gravel as the vehicle pulled over and coughed at the cloud of dust that rose. A door opened and a male voice called out.

"Hey, man. What are you doing out here?"

The bright lights faded and only the yellow ones down low on the front of what I gathered was a pickup truck were left on. It was a massive thing, jacked up high, with big tires and a shiny chrome grill.

What does it look like I'm doing? The large concrete sign with the strange name loomed in my consciousness, and though every cell in my body struggled against my purpose, I stood tall and called back, "Need a ride. To Buttonwillow."

The truck door closed, and I saw the man's shape pass in front of the dim lights. What was he doing getting out of his ride? I backed up a step, trying to play it cool. He wasn't the person I was worried about.

Then the passenger door opened, and a much larger man got out.

"Ryan, don't."

There were two of them. I didn't like my odds, but I had no choice. I had to get there. I had to stop...

"Forget it man, I'll walk."

"Wait, come back. You can't walk that far. That's, like, almost a hundred miles away."

The driver came closer, but the big man stepped in

between us. I reached for the guitar on my back. Maybe I could whack him with it and run away. I was pretty fast.

"Do you have any weapons?" Then the passenger barked an order at me. "Let me see under your jacket."

"Come on, man. I just need a ride. I don't have anything."

The driver pushed past him. "Kal, it's okay. Hey, kid, what's your name?"

"Dee Dee."

The driver held his hand out, and I shook it. "Dee Dee, I'm Ryan, and this is my husband, Kal. *Damn*," he said, letting go of my hand and slapping his together, the loud crack making me jump. "I love saying that." He turned and smiled at the large man, whose scowl seemed to lessen the slightest bit. "We just got married in Vegas." He held up a hand and the light flashed off of his wedding band.

"Congratulations?" It came out like the question it was. How were they married? Two men? Guess they really do let anything happen in Las Vegas.

"Where'd you come from?" Kal asked, standing next to Ryan as if to protect him from me. Not sure I'd ever been seen as a threat to anyone, but I didn't blame him for being cautious. Wish I'd had someone to look after *me* like that.

"Back that way. Was working at a carnival, and I needed to—"

Ryan put a hand on my chest and his eyes went wide. "Did you say carnival? Like, 'Welcome, Traveler' carnival?"

"How'd you know?" I tried to step back and my heel caught on a rock. I was about to go down, but Kal caught me —and then I was caught up in his gaze.

"I came from there, too," Kal said.

And then I heard it. In my mind. Calliope music.

I'd never gone to see it. I hadn't done much exploring. I'd only gone from my trailer to my booth and back for however long I'd been employed there. Didn't seem long, but then, time did weird things at the carnival.

"The Troubadour's Talking Board," Kal said. He gripped my arm a little tighter as he brought me back up to standing. "The booth in the arcade. I know you."

"That's right. That's me. Well, it was. I left. Got something I gotta do."

Ryan grabbed Kal's arm. "The promise. Babe, we have to help him."

Kal continued to stare down at me, and though he seemed good—the big man oozed honor from his pores—he was a scary guy. His hand could have wrapped around my bicep twice. Or my throat. He looked from Ryan to me, and then he let go of my arm.

"We shall help you along your path."

Seemed like a strange way of saying "sure, we'll give you a ride," but I'd take it.

"Thank you."

Ryan gestured to the truck. "Hop in."

Kal remained at my side and when we reached the cab, he opened the front of two doors. I'd never seen a pickup with two sets of doors before. This thing was unreal.

"You ride up here," Kal said, taking the guitar from me. "I'll be right behind you. If you hurt my husband, I will hurt *you*."

"God, Kal. That's hot, but babe, don't scare the kid. We promised we'd help him."

"Promised who?" I asked as I climbed into the tall pickup. "And I'm not a kid."

Kal shut my door after I sat, and then he climbed in. I turned my back to the door. I didn't like having him behind me. Didn't like anyone at my back, especially after what had happened to land me at the carnival in the first place.

"I think you know," Kal said as Ryan started the pickup.

"Ryan and I are married because someone else made a promise to help us on *our* path. Ryan made a promise to Mr. Ame. Now we will do the same for you."

I'd known cats who lived together, maybe even called themselves husbands, but marriage couldn't happen between homosexuals. This was all too much. It was like I'd left one odd place and wound up in another.

But what he said about promises put my purpose front and center in my mind.

I sighed and turned just a bit, still able to see Kal out of the corner of my eye as he sat in the middle of the backseat. He rested a hand on the seat behind Ryan's shoulder, his fingers tangling in the man's shoulder-length copper hair.

"Thank you for stopping," I said before I let my eyes drift closed. I needed to rest. I would need my strength when we arrived.

"What's in Buttonwillow?" I heard Kal ask Ryan.

"All I know about it is there's a pair of rest stops on either side of the highway. Creepy-ass place. Every time I stop there, I'm sure a murderer is going to jump out of the bushes."

You don't know how right you are.

As I drifted off, my last customer of the night came back to me...

A few hours before...

"Busier night than usual."

Pokey leaned against the wall separating our booths and flicked his toothpick between his teeth as he attempted to make conversation.

I'd shared a trailer with him since I arrived at the carnival, whenever that was, and he frequently complained about the few times I was able to scrounge a cigarette—said it was a nasty habit, that it smelled foul. I was so tempted to make a comment about how it was hypocritical to bellyache about *my* vices when he had that nasty piece of wood in his mouth all day, but I was trying to be the bigger person, and Pokey had looked after me ever since I could remember, which wasn't very long. He was a good enough guy.

"Sure is. My brain is like mush by now." I picked up the guitar—playing helped clear my mind—and had my back to the carnival, just picking at the strings. Another one had broken earlier so I was down to three. The challenge of playing melodies like this was good for me.

Most days, I had maybe five or six customers, but today I'd had double that and only gotten a second to breathe the past few minutes. Thankfully, it was almost closing time. I'd worked my magic and made people happy with my words, or at least the words that had come to me, through me, through the board from... somewhere.

"You the poet guy?"

I turned and found a twitchy man standing before my booth. He was ordinary-looking, in light blue jeans and a gray t-shirt, his black hair cut short, his bright blue eyes shiny, his smile wide. He rested his hands on the lip of the booth and tapped his fingers.

He took my breath away, only it wasn't in the way folks wrote love songs about. This was like the crushing weight of a knee to the chest, a garrote around the neck being pulled by strong arms, or a plastic bag pulled tight over your head.

Why those specific images came to me, so vividly, I had no idea.

"I'm the poet guy," I finally said, gripping the lip of my work table in my hands. He was a mere three feet away, and his abrasive energy washed over me and left a metallic taste in my mouth. Like iron.

Pokey turned away from his goldfish and leaned a bit more over the wall between our booths. He watched the stranger intently, as did the fish. They weren't like any fish I'd ever seen, creepy little buggers. I supposed since he was the one who'd apparently brought me into the carnival, Pokey felt the need to protect me? Normally it bugged me a bit, but tonight his presence was welcome.

"So how do we get started?" The young man pulled out his wallet and held it open to show off a thick wad of bills. "I've got money. You gonna use your board?"

He had a lot of cash for a guy dressed so plainly. Something told me it might not all belong to him.

"Well," I rubbed my hands together, "we're kind of wrapping up for the night—"

"Oh, come on. I came by several times and you always had a line. I just want a poem from the... Troubadour. That's you, ain't it? Come on. Use your talking board. Write me a poem."

His smile was too wide, like the corners of his mouth pulled out so far it looked painful. His teeth were clenched in his mouth, and he was way more excited than he should have been about a silly poem.

There was something *wrong* about him, and I couldn't put my finger on it, but I knew he shouldn't be here.

Maybe I could just make something up. I could leave the board out of it. I wished I had rhymes inside my head. I *felt* like I should have them—used to have them—but something kept them from me. I wouldn't even have to ask him a question if I could do it myself. He couldn't contaminate me with whatever darkness he was carrying if I didn't—

"Ain't you supposed to ask me for my question? I watched you do it with some people before. You ask for their question and then they tell you. I want you to ask me for my question." He'd pressed himself up against the front of my booth, and his belt buckle kept scratching against the wood, the sound like fingernails on a chalkboard. My teeth hurt at the sound and ringing started in my ear.

"Right, right," I said, rubbing my jaw. "A question. You gotta know, though, you may not get the kinda answer you think. Sometimes—"

"You're not talking me out of this. I've been waiting all day. He told me I'd find you here, so let's get going." He rubbed his hands together and the sight turned my stomach. Once more, I found myself fighting for air.

I cleared my throat and ignored the blackness creeping in around my vision. I cracked my knuckles and gazed up at the guy. He was built a bit bigger than me but was still slim, and only a few inches taller than my 5'7". He licked his lips and that smile stretched even farther. The guy was giddy. I had half a mind to make up some excuse. I wished for an interruption. Anything to not touch the planchette.

"Come on! Carnival's gonna close soon."

His smile slipped a little and his upper lip curled. The scar on my face began to itch, but I resisted the urge to scratch it.

"All right then. What's your question?"

His beady, soulless eyes flared and he licked his lips. "I wanna know how you got here."

I frowned. *What an odd question?* I blew out a breath and placed my fingers gingerly on the planchette.

The blackness creeped a little closer, sending cold spikes up and down my neck. I sucked in a breath and saw the swirl of words coming toward me.

"What do you see?" His words broke through, sending waves through the vision like disturbing a still body of water. I was about to reprimand him when his arms shot out and he planted his hands on the planchette, plummeting us both into the blackness.

On a dark night
  In a dark place

Stood the man
With the nothing face
He smiled but you recoiled
He gestured but you retreated
His smile faded
With the curl of a lip
He reached out
And grabbed your hip
He tugged and you resisted
He snarled and you receded
But he was strong
And you were weak
And the drugs you'd taken
Had passed their peak
He tackled and you reacted
He threatened and you reconciled
Just stay calm
Let him win
And when his weight shifts
The struggle will begin
He drags and you reach
Stomps on your groin and you retch
You scream
He kicks
You roll
He binds
You lash out
He growls
You plead
He strangles
You gasp
He laughs
You slip
"You shouldn't have come

You're here, let's have fun
But now you'll suffer
Before I'm done"
And suffer
Suffer
Suffer
Suffer
Endless suffering endured
Pain
Cold
Tears
Blood
Under the moon
In the dark sky
A light appears
Stinging your eye
He sees and curses
He slices your thigh
"I'll see you again"
And he flees

It took everything I had to push away from the rushing darkness, but when I could finally lift my hands, he was there. The twitchy man.

That sinister smile.

"I'll see you again." He chuckled quietly as he let go of the planchette and backed away slowly, his smile growing impossibly wider. So many teeth he had. "I'll see you again," he whispered.

Nik, the carnival's engineer, grabbed the stranger's arm. "It's time for you to leave."

The creep's entire face changed. It went soft, and he became compliant. "Sure, sure. Hey, thank you, Mr.

Troubadour." He waved like nothing awful had just happened.

Pokey's heavy hand fell on my shoulder, and I jumped. When had he come into my booth?

"I came over when I saw him touch your board. You all right?"

I brought a shaky hand up to my throat, touched my face, and took a deep breath. "Yeah. I need to quit for the night." I shook out my hands and spit on the ground, wanting the taste of blood out of my mouth. My body ached for no reason, or maybe it was like when you had a really vivid dream and when you woke up, you felt like you'd been wrestling with a demon or something.

"You should tell Mr. Ame what happened."

"I suppose, though I think he must've known since Nik showed up." I closed up my booth, which didn't involve much. I took my board with me. I knew it belonged to me, that there was some history with it, and I suppose for that reason I wanted to keep it with me. Didn't want to chance it getting misplaced, although theft didn't occur here at the carnival. Neither did any sort of wrongdoing. Nah, what just happened came from my twisted mind. He'd been a catalyst of some sort though, because I was now in possession of this memory, this awful thing that had happened.

Lucky me.

Two

alter

1982

"Mama? What's a true bay door?"

I stood in front of a carnival booth holding my mother's hand, staring up at the sign—The Troubadour's Talking Board.

"Like a singer or a storyteller, I think."

"Mama, what's a talking board?"

Mom kept looking around for Dad. He'd said he was going to get me some cotton candy, but he'd been gone for a while. She had a tight hold on my hand and a crinkle on her forehead.

"I don't know," she said, looking puzzled. "Maybe like a Ouija board?"

A man stood across from the booth, leaning against a fence post, smoking a cigarette. He had the prettiest sea-foam green eyes I'd ever seen, and his dark blond hair was long, past his shoulders, kinda like Dad's brother, Uncle Butch, had when they were teenagers. Dad and his other brother, Uncle Herman, had complained about it constantly, as they were both Marines and hated to see a Muse man not meeting the grooming standard.

The green-eyed man strolled closer to us, flicking his cigarette on the ground. I couldn't stop staring at him and the big scar he had on his cheekbone. He must have noticed, because he put a hand over it.

"Some folks call it that, but this one is special. You're welcome to come on over and ask a question. Whatever you want to ask. Your answer will be in the form of the prettiest poem I can possibly compose for you."

I looked up at Mom with my best puppy dog eyes. "Can we please? I want a poem of my very own."

Mom glanced around, looking for Dad once more. She had a hard time resisting me.

The beautiful man stepped inside the booth and perched up on a stool.

"Just for a minute," she said, smiling down at me. Mom had been extra patient and generous with me lately. I thought it was because I was double digits now, but maybe it was because Dad was struggling to hang on to himself these days.

The pretty man cracked his knuckles and gestured to the table before him that held a board with letters and numbers on it. He had a small piece of wood on top that had a hole at the point. Next to that was an old-timey typewriter, and a tin cup full of colored pencils.

"This is my talking board. Have you seen one before?"

I shook my head. "What does it do?"

He smiled at me like he was telling me a secret, and he leaned a little closer. It was the first time I ever felt funny in my tummy talking to someone. "It's like a gateway to all of the answers in the universe. It gives me the words I need to write your poem. Now, you can ask me a question and we'll see what message comes through the aether."

That gave me a little worry, like the other night when I came out of my bedroom and Dad was watching a scary movie about a little girl who got sucked into a TV. I didn't sleep the whole rest of the weekend after that. I looked up at Mom. I didn't want her to know I was scared because then she wouldn't let me take my turn.

"Mom, how 'bout you go first."

Mom smiled and sighed. "Okay. How about... how old is this carnival? It sure seems... dated." Her gaze traveled to the end of the arcade, where a cart full of balloons was being pushed by a man in a clown costume that wasn't much more than tatters.

"Now that's a clever question. Let me consult the talking board."

The pretty man placed his fingertips on the piece of wood and he focused his gaze on the clear glass hole. His eyes went kinda spacy for a moment and then he sat back and smiled at me. He turned to the typewriter and his fingers tapped the keys pretty quick for a man. I'd only seen Mom type that fast before. He pulled a small white card out of the roller, picked up a purple pencil, scribbled on the paper, and then handed it to Mom.

She read it and smiled, then she handed it to me.

Older than time
  Sooner than now
  Longer than life
  Farther than near
  Where it's needed
  When it's required

Always on schedule
Perpetually on time.

"Well," Mom said to the man with a nervous laugh. "I guess that's an answer."

"What does it mean, though?" I asked them both. It reminded me of a poem my teacher made me read in front of the class once. I hadn't known what that meant, either, and when I told her that, the whole class laughed at me.

"What do you think it means?" the man asked.

I thought hard for a moment, my belly flipping around. Please don't let him laugh at me. "Maybe it's whatever it needs to be?"

"I like the sound of that," he said, and he smiled that sneaky smile again. "Now, what would you like to ask?"

I had so many questions for him. He seemed sad, but he was so pretty, and it seemed to me that Dad had once said "pretty people don't have problems." He did seem out of place here amongst all the corny acts and games, so that's what I asked. "What kind of a place is this carnival?" I'd been ambivalent about coming when Mom told me where we were going, but ever since we'd stepped through the gateway that said "Welcome, Traveler," my curiosity was close to overflowing. I had so many questions, but I was sort of stupefied by the pretty man, so that was the best I could come up with.

He lost his smile a bit and cleared his throat. "Okay. Coming right up." He laced his fingers together and cracked his knuckles, sucked in a breath and squeezed his eyes shut before putting his hands back on the wood piece.

He jolted on the stool and stumbled back, falling on his bottom.

"Oh! Are you all right?" Mom leaned over his booth, her eyes wide.

He held up a hand and chuckled. "Not to worry. Just a little light-headed." He tried to play it off, but he looked spooked, sorta like I probably had after I'd watched that little girl get sucked into the TV.

Mom pulled me closer to her. "Honey, maybe we should leave mister...?"

"Dee Dee. Just Dee Dee. And I'll have your poem ready for you in a jiffy."

He stood and brushed off his pants before he placed his fingers on the typewriter keys. He pulled his hands back, wiggled his fingers, and cracked his knuckles again.

When he finished, he spent a little longer with the pencils before he handed me the card.

Here, there, any old where
   Exists a carnival without a care
   Behold, beware, a wild grizzly bear
   A place where creatures frolic and dare
   Welcome children, come and share
   A magic, a wonder, a splendid affair
   Your luck, your skill, or a wild sort of hair
   Make your own way at this mystical fair
   And when you leave for places elsewhere
   So does the wondrous carnival, without a care

"Your very own carnival poem. I hope you'll treasure it always."

I clutched it to my chest and nodded. I'd never had anything so special in my life, but I also didn't want to act like a goober. I handed it to Mom.

"Take care of this for me, please?"

"What are you two up to?" Dad put his hand on my

shoulder, and then he looked at Dee Dee the Troubadour—and he turned white as a sheet. "You."

Dee Dee smiled at him, glanced at me, and then looked back at Dad. "I'm the Troubadour. Care to ask a question, sir?"

Dad gripped my shoulder tight and pulled me back from the booth. "You! You're... you're him. I saw you. You..."

"Walter! Come on, let's go." Mom dragged me away with one hand and pushed Dad's chest with the other.

I looked back at Dee Dee. He was watching us leave with a confused look on his face.

2019

My phone buzzed on my nightstand, pulling me out of that unwelcome memory, and I thought at first I'd forgotten to turn off my alarm. Then I realized it was still dark.

God, I hadn't thought about that trip to the carnival in ages. It had ended with Dad having one of his episodes outside the carnival gates, and the day that had started off so great turned into a real downer. *Why the hell was I dreaming about that?*

I picked up my phone and squinted at the screen.

Caught a case. I know you're off today and headed out on vacation soon, but you might want to come out.

My buddy Dax worked opposite my day shift. I'd been his training officer at the Kern County Sheriff's Department and eventually trained him as a detective. Why on earth would he ask me to come out? Unless...

I'm at Buttonwillow.

That was why. Because in a few hours, I would have been waking up on the one day every year that I'd grown to dread, and I'd drive the hundred miles to Los Angeles like I had every year since I'd become a detective and taken over the seemingly unsolvable case.

It was 4:30 a.m. Guess the worst day of the year would start a little earlier this time.

Be there ASAP.

I took the fastest shower in history, hoping the noise from the water didn't wake Mom. She was still recovering from her hip surgery. She was mobile, thankfully, and could be left alone for a little while, but she needed her rest. Her caregiver, Kathleen, would be here at six like we'd agreed, to fix her breakfast and handle her medications for the day. She was also set to stay with Mom for the next week.

I was dressed and writing a note in the kitchen fifteen minutes later when I heard her door squeak and the shuffle of her slippers in the hall.

"Walter? Is everything okay?"

"Hey, Mom. Sorry I woke you. I got called out."

She sighed and tilted her head to the side. "On an already long day. I'm sorry, son."

I gave her a hug and a kiss on the cheek. Normally we lived like roommates, doing our own thing and enjoying the bits of time we snagged to spend together. She was an active senior, and I hoped she'd be right back to it when she'd healed from surgery. Me? I was a divorced dad of college kids and an accused workaholic.

"Can I get you anything? You should go back to bed and get some more sleep. Kathleen will be here at six."

She reached up and cupped my jaw. "Your father would be so proud of you."

I frowned a little. We didn't talk about Dad much anymore.

"I know. I love you. Get some rest. I'll keep you posted on what I decide to do with this *vacation.*" I waited while she used the bathroom and then helped her back to bed. I refilled her water glass and kissed her on the forehead. She grabbed for my hand as I stood.

"You need this vacation, honey. Between working yourself to the bone and looking after me..."

"Mom—"

"I know, I know. When will you be back?"

I groaned, and she chuckled again, though her eyes were closing.

"I've got seven days off. I don't know, I may stick around and do some things around the house."

"Take your time off *away* from here, son. And tell Mrs. Donovan I'm thinking of her today."

"I will."

The drive to the rest stop in Buttonwillow took thirty minutes, and when I arrived there were CHP and Kern County cruisers all over the parking lot. Uniforms were talking to two truck drivers outside their cabs and the K-9 units were checking the perimeter with flashlights. Floodlights had been set up, and detectives stood below a permanent light post, swatting at bugs as they talked.

I parked my blue Tacoma next to Dax's silver Explorer and got out, tucking my tie inside my suit coat. The only other vehicles were a beat up minivan and a big jacked up four-by-four.

"Hey, man," he said as I found him in the melee. He grabbed my shoulder with one hand and shook my hand with the other. "Sorry, but I thought you'd want to see this."

"Vic found?"

He gave me a hard look and nodded his head. "Out back. Follow me."

We made our way around the back of the men's room, where we were met with caution tape. Crime scene techs were still taking pictures of a blood-soaked lump propped up against a tin garbage can. I couldn't make out the words but there was writing on the can. In red.

"White male, early twenties or maybe even late teens, clothes missing, hands bound with duct tape. Femoral artery cut, probable cause of death blood loss, lacerations to the face. Victim's blood was used to write on the can."

"What does it say?"

Dax cleared his throat and rubbed his chin.

"What?" I asked again.

"'I'll C U Again DD'."

I swallowed back bile and bit down on my tongue hard enough to taste blood.

"It's been forty years, Walter. How the fuck—"

"I know." I was well aware of what day this was, how many years it had been.

"Any other similarities?"

"Kid had the same hair color, similar build, was traveling with some buddies. They thought he was having intestinal distress or something, so they didn't worry until he'd been gone like twenty, thirty minutes. They were sitting in the car listening to music, didn't hear a thing. They didn't think anything was wrong until all the patrol cars rolled in."

"That it?"

Dax blew out a breath. "Another guy called it in." He gestured with his chin toward the big black truck with three men standing beside it, talking to a CHP officer. "Blond guy with the hat found the victim. He said he saw the killer run off. Says he checked the vic for a pulse, then ran back to his friends' truck, and they called. He had blood on the hand he said he touched the body with but nowhere else, which isn't consistent with the struggle that must have gone on, though he could have changed clothes. None of the truckers saw anything or remember seeing any cars leaving. Suspect can't have gotten too far on foot. Could have had an off-road vehicle stashed on one of these dirt roads, though."

I nodded.

"I'm sorry, Walter." Dax understood better than most at the department why this day, this case, held such significance for me. He walked with me to my vehicle, which was parked a ways down from the black truck.

"Thanks for calling me. You need me to stick around?"

"Nah, we're tight here. Just wanted you to... I don't know..."

Dax had been on his own as a detective for the past year and a half, but he was young and he still asked for my opinion. Since we didn't get many brutal murders like this, he hadn't had a lot of experience. I trusted him, though. And I knew if he needed anything, our two compadres would help him out.

I wanted to walk the crime scene, but I didn't want to step on his toes. I knew he was good—he knew what to do.

"You'll call if you get anything else? I'll be on the road for the next couple hours."

"Will do. Hey, at least there should be less traffic at this hour."

I snorted. "I'll have time for coffee and a donut like a good little cop."

We shook hands, and I was about to climb into my truck when the CHP officer trotted over to us.

"Detective? Can I let these guys go?"

"Sure. Here..." Dax reached into his pockets and came up empty-handed. "Hey, Walt, you got any business cards?" His guilty grin was fleeting. I would never give him shit in front of another cop for running out, but I'd razz him later.

"Yeah, yeah." I dug in my blazer pocket, pulled out my card case and handed him one. As the paper exchanged hands, I glanced over at the truck—and had immediate tunnel vision when the smallest of the three men, the one with the long blond hair, turned to look in our direction.

He was slight, dressed in funny clothes, like some sort of corduroy bell bottoms over ratty boots, a flat-brimmed brown hat, brown vest... He stood staring after the CHP officer, and then our gazes locked.

Forty years.

"Make sure you give me copies of their interview cards?" Dax asked the CHP officer, but I barely heard him. Something about the guy in the hat had me enthralled. As the CHP officer walked back toward them, I put a hand on Dax's shoulder.

That face.

I know that face.

My dream. The poet.

The prettiest man I'd ever seen.

But that wasn't all...

The case files.

It can't be. My brain was so overtaxed, it was mixing the two faces together. There was no way.

This guy's hair was hanging in his face, but as the CHP officer approached and handed him the card, he flipped his hair back.

He had a massive scar down his cheekbone.

"Walter? You all right? You look like you've seen a ghost."

"You see him? Over there?"

"What, you mean the one talking to CHP? Yeah? What—"

"You *see* him?" I balled up Dax's shirt in my fist. "You see him, right? I'm not seeing things."

I'm not my father.

"What the fuck, Walt? You all right man?"

My gut bottomed out. *What's the matter with me?* There was no way I could even give voice to my thoughts—

They'll think you're just like him.

"Detective?" A tech stood watching us, like he didn't want to interrupt. "The crime scene is done and the coroner is ready to take the body."

Dax pulled out of my grip and shot me another funny look. "I'll be right there. Walt? You going to hit the road? Call me when you get back from LA."

I couldn't stop staring at the young man. He'd climbed back into the truck and was talking to the guy in the driver's seat, but his gaze returned to mine.

That face. *A fucking ghost is right.*

Dane Donovan had disappeared on this day in 1979, from this exact spot. He'd been twenty-seven years old. This kid barely looked worn around the edges, but the resemblance was...

His eyes flared as he realized I was staring at him. He said something to the driver, who backed out and then followed the directions of the CHP out toward the highway.

It had to have been the early hour, the dream, something. Maybe I needed to have a physical. I'd never had any issues with my eyes or heart to this point, had tried to take care of myself, but I was forty-seven and shit happens. Especially to the men in my family.

There had to be an explanation for why I just saw the ghost from my cold case.

I barely remembered the drive to Los Angeles and up into Laurel Canyon.

Of all the cold cases I continued to monitor, Dane Donovan's bothered me the most. I had personal connections to the case, and when I made detective with Kern County twenty years ago, I'd taken over the case that had seriously impacted my own family. He'd been a poster child for wrong place, wrong time, and I wanted—needed—to put the case to rest.

I still had a poster of him from his first record hanging in my home office. I could explain it away as part of the case, or that it had been part of my father's original case files. But that wouldn't be true.

No. I'd been obsessed with Dane Donovan since first hearing his music. I begged my father to tell me about him on the tenth anniversary of his disappearance, and it turned into one of the worst fights I'd ever had with him. It was the case that eventually broke my dad. It was the one that made me decide to follow in his law enforcement footsteps.

It hadn't broken me, but as the years passed, the leads dried up, and the witnesses and potential suspects died off, and since I was no closer to having an answer for his mother, maybe it just hadn't broken me *yet*.

Poor Diane Donovan.

I made the drive to Los Angeles as I did every year on this date like clockwork for our usual tea and conversation, but when we greeted at the door, she held on to our hug a moment longer than usual.

"Detective?"

"Yes, ma'am?"

She pulled away finally and patted my arm. "Come in. My assistant, Barbara, has some tea set out for us."

She led me into her small sitting room, where I'd sat on so many previous occasions. Twenty now, to be exact.

"Detective, you've looked for my boy for so long, and looked after me. Who's looking after *you* these days?"

I chuckled. During our annual visits, she always asked me this. I'd first tried to bypass that line of questioning. Then I told her about Lisa. She knew about our twenty-year marriage and divorce. She knew about my subsequent boyfriend, Brady, and that breakup two years ago. She had a way about her that got me talking about all kinds of things.

"Same as last year, I'm afraid. Work keeps me busy. Gotta pay for the kids' college somehow."

She squeezed my arm. "They're lucky to have you." Her smile turned sad. "I always wanted Dane to go to college, but I'm afraid it was my fault that he turned toward music. I couldn't exactly be a working artist while telling him he had to have a backup plan. Besides, his father was a very gifted musician. Dane never knew him. He was a man I met in London. I came back here to Laurel Canyon and raised Dane by myself. He was surrounded by art and so many talented people his whole life. He had so much potential. I just wish…"

"I know. The sheriff's department is planning to do a media blitz today. Hopefully it will turn something up, but if not…"

"You'll be here next year?" She exhaled and shook her head slowly, taking a sip of her tea before speaking. "Oh, Walter. I love our visits, but I know this tears you up almost as much as it does me."

I planted my hands on my hips and sighed. I'd tried everything for the past twenty years. At one point, we'd found remains at the rest stop when construction workers were building a new restroom, and I'd thought *finally*. Having to tell Mrs. Donovan, seeing hope light up her face alongside dread, hope that this would be over, killed me, especially when I had to go back and let her know the remains weren't Dane's. I couldn't tell her about this morning, and part of me hoped that there really weren't any connections to Dane's case. But that would be fooling myself.

A homicide on the anniversary and in the same location? Too much to be coincidence.

But then, the official police reports for Dane say "missing person"… despite what the first officer on scene, Walter Muse, Senior, saw when he arrived.

"Promise me something, Walter?"

I took her wrinkled and knobby hand in mine. Arthritis had robbed her of her ability to do the fine-line paintings she'd been famous for, but she hadn't let it stop her from creating stunning works of art. She changed her style and her admirers loved the new pieces just as much.

"Anything I'm able." My voice cracked.

"Don't come back next year. I'm not saying don't *ever* come back... but not on this day. Come see me when you've found someone to look after you, so I won't worry anymore. Dane wouldn't have wanted our sad reunions. He always gave me a hard time for allowing melancholy to settle into my work."

"From what you've told me, I think you're right." I frowned. The experience I'd had this morning was still fresh in my mind. "Is it strange that I feel I know him? From our visits? And that I feel like he's still... present?" I couldn't tell her what I'd seen. She knew what had happened to my father. Besides, how cruel would that be, to tell her I'd imagined that I'd seen her son at the place where he may or may not have been killed forty years ago.

She smiled brightly. "His presence is everywhere." She looked over my shoulder to the large painting of him hanging on the main wall in the room, the one that reached up to the vaulted ceiling. "He's always with me, Detective. His music, his smile in the photos I took of him, the paintings I did of him... he's always close. But lately?" She hesitated, and my stomach dropped.

"Yes?"

"Lately, I feel him even closer. Maybe it's *me* who's closer to *him* in this stage of my life, if that makes sense."

I didn't want that to be true. I didn't want her to go. She was, in a way, a tether to my father. A last-ditch effort to bring him peace and her closure. But what if there was something to her feeling?

"Diane, I promise. If I find... someone, I'll bring them to meet you. Maybe you oughta hang around long enough for me to do that." I didn't like the vibe I was getting from her. It was almost like she was preparing me for the fact that her time was coming to a close. That made me sadder than it should have.

We hugged again. I promised to be in touch, she reminded me of my promise to her, and we said our goodbyes.

I'd planned to meet up with my friends that evening after I got back to Bakersfield, but I needed to clear my mind before heading home. Maybe I'd go in search of some other ghosts in Laurel Canyon. I put the car in drive and took off, putting on a playlist of some of the great artists who'd once lived in this area. The Doors, The Eagles, Crosby, Stills, and Nash, Joni Mitchell... What was it about this particular piece of real estate that had such an impact on the music and culture of the time? Was it the drugs? Or the clear skies up above the smog like David Crosby claimed? The multitude of friendships between musicians, from The Monkees to The Rolling Stones?

Some of the famous places were still around, like the Canyon Country Store. There were two old women sitting outside the laundromat to the right of the old store selling hippie wares and crystals, even some pentacles and candles, from under an umbrella. I drove past them with my windows down and wondered if I should stop and talk to them. The women were out there every year when I passed by, rain or shine. They stared ahead with vacant eyes, a little tinny speaker playing The Doors' "Love Street" over and over.

How long had they been sitting out there selling their goods? Had they been in the area when Dane was riding his bicycle around?

I'd always wondered if I could get closer to finding out what happened to Dane if I could just tap into the legends of this place. So I listened to the music over the sound of the engine growling as it climbed the hill, and tried to manifest some answers.

THREE

D ane
2019

I stared down at the blood on my hands and a wave of nausea overtook me.

I was too late.

"Jesus, Dee Dee, are you all right?" Ryan asked when I opened the truck door.

"You should probably go."

He frowned at me. "What do you mean? What happened?"

"You don't get it, man." I couldn't have these guys with me. What if the man from the carnival came after me and they got hurt? "I was too late."

"Dee Dee, you're shaking," Kal said quietly. "What's wrong?"

I realized that no, I wasn't all right. My hands *were* trembling. I needed a cigarette bad. What was I supposed to do now? I had no place to go, no bread, no nothing.

No, that wasn't true. I had my life. That was more than I'd had when I last visited this place. And now I had a purpose.

"Dee Dee?"

Kal had climbed out of the backseat of the truck and stood beside me.

"I gotta go—"

"Dee Dee," he said again, this time touching my shoulder gently, as if he knew I was a split second away from running into the darkness. "I think something bad happened to you."

I shook off his hold and glared at him. "How in the hell would *you* know?" How did I explain that *I* didn't even know for sure what had happened to me, that all I had was the stupid memory that came from my talking board? And scars. Lots of scars.

"Something bad happened to me too. Before I worked for Mr. Ame. We'll help you."

Ever since I'd crossed the threshold of the carnival, feelings and pieces of memories showed up looking like... You know how sometimes when you're at the movies and the projector melts the film? How it gets burn spots in it before entirely going away? My brain felt like that. Piecemeal.

One such feeling stuck out in front of the others. Everyone I'd ever trusted—everyone I'd ever loved—had moved on, left me behind. Why would these guys be any different? But I didn't need much more than a ride. Supposed I should start from the beginning. Go back to where my life made sense.

"I came here to stop a bad thing from happening, but I was too late. He was already here."

"Wait... is someone... Is someone hurt, Dee Dee?"

All I could do was nod.

Ryan tapped his fingers on the big glass screen on the dashboard of his truck, and I heard a voice call out, "Nine-one-one, what's your emergency?"

"Hi, uh, we're at the Buttonwillow Rest Area, and my friend just found... Someone is hurt."

I stared at him and wrapped my shaky hands around myself, then realized I was getting blood everywhere.

"Here," Kal said, handing me a wet cloth. I used it to wipe my hands, then he held out a plastic bag for me to put the cloth in.

Ryan spoke a bit longer and the call disconnected.

"CHP is on their way. They want us to stay." His eyes flared when he saw the bag in Kal's hand. "Did you touch anything?"

I nodded. I had nothing in my stomach, but it burned like I was gonna throw up.

"Fuck. Okay. Hey, babe? Set that bag down outside the truck. We need to give it to the officers. They're going to want our information too. Shit. Shit! Okay, Dee Dee? Do you have identification?"

I shook my head.

I have nothing.

"It's going to be okay," he was saying. "Just tell the cops you lost your wallet before we picked you up at the carnival tonight, okay? Tell them exactly that. We'll figure this out. Everything is going to be okay, okay?"

It was as if him saying "okay" over and over would actually make it so. I didn't have the heart to tell him that *nothing* was okay, especially not for the young man I'd found behind the bathrooms. The same spot I'd seen in my—

"Dee Dee!"

I staggered around Kal and vomited in some bushes.

Kal held my hair back and talked to me in a soft voice. Then Ryan was handing me a bottle of water as a cop car came screaming into the parking lot and pulled up next to us. The sky was mostly dark but a dim light was starting to filter in around us.

"I just want to go home."

"Where's home?" Ryan asked. "We were headed to LA, but we can take you wherever—"

"Laurel Canyon." It just came out, but it sounded right. Immediately I saw the winding drives, the fancy cars, the mishmash of modest and elaborate houses cut into the hillside, hidden by trees and greenery. And then there was the music, the drugs, and the love. Once upon a time. What would it be like now?

Ryan smiled. "That's right where we're going! My producer invited us to stay at his place in the canyon while I finish my demos for my solo album. How weird. Let's give this cop our information and then we'll head there. Everything will feel a little better after you've showered, eaten, and slept. I promise. Let's just get through this."

No, it really won't.

These two men talked of promises and coincidences, but all of this *had* to have been orchestrated by the man in charge of the carnival. I didn't know much about him, but I knew he was a powerful dude.

And I'd failed him.

Earlier that night...

"Want me to walk with you?" Pokey really was a nice man, someone I might have called a friend at one point. I didn't have anyone in my life anymore other than the strangers around me at the carnival. But when I started to leave the arcade, heading in the direction Nik had taken the creepy man, my footsteps faltered. I didn't want to be alone.

Alone was unsafe.

Alone had gotten me into trouble.

"Actually," I said to him. "It might be nice if you did."

Pokey didn't say a word. Just started walking beside me.

We headed toward the entrance of the carnival, where Mr. Ame was bidding farewell to the evening's guests.

"Mr. Ame? Dee Dee's got something to tell you."

Had we somehow traveled back to kindergarten and I couldn't speak for myself? I couldn't be annoyed, though. I'd asked him to come with.

The carnival director turned to me and his freakish eyes began to swirl with color. For a moment, I thought I would find words there, like I did when I touched the planchette on my talking board. The colors were similar. But then I blinked hard and shook my head.

No. I didn't know if I could ever serve another customer again after what had just happened. What if this was the beginning of my total breakdown? What if every customer, every dive into the board, would bring me more terrible visions?

"That is not the case. But you have unlocked *your* truth, Dane."

Dane. That *was* my name. Wasn't it? Dee Dee had been a nickname of some sort, one given to me with... love. And affection.

"I don't know what just happened, but that man," I said, pointing to where I could see the back of the customer's head as he hurried away, "he touched the planchette with me. I don't let people touch it with me."

"No, you wouldn't. Two opens the portal wider. Reveals dual perspectives."

"I don't understand what I saw, exactly. It was, like a memory I guess, about me. What happened to me. But that man... he reacted strangely."

"Indeed. And he has been ejected from the premises." He tilted his head, and his gaze seemed to lock me in place. I couldn't look away, couldn't flee. "There is something else you wish to say?"

"I..." *What the hell am I doing?* "I'm afraid he was looking for something in particular in finding me. He wanted to know how I got here, but after what I saw... I think he actually wanted to see what happened to me. He wanted *guidance*."

"And you believe he may carry out something similar to what happened to you."

It wasn't a question. I didn't even have to say it. Ame knew what was in my thoughts. Had known all along what had brought me here.

"I figured maybe I should tell you."

"And you have." Ame wasn't generally rude, and he wasn't being a jerk, but he wasn't going to let me off easy.

I exhaled harshly. "But what now? What if he... does *that* to someone? It was like he wanted to see it, wanted instruction."

"I suppose if he received what he wanted, he may act upon that knowledge."

"But you can't let him! You can't let him hurt someone."

"*I* wouldn't be *letting* him do anything. I do not control the entirety of the world. I have dominion over a very narrow slice of existence. Here," he said, gesturing to the carnival, which was being packed up as we spoke. "*This* is my world. *This* I can control... to a point. No harm comes to those who cross into my world. But outside, there are others who must protect those in harm's way."

"But, we can't just let him—"

"There is no *we* in this, I'm afraid, Dane. But if you choose to act, I will support you however I am able."

I wanted to say no. I wanted to go back to my trailer and pretend nothing happened. Then I remembered what I'd seen, what I'd felt.

"I have to stop him."

· · ·

2019

The sun rose and revealed a beautiful day ahead as we descended the grade beside Castaic Lake into Los Angeles County. I was stunned by the transformation of the landscape. My head moved on a swivel. The cars were different, the road was much wider than I remembered. There were *so* many buildings...

"Unreal," I muttered to myself. Ryan had been singing along to the music playing on the radio, music I'd never heard. It wasn't like any radio I'd ever seen before, either. It seemed to be controlled by some sort of touching glass on the dashboard of the truck. The same one he'd used to call the police last night. It looked like something out of a science fiction movie. Every once in a while he'd tap it and the music would change, the cool air would come through the vents, something else would happen.

"Dee Dee?" Kal asked, leaning between the seats again. He was so big, it wasn't much of a stretch. "What is the last date that you remember?"

"Date?"

"Yeah, like the day, maybe, when you joined the carnival?"

"You mean... Oh, it was December." The further we drove from the nightmare at the rest area, the more my memories began tickling my mind, like sprinkles on a cupcake. "We'd just played The Fillmore in San Francisco. It was the last night of our tour. Tess flew back, so we dropped her off at the airport. I was riding home with the guys in our band and the crew, in the van. It was December fifteenth, I think. I know everyone was happy to be done before the holidays."

Ryan glanced at me and cleared his throat. "The Fillmore, huh? That's cool."

Kal squeezed his shoulder, then looked at me with those intense blue eyes. "What year do you think it is now?"

I turned to stare at him. "What year? It's 1979, man. What are you talking about?"

"Oh shit," Ryan muttered. He flicked on his blinker and changed lanes, letting out a whistling breath and shaking his head.

"We need to prepare you," Kal said. "Time doesn't work the same at the carnival."

"I know that. It's fucking weird there. Days seem longer because the sky is all lit up, even at night. You go to sleep in one place and wake up someplace else. People dress funny sometimes. I gave up trying to figure it out and just did my thing. I was only there like, what, a few weeks? A month maybe? I don't remember. Oh shit, is it nineteen-eighty? Man, I was looking forward to New Year's, and I missed it?"

Kal frowned. "Did Mr. Ame say anything before you left? Give you anything?"

Should I tell them about the guy? "He knew I had something I needed to do, and no. He said I could take what I needed, so I took the guitar and my board. Why?"

"Do you have a billfold?" Kal asked.

"No." *I lost everything.* "Just some borrowed clothes and the guitar. And my talking board, but that was mine from before. I think. I remember it from before." Somehow I knew that much.

"And he didn't give you a billfold? Didn't give you anything else?" Kal seemed distraught. I wondered why. *What the hell didn't Ame tell me?*

"Baby, he gave him *us*. You think we just happened to be driving through the desert in the wee hours when this guy shows up?" Ryan shook his head. "*We're* his help. Don't worry, we'll get you squared away. You were playing a show? You play guitar?"

"And piano. And I sing. Or I used to. Haven't been able to since, well... Not since I came to the carnival."

Ryan and Kal traded looks.

"I couldn't speak," Kal said to me. "When I got to the carnival, and after. Ryan and his friends helped me after I left, until I could."

"How long ago did you leave?" I asked him.

Kal looked to Ryan.

"We met a year and a half ago, when he joined the traveling music festival that my band was playing." Ryan glanced at me again and then looked where he was driving. "That was July tenth. Twenty-eighteen. Today is December fifteenth, twenty-nineteen."

My head started to pound and my vision went blurry—but instead of it being otherworldly like when I used my talking board, it was my tears.

I'd been gone? *For forty years?*

Was there anyone left? Did anyone miss me?

I didn't want to know the answer to that. All I could remember was that Laurel Canyon was a place I'd lived, and what happened right before I... met my fate, I supposed.

I looked to Kal, and his expression had changed from fierce protectiveness to just plain sad. "How long were *you* at the carnival?" I asked him.

Kal's gaze flicked to Ryan and back to me. "I joined the carnival in nineteen thirty-three."

I counted in my head as I gaped at him. "Eighty-five years?"

Kal shrugged. "It was only a year to me. I did my service for Mr. Ame, played my calliaphone and the carnival's calliope, kept them running and in good shape. Then it was time for me to go. It just so happened that the music festival shared grounds with the carnival that day." He rubbed the back of Ryan's neck. "And I met Ryan."

Ryan reached back and squeezed his hand. "He watched out for me, I watched out for him. And now we're married."

"And now we'll watch out for you," Kal said, leveling his gaze on me.

"I promised Mr. Ame," Ryan said. "When the time came, I'd help someone else like someone did for me. So we got you, okay?"

It all sounded nice, but folks didn't stay. They did their thing and went on their way.

"Well, I appreciate the ride, but I can take care of myself."

The two men traded glances once more, and Kal leaned back in the seat with a sigh.

I went back to watching the scenery go by and marveled over the changes. What had been farmland and desert was now urban sprawl, just like in the Los Angeles basin. The '70s had brought a lot of new development, but not like this. New towns, places I'd never heard of, sprouted up out of the valley floor. Finally some familiar names started to show up. Burbank, Glendale, and then Hollywood, and finally Ryan exited the interstate at Los Feliz and we meandered to Franklin and then Hollywood, and then it was a right turn onto Laurel Canyon Drive.

A sensation washed over me like waking after a hard sleep, that disorientation and sluggishness falling away and leaving—

Clarity.

This road led to my home.

A barrage of faces passed through my mind, sights and sounds, hot summer days, breezy winter nights. Laughter, screams, tears. And music. Always music. It had been magic.

"My producer, Scott Cross, he bought a house that used to belong to some folk singer chick," Ryan was saying. "I think her name was Tess something. It's a sweet pad, and we're going to have the place to ourselves, so you're welcome to stay with us."

A fresh wound in my heart opened up at his words.

Tess Miller.

Used to belong to.

I knew exactly which house. It appeared in front of my eyes like an old movie...

1967

"Oh! You're not Diane."

"She's my mom. She asked me to bring your delivery."

"Well, then. Thank you so much for coming." Tess held the door open and I scurried inside. Mom usually made deliveries herself, but she'd been locked in her studio when Tess called the house, and she told me that since I'd answered the phone, it was time I earned my keep.

"It's safe enough up here," she'd said. "No one's going to bother a kid on a bike. Just ride over and give it to her. She'll pay me later. Now run along, I've got to finish this piece. It's squeezing my brain like a vise."

I knew better than to disturb Mom during her work sessions. Her paintings were highly coveted, and lately there'd been so much demand that I'd tried to step up and help out around the house. I was trying to do my part now that I was a teenager, nearly an adult. Making herbal deliveries for her was the least I could do.

I held out the paper bag to Tess, and she put an arm around me.

"You're very sweet to bring this all the way up here. Why don't you stay for a while? There's a bunch of friends and their kids out in the swimming pool. Feel like taking a dip?"

I didn't know what to say. It was hot. A swim sounded far out, but I never did anything without asking Mom, even at fifteen years old. It was her and I against the world, and even though she'd been less and less available, I still wanted to be a good boy for her. Everyone else had deserted her—her parents, my father, her siblings. Then she'd made it big with her paintings.

She'd told me many times that it's the people who stick with you during the tough times who you should put your faith in, and since she was it for me, I would return the favor.

"Thank you, ma'am, but I would have to ask my mom."

Tess was so beautiful, it almost hurt to look at her. She had long, shiny blond hair, and wore a white mini-dress and tall white boots. But it was her smile that amazed me. Her teeth were as white as her dress, and her makeup was just like the models' in magazines. I looked at Mom's magazines a lot, admiring the clothes and the stories about the lives of people I'd never meet.

Here was one of those people, in the flesh, living just across the canyon from us.

Tess took the paper bag, looked in it and smiled. "I tell you what. You have an open invitation, Mr....?"

"Oh, I'm Dane Donovan." I stuck out my hand, remembering my manners.

"D and D, I love it. May I call you Dee Dee?"

"Sure, Mrs. Miller."

She rolled her eyes. "I'm nobody's missus, Dee Dee. Call me Tess. And if someone is home here, you're welcome in the pool, all right? You're always welcome here."

2019

Ryan made the turn off of Harlesden Court and onto the private drive where I remembered riding my bicycle. We pulled up in front of what used to be Tess's house, and my heart lifted. She might not still be there, but stepping onto the grounds felt just like the day that, to me, was twelve years ago, when Tess invited me into a life I'd never imagined. Or however long it had been.

Had I *really* lost forty years of my life? I don't know how I could have survived what happened. My skin itched in the places the scars were thickest.

"Is this Scott's house?" Kal stared in wonder at the stunning split-level wood and glass mansion. It looked different from when Tess lived there but still had the pitched roof and all the windows.

"Yeah. Gorgeous, right?"

Kal stood by the truck and Ryan moved to his side, sliding a hand around his waist and kissing his neck. Without tearing his eyes away from the house, Kal dropped his arm around Ryan's shoulders and held him close, as if to protect him from unseen enemies.

I couldn't help but watch them. They were so much in love. I never thought I'd see two men being so open with each other. The future—or present, I guessed—must not be so bad if men like me could reveal themselves to a stranger, and touch and kiss like this in the open.

"Come on," Ryan said, taking Kal's hand. "Scott's assistant had the place stocked for us, and the pool is heated!"

I followed them up the walkway... but movement at the bottom of the drive caught my eye.

A man stood at the gate we'd just come through, watching us.

"Hey."

Kal put a hand on my back, startling me, and when I looked back, the man was gone.

"Sorry," I said. "I thought I saw someone."

It looked like the man who'd stared at me in Buttonwillow. He wasn't dressed like no cop, but maybe like an investigator or something. Intense brown eyes, nearly shorn salt-and-pepper hair, and a thick mustache all added an allure to his face, and under those straightlaced clothes was a big, powerful body.

I'd *wanted* him to look at me, so imagining I'd just seen him again was probably wishful thinking. He'd looked at me as if he'd known me. Which was impossible. Wasn't it?

Kal glared in the direction of the gate, his scowl intense.

"You will be safe here. I know you're thinking about leaving, but I hope you'll stay with us, at least until you have a better understanding of this time. I had help from Ryan and his friends. Let us help you."

"You don't owe me nothing, man. I've been on my own for a long time. Far as I can tell, things aren't all that different."

We both knew I was lying. Things were very different... but so what?

"Give us a couple of days. You just landed here."

I didn't agree, but I let him lead me into the house. My whole existence up here in Laurel Canyon had required me to be invisible when necessary. It was sort of a gift. Ryan and Kal had no reason to worry about me. I could get by on my own.

"Hot damn!" Ryan shouted from the kitchen. "Who wants lasagna?"

Kal turned to me with a grin.

I knew better than to turn down food. Who knew when the next meal would come?

"I could eat."

Four

alter

As an officer of the law, I knew better than to be sneaking around the homes in Laurel Canyon, even if I had good cause. I knew the man I'd seen couldn't be Dane Donovan, but my instincts told me it was possible. And with the date, and the similarity to my father's recounting of the crime scene, I couldn't ignore what Dax called a coincidence.

"Walt, my man. You've been burning the candle at both ends lately. I know you wanted to have something for Mrs. Donovan this year. Hell, I woke you up in the wee hours to come out to Buttonwillow when I should have let you sleep."

"No, I'm glad you texted."

I'd called him from my truck on my way back to Bakersfield to update him on my meeting with Diane and to find out any news on the morning's homicide. I would *not* be telling him that I thought I saw Dane, though I couldn't get his face out of my mind.

"Whoever did this, I think it's connected somehow. What better way to celebrate the anniversary? Or maybe he really did take off that night?" Dax suggested. "Hitchhiked away from the rest stop and started a new life somewhere? Back then it would have been easier."

Dax knew I didn't agree with the theory that Dane had left on his own.

Diane had told me once that Dane often worried her because of his obsession with the folk musicians he admired. There was one woman, Connie Converse, who'd never quite made it big, though she was often referred to as the "female Bob Dylan." Converse had been frustrated with the lack of interest from a label and she eventually left New York to work on social justice issues in Michigan. Diane told me that Dane was specifically interested in the fact that, in 1974, Connie disappeared. She'd sent letters to her family members and friends saying she didn't want them to look for her, that she was just going to start a new life.

Whenever Dane got frustrated with the fact that he still hadn't broken out in the folk rock scene, Diane would find him listening to a bootleg recording of Connie Converse that he'd gotten from Tess.

I'd become a bit of an expert in folk rock, especially the artists who'd made up what became known as The California Sound. They were all contemporaries of Dane's, and he'd played with so many of the huge artists, had lived among them and opened shows for them, but every time he got close to a break, something would happen. He said in an interview once that he thought he was cursed.

Connie Converse's story seemed to fit with Dane's profile, but there were no letters, no word to anyone, and it had been the middle of the night. My father saw something, not to mention Dane's clothes being found at the rest stop, as well as a lot of his blood.

My father swore to his dying day that Dane had not walked away from that rest stop on his own, and I believed him.

"Sure, because someone would happily pick up a naked hitchhiker in the middle of the night, in the middle of nowhere. What if, though? What if he got away? What if he's had amnesia? What if—"

"Walt, you need this vacation. Are you still planning to come by the bar tonight before you leave? What time's your flight?"

I'd been forced to take the vacation time. My captain noticed I'd been pulling a lot of extra shifts and he didn't buy the old "I've got two kids in college" bit, so he told me he didn't want to see my face for seven days. "Vacation or administrative leave, Muse," he'd said.

I'd told everyone I was going to Hawaii... I just hadn't been real forthcoming about any detailed plans. And I hadn't exactly purchased a plane ticket. Nor had I booked a hotel.

The last time I'd gone to Hawaii, after Brady and I broke up, I'd booked a flight same day, found a cheap hotel, and spent the week bored out of my mind. Sure, I'd had good food, good drinks, and found a vacation fling to pass some time, but I didn't do idle well. Traveling with Lisa, and then with Brady, had been fun, but they'd both had to push me to step away from work.

Perhaps Diane had been onto something when she'd encouraged me to come back when I found someone. That would require actual looking.

I just tended to get involved in the job. In that way, I was like my father had been. I couldn't afford to become like him, though. I had to keep that side of me in check, and having a partner had always done that for me. My kids, too. I'd done all the coaching, supervising, chaperoning, whatever I could fit around my detective duties. But they were off to college now. They didn't need Dad anymore. Just my wallet.

"Early," I fibbed. I *would* get up early and do whatever I was going to do for the next seven days. "But I'll be there tonight. I want to hear what you've found out about Buttonwillow."

"Sure, sure. Yeah. I'll see you at Fallen Anchor around seven. After the day I've had, I'm going to need a drink, and so will the other guys."

I didn't tell him that I'd seen the truck in Laurel Canyon that had been at Buttonwillow. I didn't tell him that I'd just watched the man who looked eerily like Dane Donovan walk into the house that had belonged to Tess Miller. I didn't tell him because the last thing I needed was for my colleagues and higher ups to think I'd fallen prey to the same mania my father had.

I was not my father.

I hoped to emulate the good things about my dad, but I refused to be sucked into madness by this job.

Later that evening...

"Today marks the fortieth anniversary of the disappearance of folk rock singer Dane Donovan, who went missing from a rest stop off of I-5 in Kern County. Kern County Sheriff Wade Nelson had this to say..."

"Mr. Donovan's disappearance, sadly, remains unsolved. Detectives continue to monitor the tip line and are in communication with Mr. Donovan's mother. There have been no new leads, but we hope that by presenting the facts of the case to the media, along with the last-known photograph of the young

singer and an age-progressed image, someone may come forward. There is a reward of one hundred thousand dollars, offered by Mrs. Donovan, for any solid information that leads law enforcement to finding her son."

"Dane Donovan was a member of the Laurel Canyon folk rock music community. Growing up, he lived with his mother, artist Diane Donovan, in a bungalow not far from the homes of famous folk singers like Tess Miller, Cass Elliot, Joni Mitchell, members of Crosby, Stills, and Nash, and more. He was surrounded by the who's who of the music business. Donovan spent his teens learning the art of songwriting from Tess Miller and others in the scene, making his solo performance debut in 1970, but protests at college campuses over the Vietnam War overshadowed his tour. Donovan eventually joined Tess Miller's band, and performed as an opener for artists like Crosby, Stills, and Nash, and Jackson Browne. He never quite reached the level of stardom as his fellow Laurel Canyon neighbors, but he contributed several hit songs to the soundtrack of that era.

"Donovan was traveling in a van with members of Miller's band and crew, on their way back to LA after a series of shows in the Bay Area, when they stopped to use the facilities at the rest area. He never returned to the van. Authorities searched the area for weeks, but Donovan seemed to vanish into thin air. He was twenty-seven years old.

"If you have any information about Dane Donovan's disappearance, please contact the Kern County Sheriff's Department."

"Guess what we'll be doing for the next week," Detective Gene Ochoa, my best friend in the world, groused over his third beer as he sneered at the TV over the bar. I was glad our chaperone, twice-divorced former Marine turned Detective Denny Hamilton, had driven him over, otherwise it would be a fight for his keys.

"Answering phones like we're the damned Jerry Lewis Telethon volunteers," said Denny. He was the only detective who was older than me. He was mere months away from hitting fifty, which was the magic number for our pension. I figured him for a lifer though. He'd been resisting all calls to retire. "What the fuck else am I going to do?" he'd say. "Besides, who's gonna babysit *your* asses? I can still outshoot all of you and my case closure rate is second only to Junior's."

Dax Brown, Gene Ochoa, and Denny Hamilton were my closest friends. Hearing them talk, one might think they were jaded, grumpy cops, but they were some of the best law enforcement officers working today. We all had our roles to play: I was the go-getter, the doggedly stubborn and determined detective who never gave up. Gene was the class clown, but he paid attention to detail and was a great spokesperson for the sheriff's department. We all anticipated that he was next in line to be elected to the big seat.

Dax was the youngest, eager, always willing to learn and put in the extra work, and, naturally, a frequent victim of harassment from the rest of us. Denny was the most knowledgeable and experienced cop among us. After serving eight years in the Marines, he'd been a cop for twenty-three years, and he still showed up with his full attention, endless empathy, and wisdom that came with all the cases he'd worked over the years.

Denny was also the big brother I'd never had, and as much as I wanted him to be happy, I wasn't looking forward to the day when I'd be doing this job without him.

"He's gotta be dead, don't you think?" Jasmine, our favorite bartender, asked me in a low voice. "He'd be, what, sixty-seven by now?"

"Yep." I'd been nursing a dark fruit cider for the last hour, and the combination of the tangy aftertaste and the news story was starting to sour my stomach.

"If he *is* alive, you'd think somebody would have reported it," Gene said. "A hundred grand is a lot of cash."

"If he's not," I said, "his poor mother deserves to put him to rest before she goes. She's in her late eighties now. Still active, but slowing down."

"How was she today?" Gene asked with a gentle voice. The guys knew me better than anyone, and knew my history with this case and Mrs. Donovan.

"Arthritis is bothering her. She's got an assistant with her all the time now, nice woman named Barbara." I blew out a breath. "I didn't tell her about this morning, of course. I hope the message on the can and the similarities to Dane's case don't make it into the news." I downed the rest of my cider and looked to Dax. Gene had joined him after I left and they worked the scene together. I hoped they had some information for me.

"Similarities." Gene exhaled through his nose and kept his voice low. There were a few patrons at the tables along the far wall, but only one other guy up at the bar. Jasmine was down at the other end taking care of him. "Clothes were folded, same as your vic's in seventy-nine, and this kid had a similar appearance. Long hair, light brown or dark blond. But this boy was strangled and had cuts to femoral arteries leading to catastrophic blood loss. Since we have no body for the Donovan case," Gene gave me a sympathetic look, "we don't know his cause of death or the condition he was in, so it's difficult to make further connections. There were a few shoe prints around the body, but so many people have walked around there, who knows?"

"The likelihood is that we're not dealing with the same killer," Dax said. "It's been forty years, the suspect would be at least in his sixties, and how many men nearing seventy are physically capable of overpowering a much younger man? Unless he had a gun or an accomplice."

"You'd be surprised, actually," Denny said. "Both Donovan and this vic had slight builds."

"And why would he have stopped all these years?" Dax asked.

Gene shrugged. "The Golden State Killer was married, had a niece living with him at one point, and during that time he went dormant for years. Could be a lot of things."

"Could have been locked up," Denny said. "If he survived forty years locked up, he's probably in good physical shape."

"So we check recent parolees," I said. "We go back over the list of suspects. But we also look at the fact this crime could be unrelated."

The guys all nodded and grumbled as they went back to their drinks.

Jasmine came over to check on us. "Can I get you anything else?"

"I'll take a Diet Coke, thanks." It had been a long day of driving, and my brain was still working overtime.

"Let's consider one other possibility," Dax said. "Walt... what if *he's* the killer? What if he went into hiding, faked his death, and now he's back?"

I shook my head. "There's nothing in his background that even hints at that sort of behavior. I've interviewed everyone who ever knew him, and I didn't find anything to indicate he might have had violent tendencies. I'm not disagreeing that he could have faked his death and walked away, but how does anyone stay gone so long? And how would he have stayed hidden all these years?"

"What about the guys in the truck?" Dax asked. "They called it in. The one guy touched our vic to see if he was really dead. I got their info from CHP. Think I should get a DNA sample from the guy?"

"Stranger things have happened," I said. "But I don't think they would have called and stuck around for CHP to get there if they did it. Don't rule it out, but doesn't sound likely to me."

Gene pulled out his phone. "I've got the report here. Truck belongs to a Ryan Wells, twenty-nine years old, former singer of metal band Backdrop Silhouette. Did time for DUI, reckless driving with bodily injury. Released from parole in January of this year. The other guys were Kallos Alexandrou—apparently he and Wells just got married—and the third guy didn't have ID, said his wallet was stolen at work. He and Kallos worked at a carnival together outside of Vegas? Said his name was Dee Dee Miller. Worth keeping an eye on them."

That name piqued my interest. Dee Dee, could be initials? And Miller... Like Tess Miller? A relative? Seemed too coincidental.

"How in the hell does a rock star connect with a carny?" Denny asked. "None of these guys were even *born* when Donovan disappeared, but there's been enough bullshit podcasts about this kind of fuckery. Jesus, such a peculiar case. It's like Donovan vanished into thin air."

Unless you believed my father, which no one did.

"I remember that case." The grizzled old guy at the bar had moved closer to us. He'd been quietly drinking his beer since before we'd arrived, and he seemed like the type who'd be there after we left. He wore a white t-shirt under a flannel shirt-jacket, denim jeans, and work boots, none of which had the wear and tear of a day laborer. He looked to be in his late sixties, maybe early seventies.

"Shitty case," Gene said, raising his fourth beer.

The guy nodded and circled the pint glass back and forth in his hands. "I was with CHP in San Joaquin County at the time. We had a string of disappearances that next couple of years. All young, long-haired, single men. Off I-5 and 99."

I turned on my stool to face the guy. "Yeah? There was nothing in the case file. My father was the original detective on this case, and he never got wind of anything similar. Catch anyone?"

He shook his head. "We turned them over to the San Joaquin Sheriff's Department. They never had any luck, eventually considered them runaways. Heard LA County had some, too, the next year, but they never found any bodies, either so same thing. Presumed runaways."

I held out my hand. "Detective Walter Muse, Kern County Sheriff's Department."

He looked at my hand a minute before he shook it. Seemed like he might be regretting opening his mouth, but I was going to get him to talk. I was known to be pretty persuasive without having to use a heavy hand.

"John Soto. Retired CHP."

I had a million questions. "You have more details?"

He sat back and rubbed his hands on his thighs. He had some fairly heavy scar tissue on the back of his left hand, as if he'd been burned. "Not much. Back then, kids hitchhiked up and down those highways all the time. Figured they got in the wrong cars. No signs of foul play at the rest stops, no cameras back then. Lot of missing people off the highways."

"But mostly women, right?" Denny asked.

That was the issue my father ran into when investigating Dane Donovan's disappearance. There hadn't been any similar cases involving men at the time in his jurisdiction. He tried to keep up with stories from other places, but there was never enough evidence to tie the missing people together. If a missing person was male back then, law enforcement assumed they'd just wandered off. They went with friends. They committed suicide. There wasn't a whole lot of effort put into investigating the cases of missing men.

Soto shook his head. "There were several men that went

missing. All from rest stops on highways, and all we ever found were piles of clothes."

"You got a name of someone I can contact who might be able to show me the case files?"

He sighed, and yeah, he was definitely regretting his actions. "Been gone a long time. Not sure." I wondered what had happened to the guy to have him not want to be involved. Maybe he'd left on less than good terms and wanted to forget the job. My father hadn't, though, and he'd left under the worst terms a career cop could imagine. What was this guy's deal?

Denny, Gene, and I exchanged looks.

"My cousin works for San Joaquin. I can get her to hook me up with whoever's in charge of cold cases there," Denny said. "I'll also check with my other cousin, Ernie. He's in Calaveras County."

"I'll check my LAPD contacts," Gene offered. He'd gotten his start working in the Hollywood division, but when he got married ten years prior and he and his wife decided to have kids, they'd moved closer to her family in Bakersfield, so they could help out.

"You won't find him," Soto said, shaking his head. "None of them have been found. No one gave a shit back then because, at least in my department, they assumed they were gay guys hooking up at rest stops." His scowl was deep.

That was an angle I'd considered in Dane's case, but I had no clue if he was gay. Diane Donovan certainly hadn't shared anything about her son's sexual orientation, only that he was loved by everyone who knew him.

Soto's demeanor, though, wasn't flippant. He seemed truly bothered by the possibility that these victims might have been slighted. Perhaps he had firsthand knowledge.

It had taken me years of self-exploration to accept and embrace my own queerness, and being in law enforcement meant coming to terms with the fact that crimes against queer folks were often overlooked, mishandled, or outright rejected for decades. When I made detective, I made it a point to do better, and to make sure my department did better. I couldn't fix the entire law enforcement field, but I could clean up my own house. It helped that I wasn't alone.

Denny climbed off his stool and stood at my back, and Gene put his hand on my shoulder.

"*We* give a shit," Denny said. "That don't fly with us."

Soto looked between us and nodded. "All right then. I'll tell you what happened the night I interrupted a kidnapping." He rubbed at his jaw with that scarred hand.

"Let me buy you a beer," I said, signaling to Jasmine, and she shook her head.

"Thanks, fella, but this is my limit." Soto smiled at Jasmine, and she back at him.

And then he told us his tale.

"It was nineteen eighty and everyone was obsessed with *CHiPs*. Guys wanted motorcycle positions. I didn't care one way or another. I preferred working nights, and patrol cars were better at night. We regularly did rounds at the stops for safety checks. One early morning, I pulled up, no cars, creepy mist all around. I walked the perimeter of the restrooms and I heard something, like something being dragged. I shined my flashlight behind the building and caught sight of a young man on his back, being yanked by the arm into the darkness. He was moaning, there was blood on his clothes. I shouted, and whoever had him tugged again.

"I moved the beam up toward his face and he turned and ran. He ran so fast, he had to have known the lay of the land. There are rocks, hills, cacti out there, but he took off so fast there wasn't even a trail of dust behind him. I called for backup and an ambulance, provided first aid to the poor kid and waited there in the dark. I kept hearing noises, though, and my skin crawled like I was being watched. I didn't want to leave the kid, and it was so dark and misty… and yeah, I was a little freaked out. It took the longest fifteen minutes of my life for my zone partner to show up."

"There were no tracks or anything? No search was done in the daylight?"

"Sure there was, but there were a ton of footprints back there. A couple of other drag marks too, as if this wasn't the first time. That was confirmed when one of the officers found blood and two neatly stacked piles of clothes belonging to two other missing persons. But no bodies. Dogs couldn't find anything. It was like the guy and the vics just disappeared."

"You get anything from the kid?"

Soto shook his head. "He was hit over the head, that's all he remembered. He didn't see a thing. Lucky I found him. Might never been heard from again, like all the others. We had surveillance set up for weeks after and no more people were taken from that rest stop."

"How many are we talking about?" Gene asked him.

"Had to be ten or more total. About every other month that year. None of those cases were ever solved, none of the vics ever heard from again. If it was the same guy, he hid the remains well. Somewhere, there's gotta be a big pile of bones."

My skin was crawling by the time he finished.

Was that what happened to poor Dane? Had my father been right? Would I ever have answers to what happened to him?

FIVE

Dane

Ryan showed me to a guest room, which he couldn't have known was the room I'd crashed in many, many times.

"I'm going to heat up the lasagna. It'll take a while, so why don't you rest a bit?"

As soon as he shut the door, sobs racked my body. I sank down on the bed and curled up into a fetal position on top of the covers, crying soundlessly. It was as if every emotion I'd had in my whole life poured out of me at once, strangling me with the force. I'd never cried like that before. The closest was probably when everyone had left for Altamont without me. I'd been too young, only seventeen, and though I'd fought to go, Mom had a bad feeling about it. She'd said she didn't trust the Hells Angels with the safety of her son.

I'd already missed Woodstock when all of my friends had gone, but Altamont would have been the perfect opportunity to play. Tess said she'd try to get me on the lineup, or at least she'd let me play guitar with her band. It was the first time Mom ever said anything negative about the woman who'd become my best friend. They were usually close, but Diane had been livid.

"He's *my* son, Tess. I don't care that you've seduced him into this life, he's not going to play music in the middle of a field with a bunch of violent men standing between him and chaos."

"Diane, he's got a gift. I just want the rest of the world to see him play. This could be the performance that finally launches his career."

"He's seventeen. There will be other opportunities."

"As an artist, I figured you'd understood how important it is to grab a hold when you can. You can't count on other opportunities that may or may not come."

"And if you were a *mother*, you'd understand why I won't let my son take unnecessary risks. Tess, he's all I have in this world—"

"And you won't have him long if you don't let him spread his wings."

Mom had kicked Tess out of our tiny bungalow, and she'd forbidden me from going to Tess's anymore.

She'd been right about Altamont being dangerous, but I still needed to make things happen, and I couldn't do it with her breathing down my neck. The moment I turned eighteen a few months later, I was right back in with Tess's crowd and preparing to go on the first of many tours with her as a backup guitarist. Mom and I eventually reached an agreement, but I rarely slept under her roof after that.

I must have crashed hard because when I woke, the sunlight was fading. For the first time in a long time, I actually felt hunger. At the carnival, we were fed well enough. I never had a complaint. As my memories returned, I realized I'd never been a big eater. My sleep had been full of dreams, faces of those I'd met, those who'd influenced me, encouraged me. It was like putting on a suit or a uniform and absorbing that feeling of power, of knowing who you were, what you stood for.

And what your purpose was.

Mine was to stop this man who'd witnessed my almost-murder and got off on it, who wished to go out and hurt people himself. I had no idea who'd hurt me way back then, I never saw his face, but I'd seen the man at the carnival. I knew I had to find him and stop him before he hurt anyone else.

So that meant pushing the nostalgia, the tears, all the bull-shit out of my mind. I was going to need some things, and one of them was food.

I used the bathroom outside in the hall and felt the memo-ries settling in like a dog digging into its bed for a snooze. Showering in this bathroom the first morning I woke up here. Walking in on people having sex in here... doing blow on the counter. There had been so many moments.

The house looked a lot different, but the bones were the same. Walking down the hall, I could see glimpses of the old floral wallpaper. Like a flickering light leaves shadows and plays tricks with your mind, my memories of the place filtered in and out of my consciousness. The music I heard, however, was different.

"Hey, man," Ryan said, standing from the couch where he'd been playing guitar. Kal's fingers paused on the piano. "We came to check on you and didn't want to wake you. You gotta be hungry." He put an arm around me and led me to the kitchen, just as Tess had that first night spent at her house. I'd shown up in the rain with a delivery. Mom had been out of town, and I hadn't had anything to eat that hadn't come out of a can for a few days. I wondered if I'd looked more pathetic then or now, standing there in my borrowed clothes that had to be pretty ripe.

"Thank you." The response came out automatically. Guess I hadn't lost my manners.

"I can reheat the lasagna for you, or my manager, Cherish, will be here with pizza in a few—"

There was a knock at the door.

"That must be her." Ryan patted me on the back and trotted over to the front door. He was wearing a pair of what looked like pajama pants, a sweater, and his feet were bare. He was a good-looking guy, stunning really, and the way he moved was seductive. He reminded me of watching Jim Morrison.

"How are you feeling?"

I jumped, not realizing that Kal was standing beside me.

"I'm all right, thanks."

Kal's gaze was always so intense. It made you want to tell him to lighten up, but then he'd look at Ryan and his eyes would go soft. As much as he might want to help me figure myself out, he also wasn't sure how to handle having another guy around his man. Husband. I still couldn't get used to thinking in those terms.

Ryan came back in carrying three pizza boxes, accompanied by a short Black woman who was dressed in an orange turtleneck sweater, a wide belt, and blue jeans. Her arms were loaded with shopping bags.

"Dee Dee, this is Cherish. She's my manager and lifesaver, and today, she's been on a mission."

Cherish laughed. "How are you, handsome? I picked up some things for you. Ryan said you might need some supplies."

She handed me the bags, and, unlike her, I struggled under their weight.

"What is this?"

Ryan grinned as he nabbed a slice of pizza piled high with vegetables. "Clothes, underthings, toiletries. A billfold." He gave Kal a wink. "Although, we're going to have to figure out how to get you some identification."

Cherish frowned slightly. "I went by Ryan's description of

your size, so I hopefully got it right. He's an artist and a great judge. Anything you don't want, just leave the tags on and put them back in the bags and I'll take care of them. He told me, 'Dress him like non-disco 1979,' so that's what I went for."

I raised my eyebrows at Ryan, and he put a finger to his lips and grinned.

I reached into a bag and pulled out a pair of Levi's in exactly the size I used to wear, but these felt... strange. Not like the stiff material I was used to. "I don't... Thank you. You didn't have to do this."

He shrugged. "Like she said, I'm an artist. I love to dress people, draw them, take pictures. Not to sound creepy or anything. Mostly we just want you to have what you need." He gave me a pointed look at that, and then glanced at Kal, who nodded.

"Thank you."

"Eat. Shower. Then we can talk."

I nodded, and was grateful when the three of them started chatting. Kal opened all three boxes of pizza so I could make my choice, and he handed me a plate. I grabbed a slice of the vegetarian pizza. I recalled that I'd been a vegetarian at one point, before my life was nearly cut off, and the sight of the meat on the other pizza made my stomach turn. Huh. Well.

"I let Scott know that you guys made it here with no problem, and he said he'll be by next week to see how the demos are going and, if you're ready, you guys can record. I also talked to that gallery owner in Las Vegas that you met, and he wants to know when you'll be ready to do a show there."

Ryan's eyes widened. "Wow, I just thought he was being nice. He wants a whole show?" He turned to Kal. "I can't believe it."

Kal took him in his arms and kissed his forehead. "I don't know why you're surprised. He couldn't stop talking about your drawings."

"Congratulations." I hadn't meant to call attention to myself, but now they were all smiling at me. "My mother was an artist. I know how tough it can be to get a gallery to accept your work. Right on."

"Thanks, man. It all kind of happened on accident. After my band broke up, I, uh... had some legal issues and I couldn't travel. So I did the only thing I knew how to do to stay out of trouble. Turned out folks kinda liked it."

I nodded as I finished my first slice of pizza. I noticed that Kal was on his third and Ryan on his second, so I reached for another.

"You just needed some positivity, my friend," Cherish said to Ryan, bumping him with her hip. "You're so gifted. I keep waiting for you to ask me to set up some acting auditions or dance lessons. You're likely to be a quadruple threat."

Ryan rolled his eyes and threw his arm around Cherish's shoulders. "If life has taught me anything in the past year, it's that I should be open to all the possibilities. Awesome. I'm going to put in an order with that art supply place up in Fortuna that I love. They said they'd deliver anything I needed. Guess I'll be getting started on my new art pieces a little sooner than I'd planned."

"It'll be great," Kal said, smiling at him with so much love.

Kal left the room, and I finished up my second slice of pizza. It was amazing how much a little good food and friendly banter could improve my mood.

1967

The next time I made a delivery at Tess's, I decided I would take her up on the offer to hang out. Mom had been working in her studio nonstop. As long as I brought her three meals a day and snuck in to cover her when she'd inevitably curl up on the floor and fall asleep, I could do as I pleased. It was summer break, my two school friends were both on extended vacations with their families, and I had nothing else to do. Besides, rumor had it that Tess had a revolving door of rock stars in her house, and what fifteen-year-old kid wouldn't want to hang out with his idols? I'd played the piano since I could sit up, for the most part, but I really wanted to learn guitar. I thought maybe I could find someone at Tess's who would teach me.

"Hey, it's Dee Dee the Delivery Man. How are you?" She gave me a big hug, and I handed her the bag. "We've got a feast going, come on in. My brother Jimmy and his friend Kaleo buried a pig in the backyard and cooked it! We're going to have a Hawaiian luau. Can you stick around?"

I grinned at her. I was still painfully shy, but I knew there was a reason I'd met Tess Miller. "Sure. Thank you, Mrs.—I mean, Tess."

She winked at me and closed the door.

The house was full of people who were mostly older than me and a few little kids. She led me out back and introduced me to a group of women.

"This is Dee Dee. He's Diane's son. Can you make sure he gets a big ol' plate of food? Dee Dee, I'm going to make the rounds but please, make yourself comfortable. Eat, drink, and have a good time."

Three women stood, and two of them took hold of my arms.

"Dee Dee, it's so nice to meet you. I love your mom's work."

"Yeah, and her pot is to die for."

They all laughed.

"I'm glad you like it."

Mom taught art classes at Los Angeles City College, and she'd connected with some former students who made frequent trips to Mexico for supplies. There was also a farm in the valley where they grew the plants, and the farmer was kind of an eccentric guy. He loved Mom's paintings and often traded her. Though she made good money on her art and teaching, she called her herbal deliveries her nest egg. She had no one to rely on but herself, she'd say, and "sometimes you have to decide what you're willing to do to survive."

The third woman brought me a huge plate of food. "I'm Michelle. My husband John and I live just up the road. I haven't met your mom yet, but I'd love to get on her delivery list. Cass would, too, right?" She chuckled, and I took the plate, my stomach growling.

"Absolutely," Cass said. "I just moved up here, and I could definitely use a good delivery service."

"I'll tell her." Mom was really careful about who she made deliveries to, but if they were friends of Tess's? And huge rock stars? I'd make sure they got what they wanted. I loved The Mamas and The Papas. I couldn't believe these incredible women were serving *me* a meal.

A man came flying out of the house and cannonballed into the swimming pool. My heart nearly leapt out of my chest at the screams from everyone who was standing nearby. Thankfully I wasn't in danger of losing my food, because I might have eaten it soggy, that's how hungry I was for real food. I cooked for Mom and me, but I wasn't very good at it. If I never had Rice-A-Roni again it would be too soon.

When the man surfaced, I almost choked on a piece of pork. "Is that—"

"Jim Morrison, yeah," said Cass, shaking her head. "Things tend to get more interesting when he shows up."

As he pushed himself up and out of the pool, I could see why. The man was like a statue of Adonis. I understood why the magazines called him Dionysus, though, as I watched him grab a bottle of beer and drink the whole thing in one go. He wore black swim trunks that clung to his wet skin and everything beneath. I couldn't stop staring.

Yes, there were dozens of women in bikinis lying around, but I only had eyes for Jim.

Tells you something about me.

Another man came out of the house with a guitar, and he plopped down next to Michelle and started playing. My gaze was locked in on his fingers as he picked at the strings. The women went into the house shortly after, and I stayed on a lounge chair in the shade, watching him play. I couldn't move, *wouldn't* move.

Eventually, he looked up and smiled at me. "Want to play?"

I swallowed hard. "I only know piano."

He stood and slid his chair closer. Then he handed me the guitar. He went into the house, and I just stared at this piece of wonder in my hands. It smelled good, like wood polish. It was big, my hand barely fit around the neck, but my fingers were long. I pressed down on the strings and felt a shiver at the bite of the metal under my fingers.

The door opened and the man came back with another guitar.

"Nat? What are you doing?" Tess stood in the doorway, smiling at the guitar man.

He winked at her and took the chair next to me once more. "It's time you learn, son."

Tess watched as this man, Nat, taught me how to play a few chords. It didn't take long before I could hear the connections between the keys and the strings. It was like watching a zipper being pulled up. The two just came together.

I hadn't been paying attention to the time, but when I next looked up, the sky was dark.

"Oh no. I gotta go," I said, handing the guitar back to the man. "Thank you so much, Mr.—"

"Nat Greene. No problem." He set down the guitars and shook my hand. "You're a natural, kid. Come back anytime, man. I'll teach you some more."

He had no idea what a commitment he'd just made. I was determined to learn.

"Dee Dee, you are amazing," Tess said. At some point, she'd come to sit at the foot of my lounge chair. "I've never seen anyone learn that fast."

"Thank you. I've gotta go. If I don't cook for Mom, she won't eat."

"Oh, well here—come with me. I'll put some plates together for you to take back for dinner."

2019

I would have done anything for that woman. Inviting me into her house changed my life forever, and being back here without her was wrong. What had happened to her? What had I missed? What about my mother?

"I'll let you guys get back to it, then," Cherish said, bringing me back to Tess's kitchen in the present—in the house that now belonged to someone named Scott, who was also in the music business. That seemed coincidental. Perhaps in the last forty years, the canyon was still a special place, only different.

She was smiling at me, this woman who took care of Ryan, who'd bought me clothes and fed me. "Let me know if you need anything else. It was nice to meet you, Dee Dee."

"Thank you. I really appreciate it."

"I'll walk you out," Ryan said. He threw an arm over her shoulder and they turned out of sight from the kitchen.

"Dee Dee? I restrung your guitar while you were sleeping. I hope you don't mind. Scott had the right type of acoustic strings. I think I could fix it up a bit more, if you like. It's kinda what I do."

"Thank you." I wasn't sure how I felt about it. I liked that the old instrument had some defects. I liked that I had to work at it to play. The challenge appealed to me, but Kal's gesture was kind. "You guys have really gone out of your way for me. I can't thank you enough."

Ryan came back in the kitchen looking down at a small rectangular device in his hands. He raised his gaze to mine, and his face had paled. "The news is showing what happened at the rest stop."

He walked into the living room and turned on a giant screen hung on the wall. He used a small remote to flick the channels and then stepped back.

My face lit up the room a moment later.

"Dane Donovan disappeared forty years ago today, seemingly without a trace, from the Buttonwillow Rest Area on south bound I-5 in Kern County. This morning, detectives discovered a body behind the same rest area. Details are not being shared with the press while the sheriff's department attempts to contact next of kin. CHP has closed the rest area while they investigate the scene. Anyone who may have information is asked to please contact Community Liaison Detective Walter Muse, at the Kern County Sheriff's department."

Footage showed the police cars all over the rest area, and then the camera zoomed to a group of men in suits, and one in particular when they mentioned Detective Walter Muse.

"I saw him." It was the same man I'd seen at the gate, and the one who'd stared me down at the rest stop this morning. If he was in charge of the case, and he was here in Laurel Canyon, he probably knew something about me.

"Why Buttonwillow?" Kal stood beside me. The big man moved quietly, not like other big men I'd been around who didn't understand how much space they took up. "You asked us to take you there for a reason. Did you know there'd been another crime before we got there?"

"No! I didn't know until I saw... I just... That's where I last remember being. When something bad happened to me."

"I think you need to tell us what happened," Kal said, joining Ryan on the couch. "If we're going to be any help, we need to know."

"I honestly didn't remember anything about my life before the carnival until yesterday. A guy came to my booth and wanted me to do my thing—"

"What was your thing?" Ryan asked.

I chuckled but my hands were shaking again, and I needed... something. "Don't suppose you got a joint?"

Ryan gave a sad smile. "'Fraid I'm sober, friend. But if you need it, I can hit up a dispensary for delivery."

I frowned. "A dispensary?"

Ryan nodded with an amused frown. "Yeah, man. You know it's legal now."

"Wait, you mean... I was talking about weed."

Ryan laughed. "Right. Cannabis. Marijuana. It's legal in California and a few other states. We have places that will deliver it in whatever form you want. I just... I'd rather not have it here, if that's okay?"

"Fine, fine. I get it. I knew too many cats who had issues. What about tobacco?"

"That we *can't* have delivered. I can run out and get you some, but you know that shit will kill you and wreck your voice."

"So you're telling me that you can get weed delivered to your house, but not cigarettes? Like, there are more restrictions on tobacco?"

Ryan sighed. "Let's just say that a lot of research was done in the eighties, nineties, and on and on, and there are so many ways that tobacco products can kill you, it's not even funny."

I snorted. "I've already beat death once. A cigarette can't hurt you near as bad as another human, but all right I guess."

Kal and Ryan both shifted on the couch. They sat close to each other, and Kal had a possessive grip on Ryan's thigh. For some reason that caused a twinge, like a ghost of a memory of a time when I'd wished for someone to love *me* like that.

"Dee Dee, I understand your hesitance to trust. We want to help you." Kal's stare was so penetrating, I couldn't look at him for long.

"What do you want to know?"

"What happened at the carnival before you left?" Kal asked.

I exhaled through my nose and walked over to the glass wall that looked out on the patio and the swimming pool. How much should I tell them?

"My act at the carnival was The Troubadour's Talking Board. I have one of them old-timey spiritualist boards. I think I had it before I got there, but I don't remember. It just feels like it's always been a part of me. Anyway, when I touch the planchette, it's like I enter a vortex of words, if that makes sense. I don't know how it works, but there you go. I seem to remember using it to write songs, you know? I'd be thinking of something, and I'd touch the planchette and then the right words would come to me.

"At the carnival, I'd let people ask me a question at my booth, and then I'd use the board. Whatever poem came out of it, good, bad, or ugly, I'd type it up on a little card for them and they'd go on their merry way. Only, on my last night, this guy put his hands on it with me, and somehow it sucked us back into my memories."

Fear hit me like a gut punch, and I bent at the waist from the force of it.

"Hey," Kal said, coming to my side. "It's okay. Get it out

of your head. I promise it's worse in there than if you let it out."

I was panting now. "I was back at Buttonwillow. I saw the sign. I went into the bathroom and he was there, this faceless guy. I can't see his face no matter how hard I try. He came up to me at the urinal and grabbed me. I told him I wasn't interested. I didn't mess around with guys in bathrooms. But then he had an arm around my throat, and he dragged me out back of the place."

Tears pricked my eyes and my body ached like I was back there, fighting for my life. My hands balled into fists.

"Keep going. Let it out."

Kal didn't touch me, just stood beside me and breathed with me.

"I went limp, hoping he'd think I was out, and when he let up on the pressure I tried to fight back. I didn't know *how* to fight, but I tried. He stomped on my balls, man, and after that it was just..." I sank to the floor and wrapped my arms around my knees. I whispered, "It feels like it's happening right now."

"Breathe through your nose." Ryan was there, a hand on my shoulder. "It's okay. No one's going to hurt you."

"But that's just it! The guy at the carnival saw it all through my eyes. And he was *excited*. He wanted to *do* that, what happened to me. He was giddy! He was escorted out of the carnival but he said, 'I'll see you again.' That's why I had you take me to Buttonwillow. I thought he'd be there." I looked up at Kal. "And I think he was."

"He wasn't the one who hurt you, though? Before the carnival?"

"No. That man was bigger. He smelled like chemicals. But when I try to focus on his face, I see a blank spot where it should be. I knew he'd done it before, though. I could tell. He was... efficient. Even when I fought back, he anticipated my moves, man. The guy at the carnival, though, it was like he was there to learn. I don't know why he was drawn to me, I don't know why he put his hands on the planchette. No one had ever done that before. I don't know why it made the board work differently—"

"My friend Gavin had a Ouija board," Ryan said softly. "He used to use it to communicate with his ancestors' spirits. He said it worked differently when he used it with other people. I remember using it with his aunt, and it did that... it took me back to *her* memory."

I gazed at the two men kneeling beside me, and finally I could breathe.

"I have to stop him from hurting anyone else. I don't care what happened to me, but I don't want anyone else to go through what I did, and I worry that if he was so excited by watching what I went through, he'll keep doing it until he gets caught."

"Maybe we should call that detective," Kal said. "You can tell them what he looked like."

"But how can I explain to them how I know? That's going to be tricky, don't you think?"

Ryan and Kal looked at each other, and Ryan sighed.

"What choice do we have?"

Six

alter

The four of us left the bar a lot more subdued than when we'd arrived.

"I'm going to call my cousin at San Joaquin," Denny said. "Gene, you're going to contact LA?"

"Yeah," Gene said. "And I'm going to follow up with CHP. Dax, you'll keep working the Buttonwillow case?"

"Yes, and Walter's getting on an airplane in a few hours. Right?" Dax turned on me. So did the others.

"You don't honestly believe—"

"You don't have a choice," Denny said. "Captain Barnett mandated it. You haven't taken vacation in two years. Not even holidays. I know this is your baby—"

"It's not my baby," I said, trying to play this right. These men were my closest friends. They knew me better than anyone. "But I've invested twenty years in this case." More, actually, but I didn't need to remind them.

"Then let us gather the information," Denny said. "When you come back, we'll have more leads for you to follow up."

I cursed and turned away from them and took a few breaths, trying to slow my pulse. "How do you expect me to sit on the beach with a little umbrella in my drink when everything's shifted?" This information could bring me closer to finding out what really happened to Dane Donovan.

"Look, you're off the clock," Gene said. "Doesn't mean you can't do a little snooping around. How about I set him up with my LA connections? Maybe he goes down to sit by the pool at some swank Beverly Hills place with a little umbrella drink instead, while he looks over case files. Ain't no law against that."

Out of all of us, Gene was the one most flexible about interpreting policy and procedure. Most of the time it pissed me off. I was a by-the-book detective who put humanity first when dealing with victims and families. And though I knew I was dangerously close to crossing a line of professionalism—my captain had specifically told me to take a break from police work—there was no way I was going to walk away from this case now, not even for a week.

Denny looked me over, his brows furrowed. "I swear to God, Muse. Don't make me have to call your mother. You get three hots and your ass better be in that rack eight hours minimum per day, you got it? This time off is supposed to be for your mental and physical health."

"Right, of course. Gene, text me your LAPD contacts. I'll call tomorrow, see if I can set up a meeting. I'll sleep before that, all right?"

I wasn't fooling any of them, but they understood.

"Don't go off half-cocked, Muse," Gene said with a

chuckle, and he pulled me in for a bro hug. "We gotchoo," he whispered in my ear.

I hugged the other guys, making sure Dax knew to keep me posted on the new case, and I walked to my truck fully intending to go home.

My phone buzzed as I opened the door.

"Detective Muse."

"Detective, this is Taylor in dispatch. We received a call on the tip line for you. Information regarding the Buttonwillow homicide."

"That should go to Detective Dax Brown. I'm on," I ground my teeth before the last bit, "vacation."

"They specifically requested you, Detective. I'm sending the callback number to your phone. You can pass it on to Detective Brown if you like."

"Thank you," I said, but she'd already hung up. A follow-up buzz indicated a text. I finished climbing into the truck and started it up, the cold seeping in through my jacket. I blew on my hands and then hit the call button.

It rang three times before a male voice answered.

"Yeah?"

"This is Detective Walter Muse of the Kern County Sheriff's Department. I was given this number from the tip line?"

"Right. Thank you for calling. Sir, my name is Ryan Wells, and a friend of mine has some information about separate incidents at the Buttonwillow Rest Area. He'd like to speak with you."

Ryan Wells? "You were there this morning. At Buttonwillow," I said. "You spoke to the CHP."

"Yes, sir. We were there. Are you still in LA?"

I flinched. "How did you know I was in LA?" Had I been tailed? Was I that off my game I hadn't noticed? Maybe the guys were right to push me to take this vacation.

"My friend says he saw you outside the gates of the house we're staying at in Laurel Canyon."

What the hell? "What's your friend's name?"

Ryan was quiet for a minute, and then I heard him muffle the phone and talk to someone else. "When can you be in Laurel Canyon? We'll explain everything when you get here."

At this time of night, it shouldn't be a problem to get there in an hour, but it was already ten o'clock. "It would take me an hour."

"Good. We'll be up. Do you need the address?"

"Give it to me just to be safe."

I typed it into my GPS app as he spoke. Of course, the smart thing to do would be to go home and sleep and then head out in the morning.

The *smartest* thing to do would be to call Dax, Gene, or Denny. Any of them, really.

"I'll be there in an hour."

Apparently, the smart thing was not on the menu.

"Thank you, Detective. My friend, he's... well, he's really nervous to talk to you. I don't know his whole story, but it's harsh, if you get me."

Alarms started going off in my mind, but I was already pushing the go button on the GPS and putting my truck in gear. "I'll be there as soon as I can. If you could, please keep him there?"

"Yes, sir. He's agreed to let us help. Don't make me sorry I called you, feel me?"

"I do."

"Oh, and Detective? Mind picking up a carton of Marlboros?"

"Cigarettes? Okay..."

We hung up, and I drove like the devil was chasing me. He had been ever since my father was assigned Dane Donovan's case.

. . .

Forty-nine minutes later, I pulled up to the same gates I'd stood in front of earlier that day, where I'd thought I'd seen a ghost for the second time in a day.

Who the hell was I going to find at Ryan's? I ran through all of the information I'd gotten from the phone call; he'd said "the house where we're staying." What the fuck was I walking into? Wells had a record, but not for anything violent. He was a damn rock star, for crying out loud. I'd asked Siri to play music from his band—Backdrop Silhouette—on the drive down, and it almost blew out my speakers when it came on. I had to scramble to turn down the volume.

I'd often been accused of having stunted musical growth. I preferred singer-songwriter type music and the classics from the '60s and '70s. It took me back to the time when things were good... when my parents were in love and things were happy at our home, before my father had his break.

I parked my truck at the curb and got out, looking around. I texted my location to Gene, figuring he was the one person who wouldn't freak the fuck out.

Jesus, Muse. You were supposed to go home.

I got a call off the tip line. The same guys who called in the vic this morning. Tell Dax in the morning, okay? If you don't hear from me by eight, ping me. If I don't get back to you, send my last known to LAPD.

The three dots floated for much longer than usual.

. . .

Fuck you, Walter. Be safe.

"I love you too," I sent back, using voice text. I rang the buzzer on the pole next to the gate.

"Detective?" a voice spoke from the speaker.

"Yeah."

The gates opened slowly, and I made the walk up the long, dark driveway. The house had floodlights and security cameras, and it looked like it had been renovated recently. I knew this had been the home of Tess Miller until she'd passed away under suspicious circumstances. The details were sketchy in my mind at this late hour, but I remember it wasn't pretty. Diane had sure been shaken up about it.

The front door opened as I approached.

"Thank you for coming," Wells said. I stepped past him into the foyer, handed him the carton of cigarettes that set me back a pretty penny, and was startled to find a hulking blond guy standing behind him, scowling at me.

"Detective, this is my husband, Kal Alexandrou. There are no weapons or drugs in the house that I'm aware of, but it belongs to my producer, Scott Cross. If you need to search the place, I give consent as long as you know we've been here less than twenty-four hours. I can provide his contact information if you need it."

I stood with my back to the wall and raised an eyebrow at him. "I appreciate that. But you're no longer on parole, from what I understand. Is there anyone else here?"

"Me."

It was good the wall was at my back.

The ghost appeared in the entryway to what looked like a living room, and I would have fallen over backward otherwise.

My hand involuntarily went to my weapon at my right side. "*You.*"

He walked closer and stood beside Kal. He came up to the guy's sternum.

The size is right. The hair is the same. Those eyes...

And up close, he looked even more familiar, like I'd seen him before. Talked to him.

The carnival. The Troubadour.

No way.

Ryan looked between us and put a hand on the smaller man's shoulder.

"Detective Muse, this is Dee Dee."

He couldn't be a ghost, then, if these two saw him. Right?

Ryan picked up on my attempt to avoid a freak out. "You look like you could use some coffee? Tea?"

"*Please.*"

Ryan chuckled. "Kal, honey, please grab Detective Muse a coffee. You remember how to use the Keurig?"

The big man nodded but was hesitant to leave his husband's side, much less Dee Dee's.

"I'm fine," Ryan murmured to ease his concern, pushing up on his toes to kiss his cheek. Then he turned to smile at me. "Come on. Let's sit."

My brain kicked back on. "No one else is in the house?"

"Just us three," Ryan said. He put his arm around Dee Dee's shoulders, and I followed them into the living room.

Dee Dee looked back at me, his green eyes wide.

The pretty man with the green eyes.

My dream.

Had I somehow superimposed the two men together?

I shook my head. *Pull it together, Muse.* Thankfully, they took the couch facing the entryway, and I took a chair that had a wall behind it. In this open floor plan, there were at least three doorways that led off of this room and a wall of glass that looked out onto a patio with a swimming pool.

Why would Ryan take the chance of calling me here if there was something suspect going on? The way he was taking care of this Dee Dee, he seemed genuinely concerned. I relaxed the tiniest fraction.

"Detective?" Ryan asked, leaning forward with his fingers laced between his knees. "Where do you stand on phenomena that's not easily explained?"

I rested my hands on my thighs and thought of the best way to answer that. "Fairly open, although I think most things have a simple explanation once you get to the bottom of them."

He nodded and turned to look at Dee Dee. "Do you want to start?"

Dee Dee seemed so small on the overstuffed leather couch. His feet barely touched the ground. He wore a forest-green crew neck sweater and a pair of baggy jeans, with white ankle socks on and no shoes. His hair was wet, as if he'd showered recently.

"I'll talk." He brushed his hair back off of his shoulders. "I know something about the murder that happened this morning."

"Okay," I said, trying to keep my breathing even. "Thank you for coming forward. But before we go any further, I'm off duty at the moment. At some point, we'll probably need an official sworn statement from you."

His green-eyed gaze held me captive, and I watched as his mouth moved, perhaps preparing to speak, perhaps taking care with his words.

"There are two parts to the story. The first is the most straightforward."

"Okay." I was trying to be patient but I was on the edge of my seat, all of my senses honed in on this small man who looked so much like the ghost I'd been chasing for years.

"I was working at a carnival outside of Las Vegas. My routine there was to write poems for people. There's a little hocus-pocus about it, but that's all you need to know."

And there it was. The two faces superimposed. This man before me looked so much like Dane Donovan. He looked *and* sounded like the Troubadour. He worked at the carnival writing poems.

I didn't need to be a detective to put these pieces together.

Hocus-pocus? Woo-woo? Magic?

Didn't matter. I was a believer.

I was looking at my cold case in the flesh. I'd also seen him when I was ten years old, three years after he disappeared, at the carnival... though I'd been told that was impossible.

And my father? He said he'd seen a body at the scene of Dane's disappearance. He'd gone to call for backup from his patrol car, and when he returned, the body was gone. No one had believed him.

When we'd seen this man at the carnival, he'd recognized him, just as I was now, despite insisting to me later that it wasn't him.

I felt closer to my father than ever... and that wasn't necessarily a good thing.

"Go on," I said, my voice cracking.

Dee Dee blew out a breath and slid his hands forward and over his knees, probably a bit freaked out by my reaction to his story. He had beautiful hands with long fingers, but even in the dim light of the living room, I could see scars on his knuckles.

"A man came to my booth and he rubbed me the wrong way. You ever have a strange feeling about a person? I would imagine that, being a cop, you sometimes come across people you just know are *bad*."

I nodded slowly, his voice so melodic it danced over my skin like a light rain. I listened to him with my whole body.

I'll write you the prettiest little poem.

"It was late, and I didn't want to write him no poem. The carnival director, he don't let bad people in. I don't know if this guy was already bad, or he *wanted* to be bad, but he definitely wanted something. He..." Dee Dee seemed to hit a wall, and his eyes went wide. Ryan whispered something to him, and he nodded.

I tried to be patient, seeing as this guy might be able to answer a lot of questions that had plagued me since I was a kid.

"Look, I know this don't make no sense, but what I do—or what I *did*—was use a talking board, and I get messages from it. Believe it or don't, that's your business."

Oh, I believed it. I'd seen it. I held up my hand. "Please, continue."

Dee Dee exhaled in a huff and crossed his leg over his knee, exposing delicate ankles from under his jeans. In that moment, I understood why it was once considered inappropriate for ladies to show their ankles in public. I was mesmerized by him.

"Normally, I don't let no one touch the planchette with me, but this guy, he put his fingers on before I could stop him and... it took us both back into a very bad memory."

I scooted forward to hear him better, as his voice had gone quiet at the end. "Was this memory something that had been fresh in your mind?"

He shook his head vigorously and his hair fell in his face. "No, sir. I didn't even remember what happened. I only remembered the time I'd been at this carnival. They told me they'd found me... injured." He really spread that word out, like he wasn't totally comfortable admitting it. "Once I was better, they asked me what I could do, and I told them I had a way with words. Like poetry, you know? So that's what I did. But when this guy jumped into my memory with me, it was like it was happening for real. *Again.* He watched, he didn't try to help me or nothing, he just... let it happen. When I finally pulled my hands off and the memory went away, the guy was smiling, all excited like, and he said, 'I'll see you again.'"

The message at the scene this morning flickered in my consciousness.

"You don't remember this man? Do you know if you'd ever seen him before?"

"I don't know, I don't think so. I don't know how I could've, seeing as he was young and I—"

"Detective, do you take anything in your coffee?"

Kal interrupted Dee Dee and shot a look at both him and Ryan. What was that about?

"No, thank you." I accepted the mug but set it down on the table next to the chair, still not totally comfortable with this situation.

Ryan whispered something to Dee Dee, and I thought maybe he was trying to help, but I felt like I was only getting the tiniest fraction of their story.

"So you don't think you knew the guy, hadn't seen him before. What happened then?"

Dee Dee tucked his hair behind his ear, and I saw a long, jagged scar on his left cheekbone. He kept his head ducked, like he didn't want it visible.

"Nik and Mr. Ame—they're in charge of the carnival— they escorted the guy off the premises. But it didn't sit right with me. I had a gut feeling that the guy liked what he saw so much, he wanted to do it to someone himself." He slid his hands between his thighs and looked at the ground. "I wanted to stop him."

Ryan watched him, and then he looked at me. "We picked him up on the highway in Mojave at like four-thirty in the morning. Hitchhiking. He said he needed to get to Buttonwil-low, and seeing as he was like a hundred miles away, we couldn't let him walk. So we drove him, but when we arrived, we were too late."

I had so many questions.

"Do you make it a habit of picking up hitchhikers?" I asked Ryan.

He smirked. "Not hardly. Let's just say that my husband and I met last year under some peculiar circumstances, and we made a pact that if we ever came across someone who needed help like we did, we'd help them on their way."

I sat quietly with that information for a long moment. None of them could have had anything to do with what happened at Buttonwillow, if what he said was true. "Got anyone who can corroborate that you and your husband were on the road at that time?"

He thought for a minute. "We left from the parking lot at the Hard Rock Hotel in Vegas. I had to scan our key card to get out of the hotel lot, so that would show what time we left, I think. We decided to get an early start so we could miss the traffic and watch the sun come up."

I nodded. I highly doubted a rock star would have committed such a brutal, calculated murder like the one we'd seen at Buttonwillow and then invite me to his house, but stranger things had been known to happen.

"And what time did you leave the carnival?" I asked Dee Dee.

Dee Dee frowned. "I'm not sure."

"Do you remember where it was?"

"Somewhere in the desert, but I'm sure it's gone by now."

"Why Buttonwillow?"

Dee Dee's eyes flared, and I watched his Adam's apple bob in his throat. "That's where it happened to me." His gaze flicked to Kal's and back to me. "The bad thing."

His admission slammed me back into my seat. I couldn't

speak. How was this even possible? "Do you have any identification?"

"No."

"What's Dee Dee? Like a nickname?"

"I think so."

"Where do you live?"

"I don't know."

"Do you know your birthday?"

"Novem... uh—"

"Social Security number?"

"Why?"

"What day is it?"

"I'm not sure—"

"Who's the president?"

"Jimmy Carter!"

The room fell silent.

I got up and moved to his side, my movement startling Dee Dee and sending Kal rushing toward me to defend his friend.

I held up a hand to stop Kal from laying hands on a police officer and stared at Dee Dee as he sank farther into the sofa. I lowered my voice.

"Why do you look identical to Dane Donovan?"

Seven

Dane

Hearing Detective Muse say my given name stirred a longing in me. He spoke it as if he knew me. He should have frightened me. Cops weren't always trustworthy, in my experience. If you had long hair, they made assumptions, but this one didn't seem to have any negative opinions, at least not that he was saying.

I needed a break. And a smoke. Desperately.

"Hey, Detective, man," Ryan said. "Give him some space. Please."

I hated the position I'd put Ryan in. When the detective mentioned Ryan was released from parole, I felt awful that I'd dragged him into my mess. I knew how hard it was for folks who'd done their time or paid their dues and still had to walk on eggshells for fear of being hooked up again.

There'd been a time when Laurel Canyon was crawling

with undercover officers trying to get invited to parties. They'd hang around the general store and try to talk to the people who'd become like family to me. They'd ask to crash, and it got to the point where people like Tess and Cass had to be careful who they brought home. Mom had even cut back her herbal deliveries. Once I turned 18, she'd refused to let me make them anymore. "Too much heat," she'd say. "You don't want to end up in prison, baby. I won't let you."

The detective stood from the couch, where he'd sat right beside me, his knee nudging mine. I popped up, too, and maneuvered around Ryan.

"Did you bring smokes? I could really use one."

The detective's shoulders slouched a little and his expression crumbled. "Of course. I'm sorry."

He was unlike any cop I'd ever met. He seemed to genuinely feel bad for asking me questions. He was also surprisingly handsome. Nothing at all like the men I'd been attracted to in the past, but then again, they'd paid me no mind. He was so focused on me, it was both exhilarating and terrifying. Would he believe me when my whole story was out? And if he knew who I really was, what *else* did he know about me?

Kal went to the kitchen and hurried back. He handed me a pack and a book of matches.

"I'll go out back, Ryan. I'm sorry, I gotta light up."

"Hey, man, I get it," Ryan said with a kind smile. "I've been there. Don't worry about it."

I nodded and looked to the detective. "You can come. I can keep talking once my nicotine levels are back up."

The corner of his lip quirked, and he followed me. He was taller and broader than me, but not as big as Kal. The detective looked tired. Dark circles shadowed his face but his dark-brown eyes were bright and alert. He'd likely been up since he'd heard about the thing at the rest area. I'd slept most of the day.

I smacked the pack against my palm and then tore it open, shoving the trash in the pocket of the new jeans Cherish had brought me. I needed a belt eventually. They were so loose I had to keep yanking them up on my hips. I tore a match out of the book and flipped the cover backwards, pulling the match head against the strip. It flared to life, and I felt better already. The first inhale burned a bit, but the nicotine hit my bloodstream and sent a rush through my limbs, waking me up, reminding me that I was still alive.

"Where are my manners?" I held the pack out toward Walter, and he shook his head.

"No, thank you. That's one habit I haven't picked up."

I sucked in another hit and felt myself relaxing. Finally. "You have others?"

The detective shoved his hands in his pockets and chuckled, looking down at his feet in a strangely shy movement. "Butterfinger bars. Driving too fast." He looked up. "An obsession with the past."

"The past? Any particular time period?"

He stood taller and pegged me with his dark-eyed stare. "The sixties and seventies. Up 'til nineteen seventy-nine, to be exact."

"That's pretty specific," I said, feeling the tremors back in my hands. There had been times after I arrived at the carnival when my hands would shake uncontrollably. Made it hard to do my job. Mr. Ame noticed once and he laid a hand on my shoulder, telling me not to worry about it. It hadn't troubled me again. Not until that man showed up at my booth.

"It was a pretty incredible time."

I nodded. "Until nineteen seventy-nine."

"Yeah."

He continued to stare at me, and I took a few minutes to finish my cigarette and light up another one.

"Been a while since you've had one?"

"Can't remember, sometime before I left the carnival. Can't remember much. Comes in waves."

He nodded. "Dane, I'm so sorry."

I blinked at him. "Why are you sorry? You call me Dane like you know me."

"I *do* know... Dane Donovan. At least his case file." His expression was full of sorrow. "My father was the detective assigned to the missing persons case of Dane Donovan. He searched for him. Followed every possible lead. It drove him —" He sighed and planted his hands on his hips again. "I became a detective twenty years ago and lobbied to have the case assigned to me. I've done everything I could to find him since."

My eyes burned with tears. "Here I am."

"And I'm trying not to ask you a million questions."

I smiled and blew out a puff of smoke away from him. "I'll answer what I can."

"I saw you. At the carnival," he said, his voice softer than when he'd hit me with all those questions inside. "My father insisted I couldn't have seen Dane Donovan at the carnival, and I believed him. Until now."

I squinted at him. "At the carnival?"

He nodded. "When I was ten years old. You wrote me a poem. I didn't put it together for sure until now that... well, that I saw *you* at the carnival." The detective cleared his throat and recited words that resonated through me.

"Here, there, any old where
Exists a carnival without a care
Behold, beware, a wild grizzly bear
A place where creatures frolic and dare
Welcome children, come and share

A magic, a wonder, a splendid affair
Your luck, your skill, or a wild sort of hair
Make your own way at this mystical fair
And when you leave for places elsewhere
So does the wondrous carnival, without a care."

"Detective," I breathed, a tear sliding down my neck. I recognized those words. I remembered the boy, especially the look on his face after his father appeared. The guy was… unstable, is the nicest way I could describe it. The boy was caught between being embarrassed by the fuss his father made and concerned for him all at the same time. A lot for a little guy. "You're all grown up now."

The detective's smile crumpled. "And you're not." His voice hitched.

"No."

We stared at each other, him standing four feet away, his body tense as if he was holding himself back.

He was nothing like the men I'd known, but I found him irresistible. Clean-cut guy of some sort of mixed heritage that gave him dark eyes and an olive complexion. His hair was nearly black with gray at the temples, buzzed close to the scalp, which few men in the '70s did; instead, they held on to their thinning locks as long as possible. But his mustache was all '70s, thick, neatly trimmed above plump dark red lips.

He wore a dark brown corduroy blazer over a mint-green dress shirt and patterned V-neck sweater vest. The shirt had been unbuttoned at the top, showing the tiniest bit of dark hair at the base of his throat and tanned skin. I wished I could see his wrists. I had a feeling they were thick. He filled out his clothes like he was in excellent shape and his hands were big. Khaki pants were pulled tight over his thighs and hips.

Previous me—well, when I was in my mid-twenties, the years before the bad thing happened—might have gotten up the courage to flirt with him, tried to make his cheeks pink so

I'd know if I was the kind of person he was looking for, and then I'd throw him a few breadcrumbs and see if he came after me. It was so rare to have that opportunity, though. Tess insisted that I had to be careful if I wanted to have a career in music, so I was. I couldn't go to the places I'd started hearing about in West Hollywood, like Circus of Books, nor could I be seen at French Market or Studio One.

The shakes started up again.

"I shouldn't be here," I muttered.

"But you *are* here, Dane. Forget the fact that you should be in your late sixties right now and that you don't look it... what happened to you? Did you run away or did someone take you? How did you get away?"

I wrapped my arms around myself, taking care not to light my hair on fire. So many questions. "I didn't run away. I'd thought about it at one point, when yet another disappointment in my music career happened. Pull a Connie Converse, just drive off into the sunset." I flexed my hand, feeling the scars stretch across my knuckles. "No, someone took me. I did *not* go willingly."

The detective stepped closer, and though my instinct was to flee, there was something comforting about his presence. He was listening to me. He hadn't arrested me or taken me off to the psych ward. Yet.

He took a deep breath and stepped one bit closer. I still didn't move.

"I've been looking for you for a long time," he said. "I feel like I should pinch myself. Maybe I'm still in bed, dreaming about you. Wait, that was... Oh God." He looked away—and there was that blush.

I laughed so loud, I think it startled us both as much as his admission, and he chuckled.

"What I meant was—"

"They didn't catch the man who hurt me? Wait—you thought I *left*?"

"No," he said, his voice hollow. "There was very little evidence at the scene, though, and some folks in law enforcement hypothesized that you had. Only your clothes were found, and your blood. No witnesses. My father followed up on leads for years. He had search teams looking for you in the area around the place for weeks. You just... disappeared. Into thin air."

I put out the second cigarette and would have grabbed a third, but I'd calmed down some. Not sure if it was because of the detective's presence or the nicotine. "I didn't see his face. I don't remember anything between what happened and waking up at the carnival."

"Were you with the carnival this whole time, then?"

I stared at him and frowned. "Would you believe me if I said yes?"

He shrugged and rubbed at his head. "I'd have to, I suppose. What other explanation is there?"

"Beats me."

He looked down at the ground again, and then lifted only his eyes. "Are you in pain? Your scars... did you get medical attention?"

"I'm not sure what happened, but someone took care of me. I'm okay. I can still play guitar. But I haven't been able to sing. My brain... it don't work right, not like it used to. And my hands..." I held them up and they trembled, but not nearly as bad as they did sometimes. "They don't always cooperate."

"I'd say it takes time, but—"

"Time's passed. I haven't aged, but that don't mean nothing."

"Look, Dane. Right before Ryan called me, I got some information from a retired CHP officer that there were other cases like yours. We didn't communicate well back then between jurisdictions, and a lot of them were probably logged as missing persons and presumed to be runaways, but I'm going to meet with some folks and see what I can find. I don't know if the man who took you is alive, dead, in prison... but I won't ever stop looking, not 'til I find out what happened to you."

"I'm here now, though. It don't really matter anymore."

"It *does* matter. How many others did he hurt? How many didn't survive? How many parents are like your mother, living without knowing, without closure?"

Something squeezed so tight in my chest, it took my breath away. "My mom... have you seen her?" I stepped forward and put a hand on his forearm. "Is she okay?"

He smiled. "Just visited with her this morning. She lives in the same place, just up the road. She never gave up on you, refused to have you declared deceased."

"That's... sad. I feel so awful. Who took care of her all this time? If no one was there—"

"A woman named Barbara lives with her. She's her assistant, has been as long as I've had your case. Handles all of her affairs. She continues to make art, although fine line work is tough for her now." He gave me a bashful smile. "I bought a couple of her paintings. She's so good."

"I'm glad she still has her art. Always was her best friend. Never failed her like a man. Never doubted her like her family. And I guess, it must've comforted her in her loss."

"She loves you very much, Dane. She's never given up hope that we'd find you."

"Here I am," I said again, with a sort of manic chuckle. "What do you plan to do with me?"

The detective's expression briefly morphed into something hungry. Carnal. Like maybe the clean-cut officer of the law was interested in me for more than my disappearance. How intriguing. Was he... like me? My imagination went wild in that moment. What might happen if I gave him an invitation? Would he want to have his way with me? Would I let him?

I *wanted* to let him.

But then he seemed to snap out of it.

I'd had to become really good at reading men back in the day. I was out of practice, maybe, but I was pretty sure the detective was like me, and *liked* me.

"You said you left the carnival to stop this man from hurting people. We can't help the man he murdered today, but Dane... I want you to help me catch him before he hurts anyone else. If it's the same man from the carnival, you know what he looks like."

I pulled out another cigarette and tried to light it, my heart pounding in my chest. My hands shook so bad, I dropped the match, and then the pack, and then the cigarette. The detective and I both crouched down at the same time, and he scooped up the items.

"Here," he said, handing me the cigarette, brushing it off first. Then he lit a match and held it out for me, cupping the flame as the cherry glowed red.

Those hands.

"I might swoon if you keep doing that for me, Detective."

He blew out the match and tossed it in a trashcan on the patio. "I'm swooning just standing here with you." He was dead serious.

I pressed a hand to my chest, and he held up one of his own, taking a step back. I'd read the situation correctly.

"But that's not why I'm here. I'm here to help you, and, I hope, get *your* help too."

"Is that *all* you want?" I knew better than to push, but what did I have to lose? I'd nearly died. I was back in the canyon. Home... or at least it had been.

"I want to solve your case, and I want to catch this new guy." He rubbed at his jaw. "And... I want to know you, Dane.

Beyond my professional capacity. I always wondered what I would say to you if I ever found you."

I grinned at him, though I was shaking so bad I thought the ground was about to open up. "You're doing a helluva job."

He reached out like he wanted to touch my hair, but then pulled his hand back. "I want to bring you home to your mother."

I took a long drag and narrowed my eyes at the detective. "I'm not ready to see my mother. I don't know how you can help me other than to catch this guy, because I'll be a nervous wreck until he's caught. My life isn't worth saving if it means I led this man to hurt other people."

"I understand about your mother." He took another step back. "Honestly, I have no idea how I'm going to explain this to her." The detective looked out over the pool and yawned so widely, his jaw cracked.

"You need to crash, man."

He put his hands on his hips. "I'm all right. I don't think I could sleep now if I tried."

I finished the third cigarette, but the vibe was off now, like when you miss that perfect amount of caffeine or weed or coke to get you right where you want to be, and you're left wanting, jittery, disappointed.

That pretty much summed up my experience with sex, too.

Yeah, this man had me thinking about sex. Me, having sex with a cop. I'd have never heard the end of it from Tess...

1968

"How come I never see you with any of the girls here, Dee Dee?"

She gave me a hand-rolled she'd made from my latest

herbal delivery. I took a hit and coughed. I was still learning. She took it back from me with a warm smile.

Sometimes I felt like I was her pet project. Over the past year, she'd dressed me up, made sure I got all the guitar lessons I wanted, and she encouraged me to keep a journal about whatever. She said songwriters had to have stuff to draw from, so I should start writing everything down. I was on my fourth notebook.

"Don't know. Haven't really thought about it."

Her eyes bugged out. "You're almost seventeen! Aren't girls *all* you're supposed to think about?"

My cheeks flushed, but I felt brave all of a sudden. "What if I'm thinking about boys?"

I thought for a split second that I'd messed up as she stared at me, confused. Then she pulled me into a hug.

"That's okay too. Not everyone will understand, but I think you like who you like, man. Your heart decides for you." She pulled back but kept her arm around me. We were sitting on a giant piece of patio furniture that was like a big square. I'd seen interesting things happen on that square. "Let's figure out who you should talk to."

I tried to pull away. "No way, I'm not ready—"

"Oh, come on," she said, holding the joint up for me again. I took another hit and sank into the cushions a bit. "At least let's figure out your type. Who catches your eye here?"

I laughed. "Well, Peter Tork, because he's always naked. It's hard *not* to look at him." I glanced around the backyard. Joni Mitchell and Graham Nash were huddled together, wrapped in a blanket, passing a joint back and forth. David Crosby was playing guitar and had four girls around him. I was pretty sure he was sleeping with all of them.

Then my gaze fell on the man who gave me the most butterflies.

"Gram."

"Gram Parsons? Really!"

I shushed her, and we both fell to giggling.

"He's dreamy," I whispered. "I never liked country until I heard him sing it. I could listen to him all night."

Tess snickered and took another hit. "He's cute, but you need to watch out for men like him. Life of the party, death to your heart. That type of man will break you in ways you could never imagine."

I watched her closely and wondered who'd broken *her*? She always had a full house, everyone loved her, but she sort of haunted the place like a ghost, there but not touchable.

"Did you love a man like that?"

She sighed. "Too many of them. That's why I'm single." She took another hit and handed me the last of the joint. "Some of these men are so talented and yet they ride through life at breakneck speeds, flirting with their mortality. How many of us will be around when the seventies get here? The eighties? We're meant to inspire a generation, but I don't know. Sometimes I just want to take them all and shake them. Tell them to slow down. Absorb some of this life before they wind up in the next one. But everyone's gotta go their own way."

She exhaled a long time and her lashes were wet. When she turned back to me, she cupped my cheek. "Find yourself a nice boy who likes poetry and movies and music, but who wants more out of life than this."

She kissed my forehead, and then decided she wanted to bake a big ol' cake, and did I want to help her? I always did.

2019

"Dane?"

"Hmm? Sorry, just thinking."

"About?"

"Cake. Do you like cake, Detective?"

He smoothed down his mustache. "I've been known to have a sweet tooth. But you didn't answer my question."

"What's the question?" I sidled up close to him, ready to drop those breadcrumbs. What a nice distraction he'd make.

"Can I see you tomorrow?" He looked at his watch. "Today? I should let you get some rest."

"Where do you live? Are you married? Do you have kids?"

He barked out a laugh and shook his head. "Suppose I deserve that. I have asked *you* a lot of questions tonight." He took a deep breath. "Bakersfield. Not anymore. And two. Boy and a girl, both in college."

Oh, he was older. Not technically. To him, I was nearly 70 years old, after all. "Anyone waiting for you at home?"

His brown eyes went soft. "I live with my mother, but she's got a caregiver with her this week. I'm supposed to be on vacation." He shook his head.

"Supposed to be?"

"I got in trouble for working too long without taking days off. I've been laser-focused on cases the past couple of years."

"Because of me?" Here I was, standing before another broken man, contemplating taking that ride. *Oh, Tess. I guess I do have a type.*

"Partly. But I've had a few other cases that I've been really involved with. A human trafficking ring, a murdered couple and their children. Lot of people behaving badly these days."

"Human trafficking?"

"Yeah. Big problem. Sometimes they're sex workers, sometimes they're immigrants brought here and forced to work for little to no pay under coercion and manipulation. We have a lot of vulnerable populations in Bakersfield."

"You want to save them."

He frowned. "I don't know if save is the right word. I try

to help. Mitigate the damage done, prevent others from meeting similar fates."

"Okay, Detective. Let's help each other prevent those fates. Let's find this man."

His concerned expression softened. "Thank you. And let's make a pact to also catch the person who hurt *you*, or at least identify him. Then you can have the life that was stolen from you."

"Was it mine to begin with? If someone takes your life, is it yours anymore?"

"Dane—"

"I want cake, Detective. Let's go see what we can find." I tucked my hair behind my ear and smiled at him.

He might be broken.

But then, so was I.

Eight

alter

I followed Dane back into the house, where he was on a mission to bake a cake. I stood in the doorway to the kitchen while he started pulling things out of cabinets.

"What's going on in here?" Ryan asked with an amused tone when he entered a few moments later.

"I feel like cake. It's sort of a tradition in this house." He seemed a bit frustrated with his search.

"Can I help?" I asked. I did know my way around a kitchen. When things went south with my father, for a minute I thought I'd rebel and become a chef instead of going into law enforcement. It was my way of pissing him off, but by then he was too far gone to care.

"Things aren't where Tess kept them. Everything looks different. The pantry used to be over there, and she always had plenty of baking supplies. I can't find the mixer."

Ryan and I traded looks, and then helped in the search.

"There's so many cabinets now," Dane grumbled. "Ah, there it is. Detective, would you be so kind?"

He pointed to a mixer on the top shelf, and I approached to reach up for it. He didn't move. Our proximity had my body on high alert, just as it had been when we were on the patio together. Our hands connected as I set the mixer on the counter for him. Standing this close, I got a good look at the scar on his cheekbone. Probably from being struck, or his face striking a rough object.

He must have realized I was looking at his scar. He put a hand over it and turned away from me.

"What else do you need?" Ryan asked.

"Eggs, butter, baking powder, flour, sugar, vanilla, whole or buttermilk, vegetable oil. Oh, and cocoa powder and powdered sugar for the icing. Or chocolate chips if necessary."

For someone who'd been having trouble remembering things, this was a good sign. But then I noticed him looking at all of the items funny, and the oven with its digital controls had him stumped.

"What temp do you need it at?" I asked him gently.

He gazed up at me with that spooked expression, and I recognized what he was up to. He was overwhelmed with everything, and the cake baking was a distraction he desperately needed.

"Three-fifty? Please?"

The pleading in his voice had me ready to do anything for him. Anything to lessen his anxiety. He watched me push the buttons on the stove, nodding to himself.

"I don't think I've ever baked a cake before. Definitely haven't baked from scratch," Ryan said. "I've made brownies from a box a few times. Well," he laughed, "in my reckless youth. And they had a little extra kick, if you know what I mean."

Dane shrugged as he measured ingredients and mixed them like a pro. "Tess was known to add all kinds of fun to her cooking. There was one night she mixed a particularly potent batch of magic mushrooms into her midnight omelets and the whole house was full of people trippin'. I showed up the next morning and she was trying to keep everyone out of the pool. Someone was convinced there was gold on the bottom, and they were all trying to jump in to get the gold. I helped her keep the peace until the high wore off and everyone went home."

I figured it wouldn't hurt to ask him some more harmless questions while he worked.

"The stories say everyone used to go from house to house up here, and that Cass Elliot's house was a popular spot. Was Tess's house like that too?"

Dane had the ingredients in the mixer, and he was trying to figure out how to turn it on. I let him poke at it and a moment later, he had it going.

"People made the rounds, yeah. Tess's house was the place to be when Cass was on the road with the band or solo. When Tess was gone, everyone went to Joni's or Cass's. I went wherever Mom's deliveries needed to go."

"Deliveries?" I asked him.

He winked at me. "Mom never told you?"

I shook my head.

"I was her delivery boy. Diane's Herbal Remedies. She supplied most of the folks up here with weed and mushrooms." He shrugged. "Kept me fed, so I wasn't complaining."

"It was the time for it," I said with a laugh.

That seemed to put him at ease. He had to know I wouldn't hold any of that against him. Not now. It didn't surprise me to learn that about Diane, but it made me chuckle to wonder whether the octogenarian still partook of her herbal remedies? Perhaps that was why she was still producing such gorgeous artwork.

"No shit," Ryan said, his eyes wide. "You knew all those musicians?"

Dane grinned but kept his eyes on his work. "I was in the right place at the right time, I suppose. We all were. Lotta bands came out of this canyon."

"Did you tell them?" I asked him, wondering if Ryan and Kal knew just how precious the man was. Whom they'd collected from the side of the road.

He shook his head and gazed up at me nervously.

"Do you want me to?"

He shrugged and looked away.

"Tell us what?" Kal asked as he came into the kitchen. He wrapped his arms around Ryan's waist from behind and rested his cheek on Ryan's head.

I leaned in close and whispered, "I won't say anything if you're not comfortable with them knowing, but sooner or later they'll figure it out. And eventually, we're going to have to figure out how to explain who you are. We have to talk about how that's going to go. No one is going to buy you being the same Dane Donovan."

He turned to me with wide eyes. "Who's going to care?" He didn't keep his voice down, and I thought perhaps I should have brought this up out on the back patio.

"Dee Dee? What's wrong?" Kal was getting his hackles up again. I needed him to know I wasn't a threat to his new friend. This guy had a story, too, and I was curious about him.

Something behind Dane's gaze shifted, and he stood a little taller. "Okay. You can tell them. The rest we can deal with later."

"Tell us what?" Ryan's curiosity was moving into concerned territory.

I rested my elbows on the counter next to Dane and smiled at him. "You are in the presence of one of those legendary folk rock singer-songwriters that came out of this place in the 1960s and 1970s. He not only knew Tess Miller and the Luminaries of Laurel Canyon, as the latest documentary declared them, but he was *one* of them. He not only played with them live, and on a few of the most brilliant albums of the era, but he also wrote some of the songs you probably grew up listening to. Dee Dee... is Dane Donovan." I held out my hands a la Vanna White.

Ryan and Kal stared at me blankly.

Ryan rubbed at his chin. "At the risk of sounding like a huge dick, I'm afraid the name doesn't ring a bell."

Kal shrugged. "Sorry, I only know music from the nineteen thirties and before. Oh, and the bands that were on Warped Tour last year."

I wasn't expecting that answer.

Ryan laughed and kissed his husband, whispering something to him that made the big man smile.

Dane just shrugged. "Detective, you're making a big deal out of nothing."

"I am not! You've at least heard Tess Miller's 'Life of the Party, Death of My Heart?' right?"

Ryan blinked, and then he started humming. "'He'll break your heart in so many ways,' you mean that song?"

Dane grinned but continued greasing the cake pan.

"That's the one. And the song 'Taste of Midnight'? He wrote that one as well."

"Dee Dee, that's fucking cool!" Ryan was excited now. "I know those songs. I can't believe it. Why didn't you tell us?"

"Yeah, well, it doesn't matter. I can't sing anymore."

"Why not?" Ryan asked.

Dane looked up at him, and his chin quivered a bit.

Kal's eyes flared. "Because of the bad thing?"

Dane glanced at me, then shrugged again.

Kal's expression hardened, and he sighed before speaking to me. "I couldn't speak when I left the carnival. Ryan and his friends helped me. It took a knock on the head during a fight... my memories all came back after that, and then I could talk."

"No offense," Dane said. "But I don't want to get hit in the head again."

One side of Kal's lips quirked up. "Yeah, I don't recommend it either."

"Kal? You worked at the carnival too?"

He stiffened and glanced at Ryan, as if he didn't know whether he should answer me.

"Go ahead, babe. I think we can trust him."

Kal nodded. "Yes. I was there, too. For many years."

I laughed nervously. "Many years? Does this carnival have a fountain of youth or something? You look really young, too."

"Something like that," Kal answered. "Time is different there."

"And," Ryan said, giving me a pointed look, "this is what I meant by believing in things that might seem sorta woo-woo."

"Seeing as how I remember meeting Dane at a carnival when I was ten years old, I can be accused of buying into the woo-woo. It was a bizarre childhood memory that I didn't put together until today. Believe me, I tried to forget what happened that day for a long time."

"Why would you try to forget it?" Dane asked me, doing that proximity thing again, standing so close that I couldn't help but brush against him if I even breathed. "Here," he said, handing me the rubber spatula. "Would you fill the cake pans, please?" He pressed against my left arm.

I would do anything for you.

Which was why I should have left right then. Gotten in my truck and called the local police, or even Dax. I should be reporting in that I'd found the person of interest in a forty-year-old case. Not continuing to stand in a kitchen, practically playing footsies and baking cakes with the most interesting person I'd ever met, read about... I knew many pertinent details about his life, things he probably would have wished were never revealed.

But who would believe me?

Certainly not Dax, and if I told Gene or Denny, they'd give me that sad look they got sometimes when we talked about my dad. I didn't need to give anyone a reason to question my ability to do my job... or my sanity.

No. I wasn't going to call anyone. Not yet. I was supposed to be on vacation, right? I'd been given the opportunity to get to know Dane after all this time. I wasn't ready to give that up.

My personal connection to this case made me incredibly protective of him, and if there was some otherworldly element to his story? I would just have to figure out how to do my job without exposing anything that could hurt him. One look at his scars, and I knew.

I would do whatever it took to protect him, badge or no badge.

I couldn't believe the thought crossed my mind, but yes, I'd put his safety over my career. Selfishly, because I'd given so much of my life to finding him, but all I needed to do was take one look at his bright green eyes and notice the tremor in his hands and every ounce of protectiveness in me was called into action.

I took the spatula from him as well as the mixing bowl and carefully separated the cake mix into the two round cake pans as I explained. "The aftermath of that visit to the carnival was a painful part of my family history. That's all I'll say about it for now." Yes, these men could trust *me*. I wasn't quite ready to reveal that slice of family history with strangers. Not even for Dane.

"No shit," Ryan said. "Well, I had a pretty fucked-up situation as well after I went for the first time. And the second time, as a matter of fact. But never *in* the carnival. Only outside of it."

"That's because Mr. Ame doesn't let anything bad happen in the carnival." Kal handed us all glasses of water, and I held mine up.

"Here's to painful pasts and positive futures."

The men chuckled, and we all clinked glasses.

Dane put the cakes in the oven carefully with oven mitts and closed the door. "Do you mind setting the timer for thirty-two minutes?"

"Exactly? That's a peculiar amount of time."

He pressed his lips together. "It's in the middle of the suggested time range. Isn't that playing it safe?"

"Or it could be taking a risk. Using a new-to-you oven might be cause for being conservative and choosing the shortest amount of time."

"But that's what toothpicks are for. Insert and see, ya dig? It's all a delicate science, but I think a two-minute risk is worth it."

Dane's smile was downright flirtatious, more so than it had been on the patio.

How wrong was it that I *liked* it? I shouldn't have flirted back, but I had, hadn't I? I should remain somewhat professional, but I didn't want to discourage him. Young Walter had his fantasy right in front of him, but Young Walter wasn't in control. Seasoned Detective Walter had to stay in charge, despite the temptation before him.

"Well, we've got thirty minutes to wait," Dane said. "Ryan? What do you say? Want to play for us? I'm curious about your sound, man."

Ryan tilted his head to the side and thought for a moment. "Guess it would be cool. I gotta warn you, though, if you're all about folk music, I'm not sure you'll like what I do. It's not as heavy as my former band, but it's heavier than what you're used to."

"I think my son listened to your band," I said. "He had his emo phase."

Ryan cracked up. "So at least you'll be prepared. I don't know. My new stuff I've been working on isn't so emo anymore. Falling in love does that to you, you know?"

He winked at Kal, who rolled his eyes.

"You just needed someone on your side," Kal said shyly.

"Man," Ryan said, blowing out a breath. "See? He's perfect. He's magic. Oh! That's what I'll play." Ryan picked up one of the several acoustic guitars hanging from the living room wall. I recognized the song as one from the early '80s by America. He sang the lyrics crisp and clean. I was impressed. I'd always liked that song. He played it through, and I noticed that Dane was watching him very closely.

"I plan on taking a cue from my pal Maria Brink, from In This Moment, and changing the arrangement to make this cover of the song a little darker. It'll fit more with my sparkling personality."

"What happened with your band?" I asked him. "You guys taking a break, or..."

"It's a permanent break," Kal said, and that scowl of his was back. "They were awful to him."

"Aw, baby." Ryan leaned over and kissed Kal, who was sitting next to him on the couch. "It's rock 'n' roll, man. I fucked up, and they weren't able to forgive and move on. Happens all the time."

"The accident?" I asked.

He nodded. "And my subsequent prison sentence. Put a cramp in their plans, feel me?"

I shook my head. "Glad you're doing better now."

He shrugged and went back to strumming the guitar. I had a feeling he'd moved on but was still haunted by what had happened.

"That's America, right? I met those guys." Dane grabbed his guitar, plucked the strings and checked the tuning. "Thank you, Kal. It feels good." He launched into "Horse With No Name" and Ryan started humming along, trying to pick up the chords. I watched Dane's nimble fingers play the song as Ryan sang the chorus.

"How 'bout this one?" Ryan asked, and he launched into another tune that was familiar.

"Ah, Glenn and the boys," Dane said, as he started playing "Take It Easy" with Ryan. "I was there the night they asked Jackson Browne if they could finish the song. He'd been working on it for a while but he wasn't feeling it."

Ryan gaped at him. "That's so fucking cool! I love the Eagles, man. Is it true they started out as a backup band for Linda Ronstadt?"

Dane nodded and noodled around a bit more, then started playing another tune in earnest.

"Wait, that sounds familiar." Ryan started humming, and then the words came to him. "Well there's a rose in a fisted glove..." And he sang the rest of the chorus while Dane played some complicated chords. I knew the song, of course, my mom had every one of Stephen Stills's albums, and I'd followed his legal troubles over the years. He's a genius, and his lyrics and musical talent influenced so many artists of his time. But like several of his contemporaries, the drugs really fucked up everything. For him *and* David Crosby.

When they finished that song, I turned to Dane. "It must feel like yesterday."

He gazed up at me with those guarded green eyes and his

smile was sad. "I can't think about the time. I'd lost so many friends already. How many more have passed on since?"

"We can talk about it when you're ready, whenever that is. For now, probably you should check on your cake."

The timer's beep went off right then, and I followed Dane into the kitchen to be of assistance.

He carefully pulled out the cake pans and sat them on the stove to cool. "Probably I should have thought about the fact that it's two in the morning and these have to cool, but hey, cake for breakfast is always a nice treat."

"I'm sure it will be delicious," I said. He was going to have a lot of grief to process when he realized everything that he'd missed, all the history. "Whenever you get to eat it."

Dane started parsing out the ingredients for the frosting. "Might as well get this ready," he said.

"Hey, guys, we're going to crash," Ryan said from the doorway. "Detective, you're welcome to any open rooms. The locked doors are the only ones off limits, as they're for Scott's family. Dane, if you need anything, wake us up, okay? I mean it."

He smiled. "Thank you. For everything."

Ryan smiled back and nodded, and then he and Kal wandered off down the hall, deeper into the house.

"I should go," I said. "I'll be back in the morning, though, so we can talk."

"Taste this first, see what you think." He smeared some of the chocolate frosting onto his index finger and held it up for me.

What I wouldn't give to suck his finger.

Instead, I dragged my finger along his and took some of the frosting. We both sucked it off of our fingers at the same time, and I nearly moaned at the sight of his dusty-rose lips pursed, his pink tongue licking the frosting clean. "That's so good. I haven't had frosting made from scratch in a long time."

"Stick around. I'd love to feed you."

He was doing that proximity thing again, and man, did I want to close that space. I hadn't felt this charged from meeting someone in a long time. Even with the background knowledge I had of this man, he was new, he was young, and he made *me* feel young again, despite the fact that he was twenty years older. But he wasn't.

"I'd love that, too. But Dane..."

He exhaled and rolled his eyes. "You're an honest man of the law, and I'm... God, what am I? A time refugee. A flunky folky without a place."

I took his hand in mine, rubbing my thumb over his scarred knuckles. "You are an important person who's been a victim of a horrific crime, who deserves justice. And peace. I want to give that to you, whatever it takes. However long it takes."

"You want to be my knight in shining armor, Detective?"

"I want to make things right," I said, feeling something blooming between us and wishing I didn't have to fight it. Maybe there would be a time when I could give in. Now was not that time.

"Save it for someone worthy," he said, turning away from me. "Go get some rest. I'm going to do a bit more haunting of this place like the ghost I am."

"You don't know how worthy you are." I wasn't sure he even heard me, but he did give me one last small smile before he walked out of the kitchen.

I went out the front door, locking it behind me, and I walked down the long drive to where I'd parked my truck. I wasn't going to leave.

No. I wasn't going to leave these men sitting ducks when there was a killer on the loose.

Maybe the guy at the carnival had somehow known who Dane was, knew about his disappearance, and decided to pick that date, that spot to make his move. If he knew that much about Dane, he probably knew his connection to Laurel Canyon. So vacation or not, I wasn't going to leave him unprotected.

I texted Gene and let him know I was all right.

Check your email. Dax sent you crime scene photos and medical examiner's initial findings. You better get some rest. Where you staying?

I thanked him and purposely didn't answer his last question. I opened up the files on my laptop and spent what felt like hours going over every detail.

It could have only been minutes, though. I fell asleep hard with my laptop open. Disturbing dreams plagued me, someone creeping around the property. I had my weapon out and was following someone but all I could hear was something being dragged on gravel.

NINE

D^{ane}

I made it to my temporary bedroom and resisted the temptation to have another good cry. Playing guitar with Ryan, jamming to the songs my friends wrote and played, felt good, felt right, but it also brought to the forefront of my memory so many important times in my life, so many people vital to my coming of age. I wanted to weep for the loss of those times, but then I thought, things weren't going that great when, as Kal referred to it, the bad thing happened.

The tour with Tess had felt like a farewell. The crowds were smaller. There were still rock fans, but so many people were into disco and punk that us folk rockers were being pushed out of the way. Tess and I had joked that we were a nostalgia act, me at 27 and her at 35. She was tired of life on the road and thought she might take some time off touring.

She had some pretty wild ideas, especially about what her and me could get up to.

I was about to be unmoored, floating in a sea of limited possibilities for the future of my music career. I could find another band to join, start something of my own, or see if one of my mentors wanted to work with me on a new album. But time had felt like it was running out.

I'd been dropped by my first label after my debut album did mediocre. I didn't quite have the chops of Jackson Browne or Gram Parsons, the two artists I'd been compared to most often, and my music was too moody to compete with teen heartthrobs like Shawn Cassidy or Andy Gibb. Tess always told me I was cuter than both of them put together, but that didn't mean anything to me. I wanted to be taken seriously as a musician, and sure, I knew teenagers had made The Beatles famous, but they were so much more than their haircuts or cute smiles.

I wanted to be more.

I fell into bed and had a pout about the fact that I hadn't been able to snag the handsome detective, but then, I became even *more* infatuated with him when he denied me, reluctantly of course. I hadn't been let down easy. He'd wanted me too, that was obvious. But first and foremost, he wanted me to talk, and that made me twitchy.

I didn't want to be just a case to him, but what else could I possibly be?

It was complicated, and I was tired, so tired. I smashed my face into the pillow and pulled the blankets up over my head, wishing I could hide from the world, but then, that's what I'd been doing for...

Forty years. *Jesus!* I was sixty-seven years old living in the body of a twenty-seven-year-old. What would happen? Would it all catch up? Would I age overnight? That thought had me paranoid to fall asleep.

But then I thought of Kal. He still hadn't told me his whole story, but he'd said he'd been at the carnival longer than me, or at least he'd gone in much earlier than I had, and he looked young like me, though he was much older. He'd been out over a year and he still looked young, so maybe I didn't have to worry.

And sweet Ryan. He reminded me of the troubled geniuses I'd known over the years. His voice was different, much less refined than that of Graham Nash, more husky like Stephen Stills's and passionate like John Phillips's. Bet we could make some nice harmonies together... if I could ever sing again.

Somehow, I drifted off to sleep... and dreamt about a little boy smiling when I handed him his poem.

I was up with the sun, way before Kal and Ryan stirred, and I had the cake frosted and ready for them, although I'd also perused the refrigerator and saw that there was plenty I could cook for them if they wanted real food. Cooking was how I'd learned to make myself useful, first at home for my mother, and then Tess helped me broaden my capabilities until I was right next to her preparing huge meals for whoever showed up each night. She always had me take food home for my mother, but the older I got, the more time I spent at her house until I'd moved in for all intents and purposes. I'd take Mom her dinner, and then head back to Tess's to see who would be over that night.

When I turned eighteen, Tess started taking me with them to the clubs on Sunset, and then I *really* got the bug to perform music.

I wondered what the LA music scene was like now?

I looked out the front window and saw the detective's

truck was still parked outside the front gate. Had he slept out there? I couldn't decide if that was creepy or sweet.

I decided on sweet.

Back in the kitchen, I tried to figure out how to use the coffee maker, and I noticed there were little tiny cups in a rack next to it. It took a few minutes, but I realized how to open the top, insert a cup, and press the start button. I slid a mug under the drip just as the machine kicked on and coffee started streaming out of the bottom. I didn't drink the stuff, but I knew most people did. While I waited for it to finish, I sliced a piece of cake and put it on a plate, grabbed a fork, then swiped the cup of coffee. I was going to make a delivery to the detective.

I stepped outside and shivered in the damp morning. Fog hung over the hillside in patches and dew dripped from the trees above my head. What I could see of the sky was gray but everything felt fresh and clean. The ground was wet, too, as if a few showers had passed over us as we slept. I probably should have put on more clothes, or shoes at least, but I was so curious to see what the detective was up to, I couldn't be bothered.

Walter Muse.

What a coincidence. Muse. Yeah, I could see him being just that for me. For better or worse, he'd opened up a cascade of feelings I'd tamped down since I'd started to remember my life, and I didn't want to keep them in anymore. I just hoped he didn't turn me into a history lesson... or a science experiment.

That thought halted my forward progress. What would happen when he inevitably told his superiors about me? He'd said I'd have to give a statement, which, fine, but would I have to go in? They'd take one look at me and wonder how the fuck I still looked so young. Would they take me to some government laboratory and run experiments like in some sick, twisted sci-fi movie?

"Ouch."

The tremors started up again, and I managed to slosh hot coffee onto my hand. It hurt like hell and got me moving toward his truck once more. I couldn't turn back, not with the detective, and not with my purpose. I needed his help to find the bad man before he hurt anyone else, regardless of what it meant for me.

After opening the gate, I approached the passenger-side window and caught sight of the sleeping detective, his head slumped toward his right shoulder... and then I saw his gun. He had his right hand resting on it, which let me know I should approach slowly, carefully. Although he must have had a sixth sense, even in sleep. Before I could tap on the window, he lifted his head and looked at me, his eyes wide.

I held up the coffee and slice of cake, trying to keep them steady, and his expression relaxed, though I wouldn't exactly call it a smile. I heard a click and the door unlocked. He leaned over and opened the door, then he rubbed at his face and put his gun back in the holster attached to his belt.

"I apologize if I startled you," I said. "When you left last night, I assumed you *left*."

He chuckled and accepted the coffee from me, eyed the cake, and then took that too.

"Why go to a hotel when I can have breakfast delivered right to my truck?" He took a sip of the coffee and exhaled, a small sigh slipping out. "I didn't want to be too far... I don't feel right leaving you unprotected when this guy is still out there."

"Which one?" I asked, and it seemed to hit us both at the same time, the gravity of the situation.

"Right. Not only do we need to worry about this new suspect, but if word gets out that you're alive, your prior attacker may decide to see for himself. I don't like this one bit. I should put you in protective custody—"

"Does it matter what *I* want?" I wanted to trust him, but I didn't want my choices taken away from me. Again.

His eyebrows rose. "Of course it matters. It matters to *me*. I'm racking my brain trying to figure out the best way to proceed, and that has me at odds with decades of police training and procedure."

I slid into the passenger seat, shut the door, and turned sideways to face him. "So what do you think we should do?"

"A million things. I want to hold off on informing my superiors. When I do, a lot will be taken out of my hands, and I don't want you left unprotected, not even for a second. I think as much as you can tell me about this guy, the better, and we'll figure out how to pass that along to the detective in charge, my buddy Dax. I want you to work with a sketch artist, get a description of him out there so we can hopefully stop him from killing again.

"I just... I don't see how we can acknowledge you're *you*. That you're alive after all this time. It would mean bringing you into the Kern County Sheriff's Department for a statement, an examination of your injuries, even though it's been so long... DNA tests, x-rays... Dane, it would be very invasive, and you've already lost so much time. And there's your mother to think about, not to mention the media, and how to explain your absence when you look like... you. I don't know what to do about that."

I rubbed my shaky, sweaty palms on my thighs and laughed nervously. "Nowhere in there did I even hear anything about taking me out for dinner. Gosh."

The detective quirked a half smile, but his dark eyes were so troubled. That made it easier. The fact that he was trying to protect me from so much made me breathe a little easier.

"Eat your cake, Detective. You need some sugar. Let me think for a minute."

He'd set the cake on the dash of the truck, along with the coffee. He took the plate in his hands and scooped a forkful up and into his mouth. And he moaned.

I shivered at the sound.

"Oh, you've got a little—"

I reached out to wipe away a bit of frosting from his mustache, but he grabbed my wrist so fast it shocked us both. He released it quickly.

"I'm sorry."

"It's all right," I said, tucking my hair over my ear, then remembering my stupid scar, I pulled it back down. "I should know better than to lay hands on an officer of the law."

He shook his head. "If this were any other situation, I wouldn't stop you." His vulnerable gaze showed me what an honorable man he was. I hadn't spent a lot of time around men like that.

"That's good to know."

Something buzzed and startled us both. He pulled out a rectangular gadget with a glass top, similar to the one Ryan had, and it lit up.

"It's my buddy with the sheriff's department. I texted him last night. Well, when I came out to my truck."

"What is that? Ryan has one too."

"This? It's a smartphone."

"Like a telephone? How does it work without a cord?"

He grinned, and I was about to protest when he laughed. "We have a lot to catch you up on."

"I guess so. Don't think I didn't notice you stepping in last night to help me cook. Next you'll probably tell me there are people living in space."

He took another big bite of the cake and closed his eyes for a moment. "There are, but not like you probably think.

There's a space station where scientists do research. Not like a whole society or anything. It's not much more than a tin can. It's not *Star Wars*."

"I loved that movie.," I said. "I think Tess and I sat through it three times one afternoon. So no lightsabers or ray guns? No beam me up like on *Star Trek*?"

"Only toys. You can build lightsabers at Disneyland, but I'm afraid they'd only give someone a small bruise, not slice them in half."

"But you do have fancy phones. Okay. Good to know." I looked around the truck and noticed a screen in the dashboard like Ryan's had. "And these big fancy screens in your cars."

"Those big fancy screens come in handy. You've always got directions, wherever you are, no more paper maps. And any music you want right at your fingertips."

"You have music in there?"

He set the cake down and took a sip of coffee. "This is a phenomenal cake, by the way. And yes, anything you want to hear. Although, you might find modern music a bit of a head-scratcher."

"I can't wait to catch up. I just wish... I wish I could sing. That was hard last night, this morning. Whenever. When I played with Ryan. He's good."

"You're better," he said with a lopsided grin. "I'm happy to be your tour guide. Whenever you're ready."

"I'd say now, but..."

"You're not ready. And honestly, *I'm* not ready, not until we talk a little more. Are you ready to do that?"

This morning, I actually felt strong enough. "As long as you're here. I know that's selfish of me to say. You probably have better things to do."

"Dane... I'm not sure how to make this any clearer. I've spent twenty years trying to find the person who hurt you, and the twenty before that... Well, my father gave up on life when he couldn't solve your case. It drove him mad. So I'm not just doing this for you. *Now* who's selfish?"

Without thinking, I put my hand on his leg. "Detective—"

"It's Walter. Please. Call me Walter."

I couldn't help it. I wrinkled my nose, and he laughed at me.

"What?"

"Walter. It's such a serious name. A trustworthy name. Like Walter Cronkite. 'The most trusted man in America,'" I said in a deep voice, and he rolled his eyes.

"Well, he's gone now, so I've got to hold up the mantle."

I sighed. "I'm not sure I'm ready to hear who all is gone."

He nodded. "Noted. I'm sorry. I don't want to hit you all at once with stuff like that."

"It's okay. I lost so many friends so young. Cass, Jim, Jimi, Janis, Gram... You know, a thought went through my head, when the man was attacking me?"

He put his hand over mine. "Go on."

"Well. I was twenty-seven, right? I thought, maybe there was something to that superstition that we were all doomed. At least I'd had Tess and my mom to keep me off the hard stuff, and I never liked drinking much, but you know, I thought maybe our whole mountain was cursed, or anyone who lived up here for any period of time, you know?"

Walter squeezed my hand. "Those were all tough losses. But I'll tell you what. David Crosby, Stephen Stills, Graham Nash, Neil Young, Mick Jagger, and Keith Richards are still kicking around, so I don't think it was a true curse."

He said it so serious, I burst out laughing.

"Well, shit. All them guys made it? They were *way* worse than me. Okay, maybe you're right."

He was still holding my hand. I liked it a lot.

"I'll tell you another curse I seem to have." I couldn't

believe I was about to be so bold, but I'd been given a second chance at life. I owed it to those who didn't have that chance to be honest. "I seem to have a habit of flirting with unavailable men."

He looked down at our hands together and squeezed once more.

"I'm not... I'm only temporarily unavailable. Situationally unavailable. It's not by choice. Maybe... let's get through this, get you safe, and then..."

"We'll see, huh?"

He smiled, and man, I wanted to feel that mustache on my lips, run my tongue—and other things—over *his* lips, and slide my fingers through his chest hair. But I was gun shy, not just because he was what we once referred to as a "pig," but also, I'd spent my formative years around men who were open about sex, had lots of it, but not very often with each other. There were rumors about people like David Bowie and Elton John, but they weren't approachable. I was always too chicken to talk to them.

The hippies and people I knew talked about being open, loving freely, but I'd overheard plenty of conversations between my friends where they talked about a male fan getting overzealous, and they would laugh about it and be thankful they'd gotten away from the "fairy" or the other f-word that always made me cringe. Tess was the only one I was open with.

God, I missed her.

What would she think if she saw me now?

I started to slide my hand out of Walter's grip, but he held on.

"I swear I'll protect you, Dane. I won't let him near you."

"Okay." *Wow.* The shakes went through my whole body. Partly it was his promise, partly it was the promise of *him*.

I hoped I could count on both.

TEN

Walter

I followed Dane into the house with my coffee mug and cake plate, which gave my hands something to do rather than give in to the itch to touch him again.

I'd held his hand. I *had* to, wrong as it was to cross that line. I had to know he was real. I'd had a dream at one point in the few hours I'd spent in my truck, that he was actually a ghost and I was caught talking to myself at work and put on administrative leave.

My worst fear and greatest hope were converging, and I was curious which one would prevail.

"Oh my fucking God. Dane!" Ryan stood in the foyer with his keys in one hand and the other clutched at his chest. "You scared the fuck out of me! Kal woke up and said you were gone and we freaked out."

"I'm sorry," Dane said, blinking his big green eyes. "I was

taking the detec—Walter his breakfast." He turned and gave me a coy smile. "I'm glad you're up, though, because me and him are going to try to come up with a game plan, and I'd love your input."

Ryan frowned, and then raised his eyebrows as if he'd just had a revelation. "Sure. Whatever you need."

Kal rushed into the foyer and stopped short when he saw us. "Oh good. Dee Dee. I was afraid you'd left. Look, when I went into your room... I didn't mean to snoop, but I found this on the floor, sticking out of the bag." Kal held up an old Ouija board.

Dane smiled and started to speak, but Ryan snatched it out of his hand.

"Where *the fuck* did you get this?"

I stepped closer to Dane at the tone in Ryan's voice. I was willing to give the guy the benefit of the doubt about his history, but he was not going to talk to Dane like that.

"What do you mean? I..." Dane squeezed his eyes shut and winced. He put a hand to his head and blinked a few times. "I got it at a yard sale when I was a kid. These two older ladies who lived together down by the general store... they had all kinds of witchy stuff."

"That's not possible," Ryan said. "This board belonged to my best friend Gavin. He got it from his auntie's house." He flipped it over and cursed again. "I know it's his because it's got this burn mark on the back from where he almost set it on fire one night. There's no way—"

"*Ry*-an." Kal put a hand on his chest. "Remember what Gavin's aunt said. 'It goes where it's needed.'"

Ryan scowled at him, and then stared back at Dane and seemed to realize he needed to calm the fuck down. He handed the board to Dane but seemed reluctant to let it go.

"This is all the more reason we need to help him," Kal said

softly to Ryan, rubbing his shoulders. He looked at us soberly. "Why don't we all sit down and figure this out?"

He put his arm around Ryan and led him into the living room, whispering softly as they walked.

"You okay?" I asked Dane.

He frowned but didn't appear shaken. "This might look like a typical Ouija board, but I always swore it was spelled. It could do things... it shows me things. It's not just a way to communicate with the spirits." He ran his fingers over the edge of the board. "I've been through a lot with this board, but I never considered it might not only belong to me. Come on. I'll show you how it works."

"You forget, I saw it work before."

He turned and grinned. "That's right! Little Walter. Were you this serious back then? Were you ever a Wally?"

I put my hand on his back and gave him a little push as he laughed some more. "No. Junior, but not Wally."

"That's *adorable*," he said.

"Adorable. Okay." I shook my head. Not at all how I wanted to be seen, although it seemed to amuse him, so how could I take that away? He needed some amusement right now.

Dane set the board down on the coffee table, and he looked at Ryan and Kal as we both took a seat on the couch.

It looked like the board was all one piece, not foldable like the typical board-game style of Ouija boards I'd seen in the past. It was made of some sort of particle board and the face of it was yellowed with age. There were the opposites—sun and moon, yes and no, hello and goodbye—the letters and numbers, and in the bottom corners, there were illustrations of a woman from different angles reaching for the planchette, with an eerie face coming out of the shadows behind her.

The name William Fuld and a Maryland address were

stamped across the bottom, along with a patent number. It gave me the creeps, but Dane seemed totally comfortable with it. I was curious, though, how he could have been in possession of it all this time, and yet Ryan claimed his best friend had it.

On top of it was a wooden triangle-shaped item with one rounded side and a hole in the narrow portion with a glass or clear plastic insert. It didn't look as old as the board, but that didn't mean anything.

"You said your friend had *this* board?"

Ryan nodded. "Gavin. He's... no longer with us."

"I'm so sorry," Dane said, his green eyes bright with emotion. "I do absolutely believe this board could have been in both places. Kal, you know what it's like there... at the carnival? How time is different?"

Kal chewed on a fingernail and frowned. "Yes, I recall. It could have... traveled." He placed a hand on Ryan's thigh. "I've also seen some inexplicable things happen with it. There was one time, on the tour bus last year, I saw an orb of light come in through the window and it rested above the board on the shelf." He turned to Ryan. "I don't know if I ever told you that. It was unaffected by any shadows, wasn't caused by any reflections. It moved on some sort of extraordinary trajectory."

Ryan had his arms folded over his chest, but he loosened them and let them fall to his lap, taking Kal's hand. "Yeah, and when I was at Gavin's aunt's, the board showed up in my bag. I swore it was on the bus with Hush still. When I touched the planchette... I saw the past."

"Right!" Dane grew more animated the more they talked. "It's wild, right? When I brought it home from the old ladies' sale, I had to hide it. My mom was cool with crystals and stuff, but she was an atheist, and that meant no spiritualism of any kind in our house. My grandparents were super-strict Christians. We didn't see them very often, as you can imagine."

Diane had mentioned both her atheism and her

upbringing at various times over the years, so I wasn't surprised by that fact.

"But you know, I was curious what would happen, right? I knew you were supposed to do it with two people, but I didn't have a lot of friends my age, none of them were around in the summers either. This would have been shortly before I met Tess and everyone. I was fifteen, I think? Anyway, I waited 'til Mom was at a gallery showing and I pulled out the board. I remember it was a full moon. I sat in front of our big windows with all the lights off and set the board on the floor. At first, nothing happened. I sat there for a long time, until I finally blurted out 'what's the deal with this board?' And do you know what? It showed me."

Ryan and Kal were leaning in, like me, hanging on Dane's every word.

"The words just came to me. It went something like this...

"You can get lost
You can be found
You can exist underground

You can bring joy
You can cause pain
You can start your life all over again

You can do magic
You can stop evil
You can run like mad from the devil

But you can't change your soul

You can't change your fate
And you can't escape from the mess you create

Only you can know
   What there is to see
   Only you can save you"

As Dane recited the words, recognition hit me. "That was... That song was on your first album. I've never heard that explanation in any of your interviews."

Dane laughed at me. "Of course not, silly. The only one who knew about the board was Tess." He looked at Ryan. "Look, I wrote my own songs, but sometimes I used the board for inspiration. I don't know where the words come from, but the board helped me out of a rut a few times. It wound up at the carnival with me, and when they asked me what I could do for an act on the circuit, I thought, well, I can write poems."

"When Gavin used it, he said he was talking to his great uncle Heinrich."

Dane shrugged. "It is what it needs to be for each person, I guess." His shoulders sank a bit and he lost some of his momentum. "I guess that's what happened that last night at the carnival."

"How do you mean?" Ryan asked.

Dane rubbed his hands together. "I never used the board with anyone else. Only I ever touched the planchette. But when that guy came to my booth, he was impatient with me. He couldn't wait for me to get started, and before I knew what he was doing, he put his hands on the planchette with me and then we were both in my memory. He wanted to see what happened to me. The bad thing. That's the only way I can think of to explain what happened."

His face paled, and he took in a shaky breath.

"That would mean he already *knew* what happened to you," I said, a sick feeling rolling through me at the confirmation of my fear. "That he knew who you were."

Dane glanced at Ryan and Kal. "I guess that's possible, but how?"

I shrugged. "Plenty of folks are interested in society's murderous past. Why do you think shows and podcasts about serial killers are so popular?"

"Serial killers? Podcasts? What are you talking about?"

I sighed. "Right. Sorry, Dane. Do you recall how people reacted to the Manson killings?"

"Sure I do." He shuddered. "That was awful. Tess had to call the police once to get some of the Family people off her property. She was terrified when the murders happened a few weeks later, just up the road, and they showed the suspects on TV. She recognized some of them. We were *all* freaked out. What if they would have come back? Gone after any of us? My mom bought a gun, she was so afraid. That was kind of the beginning of the end of things up here. People started talking about leaving."

"Cases like Manson's, and killers like Ed Kemper, who killed hitchhikers up in Santa Cruz, and others that happened after your abduction have become quite popular. Millions of Americans listen to podcasts—which are recorded conversations on different topics—and watch documentaries on TV about them. There are even TV shows about missing persons and cold cases."

"Like me?"

I nodded. "There have been at least two TV shows about your case that I know of. There were a few persons of interest, but there was also a show that hypothesized you'd disappeared to start a new life somewhere."

Dane's face crumpled. "Oh no. Did my mom see it?"

I nodded. "She did, but she didn't believe it."

He nodded solemnly. "I'd hate for her to think I walked away from her. Despite some of our epic fights, I never would have deserted her. We were all we had." He blew out a shaky breath, and I was tempted to hold his hand again, give him some sort of tether to the here and now.

"You said you left the carnival to stop this guy from hurting people," Kal said. "What if using the board can help you do that?"

Dane shrank into the couch and stared at the board like it might attack. "I know I should at least try. It was just so awful. I never had nothing like that happen before."

"I can imagine," Kal said, offering Dane a sad smile. "When my memory came back, it was so hard. I remembered that my uncle, who was a charlatan, fled town and left me to be beaten nearly to death by an angry mob. He ran fake cancer clinics that lied to families about curing their sick relatives. Mr. Ame found me in a frozen ditch in Iowa. I relived that beating when it came back to me. It was awful, but Ryan and his friends helped me move forward, and eventually I went back to that place and found my sister. In between jobs, I'm working on making a list of people who were hurt by my uncle, and when I've saved up enough money, I'm going to try to do something to find the descendants of those people and help them somehow."

Ryan squeezed his thigh. "We're gonna do it, babe. Me and you."

Kal smiled at him, then turned back to Dane. "That's how I dealt with it, Dee Dee. I don't know if that would work for you, but if it keeps other people from getting hurt, maybe that will help you move forward."

Ryan cleared his throat. "When I used the board and saw the past, it was disorienting. Kinda like sleep paralysis. You're having a dream but you think you're awake, and you can't move? That's what it felt like. Scared the fuck out of me. But I'd do it again if it meant helping someone else."

Dane nodded.

A thought came to me just then. "You can ask the board anything?"

"Sure. The answers don't always make a lot of sense but they're truthful."

I hated to ask this, but I wasn't sure where else to start. "What if you asked it where the killer is now?"

Dane's eyes flared, but he looked at me with interest. "We'd have to be more specific, or it might show us any old killer."

"Hmm. Or if you asked it to show you the man you saw at the carnival, then we could get with a forensic artist, maybe ID him that way."

"That's not a terrible idea, although the thought of going back to that moment makes me want to vomit."

"I understand. I don't want to put you through that trauma again. I do want you to sit with a forensic artist, though. When you're ready."

Kal sat up a little taller. "What about Ryan?"

"What *about* me?" Ryan said.

"You can draw the sketch. You draw very, um, *realistic* pictures of people. Maybe you can do it."

"I mean, I usually draw nudes, but I could give it a shot."

"That would be a start, but my detective brain is also trying to figure out how to make sure we do this right. I can't ignore that part of my wiring." I turned to Dane. "What do you think? It might be less intrusive than being at the police department. I'm trying to avoid bringing you in."

"No offense, Detective," Ryan said, "but how the hell are you going to explain his existence to the police? There's no way they're going to buy that he's been missing for forty years and hasn't aged a day."

"Yeah, at least there weren't any pictures of me or anything," Kal said. "No one knew I existed, and Mr. Ame sent me on my way with a billfold and identification. That's why I asked you if he gave you anything else, Dane."

"We're going to have to get you a new ID at some point," I said to Dane.

"But I don't look sixty-seven."

"No, you don't." We'd come full circle. "And I don't know how to deal with that right now."

Dane shook out his hair. "All right. Say I use the board and ask about the guy I saw—it's going to come out in a poem, and that's not going to be real helpful."

"I'll do it with you." Ryan's gaze was steadfast. "Kal's right. I can draw him. Detective, will that work? Can you use a drawing I do, even though I'm not a cop? I did take illustration courses when I was in prison, and we had a forensic artist talk to us once."

"It's a place to start," I agreed. My phone buzzed, this time with a phone call, and I knew better than to ignore it.

"I gotta take this call. Don't do anything 'til I get back."

Dane nodded, and he and Ryan talked quietly as I took the call out on the back patio.

"Detective Muse."

"Jesus, Walter." It was Dax.

"I'm going to get a complex if you guys keep saying Jesus before my name. What's up?"

"What's up? *What's up?* You're supposed to be on vacation. What is this shit, you took a call off the tip line? And you didn't think to call *me?*"

I sighed. Of my three fellow detectives, Gene was the one who tended to lean toward the woo-woo a little more. Dax was younger, newer, still trying to be by the book—the way I'd trained him. This was going to be tricky.

"I'm sorry, it was the middle of the night. I wasn't thinking—"

"So who called? What did they say?"

Fuck. "It was the guys that called it in. The one guy, he remembered some other details." I wasn't lying, but it was killing me to not give Dax the whole story. I'd never, *ever* held back information on a case before. I was walking a thin line.

"Holy shit! Are you going to bring him in?"

"Not yet," I said, and this was where I had to hope that Dax would give me some leeway. "Listen, he's pretty shook up. I can't give you all the details just yet, but I'm going to see if I can get you a description of a possible suspect—"

"Wait, *what*? Walter, you gotta give me more than that. Where are you?"

Shit. "I'm in LA. He's with friends here, and they called the tip line looking for me after they saw the reports on the news. You gave him my card, and obviously the news didn't know I was on vacation, or else it would've gone to you. I'm still getting details from him, but I'll call you as soon as I know more."

"Jesus, Walter! Does he know anything about Dane Donovan?"

"I'm not sure." Now I was over that line. But the more I spoke to Dax, the more I realized I had a solution to the problem. A stretch of the truth might work. I'd have to talk it over with Dane. We'd have to do it just right. "He had a bizarre and disturbing interaction with a patron of the carnival who acted like he knew... Dane. Knew what happened to him. He thought this carnival guy *was* Dane." All of that was true. *This could work.*

"*Holy shit*, Walt. Okay."

I laughed. "You're telling me. I thought I'd seen a ghost when I first saw him. The resemblance is uncanny."

"You mean at the rest area. You tried to tell me—"

"Right. But this guy is shook up. I'm going to stay with him until he's ready to give a statement, okay? He needs to be protected. I think this guy could come looking for him."

"Wait, so this guy knows who the killer is?"

"I'm still working on that. My best guess? This guy knew about Dane, and what happened to him and where, maybe saw it on the news or one of the documentaries. Dee Dee said the guy was *off*. Maybe he's a copycat. The driver of the truck, the metal singer? Wells? He's an artist, so they're going to work on a sketch. I'll scan it to you when it's done."

"That's... convenient. How the fuck do these guys know each other?"

"Kal and Dee Dee worked at the same carnival, remember? Ryan and Kal gave him a ride from Vegas. Their alibi checks. They had their ticket stub from the parking lot at the hotel where they were staying in Vegas." Holy shit, the way this was just pouring out of me. I was either fucking this up royally, or this would work. It would all depend on how much Dax trusted me.

"Jesus, Walter," was all he could say again.

"I know. Trust me, I'm saying the same thing. It's been a wild twenty-four hours."

"You gotta call the captain."

Fuck. "I know. I will. Give me another day."

"Where are you staying? You better check in with me every eight hours, Walt. I don't like this."

"I slept in my truck last night. I'll figure something out and I'll let you know. I swear."

"You need someone, you call, okay? I've got PTO too."

"Save it for your family, Dax. I'll be fine. I'll check in." And with that, I turned off my location on my phone. I didn't need Dax showing up down here. It was a shitty thing to do; us four always kept it on for each other.

"Yeah. Okay. Let me know when you've got something solid."

We hung up and I took a deep breath. This had to work. I refused to cause Dane further trauma. He deserved some peace.

And yet, I had to ask him more questions, try to get this sketch done.

I hoped he could forgive me.

Because now that I had him in my sights, I didn't want to let him go.

Eleven

D^{ane}

"Are you sure you're okay with this?" Ryan asked me as we watched Walter pace back and forth outside the back door.

I wondered what he was saying about me. I hated feeling like I was at the mercy of everyone else, despite the fact that Ryan and Kal had been so nice to me. Even their assistant had brought me clothes.

Walter had been the most caring of all, but he was in a jam. At some point he was going to have to tell the police about me in an official capacity, and then what?

"I have to be. I left the carnival to stop this guy, didn't I? So that's what I have to do."

Easier said than done.

The slider opened and Walter returned to the room.

"Everything okay?" I asked him, not sure I wanted to hear the answer.

He took his seat next to me and rubbed his hands together. "I've got a plan."

With raised eyebrows, I sat back and waited for him to speak. Both Kal and Ryan straightened.

"That was one of the detectives I work closely with, Dax Brown. He's the one who caught the homicide yesterday. I was his training officer and mentor, and I know I can trust him, so as I was telling him what's been going on, it came to me. We go with as much of the truth as we can."

No one spoke for several beats—and then Ryan said, "Huh?"

"Tell them that I was attacked, left for dead, rescued by a carny, and I've spent forty years writing poems for people at a traveling carnival? Really? That's your plan?"

He held out his hands. "That's the brilliance of it. Yes, we tell them that. *Mostly* that. What if you were working at the carnival for, say, twenty years?"

I shrugged. "Okay, but how does that help anything?"

"When you gave your name at the rest stop, you said Dee Dee Miller. Why?"

I thought to myself for a minute. "Because I was thinking of Tess."

"Right. And didn't people say you two looked alike? Almost like siblings?"

"Yeah." And I missed her so damned much.

"Well, let's think about that. Who we can say you are. I think we can figure this out. But we don't need to rush into anything."

I chewed at a fingernail. "I hate that I've been gone so long."

Walter moved closer to me. "Here's the thing," he said, and he was nearly vibrating with intensity. "I had another thought. What if this guy came to the carnival looking for Dane, and he recognized you? We were just talking about the news and the TV shows about you... what if this guy was a true crime junkie and he'd seen Dane's story? What if he'd planned on making *Dane* his first victim, and he found you?"

"Fuck me," Ryan breathed, and Kal murmured his agreement.

"I don't know. He didn't say he knew me. He was really anxious, though. Excited. He said he'd come by several times earlier in the day but I always had a line. When I tried to blow him off, said it was almost closing time, he got real insistent. 'I've waited all day and I want my poem.' I felt like he might do something if I didn't say yes. But that doesn't mean he came there for that reason, does it?" My heart thudded in my chest.

"Nothing would have happened to you in the carnival grounds," Kal said, probably to ease my nerves. "Mr. Ame wouldn't allow that."

"You think *he* knew that? The guy?"

Kal shrugged. "I don't know. I don't see how he would have known anything about the carnival. True, those of us who have left might have said something to someone, but I think it's more important right now that we find out who he is and what he's planning to do next. We can't fix the past."

"Good point," Walter said. He turned to me. "Are you ready to try? It's okay if you're not—"

"I'm ready. Ryan?"

He nodded. "Let's do this."

The two of us sat forward on the couch and I moved the board to an equal distance between us.

"What do we want to know?" I asked. "We need to be specific, and even then, I'm not sure what we'll get." What else would I need? "Oh! And I need a typewriter so I can get the words down, or a pen and paper."

Ryan pulled his—did Walter call it a smartphone?—out of his pocket. "You can type it on here. I'll get it set for you."

"Or can you say it out loud? I was going to record what happened." Walter held out his own phone.

"What, do typewriters not exist anymore?" I asked sarcastically.

They stared back blankly, like "who's gonna tell him?"

"I don't know that I can say the words out loud. It's different. How about pen and paper? Stone tablet and chisel?"

Kal stood and went for the kitchen. He came back a second later with a notepad that had Disney's Cinderella on it and a sparkly pink pen.

Ryan chuckled. "Scott has two little girls, I think."

Kal shrugged and put them down next to me.

"Maybe you should ask who committed the homicide at Buttonwillow yesterday," Walter suggested. "There's always a chance it wasn't the guy from the carnival."

"That's a good point," Ryan said, making eye contact with me. "We try it and if at any point you need to pull back, you do it."

I reached for his hand, and he accepted my squeeze.

"Thank you, Ryan. You didn't have to have anything to do with this."

He shrugged and looked over his shoulder at Kal. "Every day I spend with him makes it worth it. I'm happy to help. I know what it's like to lose everything, and for that reason I'll be grateful for every minute for the rest of my life."

Kal placed a hand on Ryan's shoulder, bent over and kissed him, and then moved around to sit next to him, their thighs touching.

"Probably you shouldn't be connected to him when we do this, or you might be pulled into whatever happens."

Kal looked to Ryan as if he didn't want to be separated, not even if it meant his peril, and then he slid over a fraction of an inch. "Be careful," he murmured to him.

"I fucking love you, baby."

Kal's cheeks turned pink, and he smiled at Ryan before leaning back on the couch.

"All right. Anything else, oh fearless Troubadour? Hey, did you ever play at the club the Troubadour? I was talking to Cherish about booking some shows there after I record these demos. We should check it out."

"He did—"

"I *did* play there." I raised my eyebrows at Walter. He knew that much about me, huh? "My first time onstage was there. It's still open?"

"Yeah, man. Okay, let's do this." It was obvious he was nervous. I wanted to tell him to forget it, that we'd figure out another way, but then I looked at Walter. He needed me to do this. *I* needed me to do this, and if Ryan could draw this guy, that would help the police catch him.

"Okay."

Walter nodded, touched the screen of the phone, and held it up toward us.

I sucked in a deep breath and let it out, cracked my knuckles, wiggled my fingers, and then placed them on the planchette. Ryan did his own little dance before his tattooed fingers settled across from mine.

"Who committed the murder at the Buttonwillow Rest Area yesterday?"

I closed my eyes and waited for the bottoming-out sensation I'd usually get in my gut as the colors behind my eyes began to swirl... but nothing happened. There was nothing. Only nothingness. Blackness. No sound. Quiet. Stillness.

And then I heard it. The words began to swirl at the same time the face came into view.

Boots on gravel
Dark-carpet sky

Harvest-moon night
Bloody red dye
Wide smile grinning
Bloodshot eye
Comic-book face
Cackle and cry
Ripple-deep dimple
Burnt-face fry
Bony-shoulder slouch
Whiskey bourbon rye
Scrawny-ass hips
Follow me, guy
Wider smile still
Demon claws pry
Sharp teeth plenty
Chin like pie
Iris icy gray
Ask him why
"See you again"
When you die

Ryan's shouts rang out in the room, and I was knocked away from the board like I'd had a blow to the chest.

"What in the *unholy fuck did I just see*? Who is that monster!? *Jesus*, Dee Dee, what the fuck!"

Kal reached for Ryan, but he pushed his hands away and stormed out onto the patio.

Kal's scowl grew deep. He turned to me and said softly, "I'm sorry, Dee Dee," before going to see to Ryan.

My body seemed like it would shake until it came apart at the seams, but then there were arms around me and soft whispers in my ear.

"I'm so sorry, Dane. I'm so sorry. Please forgive me for

asking you to do this. I'm so sorry."

My teeth were rattling so hard I couldn't speak, but I could move my hands. I held on tightly to those arms until my breath came in a natural rhythm. I didn't want to close my eyes and be faced with him again.

"He's so *wrong*! What is wrong with him? He was there. He was covered in blood. The boy was naked, bleeding from his legs and his throat. Dead. Not breathing. Staring. The man stood over him. His hands... bloody. Splatters on a white t-shirt. He's smiling. He saw me, when I walked up... *he was still there*. I didn't know he was still there. In the darkness. Watching me. I touched the dead man's neck and he was *watching* me. It was all for *me*! 'I'll see you again, Dee Dee.'"

Kal and Ryan ran back into the room and knelt before me.

"That's... too close. Too close." Walter's voice was close to my ear. He hadn't let go of me, not once, and he was rocking me gently in his embrace. I could almost relax.

"Wait. The words! Where's the paper?" I pushed at Walter's arms and scrambled to the table. I began to write the words as I remembered them. When I got to the end, I put the pen down and stared at the paper for a moment before I looked up at Ryan. "You saw him?"

"Hell yeah, I saw him! That hideous piece of shit is the fucking stuff of nightmares." He looked at Walter and tapped his arm. "You watch music videos? You remember that video for Soundgarden's 'Black Hole Sun?' That creepy fucking video where the people are all smiling and then their faces stretch? Or like the fucking Joker? Fuck! This guy looks normal enough but when he smiles, his fucking lips stretch wide and he's got these fucking teeth that are all crowded in the front. *Fuck*!"

"I know exactly what video you're talking about," Walter said.

"Babe," Ryan said to Kal. "Can you grab my sketchbook

please? Thank fuck I brought one with because that delivery isn't here yet. God, I don't *want* to draw him because no one should have to see that face. I'm never going to fucking forget it as long as I live." Ryan sank down and put his hands on my knees. "Dee Dee, he wanted that to be you. He *pretends* it's you. Why? Why does this guy have a fucking hard-on for you?"

"I don't know," I whispered.

"Hey," Walter said, pulling me into his arms again, against his chest, allowing me to bury my face and breathe him in. He smelled like sunshine and honey, which surprised me. It was not what I'd expect to smell on another man, and yet it was the perfect combination for him. Sweet, warm, welcoming like a hug, but there was a spice to it, like cloves. Like kissing him would have a kick, he'd taste sweet with enough spice to balance it out and keep me wanting more.

"Walter—"

"Shhh. Don't. You're still shaking. It can wait."

I laughed against his chest. "I don't think it's going to stop anytime soon. I'm okay. Let's get this over with."

Kal had given Ryan a sketch pad, and Ryan was frantically scratching with pencils on the paper.

"You're sure it was the same man you saw at the carnival?" Walter asked me, once I could sit up on my own without my teeth clacking.

"It was. No doubt in my mind. He was standing in dirt and gravel over the boy. The man that I saw. And then he was hiding when I got there, just beyond the garbage can. Waiting." I dropped my hands to my thighs. "I was cut like him," I whispered. My hand flew to my throat, and I didn't have any major scars there. Not like on my face and my thighs.

"What else do you remember from the scene?"

"A silver garbage can with something red smeared on it. It was writing. It said DD. Like Dee Dee. Like me. There was a stack of folded clothes on top of a pair of shoes. It was like there was a light shining down on the scene, like a floodlight on a building?"

Walter frowned and ran a hand over his mustache. "Can you think of anything else?"

"The man from the carnival, he spoke. I heard him say, 'I'll see you again,' just like he said to me before he left the carnival."

"'I'll see you again'... He said that to you before?"

I nodded. "Yeah, before they led him away from my booth. Why?"

Walter shook his head and looked out the window for a moment. Like he was planning his next move. "You did good," he said, when he finally looked back. "Real good. I'm sorry you had to see that."

"Will it help?"

"I think so. Ryan's drawing could help too." Walter turned to Ryan. "Did you notice any other identifying details? Brands on clothes, a car, tattoos? Moles or scars?"

"Right. Yeah. He's got a scar on his forehead and a big dark spot on his neck, almost like a birthmark more than a mole. Splotchy hair growth on his face." Ryan continued to sketch with a heavy look of concentration. "Give me about a half hour and I'll have something for you to look at, and then Dane, you can tell me if I missed anything."

"I think we need more than chocolate cake after this," Kal muttered. "I'm going to go fix lunch."

"And I need a smoke," I said, pushing myself up from the couch on shaky arms.

Walter stood as well. "Need some space?"

I shook my head. "Not from you." I held out my hand, and what do you know? He took it. This all seemed less scary with him beside me.

Twelve

alter

I stood by while Dane chain-smoked three cigarettes. I attempted to listen and make conversation, but my mind was going a thousand miles an hour.

He'd described things from the crime scene exactly as I'd seen them. It was exactly like what my father described, too. But this suspect couldn't have been the same man who hurt Dane. I ran through the timing of the story they'd given... And Dane couldn't be the new murderer. I had no way to verify his alibi, when exactly he'd left the carnival, unless I found the carnival and spoke to someone there. Could he have gone to Buttonwillow, and then been walking back when Ryan and Kal picked him up? A hundred miles away?

"You look like you're having a crisis of faith, Detective. Don't trust the talking board, huh? Not sure you believe us?"

I stood a little straighter. "My cop brain is having a hard

time, yes, but I believe *you*. My gut tells me everything you've told me is true."

He blew out his last puff of smoke and turned away from me. "You do what you gotta do."

And with that, he pulled off his long-sleeved crewneck shirt.

"Dane—"

He unfastened the jeans and let them fall.

"Dane!"

He walked away from me, stark naked, and when he stepped out from under the patio covering and into the sunlight, my breath caught.

He was covered in scars.

His Achilles, his thighs, and his buttocks had deep, thick slash marks that were nearly symmetrical, as if his attacker had taken his time and methodically cut into his flesh. His shoulder blades had ropey scars on them as well, likely from being dragged naked, potentially on asphalt.

He walked to the edge of the pool, where he turned around to face me, and my gut clenched.

There were the deepest scars yet on his upper inner thighs, where his femoral arteries ran. The same rough scarring was on his hip bones and his pecs. None of his wounds had been stitched. It was a miracle he hadn't bled to death.

He held his arms out to his sides. "Believe what you want." He stepped backward and hopped into the pool.

I heard a gasp behind me.

"His poor body!"

I turned to find Kal staring at Dane, a tear running down his cheek.

"I know." I wanted to weep, too.

From everything I'd learned about Dane Donovan, he had a beautiful soul. He wrote incredibly heartfelt lyrics and hauntingly powerful music. He'd never hurt a fly. He'd lived most of his life on the outskirts with his mother, had few friends, and only basic formal education. He was a survivor, a self-sufficient kid who'd scratched and clawed his way into the music business, willing to take any gig in order to play. He deserved so much better than he got. That was all before he ran afoul of a murderer at the Buttonwillow Rest Area forty years ago.

"We have to help him."

"I know."

If I believed Dane, believed what he'd been through, believed what he'd seen when he touched the board, I had to accept that he and Ryan had been drawn into some kind of memory, some sort of psychic link with a killer. The question was, could the killer still be linked with Dane? Could he find him through some psychic means? Was he headed here now?

Kal grabbed my arm, and I didn't pull away. "He could come looking for Dane. Here. If he knows where he lived before, he could find us. We have to protect them."

I met his gaze and nodded. "I promise."

I stepped out of his grasp and walked over to the edge of the pool, then crouched down to wait for Dane to surface. He was swimming underwater, back and forth, only taking breaths at each end of the long, narrow pool.

He finally stopped in front of me and smoothed his hair back from his face. He rested his elbows on the edge of the pool and looked up at me.

"I've missed this pool," he said. "Lot of crazy shit happened in it, but I loved it. When no one was here, I could just swim or hang out underwater. It's peaceful."

"Dane, I need you to know that I believe you, and I'm going to protect you."

He covered his eyes to block the sun and squinted up at me. "I know. You'd protect me whether you believed me or not, though, wouldn't you?"

I gave him a half smile. "It doesn't matter. I *do* believe you, and I'm going to find this guy and stop him. I'm not going to let anything happen to you, or Ryan and Kal."

"That's a lot to promise, Detective. Maybe you oughta think about that."

"Nothing to think about. I'm giving you my word."

He smiled. "Water's nice. Want to come in?"

"That would make it tough to watch out for you. I've already accepted that I can't be objective when it comes to you, but I'm determined to keep you safe."

That seemed to call his bluff. He blinked up at me. "Walter?"

"Finish your swim. I'll be here. Watching you. Watching out for you."

"Hmm. So you're just gonna watch, huh?"

"For now."

I stood up and grabbed a patio chair, pulling it closer to the edge of the pool. I turned it so I could have a better view of the area around the pool. There was a retaining wall behind it, topped with an iron fence and surrounded by lush greenery. Off to the left was a staircase built into the hillside that led to a pool house. From my angle at the corner of the house, I could see into the master suite and the whole back patio, but there were so many vulnerable spots on this property. If we were going to remain here, I either needed to call for reinforcements or set up some rudimentary traps to let me know if someone intruded. I knew there were cameras, but was there private security? Were they any good?

"Tell me something about you."

His voice tore me from my worries. It was quite distracting having his incredibly naked form floating in the water before me, but the visible scars kept things real. He was on his back, his toes pointed together, and his hands were gently moving to keep him afloat. His golden hair spread out in the water around his face like some sort of ethereal crown. I tried to focus on his upper half and not leer at the rest of his beautiful body.

"Anything?"

"Something that has nothing to do with me or being a detective."

And there I was stuck. He'd managed to peg me with those caveats.

"There's not much else. My kids, my work... and music."

"What was the first album you ever bought?"

"Prince's *1999*."

He frowned. "I don't recognize that name."

"Prince was a bit of a genre-bender. Rock and R&B. He put out his first album in nineteen seventy-eight, but I didn't hear him until 'Little Red Corvette' got radio play in eighty-two. He played guitar like Jimi, and sang like Little Richard and James Brown and Marvin Gaye all donated to his DNA. He took androgyny to the next level and was unapologetically sexual."

The sunlight glinted off of his golden hairs, making him glow in the water. I was so grateful he was able to relax for a little while, the physical freedom to be supported in the water knowing that at least, for the moment, he was safe. It was still unreal that he was born before me. I couldn't take my eyes off of him.

"You'll have to play him for me on your pocket jukebox."

I chuckled. He had such a way of putting things. "I will."

"So that's the kind of music you liked?"

"In junior high, yes. But by the time I got to high school, my music taste had gone back in time. I picked up a copy of John Densmore's memoir about his time in The Doors and I fell hard."

Dane smiled, his eyes closed. It was the most relaxed I'd seen him since we'd met.

"John was square. He didn't hang out up here that much. Robbie taught me how to play 'Spanish Caravan' on guitar. Ray gave me my first hit of acid. Jim was my first crush."

"I can see that. Pretty sure his poster on my wall was the first indication I was bisexual. It was the one with the white background, and he's shirtless with the beaded necklace on. Maybe he's like a whole other letter on the queer spectrum. Jimsexual."

Dane laughed heartily. "He could be a huge flirt sometimes. Mostly he was quiet though, or he talked in riddles and poetry. I only ever saw him with women. I think half the men on this mountain were in love with him, and the other half were jealous as hell of him. Poor troubled soul. Tess was sure he wouldn't make it out of the sixties. He barely did."

"Such a loss."

"So many losses. But so much joy too."

"Were you happy? Your mom told me she always worried spending all your time with adults made you grow up too quick, and that she introduced you to adult stuff too early."

He frowned. "It was better than getting ignored or picked on in school. There, I was just a weirdo. An oddball. With Tess's crowd I was cute. Talented. 'A little old man,' they called me, because I didn't act like a kid." He lifted his head to smile at me. "What were you like as a kid? Serious?"

"I kept to myself in school. With my dad being a cop, a lot of kids didn't trust me. It was either become a total delinquent to impress my friends, or hang out with the brainy kids who didn't care. I was in the cadet program, planning to become a cop. Whatever I could do to please my dad. So yeah, I guess I was pretty serious."

"What happened to your father?"

I hadn't had to explain it for a long time, maybe not since I'd met Brady. Everyone close to me knew.

"I'm sorry, is that not okay to ask? I don't even know who my dad is, so..."

"No, it's okay. Just haven't talked about it in a while. He committed suicide. He fought in Vietnam and battled privately with PTSD for years. He was convinced he'd seen your body that night. He'd gotten a call about some people partying at the rest area and stopped to talk to your bandmates, who were smoking weed. They said they were waiting for you and you'd been gone a long time. He was ticked off and went looking around. He found a garbage can knocked over in the bathroom and blood. He went out back with a flashlight and followed a trail to where he found you. He claimed that when he went back to his car to call for help, you'd disappeared. Then when we saw you at the carnival three years later... well, after that, your case hit a dead end and he began to unravel. When he started to have problems on the job, they put him on leave, but he didn't want to stop until he found out what happened to you. They took his badge and it was too much for him. Self-inflicted gunshot wound."

Dane was back at the side of the pool. "Walter, I'm sorry."

I shrugged and smiled. "He would be so relieved I found you. Alive."

He held out his hands. "And mostly in one piece."

I stood from the chair and walked over to the shelf where there was a stack of peachy towels. I grabbed one for him and held it up on the side of the pool. "You're going to burn parts of you that the sun ain't supposed to shine on."

He ducked his head back, laughing, and smoothed down his hair once more. He pushed up and out of the pool. Thankfully it didn't appear to cause him pain, though the action made his skin stretch tight over the scars on his legs and shoulders.

Instead of taking the towel from me, he walked into it so I could wrap him up and hold him in my arms. He was shorter than me, maybe 5'7", and thin, but his bones were thick and strong. He exuded such resiliency. It shone so brightly in his eyes, giving him a fierce gaze. I'd never consider him fragile or unable to take care of himself. It was as if he was too stubborn to let what happened to him bring him down.

"See anything you liked while you were watching over me?" His eyes widened. "I can't believe I said that."

I let my hands settle at his lower back with the two ends of the towel. I'd trapped his arms inside, but he didn't seem alarmed.

"You know I did," I murmured. "You're beautiful, Dane."

He wrinkled his nose. "Not so much anymore. The scars kind of detract—"

I pulled him in tighter, and he gasped.

"They show your strength. They mark you as a survivor, and that enhances your beauty in my eyes."

He lost a little of that bravado and let me see a glimpse of his vulnerable side. "Really?" His voice was so quiet, I might have missed what he said.

"So beautiful," I whispered, smoothing his hair behind his ear with one hand. "So strong."

He pushed up on his toes. "Beautiful enough to..."

It happened so fast—our lips found each other's across the decades, between the moments, and it took us both by surprise. But when I would have pulled back, he snaked his arm out and pulled me back in for a second, scorching kiss. Hotter than the sun. Face-meltingly hot. He was living heat like fire in my arms, molding against my body, filling in the spaces until there was no question.

Dane was real. He was alive. It was a miracle—*he* was a miracle—and my lips were drinking in the good news.

"I still feel like I'm dreaming," I spoke against his lips. The glide of his tongue over mine made me shudder. The feel of his fingers digging into my neck made me desperate for more of him. I wanted to devour him. I sucked on his bottom lip until he gasped, and then moaned happily.

"This isn't a dream, Walter. You're awake." He ground his pelvis against mine, and *oh*, was I awake. I felt more alive than I had in years.

"You've awakened me."

"Why do you smell like honey?"

"I—oh! My lotion? Mom volunteers at a co-op for seniors. One of the ladies makes it."

"I could just sink my teeth in here," he said, fingering my neck underneath my collar. He pushed up on his toes to nibble my jaw, and then he pressed his fingertips into my mustache. "And I love this. Feels so good."

"You're incredible." I held his face in both hands and gazed into his eyes. "I can't believe—"

"Believe it. Touch me. Feel that I'm—"

"*Ohhhh, naked*. Oh shit. Sorry, guys. I didn't mean to interrupt." Ryan laughed nervously as he covered his eyes with his sketchbook. "I just wanted to show you the sketch."

I wrapped the towel as much as I could around Dane and pulled him behind me. "Thank you, Ryan. We'll be right in."

"In any other situation I'd tell you to take your time, but I figure the sooner you find this guy, the sooner you two can—"

"Right. Yes. Thank you."

"Thanks, Ryan." Dane placed an arm around my chest and peeked over my shoulder.

I reached behind me, giving his hip a squeeze. He gasped and buried his face in my back with a surprised laugh.

Ryan's cheeks reddened. "I'll just be inside."

When he turned, he whistled through his teeth, which had Dane laughing again. "I know you're going to tell me to get dressed, but Walter…"

"I know. It'll have to be enough for now." I bent and took his lips once more, nibbling and sucking as I went.

"God, I love that mustache," he moaned. "I'm going to get dressed, but later? I need to feel it all over, you understand me?"

"Whatever you want, Dane. It's yours."

He grinned and backed away from me, wrapping the towel around his hips and tucking the end into the fold. "Promise?"

He turned and went in the house before I could answer, which was probably for the best. I could barely think straight around him *before* he'd shown himself to me. Now that I'd tasted him? Anything less would be unbearable.

And I was ignoring the alarms shrieking in my head.

You're so going to get fired.

Dane came out of the bedroom a few minutes later in a black and white flannel shirt open to his navel and a pair of rust-colored corduroy flared pants. He'd put socks on and was combing his hair.

"Okay. Let's see what you've got," he said to Ryan. He plopped down on the couch next to him, and Ryan opened the sketchbook.

Dane visibly lost color in his face. His cheeks had been rosy when we were outside, that ruddiness that fair-complected people tended to get, especially after kissing, but now his skin was sallow, his dusty-rose lips colorless.

"That's exactly him. God, this is so real, like he could climb out of the picture." Dane pulled his hands back and curled them in his lap to avoid touching the paper.

"Here," Ryan said, turning the book around toward me.

"Jesus," I breathed. "He's a fucking horror show."

Ryan pointed out the attributes he remembered. Scars, moles, a cowlick in the front of his hair.

"The thing is, he'd probably blend in if he wasn't smiling. Here..." He flipped a couple of pages and turned it around again. "This is him without that creepy smile. You should probably send both."

I rubbed at my mustache. "Probably send it to local dentists too. They'd remember that smile if they ever worked on it."

Ryan used a ruler to rip the drawings carefully out of his sketchbook. "Might have to burn my book after this. Fuck. Hey, Scott's got a scanner if you want to use it, it's in the office." He stood up to show me, and I followed.

"I'll be right back," I said to Dane, who now sank into the couch with his knees pulled up to his chest. I wasn't leaving the house, but he seemed on the verge of slipping away. I needed him to know I wasn't going anywhere.

He nodded slowly but didn't speak. The "hurry back" was in his eyes.

I followed Ryan to the office. He sat down at the desk and fired up the computer and three-in-one machine. "If you want to give me an email address, I can send it directly."

"Hey," I said, now that we were alone. "You okay?"

"Yeah, yeah," he said, rubbing at his neck. "I don't usually get spooked. I mean, there were some guys in prison I steered clear of for sure. I got my ass kicked, but the real creepy ones I was able to stay away from. This guy... I've never felt so repulsed. Like I said, he's normal-looking until he smiles, and then..." Ryan shuddered. "I don't ever want to see him again, and yet now that I've drawn him, he's like burned into the back of my eyelids."

"Is there anything else you remember? Like how tall? Weight?"

Ryan frowned. "Maybe like my height? Under six feet, I'm pretty sure. Not real muscly, but like one of those skinny guys who are freakishly strong, you know what I'm talking about?"

"Yeah. And his voice? Any accent?"

"Nah. He talks fast. Maybe he's got like a slight speech impediment or a lisp. There was something off about the way he talked."

"Could be all those teeth." I handed him my business card so he'd have my email address. "I'll forward it to the detective in charge and he can distribute it."

He turned around in his chair. "And how are you going to explain all this?"

I planted my hands on my hips. "That Dane described him to you, and you drew him. It's stretching the truth, but it's mostly true."

"I gotta say, you're the most chill cop I think I've ever met. Is that for real or are you just fucking with me?"

I laughed. "I haven't been accused of being chill before. You're catching me at the weirdest moment in my career, so I guess I'm off my game."

"How so?" He crossed his arms over his chest and leaned way back in the chair, dangerously close to having it tip over.

"I was a decent deputy in the county jail, a good street cop. I'm a great detective. My case closure rate is the highest in my department. But this one... this is the case that's haunted me for my whole life, and to have this guy get plopped in my lap forty years later? With a wild tale to tell? And as much as my cop brain is like, 'take him in for questioning, do this by the book,' I don't quite think the book was written for this situation."

"No, it wasn't." He grinned. "You like him."

"I do, but it's more than that. He's a living puzzle, a mystery that I've spent most of my life trying to solve. Never in a million years would I have imagined that I'd find him alive and well, or that, you know..."

"You'd find him fine as fuck."

I pressed my lips together and closed my eyes as Ryan laughed at me.

"I mean, what the fuck are you supposed to do with that?"

"That's the sixty-four-thousand-dollar question, Ryan.

The smart move is for me to recuse myself, admit to my superiors I have a conflict of interest, and take a leave of absence."

"So will you? Let someone else take over?"

"No one else is going to believe him. Who's going to take care of him through the process? Who's going to keep him safe?"

Ryan nodded and bounced in the chair. "You. You're right. When I met Kal, it was not a good time. My band was on the verge of self-destruction, and he shows up all gorgeous, can't talk, and he's trying to protect *me*? I knew something was off about him. I just knew. I had to make sure he was okay, and when I couldn't do that—I got my ass kicked and my band got kicked off the tour—I had to trust my friends to take care of him, and thank the goddess they did." He stood up and placed a hand on my shoulder. "You can trust Kal and me to take care of him, but I think he wants *you*."

"I want him, too." And I had no business admitting that.

Ryan's grin wasn't sleazy. It was sweet. I appreciated that.

"I'm worried. If this guy saw you and Kal at the rest stop, you're not safe either. You're high profile. He could find you. I don't like it."

"Maybe it's time to call in some reinforcements?"

My phone buzzed in my pocket.

We need a sitrep

It was Dax on the group text, looking for a report.

"I think you're right."

THIRTEEN

D^{ane}

I tried smoking. I tried pacing. I almost jumped back in the pool, but I didn't want to hassle with clothes, drying off, none of that nonsense. But this house, these walls, the assault of memories, the terror of the killer's face, all of it had me in a state of agitation.

Then I walked by the piano. I didn't think it was the same one Tess had, but it could have been. I lifted the lid and tapped a couple of keys.

1970

"Oh hey, Dee Dee. I'm just going to fix breakfast."

It was the morning after I'd had a huge fight with Mom, and I'd told her I was leaving for good. I'd probably go back, but Tess's house was the only place I wanted to be, the only place where I felt like I could be myself. Mom would argue that was because I spent all my time there instead of with kids my own age, and I would be better off not spending my days with a bunch of drugged-out hippies. I retorted that they were drugged out off of her weed, and she didn't have a lot to say about that. We both knew her herbal deliveries kept a roof over our head when her art wasn't selling as well.

"Hey kid, if you're going to start playing that thing, you should bring me coffee first."

His voice startled me. I hadn't noticed that Gram Parsons had crashed on Tess's couch in a low-cut pair of pants unbuttoned at the waist, and nothing else.

"Sorry," I said, closing the lid.

He sat up, and his dark hair fell in his face as he reached for a beer bottle on the coffee table. "I didn't say *not* to play, only that you should bring me coffee first." He gulped down what was left of the beer, made a face, and then put the empty bottle back with the vast number of dead soldiers.

"It's okay," I said. "I haven't played in a long time. I can get you some coffee, though." He'd never talked to me before. Or not *just* me. I was a little tongue tied. He was so handsome. Smart, too. And there was so much skin on display. I'd never really liked country music, but if he was playing it, I'd listen for hours. I couldn't deny his genius. His lyrics were the level I aspired to write someday.

"Bring me some coffee and I'll teach you a song." He grinned up at me with his dark hair falling over his big blue eyes that always had that lazy way about them.

I scurried into the kitchen and watched the pot fill way too slowly for my liking.

"Here, taste this," Tess said, holding up a spoonful of oatmeal.

"Oh, that's good," I said. "It's sweet."

"Maple syrup! Nat brought some back from New England. Thought I'd give it a try."

"It's really good." I accepted the bowl she'd scooped for me and then reached up for a coffee cup. As much as Tess protested being involved with anyone, Nat seemed to be extra nice to her, and it seemed like maybe he was wearing her down.

"You don't drink coffee," she teased me.

"It's for Gram," I said, my back to her. I knew she'd have that pitying look in her eyes when I turned around. She knew I had a crush on him, and she always told me to be careful.

I'd had enough of careful. I knew better than to get my hopes up, but if he was going to teach me anything on the piano, I was going to learn whatever I could from him.

I turned and grinned at her, then I carried the bowl and the mug into the living room. I found Gram sitting at the piano, his low-slung brown corduroy pants barely covering his ass as he sat on the bench. He played a few bars of "Hot Burrito #1," his body swaying side to side as he played.

I set the mug down on the table nearest the piano and stood behind him, watching his fingers dance over the keys.

"Here," he said, shifting on the bench. "Sit."

He demonstrated a few things, but I was mesmerized being so close to him, watching him speak, watching his long fingers stretch and curl, watching his dark hair brush the sides of his throat.

Poetry in motion.

"How 'bout you try?"

I put my hands on the keys and I tried to do what he showed me, making it painfully clear that I hadn't been paying attention to his instructions. I faked it well enough and caught up as he played beside me.

"You know the words?" When I nodded, he smiled. "Let's hear you sing it."

His smile was so genuine, so encouraging. I understood how he'd come to town and was instantly tight with most everyone in the canyon. He just made you feel like you mattered, and he chattered on about how he learned to play as a kid in Florida, how he'd started a band when he was at Harvard, and how he couldn't wait to leave in a couple of weeks for London to hang out with the Stones. Him and Keith had become good friends.

"You've got a great voice. You sound older," he said with a laugh. "Play me something you've written. Sing for me."

We played for a couple hours more, my oatmeal and his coffee long forgotten. Tess eventually came out and sat on the couch, listening.

"We gotta get you a gig at the Troubadour. You need to play live. Tess, he's great. You should have him play for you."

She raised her eyebrows. "I could use another touring musician. I've got bass and drums covered, but if I play piano, I can't play guitar, and vice versa. What do you think?"

She was offering me a job. A way to stay with her and my friends when they were on the road. A chance to make music, which was increasingly all I wanted to do, all I cared about.

"I think my mom will hate it." And she would, but she had no room to talk. Since I'd turned 16, almost three years ago, she'd been traveling a lot more, leaving me to watch the house... and hang out at Tess's. "But I'd love it."

"Me too!" Tess gave me a big hug.

Gram patted my back and smiled at me. "Greatest life ever, man. Come on, let's teach you some of Tess's songs."

I'd have agreed to just about anything with Gram playing piano beside me. I learned that he'd actually written two songs for Tess previously, and she planned to have him produce her next album. That had me thinking about possibly playing with her in the studio—under Gram's spell. I'd love it indeed.

"We start our next tour in about six weeks," she said. "Gives you plenty of time to learn."

"Thanks," I said.

"Don't thank me! I wasn't looking forward to auditioning people. You're helping me out, and it will be so fun to have you with me on the road! You make everything better, Dane."

That tour was my first time away from home, the longest I'd ever been away from Mom, and the best time of my young life. It was also the start of my musical journey. I learned so much, and every night that I performed and met new people, I was more determined than ever to figure out how to keep doing this forever. I started writing in earnest, and by the time the summer was over, I was ready to start recording my own music and play my own shows.

I owed it all to Tess, and to Gram, and everyone else who'd ever talked to me at Tess's.

I felt fortunate. Hopeful. I was ready to take on the world.

2019

I felt fortunate once again—getting a second chance at life, meeting good people like Ryan and Kal, and of course Walter, who kissed me like there was no yesterday, no tomorrow. However, this situation was too scary to feel hopeful, and I definitely didn't feel ready to take on the world. Although, with Walter watching over me, things were starting to feel doable.

"Hey," Kal said quietly. "I made you some food. I thought maybe things would feel a little better after a meal."

"Thank you," I said, looking over the tray. There were cut-up strawberries, carrots and celery, and cheeses, along with some crackers. "Food really does make things better, doesn't it? My friend Tess, who used to live here, taught me that."

"She sounds like a wonderful person."

"She is, was… I wish I knew what happened to her."

Kal's big blue eyes widened. "I'm sure we can find out." He reached for a flat silver rectangle, bigger than the thing they called a smartphone.

"When I left the carnival, I had to learn fast what all of this new technology was. I didn't want to stick out more than I already did. This is a laptop computer. It's connected to a system called the internet, which uses some sort of waves to send infinite amounts of data anywhere around the world with a connection. I can find just about any information I need, send messages, listen to music. Would you like me to look up what happened to her?"

"I have no idea what that means, but yes." I needed to know, and though everything felt raw, perhaps getting the pain out of the way now might allow me to feel hopeful again.

Kal gestured for me to sit down with him on the couch. He opened the lid and a screen came to life.

"How do you spell her given name? And do you know the year and date of her birth?"

I gave him the information he asked for and he typed it in.

"So there *are* typewriters, only they're fancy too."

He chuckled. "I understand. I'm still surprised daily by things that exist today." The screen displayed a picture of Tess from her biggest-selling album, *Laurel Lady*. "She's beautiful."

"Yeah."

"It says she… oh, no. It says her cause of death was a homicide, which means it wasn't accidental. The police arrested a man named Virgil Evans and charged him with manslaughter. He spent twenty years in prison."

The images on the screen began to move up until they were replaced by a picture of a man—

"Hey, I know him! He was here a few times but Tess didn't like him. He brought a bad vibe, you know what I mean? I remember she threatened to call the cops if he didn't leave. He wouldn't, so she did, but they wouldn't do anything except make him go home that night. He came back a few times, even came in once while she was sleeping. She never wanted to stay alone in the house after that. I remember..." *Oh, God!* "What's the date on that?"

"December fifteenth, nineteen eighty-two."

"Three years to the date after I went missing? What if..."

"What if, what?" Ryan asked, as he and Walter returned to the room.

Walter came to my side and knelt beside the couch. "What's wrong?"

"Look," I said, pointing to the screen. "Did you know?"

Walter read over the details, and he frowned. "I did."

"What if *he's* the one? He was really creepy. She told her manager several times, and some of the other guys, but they'd just tell him to leave when he came around. They thought he was harmless. What if...?"

Walter studied the picture of the guy. "My father interviewed her after your disappearance. She was distraught. She swore you'd never go off alone."

I was glad she'd stuck up for me.

Kal continued reading from the fancy screen. "It says she quit the music business abruptly in early 1980 and became a recluse, no longer having parties or allowing friends to come around. There was talk that it was because of you... and there were even rumors she'd had a baby."

I frowned at that. "She'd told me at the end of the tour, the night before that last show, that she wanted to take a break but wasn't sure her manager would be okay with it. She joked to more than one person that she should just get pregnant like Cass did, so everyone would leave her alone." I felt my cheeks get hot. "She had a lot of crazy ideas, including *me* getting her pregnant." I shook my head. That had been a ridiculous conversation. I'd told her she should ask Nat, but they'd broken it off and she said he would never let her go again if she went back to him. She thought I'd be perfect because I'd make a great uncle, and because I didn't want her as a wife to try to control.

Oh, Tess. What did you do?

If I'd thought she was serious, would I have given her a child? If I hadn't been nearly killed?

I made room for Walter to sit between me and Kal so he could see the screen better. "She did tell my father that there were some people who'd hung around her circle that she didn't trust, but I don't think my dad put it together that you could have been attacked by someone you knew. Did this guy ever go to shows? Did you ever see him anywhere other than Tess's?"

"One time that I remember for sure. He tried to get backstage at a show in Phoenix, and I told him that Tess didn't feel up to company. He didn't take it well." My hands were shaking out of control again as I suddenly recalled what happened next. "He said, 'All right. I'll see you again.'"

Walter stared at me for a few beats, then he pulled out his phone.

"Gene, hey. It's Walt. I sent you… yeah, you got it? I also have another lead I need to check out. You got someone with LAPD I can call? No. You don't have to— No, I'm fine. You don't need to— *Fine*. I'll text you the address. See you soon." He tapped the screen and sighed. "That was my partner, Gene Ochoa. He's already on his way down."

Everyone looked at each other.

"What are you going to tell him? About me?"

"Yeah. We need to decide." Walter frowned and tapped his thumb on his thigh for a few moments. Then he stilled. "Back up. You said Tess joked about having a baby. With you."

"Yeah, but it was a joke. Everyone knew we were like brother and sister."

"But you *weren't* brother and sister. Dane... what if she *did* have a child no one knew about? That would have been... eighty? That would make the child thirty-seven? Thirty-eight by now?" Walter looked at Ryan and then at Kal, and then he turned his gaze on me.

Ryan's eyebrows went up. "Could work. A young-looking thirty-eight maybe, but possible."

"Hold it. You want me to say I'm Tess's *kid*?"

"Tess and Dane's kid."

My head twinged at this new information. Too much. There was too much to think about.

"Are you serious? You want me to *lie*?" My heart was pounding in my chest. This was outrageous!

"I want to come up with a story that isn't going to make this situation worse," Walter said. "I can't believe I'm even considering this, but it makes sense. Tess and Dane had a son, Tess has the baby after Dane disappears, and she's distraught. She leaves the child with relatives, and eventually, the child grows up, goes looking for his father, and finds the carnival, and he goes to work."

Ryan blew out a breath. "I mean, for some wackadoo made-up shit, it makes sense?"

"But I would never... *me*? Have a child?"

"It also means my father's story about seeing Dane's body at the rest area will also be assumed to be part of his mental illness." Walter looked down at his feet and put his hands on his hips, taking a moment to breathe.

That added an uncomfortable weight to the room, an oppressive force that felt strong enough to push me into the couch until I was no more.

If Walter was willing to tell this story, even when I could tell it would hurt him to do so, I could lie. Say I was someone I wasn't. There would still be questions, but I wouldn't be a freak of nature.

"The strangest things usually have a simple explanation," Walter said, a tinge of sadness in his voice.

"Okay," I whispered. "How do we make it so?"

Kal hopped off the couch and pulled on the chain hooked to his belt loop, and out came his wallet—billfold, as he called it. He took everything out of it and carefully lay the cards and cash out on the coffee table. When it was empty, he unhooked the chain and held the wallet out to me.

"You need this more than I do," he said.

I stared at his outstretched hand. An empty billfold? "I don't mean to sound ungrateful, but how is this supposed to help?"

"Babe?" Ryan reached for Kal's free hand. "Are you sure?"

Kal smiled. "I'll be okay. I have my work with Hush, and I can find other places that need me if—"

"Don't be silly, babe. We're married now. What's mine is yours. I'm going to take care of you for the rest of our lives. I just mean, that's your last tie to your *old* life."

Kal smiled down at him. "I don't need it anymore."

Ryan stood, and the two men embraced tightly for several long moments. I felt like I was intruding on their privacy.

I caught Walter's gaze, and I saw there what I'd felt my whole life.

Longing.

The desire to love and be loved.

To belong.

We had more in common than just being broken.

We were both lonely.

Ryan and Kal broke apart, and both Walter and I breathed in at the same time. I noted the shadows under his eyes and thought, *I need to save him, too.*

"Here, Dee Dee. Take this."

I took the wallet from Kal and looked up at him. "I don't understand."

That crinkle between his brows was back. "Mr. Ame gave it to me so I would have everything I needed. I have that now. You're in need now, so I give it to you. I think he would approve."

I had a glimmer of a memory, but I couldn't make it out completely. I was in a tent on a cot, I was cold. Everything hurt. Someone brushed my hair back from my face, a gentle hand followed by a gentle voice.

"You shall have all you need to recover here, my friend. You are among friends. Welcome, Traveler."

"Thank you." My voice came out hoarse as I took the wallet from Kal. I ran a thumb over the soft brown leather and looked up at him. I clipped the chain to my belt loop like Kal had done and tucked the wallet into my back pocket, unsure what else to do with it. It wasn't like I had any money or anything. Not even a picture.

Kal nodded at me, and then he sat beside Ryan and folded his hands between his knees.

I had no idea what was supposed to happen. We all exchanged glances for several moments, and then Walter rubbed his hands together.

"Let me see what else I can find out about this Virgil Evans."

I nodded. "Okay."

Walter ran out to his truck and grabbed his own fancy typewriter. I took a moment to stand and shake out my hands. I needed a cigarette. I went out to the back patio but stood just outside the door so I could hear what was going on.

Walter returned and was doing something with his fancy typewriter. After a few moments and several screen changes, he started to speak.

"It says here that Virgil Evans did twenty years for

manslaughter in a plea deal. He was released fifteen years ago, and it says... now *this* is interesting. His last known address is in Los Angeles—and his occupation? He's an assistant manager of a damn halfway house."

"How the fuck does *that* happen?" Ryan asked.

"What's a halfway house?" I asked Walter as I returned to the room. I placed my hand on his forearm as I sat down. I needed all this information to slow down and make some sense. My head throbbed from all the information that had been thrown at me the past hour and I was getting shakier by the minute. I didn't know how much more I could take.

"It's a house where people released from prison can stay for a limited time, until they have a job and a place to go. Sometimes parolees are mandated to stay at a halfway house, or a residential re-entry center, for a period of time so they're supervised. It's unusual for an ex-convict to be in any sort of supervisory position, though."

"This guy must have made a miraculous recovery." Ryan ran a hand through his hair. "Or he's a smooth operator."

"I'm thinking the second," Walter said. He tapped on the keyboard a few more times and then pulled up a mug shot. "Do you recognize him here?"

I looked at his computer and appreciated the feel of his hand on my back. "I do remember him, but I didn't see the person who attacked me. I might remember a voice, but I didn't see a face."

Walter rubbed his hand up and down and in gentle circles. I leaned into him, his touch keeping my shakes at a minimum.

"When Gene gets here, I'll see if we can get any video footage of him, maybe get a voice for you." He slid his hand around to my shoulders and pulled me against his side. "I hate putting you through this."

"Keep holding me like this and I won't mind." I smiled up at him, trying to look braver than I felt. I lowered my voice further. "If it gets me more of that mustache, I'll do it."

I loved his smile, his dimples, his kind eyes. I felt like I could handle anything if he'd keep looking at me like that.

"Whatever you want," he whispered back, and he gave my arm a squeeze.

"You know what else I want? Some more of that pizza."

He removed his arm. "I'll get you some."

"No, that's okay. I can get it." I needed some food, but I also needed a break from this heavy shit. I needed to get out of there, and the backyard wouldn't do. I knew it wasn't safe for me to just go traipsing around town, but I wanted to rip the Band-Aid off. I wanted to see what, if anything, was left of the city I remembered.

I'd gone from one mandated stay to another, and it was starting to chafe. I wouldn't be free until these killers were caught, and I knew a sure-fire way to get the information we needed.

"Well, it worked once," I thought to myself as I walked into the kitchen. I needed to use the board again.

And there it was, on the counter in the kitchen, waiting for me as I knew it would be.

I approached it cautiously, my heart pounding in my chest. I didn't want to see these awful things, experience these awful events again, but if it helped Walter and his friends catch both killers, I would do it. We had a face now for the guy at the carnival, but if the man who'd attacked me—who was also likely to be the man who'd killed my dear Tess—was still out there, still actively hurting people, he had to be stopped.

I took a deep breath, my shaking hands hovering over the planchette.

"Where is the man who hurt me?"

I heard a shout just as I lowered my fingers, and then

another set dropped onto the planchette as I was yanked forward into the blackness.

FOURTEEN

I realized Dane probably didn't know how to work the microwave, so I followed a few beats after him. When I turned the corner and started to speak—I also reacted.

He can't do this alone!

I dove toward the counter and put my hands on the planchette just as he did.

The ground dropped out from under me, and my stomach turned as I spun out of control. When the sensation stopped, I stood in total blackness. I tried to call out for Dane, but I couldn't move, couldn't speak. I could see and hear, which I realized as soon as I heard footsteps and someone whistling. A light appeared, like at the end of a stone hallway, and it shone off of a bald man's head. His face was in shadows, obscuring any identifying features.

My chest felt as if it was being constricted, but I tried to put my rational/logical brain in charge and ignore the panic setting in.

The tune he was whistling seemed somewhat familiar. It was old, like a Frank Sinatra kind of jam. Maybe older. The bald man approached and stopped a few feet away. Still no facial features.

"You've done very well," he said, his voice like a cross between that of an Alfred Hitchcock movie villain and the evil emperor from the *Star Wars* movies. "You found him. The one that got away. I knew he was still alive."

"He's still alive. And I made sure he saw what I did."

The second male voice came out of the darkness and all I could see was his eyes.

I felt Dane's presence beside me, but he appeared unable to move either, except for the tremors running through his body. His poor battered body.

"I sent so many sentinels out to find him, and you, Smiley, you were the one. Such a good soldier."

He reached out and patted the shoulder of the man with the eyes.

"You want more, don't you?" the bald man asked.

"I want *more*," the man with the eyes said. "When they're afraid? I fucking get off, man. It's such a rush!"

The bald man chuckled softly. "Know that you're putting fear into him as well. He knows you're out there, watching him. Waiting for him."

"When do I get to kill him?"

"When the time is right, I'll let you know. And I want to watch, of course."

"Why ain't you gonna kill him yourself?"

"I've accepted that I can have so much more fun *out* of prison. With sentinels like you, I can go on enjoying the capture forever and remain free. I can wait. I've been so patient. But watching him bleed again will be my greatest joy.

It won't be long now." The bald man turned his faceless shape toward where we were standing, almost like he could sense we were there. Then he walked away, singing this time, and I could make out the words. "I'll see you again... I'll see you... again... Dee Dee."

The light went out at the end of the hallway, and I felt the hold on me loosening. I grabbed Dane and pulled him against me, pulled him away from that place—

"Wake up!" Someone shouted. "God, wake up, please!"

When I came to awareness, I was on the kitchen floor, my back against the oven with Dane in my arms, shivering, his teeth clacking together so loudly. Ryan and Kal were there, along with... Denny? Kal tried to take Dane out of my arms, but I pulled him tighter.

"No!" I practically growled. Dane clung to my shirt and squirmed to get closer to me.

"Walter, buddy, you okay?"

I nodded. "Ryan? Get him a blanket. He's freezing."

Ryan darted away at my request, and I kept rocking Dane, rubbing his arms that were covered with goose bumps. I felt him take a few deep breaths, and then he lifted his head and pegged me with his intense gaze. Ryan returned with a crocheted blanket and wrapped it around Dane.

"Why did you do that?" he asked. His voice was hoarse and it sounded like it hurt him to speak. "Why, Walter?"

I smoothed back his hair and kissed his forehead. "I couldn't let you go alone. Hold on to me." He wrapped his arms tight around my neck, and I somehow managed to get to a crouch. I lifted him in my arms and carried him to his bedroom. I lay him on the bed, but he tensed up when I tried to stand.

"No! I don't want to close my eyes. I don't want to—"

"I'll be right here," I said. "I won't leave you." I stretched out beside him and wrapped my arms around him once more.

My promise allowed him to relax. He fell into a deep sleep, but he never let go of my shirt.

The door opened with a small creak a few minutes later.

"We let him out of our sight for one damn day…"

I peeked over my shoulder and found Gene and Denny both standing over the bed.

"You both came?" I whispered. Dane shifted in my arms but he remained asleep.

Denny patted my shoulder. "I have way too much PTO. Ochoa's heading back tonight. We can't all of us be gone, plus Dax needs his help tracking down your suspect. Nice drawing, by the way."

"That was Ryan," I said.

"Cool guy. Talented motherfucker," Gene said.

Dane rolled over toward the wall, freeing my arm, so I sat up.

"Junior, you got some splainin' to do," Gene said softly, gesturing toward Dane. "I swear we saw you less than forty-eight hours ago and you didn't mention having a sweetheart."

I placed my hand on Dane's leg, so he'd know I was still there. "I know." I ran my other hand over my face and rubbed at my hair. "How much woo-woo are you two willing to hear?"

Gene smiled and wiggled his eyebrows. "I love me some woo-woo."

Denny, however, let out an exasperated sigh. "What the fuck, Junior?"

These were my two best friends in the world. They knew me better than anyone, including my history with Dane Donovan. They'd know if I was lying. Then I would tell them my plan.

"Take a good look at him."

The two of them leaned over the bed, their heads cocked in the exact same manner.

"He's cute," Gene said. Then his eyes flared. "He's...
holy—

"Fuck me." Denny's mouth hung open. "What in the
cuckoo for Cocoa Puffs realm of fuckery am I looking at?"

"I found him," I whispered. I turned and brushed Dane's
hair farther out of his face to give them a good look at him...
and his scars.

"My God, Walter. What the fuck happened?"

"Jesus, Walter," Denny breathed as he noticed Dane's
hands. "You down here summoning revenants or some shit?"

"He's been working at a carnival. He's got some form of
dissociative amnesia, and he's only just remembering what
happened to him."

"But he looks *the same*, Junior!" Gene said in wonder.
"How the fuck does he look the same?"

"Are you sure it's him?" Denny was frowning, but it
wasn't his Marine Corps Scowl he tended to get when he was
disturbed by something he didn't quite understand.

I nodded. "My dad was right all along. He's got scars in
the same places as the vic from yesterday, except the neck. This
carnival... it's not a regular carnival. They found him, healed
him, and kept him."

"For forty fucking years?" Denny said, shaking his head.
He plopped down in the chair in the corner. "As much as I
wanted you to solve this case—we all wanted that—this is not
how I saw shit going down."

"I know," I whispered. I couldn't stop touching Dane.
Even in sleep, he searched for me. He turned over and reached
for my hand, squeezing it as though he was still terrified. I used
my other hand to touch his hair again. *Like silk.*

"He's beautiful," Gene whispered.

"So what do we know so far?" Denny pulled the chair
closer and Gene sat on the floor next to the bed. I slid down
next to him, keeping my hand on Dane's.

"Well, we know he's alive. He met the suspect from the Buttonwillow killing at the carnival. I'm pretty sure there's a link between the person charged with Tess Miller's homicide and Dane's abduction." I took a deep breath and rubbed my eyes. "You're going to ask me how I know these things, and you aren't going to like the answers."

Denny frowned, but Gene nodded knowingly.

"That board, huh? He psychic or something?"

"Something. I think so. The board..." I shuddered. What an awful feeling. And it was having an effect on Dane. He'd crashed hard after this last time. "It's gonna be tough to use any of this information to make a case, but it's a place to start."

Denny leaned forward. "That CHP guy's story checked out. I've got a list of seventeen disappearances that match Dane's, from San Joaquin and LA County. All with the folded clothes and traces of the victim's blood. No remains. How the fuck did no one ever pick up on the similarities in these cases?"

I shook my head. "We need to look at Virgil Evans. He knew Dane. They had words."

"But all you've got is..." Denny gestured toward Dane.

"Yeah. I wish I could explain it in a concrete, solid way, but I can't."

Gene stretched up and looked toward Dane. "How the fuck does he still look the *same*?"

"He's covered in scars all over, G. I don't even know how he's *alive*."

Gene frowned, but then he raised an eyebrow. "All over, huh?"

"Fuck you," I said, though I'd have done the same thing if I'd walked in on what they just saw. "I'm going to have to recuse myself. Take a leave, whatever I have to do. I'm not leaving his side. Not 'til he's safe. And I can't waltz into the department and say 'look! I found him' when he looks like a twenty-seven-year-old... but I have some ideas about that."

Denny nodded, and Gene cursed.

"We'll figure it out," Denny said, elbowing Gene. "Who else knows?"

"Ryan and Kal. You guys. I can't tell Dax. He's pissed at me already, and he won't go for any of this. I haven't told Dane's mother yet. He's not ready. I don't know how we're going to explain it."

"No shit. He barely looks twenty-seven." Gene snorted. "Doesn't look much older than Stacia and Stef."

I groaned. Leave it to Gene. My twins were twenty-one, so yeah. Dane wasn't much older than them. But this situation was something else altogether.

"You got a change of clothes?" Gene asked. "Cause if I'm not mistaken, that's the same shit you had on at the bar."

"Yeah, in my truck." I handed Gene the keys. "Mind grabbing my duffle?"

He took them and headed out.

"Listen," Denny said. "I'm only saying this once, and I'm not trying to be an asshole. You sure this is how you want to play it?"

"What choice do I have? He needs protection. I can't be objective. I'm too invested. If I tell Cap any of this, he'll think... he'll say..."

"Walt, you're not your father. I'm right here. I see him with my own two eyes, and no way is *anyone* saying anything about my mental fitness. Although, man. How...?"

"I know."

He sighed. "For now, you're on vacation, so Gene and I will handle shit. You found... information relevant to the case. I'm taking over the case. You okay with that?"

I nodded. I had to be.

"You trust me to handle it?"

"Yeah," I said. And I did.

"Good, because I'm not having you lose your fucking job

over this. You gotta trust me to not let you throw the rest of your life away, got it?"

"Denny, this isn't how it looks. I haven't... we haven't... I wouldn't."

"Not yet, anyway."

"Yeah," was all I could say. Dane and I had forged a connection that was about more than just me trying to close his case. Our lives intertwined in so many ways—ways he wasn't even aware of yet—and I didn't want to let go. I also didn't have high hopes for any kind of future with him. He was going to figure out this life and move on. I didn't have much faith that I would be a part of that. He deserved to find happiness, and I wouldn't stand in the way. I'd be here as long as he needed me, and then...

I felt as if I was on a collision course with forces that would change my life forever, and at this point, I couldn't fucking guess whether or not those forces would do good, or would destroy me.

It didn't matter.

Only Dane mattered.

"You slept?" Denny asked.

I shrugged. "Not really?"

He leaned forward and squeezed my shoulder. "Get some sleep. We'll figure this out when you wake up. Gene will be taking off late tonight but I'm here for the duration, so you can relax, all right?"

I accepted his hand and allowed him to pull me into a big, back-pounding hug.

"I can't thank you enough," I murmured.

"Fuck off," he said. "You've been there for all of us countless times, not to mention that fucking bullet you took for me. You'd do the same if I was going off the rails."

It was true. When he was my T.O., we were serving a warrant on a county-wide domestic violence sweep, and the abusive husband we served decided he'd rather kill himself and take us all with him than go to jail. I stopped his bullet, and then him, allowing the rest of the team to take him down. He cried more than I did. It was a clean through-and-through of my left biceps. Barely left a scar. Hurt less than the time I tore my rotator cuff wrestling a guy to the ground when he tried to stab Gene. Or the time Dax was a rookie and I shoved him out of the way of a car that tried to run him down, getting clipped in the hip in the process.

I wasn't as marked as Dane, but I'd shed blood for my colleagues and had my own map of battle scars to prove it.

"Get some rest, Junior. We'll figure it all out later. Don't worry about this," he said, looking at Dane. He smirked as he walked out the door.

I muttered something about him only calling me Junior when he was pissed, and I eased myself down on the bed. I kicked off my shoes, pulled off my coat and my sweater, took off my holster and set it under the nightstand, and then I stretched out next to Dane in time for him to wrap himself around me.

I drifted off thinking we fit really nice together.

When I woke next, it was dark in the room. How long ago had I entered this house? Had it only been twenty-four hours? My whole life had been turned on its head by the man I'd been looking for—

"Mmmm, is this a dream?"

—the man who was currently pressed against me with his hands inside my shirt.

"I feel like I'm still at the carnival," he whispered. "Time is weird, man. It seems like I've been here ages, not just a day."

I slid my hand under his shirt and grazed my nails up his spine, causing him to hiss.

"You're here. You're safe."

"You're in my bed," he said, and when I started to let go, he pulled me tighter to him. "Give me that mustache."

"Fuck. *Dane*." There was no resisting him. He kissed me as if I held the power in my lips to convince him he was alive, tangible. Real. It was enough to convince both of us.

He went to work unbuttoning my shirt and opened it wide, and only then did he pull away from the kiss.

"God, you're perfect." He pulled off his shirt, and then we were chest to chest, his mostly devoid of hair, mine not at all. He unfastened my pants next, and I could barely breathe when he slid his hand inside and grabbed my erection. "All of you. Perfect. Walter, please, touch me. Make me real."

His pants were loose, too loose. I slid my hands underneath and over his ass, pulling his hips closer to mine. He hooked his leg over my hip and ground his equally hard erection against mine.

"Dane, are you—"

"Don't ask me if I'm okay. Just please, make me forget for a little while."

I gave his dick a squeeze, and he gasped.

"I'll make you forget everything but this." And then I completely gave up on any sort of professional discretion. Right or wrong, I was going to give him what he asked for.

I tugged his pants down to his knees and grabbed his hips tight, pulling him up on the bed and flipping him onto his back. He asked for mustache? He was going to get everything he wanted.

He let out a long, low moan as I sucked him down. I was grateful Denny had shut the door and that we were far from the sitting room and kitchen, because his sounds of desire drove me into a frenzy.

He wanted the mustache, but he was getting a lot more. I touched him everywhere I could get to; tweaked his nipples, squeezed his ass, stroked his balls until his body was overcome by the good kind of shakes. When he started to thrash beneath my hands, I loosened my grip. The last thing I wanted was for him to feel trapped.

I pulled my lips off him and switched to stroking with my hand. I slid up the bed next to him to kiss his throat, his earlobe, his eyes. He was panting, and the needy sounds coming from him were frustrated, pained. I slowed my movements down and stroked his hair.

"Come, Dane. Come for me. You can let go."

"I don't... No one's ever done that to me. I don't know how—"

"Shhh." I ran my fingers lightly over his chest. "It's okay. I didn't know."

"Yeah. Twenty-seven-year-old virgin here. I mean, I did that to someone else, but no one..."

"No one ever took care of you. I will. I want to. You can let go with me. Take as long as you need. Tell me what you liked."

"God, your mouth. Your mustache. Feels so good."

"You *taste* so good. Let me try again," I said, kissing my way down his stomach. "Move however you want, I'm here for the ride. Tell me what gets you off."

"You, Walter. You get me off. You're so... *Ohhhhhh.*"

I tried to be gentle, using my tongue and light pressure from my lips on his crown, and soon he started thrashing again. He kicked off his pants the rest of the way, brought his legs up, and gripped the back of my head as he thrust deep into my mouth, hitting the back of my throat until my eyes watered. He slowed his movements down, but he gripped tighter as his legs started shaking again. He moaned once more, long and low, and filled my mouth as he spilled over and over.

I released his cock and let the last few spurts land on my lips as I gasped for breath. A few tugs on my own dick and I filled my hand, the shudders bringing pleasure to every synapse in my body in their wake.

"Kiss me, please. I need you."

I wiped my hand on a tissue from the nightstand and pulled him into my arms, taking a moment to catch my breath.

Dane reached up and touched my lips, sucked his fingers and moaned. He crawled on top of me, straddled my waist, and licked at my mouth, tangling his tongue with mine. He sighed happily, and I felt him growing hard again.

"You might technically be older, but I'm the old man in this bed. I need to catch my breath." I chuckled as he snuggled into my neck.

"You're incredible," he whispered, and then he started humming against my throat. And then he was singing...

"'Hello,' you said to me time and time again, did you ever wonder what I would say then, if you stopped a while, shared a smile..." The words to one of my favorite songs off of his first album poured out of him, his voice quiet but strong. I held him close, wondering if he realized what he was doing. When he finished the song, I turned his face to look up at me.

"Do you realize what you just did?"

His eyes widened and he smiled. "I sang. My... Oh! Walter! You—"

"Do *not* say I cured you with a blow job."

He burst out laughing and rolled off of me.

"I would never. I'm the magic one, remember? But you saved me. My voice. You got me out of my head and into my body—"

"Or, it was the trauma you just went through..."

He sighed, and I thought, *Dammit, Walter. You just ruined it.*

"Or, maybe for the first time since this all happened, I felt safe."

FIFTEEN

D^{ane}

What are you doing, Dane? "I'm sorry, I know that sounds totally unsexy, but..."

I should have known Walter would understand. He kissed me and brushed back my hair. "I *want* to be safe for you. I want to be whatever you need. If that means being the one you explore your sexuality with, I'm fine with that. If that means holding your hand through all this until you're settled, I'm fine with that too."

"You're exactly what I need, Walter. I don't think I could do this without you here."

"Well, you don't have to, but when you're ready to stand on your own, I'll understand, okay?"

I pushed up on an elbow. "What do you mean?"

His dark eyes had been so sultry throughout this whole encounter, all hungry and turned on. Now they were back to that do-the-right-thing gaze. He ran his fingers down my arm and then dropped his hand.

"I mean when you're ready to move on. Start living. You have your whole life ahead of you now. Once we catch these guys, you can..."

"What? Find my old friends? They're dead. Start my music career over? I don't even know how to use one of those smart fancy contraptions, how the hell am I supposed to—"

"Dane, I'm going to help you."

"I don't want you to *help* me! I want you to— Forget it." I sat up. I was going about this all wrong, and here he was, starting to take pity on me.

"Hey." He sat up next to me and placed a kiss on my shoulder, so gentle, such a loving touch, it nearly broke my heart. "I'm glad I can be here for you right now, however you need me. You are going to have a lot of emotions. You're going to want to be held, you're going to want to hit something, you're going to scream, or not understand why the hell you're crying over a hole in your sock. I want to be here for you through all of it, okay? I can take it, I *want* to take it. When you're safe and able to do what you want, I'll be there to help you take those first steps, if you want me there. I'll do *anything*, Dane. Even step back... if that's what you want. I think you're incredibly strong, and I'm honored to be the one beside you right now." He rubbed his lips and mustache on my bare shoulder as he gazed up at me.

"I'm sorry." I took his hand in mine and held it, mostly to keep mine from shaking. "You're probably right about it all. I'm so grateful you found me. That you believed me no matter how ridiculous all of this sounds. And..." This was the hard part to admit. "I'm so glad you were my first. It was a different time back then. The only times I ever got touched by a guy were in secret. They were rough, and none of them cared for me when it was over, you know? I suppose I could have gone to places where things might have been different, but I didn't trust people, and Tess warned me that if I was open about who and what I was, it would hurt my career.

"She wanted me to be patient. She wanted me to be *me*, but she wanted me to play the game, so I did. It wasn't like I could have the men I wanted back then anyway, and I didn't really meet anyone who I knew was like me, at least not that they let anyone know. I never let it go any further than hand-jobs except with one guy, who I thought... It was on tour, and he was young like me, but he wasn't *like* me, didn't *like* me like I wanted. I'd rather forget about him."

"Things weren't a whole lot different when I was growing up, where I grew up. No one was out in high school. And then, well, there was AIDS, a disease that killed a lot of gay men, and that kept me from exploring that side of myself."

"What do you mean?" I asked him.

He sighed. "It's a virus, it's called HIV. It spread through the gay community in the late eighties and early nineties. It killed thousands before the government would do anything about it. When it showed up in straight people, then they paid attention. Now there are medicines and a lot of people that are infected with it have survived for decades. It was terrifying to me and kept me in the closet for a long time."

"So you dated women, then?"

"Yeah. I met Lisa, my ex-wife, at the beginning of college, and we got married pretty quick. At that point, she was happy being a cop's wife and a stay-at-home mom, until the kids started high school and they didn't need her around as much. She decided to go back to school and get her master's degree. She met new people, decided that she wanted more than a best friend for a spouse, someone who could give her more than I could."

"What happened?"

He smiled. "We parted as friends, we encouraged each

other to explore other opportunities. She knew I was bisexual. I'd told her early on in our marriage. She asked me then if I wanted to see other people, and I totally didn't. I loved her and our kids and our life. It was enough for me."

"So did you? Explore after you got divorced?"

He laughed. "Not really. The first guy I went out with, we ended up dating for two years. Brady. He also didn't like being attached to the cop life, and he never totally got used to being second to my kids either. Me working weekends and holidays, late nights, early mornings, with no sense of normalcy bothered him. Since him, I've hooked up exactly one time, two years ago. I threw myself into work and tried to spend as much time with my busy college kids as they would allow, and that's my story."

"Your work led you to finding me, so I couldn't ever be mad about it."

He laughed and lay back on the bed. "Oh, don't be so sure. The first time I had to cancel plans on your birthday, you'd be singing a different tune."

I spread myself out on top of his gorgeous body, loving the way his hair tickled me everywhere. "Maybe I'd just sing a little louder. Change my tune. You're worth it."

His lazy smile faltered, and I caught the most vulnerable look in his eyes. He could say he was okay with losing his relationships but the truth was right there. He'd been abandoned, just like me, and that made me want to hold on a little bit tighter. He knew what it was like to be alone. He understood me beyond my trauma, as he called it.

"Maybe there was a reason you never stopped looking for me. Maybe *you* needed to find me as much as I needed to be found."

"I did. You have no idea."

"I do. You're here." I kissed him gently, staring into his

deep brown eyes. "You want to save me, Walter. That means more to me than I could ever say."

He ran his thumb along the curve of my spine and down to my tailbone. He had the most sensual touch. I never wanted him to stop.

"Maybe you saved me a little bit too." He brought my hand up to his lips and kissed my scarred knuckles, bringing a bit of reality back into the forefront. "Let's see what we can do about giving you back the rest of your life."

"After you shower," I said with a laugh. "If you go out there right now, this whole house is going to smell like sex."

"You don't think the newlyweds will mind, do you?"

"Yeah, but your friends are here."

His smile fell a little. "They are. You can trust them, Dane. I promise. I trust them with my life. They're going to help."

"I'll *have* to trust them. Since we've clearly established you can't keep things professional with me, they have to be the cops, huh?"

"Right." He rubbed a hand over his face. "I'm sorry."

"Do not apologize, Detective Muse. There is no part of what just happened I'd want to take back. Well, except my little freak out, but even that... you get me, Walter. Thank you."

He grinned. "You're welcome."

We took turns showering in the attached bathroom. I wished I had a notebook. I was bursting with thoughts, ideas. Words. Maybe I could write again, but would today's world have any interest in what I had to say? A folk singer stuck in 1979?

When we went out into the living room, Kal was beside Ryan on the couch. Ryan had the guitar in his lap, laughing and chatting with the two cops. Gene and Denny. They were more than co-workers to Walter, I could tell that. The men greeted him with hugs and soft words of concern before Walter took a seat next to me on the other couch.

"You ready for an update?" Gene asked.

Walter took my hand in both of his and looked to me for confirmation. I was shocked that he had no reservations about touching me in front of his friends. It was all too good to be true.

"Sure." *No.*

Denny smiled at the two of us. It was tinged with sadness, which had me wondering which one of us he was sad for. He wore a tight t-shirt that had the Marine Corps logo on it, which made my stomach tighten a bit. Military guys had made me nervous ever since they started showing up in LA after Vietnam, but Denny had a warmth about him that made me think maybe he was different. Or maybe I felt safe next to Walter and knew he wouldn't have brought someone around me he couldn't trust.

"While you were sleeping, I've been reading over the file on Evans," Denny said. "Born in nineteen forty-seven in Los Angeles County. Youngest of six. Father was military, he attempted to enlist but was designated 4-F. Convicted of Tess Miller's death in nineteen eighty-four. He spent twenty years in the California State Prison at Lancaster, was released fifteen years ago. Before that, he worked for CalTrans as a maintenance supervisor, which means he had access to a lot of facilities along the highways, including rest areas."

"That gives him means," Walter said. "How about any records prior to the murder?"

Denny and Gene looked at each other before Gene spoke. "He's got a sealed juvenile record."

Walter squeezed my hand. "All right. How about video? Recordings?"

"I didn't find any so far, but I'm going to keep looking. I

also thought we might go pay him a visit tomorrow. Maybe we *get* a recording."

"That's a good idea." He rubbed his hand back and forth over mine. "I don't want to leave Dane."

I leaned closer to him and spoke quietly. "I'll be okay. You can go."

He frowned at me and shook his head. I liked that he felt protective over me, but I didn't want him to think I couldn't take care of myself. That would be the absolute wrong reason for him to want to be with me.

"I'll call him in the morning. I've got some local contacts. I can have someone sit on the house here while we're out."

Walter nodded. "Okay, what about the sketch?"

"Nothing yet," Gene said. "Dax is up to his eyeballs in crime scene photos and most likely useless evidence. Vic was nineteen years old. Christopher Gilman. Was on his way to a music audition in Los Angeles." Gene gave Dane a glance.

I swallowed bile. *I should've gotten there sooner.*

"Parents identified his remains." Gene cleared his throat and gave me an apologetic look.

"No other recent cases like this?" Walter asked.

"Dax says no, he ran it through state and federal databases. No hits. No missing persons reported around that rest area or in Kern County who match similar characteristics. Maybe this is totally unrelated."

"The 'I'll see you' and DD had to have been directed to Dane. Dee Dee is his nickname."

Gene and Denny both looked at me with interest.

"I saw him at the carnival. Before I left," I said. "We had a strange encounter, and then he said, 'I'll see you again.'"

"You get a name for him?" Denny asked.

I shook my head.

"It's okay. He definitely sticks out. We'll see if we get anywhere with the sketch." Gene pulled out his phone, which was buzzing. He stood and answered it, making his way out onto the patio.

"We were wondering," Ryan said, looking to Kal. "Dee Dee, do you think you're ready to go out? We thought we could grab some dinner on Sunset, take you around?" He looked to Walter. "You think it's okay?"

Walter squeezed my hand and I turned to him. "I think I'd like that. What do you think?"

He gave me a small smile, his mustache quirking up on one side. "Probably safe enough. However, I think some sort of disguise would be good for both you and Wells. If anyone recognizes him, there could be pictures of you taken." He turned to Denny. "And I should call Cap."

Denny nodded. I figured that meant Walter needed to tell his boss what was happening. I tried not to think about what that meant for either of us.

"Good call," Ryan said. "I'll hook you up," he said to me. "Let's go get dressed."

I stood to follow him, but I looked down at Walter. "I'm a little bit nervous," I whispered.

He grabbed my waist with one hand. I loved how he handled me, which got me thinking, and blushing...

"Only if you're ready."

I could do this. I was so curious. Walter would be there, along with my new friends. It would be fine.

"Okay." I followed Ryan back to his bedroom, and I heard Walter and Denny start talking over each other.

"The good news is that your style isn't too unusual for SoCal these days, but let's see what we can do to make you look totally not like you. It's too bad I didn't get my art supplies today but hopefully they'll be here tomorrow. I had them throw in some theatrical makeup and body paint. I had some ideas... We could have done something wild to disguise ourselves."

He handed me a black hooded sweatshirt with the word Slipknot written in red across the front and a picture of a person painted like a skeleton underneath. I pulled it on over the plain white t-shirt I was wearing.

"I don't think I have a pair of pants that will fit you..."

"I can wear the ones Cherish brought if you have a belt?"

"Oh sure." He dug around in his suitcase and brought out a black leather belt with a load of metal studs on them.

"Whoa," I said, fingering the silver bumps. "You've gotta tell me if my head starts spinning while we're out. I can't imagine how different everything is." I slid the belt through the loops and luckily it had enough holes to yank the Levi's tight enough they wouldn't fall down.

Ryan laughed. "Can do. Here," he said, moving around behind me. "I'm going to put your hair up and we'll tuck it inside a beanie, okay?"

I turned and frowned at him. "Put my hair up?"

He nodded. "Trust me. My hair was longer until last year. Guys with long hair put their hair in messy buns and ponytails all the time."

I shook my head as he started to brush my hair. It was nice. He was very gentle. He did some sort of twist with my hair and wrapped a thick, stretchy band around it. My hair was down past my shoulders when I arrived at the carnival and it hadn't grown or changed... what would happen to it now? I still needed to ask Kal about how the carnival had affected him.

"It's cool outside so this won't look out of place at all." He pulled a stretchy cap over my head and pulled some of the shorter bits of my hair out from under it in front. "Okay, take a look."

He turned me to face a full-length mirror. I immediately reached up and touched my scar. I knew it was there, of course, but I hadn't seen myself in the mirror much.

"People will think you're a badass," Ryan said. He pulled off his t-shirt and sweatpants and stood in just a pair of tight shorts-like underwear. "Makes you look dangerous. Trust me, no one will fuck with you if they see that thing. They'll know you survived something major."

"That's one way to look at it," I muttered. "I used to be told I was pretty."

"Me too," Ryan said. He pulled on a long-sleeved red and black flannel shirt and slipped into a pair of skin-tight black jeans that clung to his muscular legs all the way to the ankle. "Didn't help that my band used to wear a lot of makeup. Then I was in a car crash and went to prison. The scars messed me up enough to where people stopped calling me pretty. Except my buddy Silas. He still calls me pretty. Asshole."

I looked a little closer and could see that, yes, he did have a few scars and a chipped tooth. He also looked like he spent a lot of time out in the sun, but he was striking. He looked like a star, like the men I'd known in my past. "How old are you, Ryan?"

"Just turned thirty," he said. "Never been happier."

I smiled at him. "I'm glad. I'm really happy that you and Kal have each other."

"Thanks. Me too." He raised his eyebrows. He looked in the mirror and put some goopy stuff in his hair and started using his fingers to make it look carefully messy. "Things seem to be progressing with the good detective, huh?"

My cheeks got hot and I looked at myself in the mirror again. The clothes were so big on me, but at least I didn't look too scrawny. And the scars were mostly covered. "He's pretty great."

"Yeah. I gotta say, I never thought I'd feel comfortable hanging around a bunch of cops, but him and his buddies are cool guys." He leaned over the counter in the bathroom and applied black eyeliner, which made him even more striking.

He had tattoos all over, from his fingers to his neck and down his whole chest. That had to hurt. "And they don't treat me like a loser," he continued, "you know? It's been a long time since people were cool with me."

"I don't know what you were like before, but you've been so nice to me. I can't thank you and Kal enough."

He patted me hard on the shoulder. "No thanks needed. Kal is the greatest gift I've ever been given. Even without the promise we made, I think we'd have stopped for you. He's just good like that. He makes me a better person, you know?"

"I can understand how that's true. Hey, um, all I have are those dusty boots?"

"What size?"

"I don't even know. I don't remember. Maybe eleven? Ten? Nine?"

He laughed and shook his head at me. "Let's see what Scott's got." He opened a door and walked into what looked like a small bedroom but was actually a closet. "He's a thirteen. Wait, his wife's got some Chuck's. Here, try these."

He handed me a pair of sneakers that I actually recognized. They were dark green and they actually fit pretty good.

"How do they look?"

Ryan grinned. "You look just about perfect. Here," he said, handing me some aviator sunglasses. "You'll look cool enough to fit in, enough for people to look twice and think you're in a band."

"I feel kind of ridiculous."

"That's precisely the point. Let's go grab our men."

When we went back out to the living room, Kal's eyes lit up when Ryan walked in. They embraced and Ryan kissed him, then whispered something in Kal's ear.

Walter was having a heated conversation with Denny and Gene, but when he saw me, his eyes went wide. I didn't know if that was a good or bad reaction.

"Everything okay?" I asked him.

He nodded, looking me up and down. "Yeah. Very."

"How does the Rainbow sound?" Ryan asked. "That place opened while you were here, right?"

I brightened up. "Yes! We went to the grand opening. They threw a party for Elton John, you know, that English singer?"

Denny snickered. "You mean *Sir* Elton John."

I blinked. Wasn't that what I'd said? "What a wild night. We'd go there sometimes after we played at the Troubadour."

"Well, you're in luck. It's still very much the same, and there are pictures all over the walls of the folks who've eaten there over the years." Ryan patted my shoulder as we headed for the front door.

I turned to Walter, who was at my back. "You up for this?" I asked him quietly. Denny and Gene had gone out the door ahead of us, followed by Ryan and Kal.

"Yeah. It'll be good."

"What's wrong?"

He sighed as we went through the door, and I pulled him aside.

"Talk to me."

He put his hands on his hips. "I talked to my captain. Told him I'd been doing some work on your case while I was on vacation, but that I was stepping back, handing things over to Denny. He stopped short of ordering me to hand over my badge and service weapon to Denny, but I'm mandated to meet with the department shrink when I return to Bakersfield."

I put my hands on his arms. "Why are you in trouble? Because of me?"

"I'm not in trouble necessarily. He wasn't happy with me, but he commended me for taking a step back and admitting that I was too close to your case."

"But what does this mean? Did you lose your job?"

"No, Dane. No. I might be written up for not getting your witness info to Dax in a speedy manner. It'll go in my file, but I shouldn't lose my job."

"You can't lose your job, Walter. It's not right!" After everything he'd done for me, after losing his *father* over my case, I couldn't let him lose anything else because of me.

"Hey," he said, putting his arms around me. "Everything's okay. I'm going to protect you, and Denny is going to stay with me until we figure out if this Evans guy was involved and we locate the Buttonwillow suspect. You *will* be safe, okay?" He held me tight to him, and I swore I felt a tremor run through his body. "We're going to figure this out."

He always had a reassuring answer. But I didn't want him to be hurt because of me.

It was more important than ever that I find these men. If that meant using the board, I'd do it again. If it meant protecting Walter from his need to protect *me*, I would do it.

"Ride with me?" he asked as he dug his thumbs into my lower back.

"Anywhere."

Sixteen

alter

The captain hadn't really been that upset. In fact, he'd handled me with kid gloves, which made me even more nervous. Had command just been waiting for me to lose it like my father? Were they sitting around worried I would eventually embarrass them? Or worse?

And now, I had irrefutable proof that my father had actually seen Dane's battered and bloody body, and I couldn't tell anyone in an official capacity. That was probably the worst part.

Dane and Denny climbed into my truck with me, and Ryan and Kal rode in their truck with Gene. I appreciated how my guys had shown up and taken over, taken on the protection duty for not only Dane, but also Ryan and Kal, who were a couple of good Samaritans who didn't deserve to get hurt because they were trying to help a guy out.

I'd been a little skeptical of Dane's talking board when I'd watched him and Ryan use it together the first time, although their explanation had made sense. But when I'd jumped into Dane's second attempt, I hadn't been prepared for the visceral reaction I'd had to what I'd seen. It was horrifying. The man's voice was playful in a Hannibal Lecter way that had my stomach turning and its contents wishing to check out of Motel Walter Muse. It was realer than any nightmare I'd ever had, and the thought that Dane had been through it multiple times already had me worried about the aftereffects this board's power would have on him.

I suppose my interaction with Dee Dee—The Troubadour and his Talking Board—all those years ago had me open to believing what I'd seen. Dad also used psychics when he was looking for missing people. I'd gone with him once when I was in the cadet program. I was probably seventeen years old. He worked with a woman named Charlene who lived in Grand Teton in the Grapevine, a small community in the mountain range that was famous mostly for the necessity to drive through it if you wished to take the quickest route between Southern and Northern California. We drove out to her house one Saturday, and he made me promise not to say a damn word to anyone that he'd taken me.

"This woman knows things she shouldn't, but she knows things that help in my cases sometimes. I don't want her knowing nothing about *you*, is that understood?"

I'd agreed… but my curiosity got the better of me.

When we got to her house, which wasn't more than a shack amidst high desert brush and the wildflowers brought on by a winter with heavy rains, I forgot myself. She met us at the door and I stuck out my hand. I'd been taught manners, and if Dad didn't want me to use them, he shouldn't have brought me.

"Walter Muse, Junior. Pleased to meet you."

Charlene took my hand in one of hers, ran the other one over the top, and led me to her table. My father cursed under his breath, and I knew this was exactly what he hadn't wanted to happen. If he really didn't want me to be read by her, he wouldn't have brought me, though. Looking back, I wonder if he was looking for answers about his son as well as his case.

"You are so like your father. You carry a lot on your shoulders," she said. She didn't look like a fortune teller or a witch or anything. She was a tough old woman in a US Army Veteran ball cap, an SF Giants t-shirt, and a pair of gray sweatpants. Her hair was cut short, the way my dad had always worn his since his USMC days.

"Charlene," my father said, more in exasperation than in warning. "He's just a kid."

"A kid who has a big warrior's heart. He's an empath. He's going to be a hunter and protector, just like you."

Dad just exhaled, and I could tell he fought not to roll his eyes. "We're not here about him." But was that the truth?

She hadn't let go of my hand, though, so I stayed riveted, waiting to see what else she would say about my future.

"One hunt will take you a particularly long time, but you shall reap rewards both personal and professional. Don't give up. Don't be deterred, no matter the cost."

"Yes, ma'am." She let go of my hand with a pat and I sat back in my chair. When I looked at my father, somewhat apologetically, he didn't seem mad like I thought he'd be. Instead, he had a haunted expression on his face. I knew his work, his search for missing people, including Dane Donovan, really affected him. He spent more hours in his home office by that time, talking less to Mom and me and more to himself. And in a few short years, he'd be gone.

On that drive home, I'd asked him, "Why did you bring me?"

He didn't answer for a long time, just twisted his hand

back and forth on the steering wheel, making a squeaking noise that hurt my ears but I refused to say anything.

"Some people say that psychics are a hoax, that they're useless to police. I think the right psychic can help you if you're open to it. It's only part of the investigation, but a valuable one. I've found three missing kids based on tips I've gotten from psychics. You have to be willing to use anything at your disposal, and frankly I'd rather get information from a psychic like Charlene than from a doped-up informant on the street. She knew what I'd seen... she saw what I saw. She believed me when no one else did." Dad couldn't bring himself to talk about what he saw at Dane's kidnapping site, but I knew what he meant. "She's got nothing to gain from helping me. An informant is looking for some quick cash so they can get high again."

Dad had no tolerance for drug users, but I felt sorry for most of them. We argued about a lot of things in law enforcement, and while we didn't see eye-to-eye on many of them, I valued every bit of guidance he'd given me. It had made me a good cop.

His DNA, however, had me petrified, looking around corners, second-guessing myself at times, always afraid that the madness that plagued him would come calling. His official diagnosis had been psychosis brought on by PTSD, but his doctors hadn't ruled out schizophrenia. He'd refused to be treated further, refused medication because he thought it would lead down the road to addiction, so he suffered in silence... until he'd opted for permanent silence.

If I were to believe Charlene, though, perhaps she saw that I would eventually find Dane. Her prediction had been vague, but I think in my subconscious I always believed she was right, that I would eventually solve the case. I just had no idea it would end up like this, with Dane alive and breathing, sitting next to me... everything I'd ever dreamed he'd be and so much more.

I needed to stop thinking about Dad and focus on the man sitting next to me.

I'd about fallen over when he'd come out of the bedroom with Ryan, dressed like a skater or like he'd just stepped out of *Feedback Magazine*. I also thought the choice of Slipknot was interesting. Wait 'til Dane actually heard the hard rock and heavy metal music that was popular with kids who dressed like he was now. I desperately wanted to close this case and move on to things like playing music for him, talking to him about his past, about current trends. Watch movies with him. Travel. Together?

What a group we made, with him and Ryan dressed like rock stars, Gene still in his suit, and Denny in a USMC t-shirt and faded Levi's. I'd gone with a black crew-neck sweater over a white button down and jeans, which was what my kids called my leftover '80s preppy look.

My kids. I needed to give them a call. It had been too long. I usually talked to them at least once a week. Stacia was in her last year at UC Santa Barbara majoring in Psychology and Steffan was a year behind her at UC San Diego majoring in Biology, with a desire to go into medicine. He'd needed an extra year of community college before transferring due to some health issues he'd been plagued with, since they'd been born a bit premature.

We'd been lucky with the twins; though they had a bumpy start, they hadn't suffered like so many twins born premature. They were becoming their own people, but I was glad we were still close. When Lisa had gone to graduate school, it allowed me to get closer to them, as she wasn't on call for them all the time anymore. I became the Dad Uber, I coached their swim team, and I even drove them to prom and college visits. I'd cherished that time with them.

"You okay over there?"

I turned to look at Dane, and my heart skipped around a bit in my chest. His shy smile warmed me, reminded me that I, too, was my own person. That was something I forgot a lot. Usually, I was Stacia and Stef's dad, or Detective Muse. Tonight, I wanted to be Walter, a guy who was falling into something special with a miracle man.

I almost forgot Denny was in the backseat. I wanted to lean over and kiss Dane like he was mine, but that was out of character for me and would definitely earn me a ration of shit from Denny. Instead, I gave his thigh a squeeze before putting the truck in gear.

"Yeah. I'm good."

I followed Ryan down the hill on Laurel Canyon Boulevard from the house to Sunset Boulevard, while Denny got serious.

"I have some really important questions, Dane."

"Of course. What do you need to know?"

I knew from Denny's tone that there was about to be an interrogation, but of the fun kind.

"You're telling me that you met The Beatles. That you actually *knew* Mick Jagger and Keith Richards?"

Dane's posture relaxed, and he turned around to face Denny. "I did. The Beatles were fun. Good guys. They were only here for a while, and they only came by Tess's occasionally, but yeah, they were around. Ringo eventually moved into Cass's house. I guess he had a bad fire. We were on tour when it happened, but we heard about it, it was all over the news. I talked to Keith and Mick a few times, when they weren't too messed up, but I didn't know them well."

"And Eric Clapton?"

"Yeah, I met him. He hung out at Joni's. I went over there a few times."

"And did you ever play with Gram Parsons?"

"Denny, I didn't know you were such a Laurel Canyon aficionado." This side of Denny cracked me up.

"Fuck off, Junior. I watched the documentaries."

Dane laughed, and it sounded so light and joyful. It was probably the first time he hadn't sounded like a victim of trauma who was trying to get a grasp on his life once more.

"Gram," he said with a sigh. "Not onstage, but he taught me a few songs on the piano, and when I played on Tess's album in the studio, he was there as a producer."

"Was he as knowledgeable about music as everyone says?"

Dane grinned. "He was. More, probably."

"Did Gram Parsons write 'Wild Horses,' or is it true that the Stones already had the song recorded?"

"That I don't know for sure. I know the Burritos' version of it came out first, and a lot of folks said Gram wrote it with Mick and Keith and didn't want any credit on it. He was like that. He wrote a couple of songs with Tess but didn't want to be credited on those either. He told me he'd work with me when I went into the studio. He was gone before then, though."

"Such a loss," Denny said, shaking his head.

I looked at him over my shoulder. "I didn't even know you listened to any of that music."

"Fuck *off*, Junior. You played it all the time. I had to give you shit about it, but I love that old stuff."

Dane snorted, and I thought, *how bizarre for him*. He had no idea how much music had changed, come back around, and then changed again since he'd been gone.

"Okay, one more and I swear I'll stop. Did you ever meet Jimi Hendrix?"

"Only a couple times. He'd show up after I'd gone home. That was earlier, when I first started making—Uhhhhh..."

"It's okay, Dane. Denny's quite open to the medicinal properties of plants." It was true. He'd often say he thought about retiring just so he could see if marijuana really did help with his pain and insomnia. Law enforcement personnel still weren't allowed to partake, even of the legal stuff.

"Oh. Okay. Yeah, I made herbal deliveries for my mom. That's why I was over at Tess's place, Joni's and Cass's. I started when I was fifteen. Mom made me stop, though, when I turned eighteen."

"That was smart. You could have ended up in prison for a long time."

I followed Ryan as he turned onto a side street and pulled over to the curb. It was near seven o'clock, so parking was tight on the street, but we managed to park together.

Dane went to open his door, and I laid a hand on his arm.

"Wait for me?" I asked in a low voice.

His smile and subsequent blush were just what I hoped for.

I got out and met Denny on the sidewalk.

"He's something else," he said. "Really. I totally get it. You done good, Junior."

"Thanks," I said with an eye-roll, but Denny knew the truth. I did want his approval. It was nice that he wasn't telling me I was ignorant for taking such chances with my future.

I opened Dane's door, and he slid down from the cab, brushing against me. He smiled up at me, and man, did I want to kiss the hell out of him.

But more than that, I wanted to feed him. He was so thin.

Denny took the lead, followed by Kal, who walked with Ryan at his right rear, and I maneuvered Dane to walk next to Ryan, with me at his side and Gene behind us. To an outside observer, our protective flanking probably called more attention to us. We looked like bodyguards for a couple of celebrities, which wasn't too out of place on Sunset, but exactly what paparazzi would be looking for.

"Keep the sunglasses on 'til we get inside," I said to Dane.

"If anyone takes pictures, I don't want them getting your face."

"Okay," he said nervously. He pulled the hood up over his head and I noticed his hands shaking out of the corner of my eye. I put a hand at his lower back, and he took a step closer to me. "Thank you," he whispered.

"You're safe," I told him, keeping my hand on him and my eyes on the neighborhood around us.

The restaurant was busy, but we didn't have to wait too long for a table. The hostess recognized Ryan and got her staff to pick up the pace bussing tables, so they could get us seated. Dane's head was on a swivel, his eyes flicking all over from behind the glasses at the people, the photos on the walls, and the general activity. I worried it would be too much for him, but then he turned and grinned at me, and my tension level dropped a tad.

We were led to a booth in the corner, which would thankfully have our backs to the wall and a clear view of the restaurant. Ryan, Kal, and Dane climbed in first, and my friends and I took the outsides of the booth.

"This is the same but different," Dane said. He pulled down the shades and looked at the pictures all up and down the walls. "Deep Purple, Rainbow... Who are Guns and Roses?"

Denny and Gene chuckled, and Ryan smiled.

"They kind of ruled the Strip in the mid-eighties," Denny said. I let him be the elder statesman when it came to music. "Most of the bands that played here were more appearance, less substance, but they were the whole package. Slash is one of the greatest guitar players of all time."

Dane looked closer at the picture. "Which one is he?"

"You might have known his parents, actually," I said. "Ola and Anthony Hudson. Anthony did album covers for—"

"That's right! I *do* remember him. He did one of Tess's

album covers. Henry Diltz did her second one. Wow. I bet he was one of the kids swimming in Tess's pool. That's great. You'll have to play some of their music on your pocket jukebox."

Denny and Gene cracked up at Dane's terminology, but I loved it.

"Absolutely."

"What can I get y'all tonight?"

The server was a young guy with all the piercings and tattoos.

I couldn't wait to see how Dane reacted. He was reading the history bit on the menu, and when he looked up, the sunglasses slid off his face and he let them fall in his lap.

"I..."

I squeezed his thigh, and he looked at me.

"I... wow... I haven't even looked at the menu." He was staring but not gawking.

"How about waters all around while we take a minute?" Gene said to the kid with a flirty smile.

The kid gave him a once-over. "Sure thing, Daddy. Anything stronger?"

Denny snorted, Ryan laughed, and Gene rubbed at his goatee with his left hand, flashing his wedding band. "I don't think so, sweetheart, but if you keep our glasses full and any photographers away from the table, there'll be a big tip for you."

The server checked out Ryan and Dane, then his eyes flared when he got a look at Kal, who was staring him down just short of menacingly.

"Sure, no problem. Take your time. I'll be back with waters."

He moved with a quickness away from the table and straight to the bar.

"Now was that necessary?" Denny said to Gene. "You toying with the poor guy's emotions?"

"I let him down easy," Gene said, straightening his tie. "You be sure to let my wife know I behaved."

I shook my head, and Denny groaned.

Dane leaned toward me. "He's... like us, too?"

"He's bi. Like me, but still married to his wife. She's long suffering."

Gene winked at Dane, and I kicked him under the table.

"Watch the shoes, Junior."

"It was odd for me, too. The openness," Kal said to Dane. "Things are much better than they were when I was young. But it's still not perfect."

Denny gave Kal a look, and Ryan reached for Kal's hand. "Kal worked at the carnival too. That's all you need to know."

Denny held his hands up and turned to me. "You been to this carnival?"

"When I was ten years old. With my parents. I saw Dane then."

"No shit!" Gene said. "Your dad go too?"

I nodded and looked down at my hands. "He did. Mom made us leave, they had a fight, and when he went back the next day, the carnival was gone. No trace. No forwarding information. He looked for years to try to find it again."

Dane put his hand on my arm. "I didn't know."

I put my hand over his. "He never stopped looking for you. I vowed I wouldn't either."

His eyes filled and he blew out a breath, then wiped his eyes and put the sunglasses back on.

"Here's some waters for you," the server said as he started setting glasses out. "I brought you a couple of carafes to make sure you don't run out if I get behind." The poor kid seemed nervous as he looked around. "Do we know what we want?"

Gene ordered first, giving me a minute to check with Dane.

"You know what you want?"

"Can you order for me? I'm sorry, I'm, um—"

"Of course. Anything you don't like?"

"I'm vegetarian, or at least I was."

"How about pasta? Fish okay?"

He nodded and put his shaking hands in his lap.

I ordered for both of us—shrimp fettuccine and spinach tortellini, thinking he could eat whichever meal he preferred. When the server was gone, Dane asked me to let him out to use the restroom. Denny stood, and then I followed. Dane scooted out of the booth.

"I'll go with you," I told him, and he nodded.

"I'm sorry, I just needed a minute," he said as I led him to the back and up the stairs to the restrooms.

"Don't apologize. This is a lot. Let me go in first and check things out, okay?"

He nodded, staying right behind me.

Dane looked around at the walls and smiled, but he was quiet. I opened the door first and then let him in.

"I'll wait out here for you."

"Walter?"

"Yeah?"

He held on to the door with both hands and kind of hid his face inside. "Thank you for bringing me here," he finally said. "It's nice to be around familiar faces."

He smiled at me then shut the door. Did he mean memories? Ghosts? Probably they were similar for him. I'd spent years obsessed with that period of time, read all the articles, watched the documentaries, poured over the memoirs and the music... but these people, these places were real to Dane, and for him they were only a few years past. Us asking him questions could help *and* hurt him.

I needed to tread carefully. I wanted him to come out of this experience strong enough to endure the rest of his life, not send him into a downward spiral of depression. Not that I had a whole lot of control over that, and no one knew that better than I did.

All I could do was watch him, be there when he asked, and be patient. I prayed he would ask, and I prayed he'd let me hold him, because being with him had been the best thing I'd had in my life in so many years. It reminded me how alone I'd been, how driven I'd been to solve his case, as well as the others that passed my desk. My drive had pushed Lisa and Brady away. If I were to have a shot with Dane, I didn't want to make the same mistakes.

I wanted him to be safe.

I wanted *him*.

Seventeen

D ane

It was nice to know that not *everything* had changed. Yes, the Rainbow was different, but I could still feel the same energy within the walls of the place as I did in the early years. The owners had lovingly preserved what I cherished about the place. I thought about the small bar upstairs, and the tiny corner Alice Cooper, Mickey Dolenz, and others had made their own. The Hollywood Vampires lair.

I hadn't made it in the door. I wasn't much of a drinker, and I was afraid of what I saw happening to the people who were drinking so heavily. Marijuana was different. Even the mushrooms my mom peddled didn't have the same effect. People like Jim Morrison and Keith Moon did some wild things while drunk, and it scared me. I didn't want to be out of control like that. What if I acted on my true desires? What if I slipped up and everyone found out I was homosexual?

As much as I missed my friends and the life I had back then, how wonderful was *this* time? I could touch Walter in public! I could tell him how I felt, ask him for what I wanted... The closeness I'd craved when I was young, a love like Joni and Graham, or Ray Manzarek and his wife, it could be possible now. I could talk about music with him, and he could introduce me to all the new things.

As long as the man who attacked me or this new blood-crazed maniac didn't find me first.

I made up my mind. When I got back to the house, I would use the board again. Whatever I had to do in order to end this as quickly as possible and move on with my life.

I used the toilet and washed my hands, taking a moment to look at myself in the mirror. I could live with the scar on my face, especially since Walter didn't seem to mind it. The others on my body bothered me, though. It was hard to look at myself and not think about what happened.

I opened the door, and Walter's gaze flicked to mine. He held out his hand to me with a warm smile on his face.

"Dane. Look." He pulled me in front of him and pointed at the wall above our heads.

It was a framed photograph of a group of what folks used to refer to as "long-haired hippie types," but when I looked closer...

"Oh Walter! It's Tess and me! And Nat, and that was Buddy, Tess's drummer, and Roger, her bass player. It's our band. Oh my God. It's us!"

Walter looked around before reaching up and pulling the picture off the wall. The frame was worn and the image was faded, but it was us. I was wearing a cream shirt with a big collar, my funky brown hat that I thought kind of made me look a little like David Crosby, even though I couldn't grow a mustache to save my life. Maybe that's why I loved Walter's so much.

I ran my finger over the image of Tess, and my eyes burned with tears. I couldn't believe she was gone. In my mind we'd barely been apart. When we dropped her at the airport, I assumed I'd be seeing her in a few days. Then I forgot everything while I was at the carnival, but still. It only felt like weeks that I'd been gone.

Tess had been my confidante, my best friend, my biggest fan for twelve years. What would she say if she could see me now, in these borrowed clothes, with this wonderful man who took such good care of me? I would have done anything for her. Maybe finding these killers would be a way to honor all she did for me.

"Here," Walter said, taking the frame from me. "Let me get a picture for you." He set the frame on the railing, and he held his fancy phone over it. He tapped the screen, then looked at it. "See? Now you can take the picture with you." He handed me his phone and reached up and rehung the frame.

"That's amazing. You can take pictures of pictures! Can you print them out from this thing too?"

He shrugged. "You can still get prints made, but they have digital frames now so you don't even have to have the paper copies if you don't want. Are there any other pictures you want me to take?"

I perused the pictures along the wall and laughed. "I remember that night! John Lennon wanted to join the Hollywood Vampires drinking club. They all got so drunk. We left early and they were still drinking." I shook my head. "Amazing that any of them survived."

"Well, Alice Cooper stopped drinking. Some of the others weren't so lucky." He glanced at me. "I'm sorry, I know you weren't ready to hear that."

"It's okay." I looked around to be sure we were alone. "Thank you, Walter. For everything. For making this easier."

He smiled almost shyly and took my hand. "I'm happy to."

"Can I kiss you again?" I whispered, leaning closer.

He licked his lips and took my jaw in his other hand. "You can have whatever you want," he whispered back before he pressed those plump lips against mine, slid his tongue over mine, and moaned softly. He pulled back, searching my eyes. "This okay?" he asked.

"I want more."

Oh, he gave me more. He pressed my back against the wall, nudged my thighs apart with one of his and he grabbed me by the belt, holding me in place while he licked and sucked at my mouth, his stubble rubbing me raw in the best way. My hard cock was caught between us and the friction of his movements heightened every sensation.

"Please say what happened earlier can happen again? Soon?"

He chuckled and pulled away. I was glad to see him breathing hard, as well.

"I would love that. But I need to feed you."

I moaned. "Yes, I'd like that, too." Okay, maybe licking my lips was overkill.

His laughter froze and his eyes went all hungry again. "Oh God, Dane."

He took my face in his hands just as laughter broke out at the top of the stairs, followed by the gasps of a couple of teenage girls.

"Oh! Sorry, we didn't—"

"It's okay," Walter said. He took my hand. "Our food should be there by now," he said very seriously as he led me past the girls.

"Aw, they're so cute," one of them said to the other as we descended the stairs.

"I wish *my* boyfriend would kiss me like that," the other said.

"Sorry about that," Walter muttered.

"Do *not* be sorry. As long as no one's going to call the cops on us or kick our asses, you can do that anytime, anyplace."

He stopped me at the bottom of the stairs. "One, I *am* the cops. And two, no one will ever lay a finger on you ever again, you understand me?"

I got the flutters all the way down to my groin at his fierce tone. *This man.*

I nodded and smiled at him as he scowled and led me by the hand back to the table. I hiked up my pants as I trotted after him and prayed the whole restaurant couldn't see just how turned on I was.

Gene's knowing smile when we got back to the table answered that question.

"Find the restroom okay?" he asked Walter, who flipped him off.

"Great! Food just got here," Ryan said. "Never fails. Food always comes when someone goes to the bathroom." He winked at me as I sat down next to Kal.

"Everything okay?" Kal asked me quietly.

"Yeah," I said. "Walter? Can I see your thingie?"

Denny shook his head while Gene snorted. "Thought that's what upstairs was for?"

"Fuck off," Walter said, his cheeks so red, but he laughed. He pulled his phone out, tapped it a few times, and then handed it to me with a shy smile. I loved how flustered he got.

"Look what we found," I said, showing Kal and Ryan the picture.

Their eyes went wide, as if things got a little more real for them right then. I'd had no doubt that they believed me before, especially Kal, but now there was photographic proof in this historical place.

"Let me see that," Denny asked, so I handed him the phone.

"It was upstairs near the bathrooms," Walter said.

Denny looked between me and the photo, then passed the phone to Gene, who muttered "holy motherfucker" or something like that, and shook his head before handing Walter back his phone.

"Unreal," Denny said, and Walter nodded.

"Henry Diltz took that, I think, if I'm remembering the night correctly. He used to hang out with Tess a lot," I offered. "He used to get pictures of everyone."

"Right," Denny said. "He's good."

"Yeah," I said. "I wonder if he's still around? He took pictures at Tess's place. Maybe there are some of the guy—"

The server came with the rest of our plates, and I decided maybe I didn't want to be discussing this in front of other people.

The pasta looked amazing, and Walter offered me bites of his. "Whichever one you prefer. I'll eat whatever you don't want."

I pressed my hand to my chest, I couldn't help it. He was so damned kind.

Denny and Gene both looked between us, worry on their faces. I wondered why?

"It was just a thought," I finished.

Walter slid his hand onto my thigh and squeezed gently. I liked the weight of it, the warmth through the denim. His hand was huge. It practically encircled my whole leg.

Denny leaned closer and said, "We're going to see Evans tomorrow. I'll get a recording of his voice and then maybe we'll know something more, okay?"

I nodded and glanced at Walter, who was suddenly very focused on his food.

Ryan entertained us with the story of the first time he and

his band performed in LA, how he messed up the words to one of Guns 'n' Roses' songs, "Night Train," in front of Slash because he was so nervous, and then ended up partying with the band late into the night.

"I apologized profusely to him. He shrugged and said, 'One of the reasons I don't sing, man. I'd forget the words to the songs I wrote.'"

"Try singing a Bob Dylan song in front of Bob Dylan and fucking it up," I murmured—and the whole table erupted in disbelief.

"Are you *fucking kidding me* right now? Bob fucking *Dylan*?" Denny's mouth hung open while Walter shushed everyone.

"Yeah, at the Troubadour," I said in a lower voice. I got the giggles at their expressions. "He came a few times. I'd been practicing 'Subterranean Homesick Blues.' It's a hard song to sing, but I loved it. I didn't know he was there, but then I spotted him, and I just lost it. I played some complicated guitar solo that didn't even make sense with the song and then left the stage, even though I was supposed to play three more songs. Tess met me backstage with a joint and a hug and she took me home, told me not to worry about it. Said so many people were mobbing him, talking to him about nonsense, that he probably couldn't even see who was onstage." *Poor Tess.* "She was good like that."

The server came back and asked if we wanted dessert, but everyone said they'd had enough. I'd noticed that the restaurant had filled considerably while we were eating, and there was a line outside the door. Denny and Gene were getting a bit twitchy.

Walter reached for the check, and my stomach dropped.

"I'm sorry," I whispered to him. "I can't pay. I had money at one point. I wonder if the label gave it to my mom?"

Walter slid his credit card into the folio and handed it back to the server. "Don't worry about it."

Kal leaned over. "Check the billfold."

I didn't want to remind him it was empty in front of Walter and his friends, so I did as he asked.

I leaned a little to the side and slid the leather from my back pocket. When I opened it, I saw that, no, it wasn't empty.

"Whatever you need will be there." He nodded and then went back to listening to Gene and Ryan talk.

I ran my finger over the... California Driver's License?

Dee Dee Miller.

And my mom's address.

There was also a Visa card, and in the long pocket, several green bills.

I closed it quickly and slid it back into my pocket before Walter noticed.

Holy shit.

Walter finished filling out the receipt and he turned to me. "I don't know for sure, but since you were never declared deceased, they should still be paying your royalties. Anything that was in your accounts should be there. Was your mother's name on them?"

"Yeah, actually. I wasn't eighteen yet when I signed my first band contract so everything had her name on it. Never got around to changing it. I hope they're still paying. Otherwise, I left her with nothing—"

"Oh, trust me, she's doing just fine," Walter said, resting his hand on my leg once more, this time sliding his fingers along my inner thigh. "Her art continues to fetch her up to hundreds of thousands of dollars. Not to mention she owns her house outright, and those houses up there are worth millions."

"In the canyon?" I gawked at him. "That funky place?"

"Thanks to you and your pals," Denny said with a laugh.

"It became some of the hottest real estate in one of the most expensive cities to live in."

"Yeah," Gene said. "There's a reason my wife and I moved from here to Bakersfield, and it ain't the scenery."

Walter and Denny laughed at him, and Ryan joined in.

"Yeah, I sold my place in Lauren Canyon last year for close to seven mil. Not that I saw any of it, thanks to my asshole fucking bandmates. We had fines to pay after we got dropped from Warped Tour and then broke our contract. It's fine, though. All worth it, right, husband?" He leaned over and nibbled on Kal's earlobe, making the big blond man blush profusely.

"It wasn't your fault. I still think it was wrong what happened." His gaze flicked around the table before he gave Ryan a sad look.

"Are we ready to take off?" Gene asked, standing up from the booth and letting Kal and Ryan out. "Speaking of spouses, I told mine I'd be home before midnight."

"Thanks, man," Walter said to him. He and Gene hugged, and they spoke quietly to each other.

"Stay beside me. Close," Denny said, grabbing my arm firmly, and as we moved away from the table, Walter stepped in behind me, right on my heels. Gene took the lead and Kal once more blocked Ryan with his body. Their movements made things real again. It took the lightheartedness out of the past hour.

Once we were on the sidewalk, I looked down the street and exhaled.

"You okay?" Walter asked me.

"The Whisky and The Roxy are still here," I said, breathing a little easier. "And Ryan said the Troubadour was still open too. Some things made it."

"*You* made it," he said. "Let's get you home. Did you get enough to eat?"

Walter suddenly stumbled and pushed me against the wall of the Rainbow as Denny shouted and blocked me with his body.

A man with a hooded shirt like mine had knocked into Walter as he passed.

"Everyone okay?" Gene asked.

"I'm okay," I said, though my hands had started shaking again.

"Walter?" Denny said, looking him over.

He nodded, but when I looked down, I noticed he had his gun in his hand.

He tucked it into the holster on the belt of his jeans. He and Denny spoke to each other in hushed voices, and then they moved us all toward the vehicles. When we reached the truck, Walter held open the door for me and took my hand as I stepped up and into the cab.

"Thank you," I said, but he only nodded and closed the door before he and Denny went back to their discussion.

I looked up the block, and I could see the guy who'd run into us. He was standing on the edge of the sidewalk watching the traffic go by, and then he darted across the street, causing cars to honk and swerve around him.

"What is he doing?"

Once he reached the opposite side of the street, he turned and faced my direction and stood there, motionless.

Then he smiled.

My pulse sped up. *It can't be.*

Walter and Denny climbed into the truck, still arguing, and I grabbed Walter's arm.

"Do you see?" I pointed as he started the truck. As the engine caught, the lights flicked on and illuminated the hooded figure. It reflected off his eyes. And his teeth.

"Fuck me." Walter put the truck in gear and it lurched forward. The man turned and ran.

"What the—" Denny hadn't put his seat belt on, and he was tossed to the side.

"It's him."

"Jesus, Walter—"

"*It's fucking him!* Hang on."

He pulled the truck up to the intersection, but there was no traffic light and no way to get across the heavy traffic.

"He turned down that next block," I said, watching the hooded figure disappear around the corner. I wanted nothing to do with catching him, but I knew that was the end game.

"How the fuck did he find us?"

"He had to be watching the house and saw us leave," Walter said. "He was probably watching us in the restaurant. *Fuck*, that was too close."

Denny called Gene in the next vehicle and told him what we were doing. "Get the others back to the house—"

"No," Walter interrupted him. "He probably knows where we're staying. We need to hole up somewhere—"

"Wait, Walter," I said. "Wouldn't this be a good way to catch him?"

Walter was stuck. He couldn't cross the busy street and he couldn't back up, and the people behind us were honking. Ryan's truck was still at the curb.

"Shit. Tell Gene to follow me. Let's at least get out of this area. If he's on foot, he won't catch up to us right away."

Walter turned onto Sunset and went around the block, then turned left at a traffic light on Sunset, which would take us back to Laurel Canyon. But instead, he turned right into the parking lot of a store called Trader Joe's. Denny told Gene where to find us and Ryan's truck pulled in a moment later.

"Dude," Ryan said when he pulled up next to Walter's side. "You can't have me driving like a maniac. You do remember what I went to prison for."

"You're fine," Gene said. "Cop, remember? Now, what the fuck was that?"

"Pretty sure that was the Buttonwillow suspect," Walter said, and hearing it come out of his mouth had me ready to—

"Dane!"

I opened the door, took three steps out, and hurled into the bushes. The whole time my body was purging itself, I was cursing my weak constitution. I needed to get it together, and I needed to be insistent.

Walter was at my side when I stood.

"I'm sorry to waste dinner," I said, and when he went to argue, I held up my hand. "I can't live like this, Walter. I can't run. I need to face this. If he knows we're at the house, then he'll come back, right?"

"Dane, you can't—"

"Send Kal and Ryan away but let him come for me."

"*Dane*—"

"He's right," Gene said. "Fuck this. Let's get some guys up here in hiding. Let's fucking invite him in. If he's coming for *us*, then he's not out there killing anyone else."

Walter looked like he was about to explode.

"Let's take it a step further," Denny said. "Hear me out," he added, holding up a hand to Walter. "Let's announce we've identified a person of interest in the murder at Buttonwillow, and he's been seen in Los Angeles. On the news. He won't be able to hide if everyone is looking for him, and if LA can be counted on for anything, it's for catching killers."

"Fuck yeah," Ryan said. "Like they did with Richard Ramirez. Let's do it!"

"*Have you lost your fucking minds!?*" Walter got up in Denny's face. "I'll take Dane away from here! I've got a guy with the marshal service. I'll get him into protective custody—"

"Walter?"

He turned on me, and the whites of his eyes were completely visible. He was vibrating when I put a hand on his arm.

"Can you guys give us a minute?" I asked Denny and Gene. They moved a few steps away to check on Ryan and Kal. Walter led me closer to the truck so we'd have cover.

"I'm sorry, my breath must be terrible—"

"Forget it," he said. "Dane, I'm not using you as bait. We'll catch him some other way."

"But I left the carnival to stop him. I came here to stop him. I *have* to do this. If he hurts anyone else, then I've failed."

"I can't lose you!" he whispered fiercely.

"And I can't live like this," I whispered back. "I don't want to hide. I won't be able to have any sort of life until he's caught, and I want that." I wanted all kinds of things—most importantly, I wanted more time with Walter.

His expression was unreadable, but then he yanked me to him and wrapped me in a vise-like embrace. "I want that, too. But I won't put you in danger."

"We're *already* in danger."

He pulled back, gazing into my eyes with an expression of helplessness. It was the first time I felt like we were on an even playing field... for all the wrong reasons.

EIGHTEEN

Walter

Everything happened so fast.

We went back to the house and Gene and Denny got on the phone. Fifteen minutes later, a detective from the LAPD who Gene knew was knocking on the door. Gene went to answer, and Denny took that opportunity to calm me down, or at least attempt to get me on board with their plans.

"Junior, I know you don't like this. But we'll be sure Dane is never in danger for a second. You stay on him like you have been, and let us handle the rest."

"Denny, I'm not trying to be unreasonable here—"

"No, but you're compromised. You did the right thing stepping back, now let me do the rest, okay? I won't shut you out, but you have to follow my lead."

I nodded, but I didn't like this one bit. And he knew it.

"What's happening?" Dane asked me. He'd gone straight

to the bathroom to clean up when we got back, but then returned to my side.

I took him by the hand and started to lead him to the kitchen, but he tugged my hand.

"Can we go out back? I need a smoke."

I let him lead the way and we went out the slider. Instead of standing near the pool, he took me around the corner into an area enclosed on three sides by retaining walls. He took out a cigarette but like the first time, his hands were shaking so bad, he couldn't light it.

"Here," I said, approaching him slowly. I took the matches so I could help him. "I hate what this is doing to you."

He sucked in the smoke and squinted. "The smoking?"

"No, all this. Your hands, the shaking."

He shrugged. "It started after... the bad thing. Mr. Ame at the carnival made it stop for a while, but I have a feeling it's going to be like this until... I don't know."

I wanted to offer him some sort of comfort. I stepped behind him and placed my hands lightly on his shoulders. "May I?"

He nodded and blew out a huge puff of smoke.

I began to apply light pressure with my thumbs at the base of his neck, and he moaned softly.

"That's nice," he said, and he let his head hang forward. "It's been so long since I've had any sort of physical contact with another person. Not even a hug. But you touch me a lot, and it's... so nice."

"I'm glad. I get it. My parents weren't affectionate with each other, and when I married my wife, she used to get on my case about me being the same. I went to see a therapist when we had our twins. I had all kinds of worries about whether... Let's just say my father had a lot of issues, and I didn't want to repeat those patterns. It was important to me that my kids always knew how much I loved them." I laughed.

"I wasn't great about it with my wife, but my kids always knew."

"I bet you're a great dad." He rolled his head from side to side and then crushed the cigarette out in the dirt. "Your kids are lucky."

"I'm the lucky one. They helped keep me tethered to the good things in life when my work led me to dark places."

He sighed. "You really are a poet at heart, aren't you?"

"Nah," I said, sliding his hair to the side and kissing his neck. "You're the poet. You've written some beautiful songs. I listened to your music a lot when I was frustrated and didn't know how to deal with my life."

He turned to face me, but then stepped back. "Shit. I forget you don't smoke. I should brush my teeth. Sorry."

"Don't even worry about it," I said, pulling him into an embrace. "I might not smoke, but between picking up sweaty kids from sports practices, and long stakeouts in small cars with stale coffee and cigarette smoke from my co-workers, smells don't bother me."

He chuckled but rested his head on my shoulder, his face away from mine. "Were you a hands-on parent? I didn't really see many fathers with their kids growing up. Cass had Owen, but no one knew who the father was. I wasn't close with the other people in our circle who had kids. They didn't stay late."

"I wanted to be involved in everything. My kids were the most important thing I'd ever done, and with twins, Lisa needed me. My mom helped, but she isn't a real nurturing type. She's more like a good buddy than someone to take care of your boo boos. Lisa and I figured the parenting stuff out together."

"You're a good man, Walter. I'm sorry to lay all this heavy shit on you."

"No way," I said, hugging him tighter. "I chose this. I chose to take on your case. I chose to come when Ryan called.

I chose to... to lead with my heart when I met you, whatever the consequences. But Dane? Don't choose *this*. Putting yourself in danger. I'm begging you. Let me take you away from here."

Dane put his hand up to my face and stared into my eyes. He was so strong. Ever since the close call outside the club, he'd seemed more determined than ever to do what he came here to do. It hurt my heart.

"I made my choice before we met, Walter. I decided to leave the carnival and come after this guy to stop him. That's why I was at Buttonwillow. I was too late that time, but I'm still gonna do it. I'd like you to be with me, but I understand if you can't." He stood a little taller and kicked his chin up. So brave.

I stepped away from him. I needed some sort of clarity, though I should have known I was beyond getting it from a few feet of separation. My obsession with finding Dane, and then finding him to be so much more than I imagined, had completely clouded my judgement. I knew I needed to let Denny and Gene run this thing, but my instincts told me this was *not* the way. I just didn't know if that was the detective talking, or the man catching feelings.

"Hey, you two," Gene said as he came outside. "I've got a reporter coming from the local news channel tomorrow, a friend of my wife's from when she used to work here. He's agreed to do a story on the Buttonwillow case and the history of unsolved disappearances on the I-5 corridor. It'll run on the evening news. Detective Ramos from the LAPD has three of his guys scouting out the perimeter of the property as we speak, and they'll be set up out there, out of sight, in case this guy shows up. These guys are former military. They're good. I've met them before. Dane, you'll be safe, all right?"

Dane nodded at him but gave me a wide-eyed look.

"Are you heading out?" I asked Gene.

He shook his head. "Sam knows I'm staying now. She wanted me to, said to tell you to let us help, and that she loves you."

I couldn't look at him. I couldn't stand the fucking pity in his voice. I'd had no choice but to turn things over to my two closest friends, I knew that.

"Thanks," was all I could say.

He squeezed my shoulder. "So, Dane. Since we've seen the Buttonwillow suspect here in LA, Detective Ramos would like to ask you a few questions about this guy we're looking for. Can you tell him what you told us?" He turned and looked over his shoulder, and then spoke quietly. "You know, what we decided?"

"I can, but is he going to believe me?"

"Maybe stick to the facts that matter. You were working at the carnival, he came to your booth, he was pushy, made you uncomfortable, and then he said, 'I'll see you again.' That ties him directly to our crime scene. We'll, uh, have to figure out what to do about your identity."

"We have a plan about that." I turned to Dane. "Are you okay with what we talked about earlier?"

He nodded. "Yeah. And look." He pulled out the empty billfold from Kal and opened it.

Gene and I leaned in—and stared in disbelief.

"Holy... where the fuck did that come from?" Gene reached for it and looked at it closely. "You didn't tell me you got a fake ID for him."

"No, he didn't do this," Dane said. "It's, um... It came from the carnival."

"Dee Dee Miller, born August twenty-ninth, nineteen eighty. What—"

"Tess Miller was my... mother," Dane said, his words halting as if he wasn't sure how far to go. "Dane Donovan was my father. He disappeared when my mother was pregnant with me, and before she was killed, she sent me to live with an aunt and uncle of hers in…" He looked to me with his eyes wide.

"We'll figure that out. What about Dane?" I asked. I hated this plan, but I knew we needed to have a cover story for him.

"No one knows. He disappeared. When I turned eighteen, I went to work at the carnival."

"And someone attacked you when you were traveling," Gene said. "You gotta have some way to explain the scars."

Dane nodded, touching his cheek and looking down at his hands.

"Yeah. I wanted to know more about him, so I went looking for information about his life. I got jumped along the way. The guy from the carnival found me, and I stayed on." He kicked up his chin. "Bob Dylan told stories about traveling with a carnival and since I knew Dane loved Dylan, I thought I'd give it a shot. Guess it grew on me."

I exhaled as I felt the weight of that explanation. I was familiar with Dylan's tale, which apparently was false, but it gave us the perfect explanation.

"It's brilliant," I breathed. "Makes total sense given 'Dane's' history." I used finger quotes, and Dane grinned at me.

"Then you gotta start calling me Dee Dee," he whispered.

I took his hand and tangled our fingers together, ready to forget the chaos around us and let the spell this man had cast on me take over.

"Great. Fucking carnivals. Got it," Gene finally said. "Just make sure you've got that story down and find some relatives somewhere. I'm going inside. I'm getting a headache from all this woo-woo."

"You ready to go in? Dee Dee?" I asked, and he laughed that big, loud laugh of his that had happened so infrequently since I'd met him. I wanted more.

"Thought you loved woo-woo?" Dane asked Gene's retreating back.

He flipped us off as he turned the corner.

Dane moved closer to me as we walked inside. "I just need a minute to use the bathroom." He smiled at me, and I had to admit that he was doing better with all of this than I was.

"Sure," I said as we stepped into the house. I watched him walk to his room, and then I found Gene.

"You good with all this?" Gene asked.

I stood a little taller, making myself eye level with my friend. "I guess I have to be. I don't like it."

"Walt, man. We've got it covered—"

"And as much as I trust you with *my* life, I don't like it for *him*."

Gene narrowed his eyes at me. "I'm not going to take that personally, since I can see you're hung up on this guy."

"Let me ask you this—would you put Sam in harm's way if the situation called for it?"

"Jesus, Walter—"

"Yeah, fuck off, because you wouldn't."

I walked away from him before I said anything else. I still needed to be sharp because despite their assurances that the place was protected, if anything happened to Dane, I'd still consider it my fault... and it would break me.

Before I rounded the corner, my phone buzzed. It was Dax in the group text.

There's been another homicide.

"Walt," Gene called out, and I returned to him as he dialed Dax's number.

"Where?" I asked.

"Dax, where?" Gene said into the phone.

"Lebec. Tejon Pass Rest Area. Before dawn. Like the last one."

Gene and I both cursed. "Same MO?"

"Yeah," Dax said, "and he was caught on surveillance camera. It's the guy. We didn't get a vehicle but he had to have one."

"We saw him on foot here just a bit ago."

Dax cursed. "And you didn't think to fucking call me?"

Gene frowned and held the phone away, like *are you kidding me right now*. "It just happened, *kid*," he said, putting Dax in his place. Gene and Denny still treated Dax like the youngster he was. "We were out to dinner, we saw him, we called LAPD, and we were going to call you as soon as we came up with a plan."

I hated that I now had Gene and Denny involved with keeping information from Dax.

"Well, I just wish... I'd like to have any information you've got that is relative to *my* case." His tone changed quite a bit, from whiny to formal and recalcitrant.

"Okay. That's better. As for *your* case, we are currently trying to determine how the suspect found out where we—"

"Who's we? Walter? And those guys from this morning? Who the hell *is* this Dee Dee person? I can't find anything on him."

"I'll send you my notes in a few minutes. That'll answer all of your questions. Now, if you would please let me get back to work?"

"Uh, yeah. Thanks."

"Thank *you*, Detective Brown." Gene hung up and cursed at the phone in his hand. "That little twat. Talking to me like that."

I knew it was time for me to get over my snit.

"Gene, I'm sorry, man—"

He didn't wait for me to finish speaking. He pulled me in for a hug and pounded on my back.

"We got this, brother," he said in my ear. "You let me deal with Detective Pissy Pants, all right?"

"Thanks, man. Go easy on him, would you? He's not used to being on his own, and this is a big case."

He raised his eyebrows. "Little shit's not going to get snippy with me and get away with it if he wants to be treated like a big boy. And relax, I was just reminding him of his place. Now, we good?"

I exhaled. "Yeah, man. I'm sorry. I appreciate you and Denny coming down here. I've never... I can't think straight around him."

Gene smiled and squeezed my shoulder. "We gotchoo. I love you, man, Don't ever doubt that."

I just nodded, not trusting my voice.

Dane stepped out of the hallway as we entered the living room.

"You ready to talk, Mr. Miller?" Gene asked.

Dane looked to me, and I went to his side. "You want me here?"

"You have to ask?"

We sat together on the couch after shaking hands with Detective Efrain Ramos.

"We want to help your guys catch this man before he tries to pull this bullshit in our city, so whatever you can tell us will help."

Dane nodded and folded his hands in his lap. With the beanie off and his hair down, he looked vulnerable once more. I fucking hated putting him in this position.

"Great. I already spoke to Mr. Wells, who drew the sketch of the suspect, and I just received a photo of the suspect from Detective Brown with Kern County. A surveillance camera caught him leaving the Tejon Pass Rest Area, where another victim was found."

Dane flinched, and I reached for his hand. He took mine in both of his, and I felt him fighting the shakes.

"I'm sorry," he said, looking down. He tucked his hair over

his ear, and I noticed Ramos's reaction when he saw the scars on his face and hands. *Good*. I hoped he understood how delicate this situation was.

"Not your fault, son. We just want to make sure he doesn't do it again." I appreciated that Detective Ramos was being gentle with his questioning. He was probably close to my age, but without sounding vain, he definitely carried himself older than I did. "Now, I know the basics of your situation, and I don't want to drag you through the horrible scene you witnessed again, but can you tell me what you know about this suspect?"

Here goes.

"I've been working with a traveling carnival for a long time now, since I was eighteen or something? The other night, this guy came to my booth and he was just... strange. Something about him set me off, and I told the carnival boss."

"Can you elaborate? What about him was strange?"

"He was real pushy. When he left, he said, 'I'll see you again.' Wait..." Dane got quiet for a minute, and he rubbed at his head, wincing as if he was having another memory.

"Did you remember something else?" I asked him in a low voice.

Dane whispered to me, "He said, 'He told me I'd find you here.' I forgot that part before."

Detective Ramos looked at me with interest. "We all sort of wondered if there was a link between this suspect and what happened forty years prior to Dane Donovan."

Dane cleared his throat. "He was my dad."

Detective Ramos's eyes flared, and then he coughed into his fist. "You said Dane Donovan was your *father*? Are you aware that he's a missing person?"

Dane nodded. "I am now. I mean, Detective Muse explained it to me. All I know is he disappeared while my mother was pregnant with me."

"And your mother..."

Dane cleared his throat. "Tess Miller. My aunt and uncle raised me. I lived with them until I was eighteen. I went looking for information about my father, more than the little bit I knew, and I ended up going to work at a traveling carnival. I liked it so I stayed. 'Til now." Dane's hands shook as he brushed his hair out of his face again, and I noticed his lip trembling.

Ramos turned to me. "You check this out?"

"Detectives Hamilton and Ochoa have been working on it. I'm on vacation and, after everything that's happened, I've recused myself from the Donovan case."

He frowned. Yeah, it was unusual for a detective to step back from a case. I knew this guy was going to have a lot more questions.

"So, your dad went missing, then your mom is murdered, and you've been working at a carnival?"

Dane just nodded, and his eyes were wide, as if he was terrified of making a misstep.

"And where did this aunt and uncle live?"

"Minnesota."

A shudder ran through his body, and I leaned against him to offer what I could.

"You go to school there?"

"Uh, my aunt homeschooled me."

Ramos nodded, but there was something he wasn't buying about the story.

"Your aunt never mentioned that people were looking for your father?"

Dane shrugged with one shoulder. "They didn't really talk about him."

Gene cut in. "We've got no evidence to support it yet, but there's a possibility that Tess Miller's killer may be connected to Dane Donovan's disappearance, as well as the Button-willow suspect."

"You mean that piece of shit Virgil Evans?" Ramos made a disgusted face. "Excuse my language, Mr. Miller. That case was before my time, but I'm familiar with it. We've had several run-ins with him since he was released. A few of his wards at the halfway house have gone missing in the past couple of years, and when the parole officers go in to follow up, they get nothing but pushback from him."

"I remembered his name when Detective Muse mentioned it. My aunt and uncle told me when I was old enough about my mother's murder."

That was a great angle. Dane was doing really well with this.

Ramos sat up taller at that piece of information. "You think," he said to me, "this guy might be responsible for Mr. Donovan's abduction?"

"It's a strong possibility. It's the closest I've come to identifying a suspect. Her murder was three years to the day after he disappeared." A thought occurred to me. "You've got the suspect's picture. You have an ID yet? I wonder if maybe he passed through that halfway house, or maybe they served together in prison."

"It's worth checking out," Ramos said. "You know, when they interviewed Evans after she was reported missing, he made out like they were a thing, said he was the caretaker of her house. He said she'd been in mourning ever since Donovan disappeared and hadn't been taking care of things. Guess by things, he must have meant you. Her son."

Dane didn't speak, but two tears ran down his cheeks.

What a horrible bit of information to lay on him.

As if Ramos realized it, he said, "We didn't buy his story, hence the twenty years he spent in jail. He pled guilty in an

Alford plea deal." When Dane frowned, he said, "It's a plea without admitting guilt."

"They never found her body?"

"That's correct," Ramos said.

"Detectives Hamilton and Ochoa are going to interview Evans tomorrow. They'll see if they can find a connection between him and the suspect from Buttonwillow."

"Sounds good. My guys are set up on the hillside surrounding the house and we've got drop cams at every entry point. Mr. Wells called Mr. Cross, the owner of this property, to get us access to the security feeds for the twenty-four hours leading up to their arrival and since they arrived, to see if anyone has been poking around."

"I was wondering, are you able to put a patrol car on Diane Donovan's house?" I smiled at Dane apologetically. We hadn't had time to talk about it, but if anything about him ended up on the news, it was better his mother find out from him than the TV. "She doesn't know about Dee Dee, and since that's also a significant location—"

"Of course, yes. I'll get someone there right away." He put out his hand for Dane to shake. "Thank you, Mr. Miller. We'll talk again, but I want you to be assured that we're doing everything in our power to keep you safe. Is there anything else you need?"

Dane shook his head, murmured his thanks, and then curled up with his knees to his chest on the couch.

"I'll be right back," I said to him as I went to walk Detective Ramos out.

"Thank you," I said to Ramos out of earshot, and the detective shook his head.

"Un-fucking-believable," he said. "Ochoa said Miller's pretty shook up?"

"Yes," I said. "And I appreciate you going easy on him."

"He's got a lot of scars. He tell you what happened?"

I shrugged. "Got jumped when he was out looking for his dad, is all he's said." Fuck, here I was being dishonest to another fucking cop. I was sliding down a slippery slope of deceit, and who the fuck knew how this would all play out? I could end up in jail for obstruction at the rate I was going.

Ramos pulled out a business card. "This is for victim's services. I know his case is with Kern County, but if he's going to be living here, we have services he could be eligible for. I'll keep in touch and if you need a referral, I'm happy to give one. He's got a long road ahead of him."

I shook Ramos's hand. "Thank you, I appreciate it."

He held on a moment longer, and looked to Dane and then back at me. "I understand he's more than just a case to you?"

I cleared my throat. "Yeah."

He smiled. "I'm glad he has you. I've seen the documentaries about his father. They look fucking identical."

"Yeah. It was a shock, honestly."

Ramos shook his head. "And you didn't know Donovan had a love child with Tess Miller?"

"No clue. Hamilton and Ochoa will follow up on it, but no, I had no idea."

"Wild shit with these artists up here in the canyon, huh? A lot of history. Stay frosty," he said, and then he let go of my hand and went back over to Gene and Denny, who were talking to another detective in the foyer. I recognized his move for what it was. He was trying to see whether or not I was bullshitting him. I hoped, after how good Dane had been, I hadn't just blown it.

When I came back in the room, Dane had picked up the acoustic guitar and was playing softly. I sat on the same couch but with enough room for him to have space, and I just listened. He drifted away into some state of consciousness where hopefully nothing could get to him. He had such an intense look of concentration on his face, it was as if he had the ability to shut out the whole world, and I wanted that for him right then.

A flurry of movement in the foyer caught my attention, and I stood when I saw Ryan waving me over frantically.

"What is it?"

"Scott, my producer? He had his security company go through the footage, and look what he found."

I glanced back and was glad to see that Dane was still playing guitar, not paying attention to us. I leaned in and looked at the laptop Ryan was holding up.

"Fuck me," Denny said, as we all watched the creepy motherfucker go from camera to camera along the perimeter, smiling and waving.

"When was this?" I growled.

"The night you got here, just before you arrived."

Which meant the guy was potentially creeping around while I was sleeping in my truck with my dick in my hand.

"Then there was this," Ryan said, as the cameras caught him again, passing by late the next morning...

"When Dane was in the pool. Goddammit, he was watching."

"Thankfully, the gate out front caught this when we left for the Rainbow."

The video showed us getting into the trucks, both of us pulling away, and a few short seconds later, a motorcycle appeared out of the bushes across the street from the gates, and the guy sped off after us.

"At least we know what he's driving now, and we can get plates off that image," Ramos said. "That should at least get us a name."

"It also means he knows where all the cameras are, probably followed us back up here. He probably knows we've got people on the property. He's likely not going to come here." Denny cursed, and Ryan closed the computer.

Gene sighed. "I still say we go through with our plans for the news clip. We sleep in shifts tonight. Can you give Mr. Cross our numbers so he can get them to security? I want to be alerted if so much as an unusual bird flies by or a spider makes a web in this yard."

"I'll take care of it," Ryan said as he returned to the kitchen. Kal was in there, banging pots and pans around. I could tell he wasn't happy with any of this either. He and Ryan began arguing in hushed voices.

"You want us to break it to Da—Dee Dee?" Denny asked.

"I don't know. He's had so much to process today."

"Why don't you see if you can get him to eat something and get some rest?" Gene offered. "Poor man won't sleep if he knows the guy was fucking watching him."

"It's more likely to piss him off," I said, watching Dane play. "He's angry already."

"That could help," Denny said. "It'll definitely help him get through tomorrow."

"I'm going to leave Diane's assistant a message, let her know I want to come by tomorrow."

"Good plan," Denny said. "Let us hold the fort down. You and Dane get some rest."

"Thanks guys," I said. "I'm sorry about earlier—"

They both hugged me and told me to shut the fuck up.

Some things you could count on, and these two men were solid.

Nineteen

Walter came shuffling back into the room and sat down heavily on the couch next to me. I'd been working my way through Bob Dylan songs, trying to zone out on all the shit that had happened. I needed to find that empty space or else I was going to have to welcome the full-body shakes back until I was in pieces on the floor.

I'd finished "One More Cup of Coffee" and was about to start playing "Simple Twist of Fate" when Walter reached over and squeezed my knee.

"Can I get you something to eat? Kal is in there cooking late-night breakfast."

I shrugged. "I don't think I could get anything down." I looked toward the foyer. "Those other cops leaving?"

Walter seemed jittery. He kept rubbing his palms on his pants and looking around.

"Detective Ramos is leaving, but he's got his people staying outside. He's got some leads to go on, including a possible sighting of the suspect on a motorcycle. They're going to see if they can get a name."

"That's good." I adjusted the tuning a bit on the guitar and strummed it a few times.

"Hey, what were you playing?" Ryan asked as he and Kal came in. Kal set a plate of eggs and toast in front of me, the intention clear. He was a caretaker, that one, and he knew I should eat. I smiled at him and tried to make myself eat a few bites. Not even a cigarette sounded appealing.

"Bob Dylan. I have a few songs I like to play when I'm in my feelings. The man had a way of making you feel small in the best way possible, like your so-called big problems are nothing compared to that of your fellow man and for that you should celebrate, take them in stride."

Ryan picked up his guitar. "I know this probably sounds sacrilegious, but I don't know any of his songs. I mean, of course I know 'All Along The Watchtower,' but mostly because of U2."

"Me too?"

"U2," Walter said. "An Irish rock band. Their first album came out in eighty-one here."

I nodded. "Well, then. Let's learn you some Dylan. Hmmm... where to start?"

"'I Want You'?" Walter asked. "I always liked that one, although I have no idea what it's about."

I shrugged and started to play the intro. "Like all Bob's songs, if you ask him, his answer changes. And he never plays them the same way twice, it seems. I know it as D, F sharp major, C sharp, B major, and A7."

Ryan was able to keep up and we played through the verse and the chorus. He was a quick study. We started it again, and then I began to sing. When I got to the I want yous, I couldn't help it—I stared right at Walter. I was exhausted, and the only thing keeping me together right now was playing the songs I'd always found comfort in and having this man sitting beside me.

We played the song all the way through, and I only flubbed up the lyrics once, which was pretty good for not playing the song in... how long?

"Not bad for a sixty-seven-year-old man," I said as I finished out the tune.

Ryan was all smiles. "Dylan himself would be proud."

I had a moment of fear, but Walter stepped in. "He's still with us. Still touring, too, at seventy-eight years old. Still putting out albums."

"Thanks, man," Ryan said. "I never had anyone around who could teach me the old—uh, I mean the classics."

We all laughed at his choice of words. "I'm happy to teach you anything I know, but you've got to catch me up on everything I've missed."

"Deal."

I was profoundly grateful to be communing with another musician, in this house, at this particular moment. The years between us didn't matter as we found common ground. Eventually Kal joined us on the piano, Walter kept our glasses of water full and watched us with what seemed like quiet joy. Denny and Gene were in and out, mostly huddled around a computer in the kitchen, and though I knew there were other police officers hidden around the property, all that mattered were the three men in the room with me. They'd rescued me, watched out for me, and now, they were making me part of their trusted circle.

Being raised by a single mom and then spending so much time with Tess meant that I was mostly around women. There were a few men I was friendly with, like the guys I played with in the band, but I didn't have traditional male friends. I think

I was nervous that if I got too close to men, they'd figure out my secret.

But with Walter, Ryan, and Kal, I could be myself. Even Denny and Gene seemed to be accepting, and protective of me for that reason. There was something to be said for getting this ride to the future, to a time that was much more accepting of all the parts of me.

Eventually, Denny retired to one of the guest rooms and Gene kept watch, wandering from room to room and checking on the computer in the kitchen, which I could see from my vantage point. Walter had explained that there were cameras all over the property and they were all broadcasting to the laptop. I couldn't imagine what this internet thing was that they kept talking about, but it seemed like they had answers to any question at their fingertips. Computers, in my mind, were giant boxes in a sterile room of an office building with blinking lights and buttons. I didn't even know how the smartphone worked, much less a laptop computer, but they seemed to be able to do anything they wanted with them. To me it was some kinda magic.

Gene called Walter into the kitchen with him, and Walter patted my leg before he left.

"You're something else, man. Hey, when this is all over... what would you think about playing on my album?" Ryan's eyes flared. "I mean, I know it's beneath you—"

"What? No, not at all." I laughed. "You're the rock star. I'm just the guy you picked up in the middle of the desert. No one will have even heard of me. Well, definitely not Dee Dee Miller."

"That's not true," Kal said, coming back to the couch. "Walter says you were a big deal. And you were on the television. I may not know a lot about popular culture, but I do know that not just anyone has TV programs made about them."

"I love that *that's* what you've picked up in the past year and a half," Ryan said. "I would challenge that assumption, however. Reality TV and social media have put all kinds of questionable people in the spotlight. You, Dee Dee, are not one of those, though. I fault my own biases for not knowing your music. I was such an asshole coming up as a musician, only listening to 'the right rock bands' and poo-pooing all other forms of music."

"Oh, come on. Folkies were total snobs. There were people who wouldn't listen to us, and places we couldn't play if we played electric. And we hated bubble gum rock music. Your songs had to mean something, even if you were the only person who knew what you meant. I hated disco when it first started—"

"Everyone hated disco," Walter interjected as he returned to the room. "But then when KISS did it, people still listened to it."

"KISS? Those guys from New York, right? With the makeup?"

"Did you fucking meet them too?" Ryan asked, shaking his head and putting his guitar down. "I bet you hung out with Zeppelin."

I grinned. "Robert Plant was dreamy." I wiggled my eyebrows at him, and he threw a pillow at me.

"If you tell me you met David Bowie—"

"He was a fucking *god*," I moaned. "He came to a party here, just once, and I almost died when I saw him kissing another man. I made Tess take me to his concert at the Santa Monica Civic Auditorium in seventy-two. Ziggy Stardust. I was in awe. I wished I'd had the guts to do what he did."

I glanced at Walter, and he had that shy smile on his face. He'd been very quiet during this conversation.

"We're going to crash. We'll be here for whatever you need tomorrow, okay?" Ryan stood and moved to my side. He surprised me by bending over and giving me a hug, which he held for a few moments, giving a squeeze before he stood. He slapped hands and did a strange sort of hand-clasp shake with Walter, and then he hopped on Kal's back. Kal carried him down the hallway to their bedroom, with Ryan slapping his ass the whole way.

"You kids should get some sleep too," Gene hollered from the kitchen.

"Okay, Dad," Walter muttered. He stretched his arms over his head. "Want a piggyback ride too? I can drop you off at your room."

I laughed, but then I realized what he was saying. "Oh, do you not want to sleep with me?"

His eyes flared. "God, yes, but I didn't want to assume. I was just going to crash on the couch."

That wasn't going to do. Guess it was time for some bread-crumbs. "I would love a ride."

His hungry look was back. He stood up and gave me his back. "Hop on."

I stepped up on the couch and put a hand on his shoulder. "Turn around." I pushed at his shoulder until he was facing me. Then I linked my arms around his neck. "Are you ready?" I wrapped one leg around his hip, and he caught the other one, his hands under my thighs for support.

He didn't strain under my weight as he walked, but he did look as if he was struggling with *something*.

"This is nice," I said, sliding my fingers into his hair, loving the way the short hairs tickled my fingers. "Tonight, playing, and earlier. I mean, except for the whole maniac on the loose."

He shrugged. "Minor detail."

"Totally minor. But the restaurant, that kiss... This."

"Mmm," Walter murmured as he stared up into my eyes. "*So* nice. Listening to you play and sing." He opened the door and let me slide down his body.

"Thank you for the ride," I said, not letting go of his neck. I pushed up on my toes and kissed him gently.

He moaned and took the kiss so deep, my knees buckled. He clutched at my ass, pulling our groins together so tight, every movement sent fireworks through me.

"You *taste* good," he said.

"Don't leave," I said, tired of worrying about what I said, what I did. "Please stay with me, Walter. I promise... it'll be nice."

He dropped his head back and closed his eyes. "I'm trying to *be* nice."

"Walter... wouldn't it be *nice* to not be alone? To feel something real together?"

"So nice... *too* nice." He seemed to snap out of his lust for a moment.

"Walter? What's wrong?"

He sighed and slid his hands around to my lower back. "I keep thinking of a line from a cheesy nineties movie—"

"Tell me."

He chuckled and looked up at the ceiling. "It's this cop, and he's on this bus trying to save people from a bomb—"

"A bomb? Is this like a Clint Eastwood movie? Like Dirty Harry?"

That made him laugh harder.

"Not exactly. Anyway, the cop and this woman who's driving the bus, they have an intimate moment, and she says something to him like, 'you know, relationships that are formed during intense circumstances never work out.'"

I had an idea of what he was trying to say. We were going through a horrible experience together, and sure, I'd somehow missed out on forty years of my life, although my body still looked twenty-seven years old. But he was real to me, and he was here. I couldn't spend another minute worrying about whether I had a future. All I had for sure was right now.

"In the movie? Do they get together?"

He laughed. "Well, yeah. But then in the sequel, she's with someone else—"

"Walter, we can't worry about the sequel. I'm *living* the sequel. I shouldn't even have this time right now, but somehow I do. And I want to spend it with you."

He frowned and pressed his lips together. "Fine. You should know then that there are certain people who are convinced that I'm like my father. That I may succumb to mental illness. I see a therapist on a regular basis and I—"

"Walter, we're in this together, right? Isn't that what you said? *I'm* in this. *You* have a choice."

"And I made my choice."

"Then what are we waiting—"

"I'm trying to be the nice guy here."

"Nice is so nineteen seventy-nine."

He laughed again. "God, now you've got me quoting another movie in my head. 'Be nice, 'til it's time to not be nice.' Patrick Swayze, *Roadhouse*."

"Walter?"

"Hmm?"

"It's time to not be nice."

It was good to know I could still evoke emotion with my words.

Walter had me undressed in a few quick moves of his hands. It took me longer to get to his skin through his sweater, his buttons on his shirt, his under shirt... So many layers, but once I did, I was in heaven. We stood facing each other, drinking in each other's curves, angles, and planes. And scars.

I ran my finger over a long one on his right shoulder and looked into his eyes.

"Surgery."

I gripped his left biceps and ran my thumb over a round scar there.

"Bullet."

My eyebrows shot up. I looked down and ran my palm over his left hip. "And here?"

"Got clipped by a car."

I knelt before him, keeping my gaze locked with his. I ran my hands over his velvety-soft skin covered by luscious dark hair, and I pressed a kiss to his scar there, taking time to nuzzle his hipbone before trailing kisses to his navel and below.

"Dane," he breathed as I ran my lips over the head of his beautiful cock. I rubbed my face in that nest of hair and inhaled his incredible scent.

"Please?"

He muttered something incomprehensible and nodded. As I opened my mouth and took him inside, I knew what Heaven tasted like. I knew what it felt like, and I wanted more.

Walter gently cupped the curve of my skull with one hand and caressed my scarred cheek with his other. "You good?" he whispered.

"So good."

His lips quirked under that mustache, and I remembered what it felt like when he'd treated me to such an incredible experience. I wanted to make him feel as good as he had me.

"So nice," he whispered back, and then moaned as I used my tongue, lips, and hands to work him and make him quake in the best way.

"Dane... Dane... *Dane. God... Dane!*" His back arched, his hips curled forward, and his grip tightened on my hair as he came, and I got to watch it all, taste it all, *feel* it all. I took it until I had to breathe. I sat back on my heels and laughed, so grateful to be alive.

"That was... *nice.*"

Walter rolled his eyes at me and took my hand to help me up. He pulled me into his arms and held me tight, his breath coming in pants. When he seemed to have recovered, he walked me to the bed, pulled back the blankets, and directed me to lay down. He climbed in beside me and sprawled across my chest.

"I'm not done, don't worry. Just need to catch my breath."

I ran my hands over his back and sighed. "If I'm dreaming, don't ever wake me up."

He pushed up. "If you are, that makes two of us." He reached under the blanket and gripped my cock, making me arch up off the bed. "If you are, then you'll have to tell me if this is okay." He lightly grazed my balls with his fingers, and I sighed happily, spreading my legs to give him access.

"Very... nice."

He shook his head. "Only nice? I guess I'll have to up my game."

He disappeared under the blanket and a moment later, I felt him someplace new—

"Walter!"

He peeked out from under the blankets and held a finger to his lips. "Was that not okay?" I narrowed my eyes at him, and he ran his fingers over my sac and down to my hole. "Have you never?"

I shook my head. "Never."

"It'll be good. I promise."

"I trust you."

He smiled and disappeared. I felt his hands on the backs of my thighs as he pushed my knees up and then... oh, the man did things with his tongue that I don't think any definition of the word *nice* would cover. He took full control of my body with every kiss, every touch, until there was nothing but slick sounds and the most incredible sensations.

I didn't think it could get any better, but then he took my cock in his slippery hand and began to stroke in time with his tongue, and then he pressed a finger against my hole, and then the pressure grew so intense and I felt... full. It was so much, I couldn't make out individual sensations. And then I was coming. It was effortless, the pleasure erupting from so deep inside me, it stole my breath. I felt I would either fly away or perish in the best way possible.

Then Walter was there, stroking my chest and kissing me, his mustache wet against my cheek.

"Tickles," I slurred, barely able to form words. I couldn't open my eyes or lift my limbs.

"That's it? It tickles?"

I chuckled, he sounded so exasperated. "Your mustache. It tickles."

"You said you liked my mustache." He reached for several tissues and cleaned up the mess we'd made, but I didn't even care. I didn't want to move.

"I love your mustache," I think was the last thing I said. The last thing *he* said made my breath catch once more.

"I love... *you*."

It was so soft I might have imagined it, might have attempted to will the words and the sentiment from him.

I drifted to sleep holding on to that thought, that maybe he really could love me, and wouldn't *that* be nice.

TWENTY

alter

Walter, you're too damned old to be making such proclamations.

Yes, I *was* old, and with my age came the wisdom to know that when something special comes your way, you fucking hold on to it because life isn't guaranteed to wait for you to figure it out.

I was older than my father was when he'd lost his battle, the one between his will to remain with his family and his distress over perceived failures in his career, in addition to PTSD and the mental illnesses he was dealing with. Dane's case was the catalyst, but according to my mother, my father was never the same after he returned from Vietnam.

I knew what it meant to love and be loved. I knew what it meant to perceive failure in love, and then to come back from it, only to fall again. I knew I tended to love hard and fast, but I also knew better than to try to fight it.

Was it fair to say those words to Dane? I didn't know, but I wasn't sure he'd heard them anyway. I'd turned the man inside out, and I knew from how he'd reacted that he'd never had an orgasm quite like that. The benefit of my first and only relationship with a man had been that Brady was a licensed sex therapist, and he *loved* to bring his work home. I couldn't have asked for a better man to have my first male-to-male encounters with, and I had no regrets. Our split had been mostly amicable, leaving me with all sorts of knowledge and experiences I never dreamed I'd have, so I was thankful for that.

I bet Dane wakes up thankful as well.

It was enough to make me smile despite this off-the-rails roller coaster ride we were on.

I cleaned up in the bathroom and threw on my jeans and sweater to go check in with Gene and Denny.

I found them huddled around the computer.

"Either of you get any rest?" I asked them.

Gene snorted at me. "About as much as you." He glanced over his shoulder toward Dane's open door down the hall. "You destroyed that poor man, didn't you."

I pressed my lips together for a moment, determined not to gloat. "Anything new?"

Denny laughed. "I'll take that as a yes. And yeah, we have a name. Fucking guy's name is Hunter Holland. Ex-Army, served time for aggravated assault, and guess which halfway house he stayed at?"

"Same as Virgil Evans. They knew each other."

"Indeed," Gene said. "Holland's been out about two years and his current address is still the halfway house. Ramos got a warrant to search the place tomorrow morning, and I'm going with him and his guys. Dax is coming down, too." Gene paused, and I could tell he didn't like saying the next part any more than I wanted to hear it. "You're staying here. With Denny—"

"To babysit me?" I knew as soon as I said it that it wasn't fair. "I know. I'm sorry."

"Hey, I get it," Denny said. "Remember when I had ACL surgery a few months ago and got sidelined on that trafficking case? I hated it, and you guys had to hear it from me every day."

"We really did," Gene said with an exasperated sigh. "Walter complains the least of us, though, so I guess he's entitled to some grousing."

"Thanks," I answered sarcastically. "I'm still hoping to hear from Barbara. I want to take Dane to see his mom, but she hasn't gotten back to me. I'm thinking we go late morning."

"That's good. Sam's reporter friend will be here around noon to record the interview with Da—Dee Dee Miller. Damn, I need to get that right." Gene exhaled and shook his head.

These two really were the smartest men I knew. "Any other background on the suspect?"

"Well, he was dishonorably discharged from the Army for some 'psychiatric concerns' that showed up when he was serving in Afghanistan," Denny said. "Probably they were overlooked when he enlisted. Last thing we needed over there was unstable soldiers."

"The military needs a better way to weed them out," Gene said. We'd had this conversation before. At least now that we were older, it didn't end up in a big fight.

"Yeah. Lotta things we should do different." Denny gave Gene a pointed look that meant conversation closed.

"I'm going to get some shut-eye," Gene said. "I suggest you go crawl back in there with your man and actually sleep this time."

I felt my cheeks get hot. "I'd be happy to give you some pointers."

Gene shoved me, then he pulled me back in for an embrace. "Let's get through this fucked-up situation before you get me all tantric with my wife."

Denny chuckled as I gave him a hug too. "Thanks for being here."

"Of course. See you in the morning."

I did as ordered. I crawled back into bed with Dane, leaving my pants on and my weapon within reach this time.

In the gray early morning light, I reached for Dane and came up empty-handed.

I shot up off the bed, grabbed my piece, and crept out into the hall. The lights were out and no one was in the living room, but I caught sight of a cherry glow on the back patio. I breathed a little easier, realizing Denny was out back with Dane. The two were chatting... and both were smoking.

"Naughty, naughty," I said as I pulled open the slider.

"Fuck off, it was just one," Denny said as he put out his cigarette. "At least I eat clean, unlike your steak-loving self."

I shook my head and took Dane's hand in mine, pulling him close for a kiss on his cheek. "You okay?"

His smile was more relaxed than it had been when we'd gotten back from the restaurant.

"Sorry, I couldn't sleep, and I didn't want to wake you." He seemed a little shy, and I thought, *Oh hell, did I take things too far?*

Then he winked at me.

"Plus, I'm a better conversationalist," Denny said, puffing up his chest.

"Oh, for sure. And you're closer in age," I said, and Dane

barked out a laugh. He covered his mouth as the sound echoed off the hillside.

Denny shook his head and looked utterly disgusted with me, but Dane continued to laugh. He wrapped his arms around one of mine and shivered a little.

"You cold? We should get you back inside—"

A loud crack and a rustling in the bushes startled all of us. Denny pushed us behind him and pulled his service weapon. There was a flash of movement just beyond the floodlights above the pool, and a shout rang out.

"Get down!" I pushed Dane into the living room and to the floor behind the couch. Denny took a flying leap and scaled the retaining wall, and then the iron fence at the top, where he joined a man dressed in all dark clothes. I couldn't hear them but a few moments later, Denny made his way to the natural stone steps that led down the hill from the pool house... and he was smiling.

"What the fuck?" I asked when he opened the door.

"A fucking mountain lion scared one of Ramos's men half to death. The two came nose to nose in the bushes and the guy jumped up, broke a tree branch with his head, and the cat went running. All these houses up here, you wouldn't think they'd be lurking around."

"Oh yeah, they're up here," Dane said, standing up from behind the couch. "There was one summer when I was a kid that I wasn't allowed to go outside alone because a mama and her cubs were in our backyard. Wildlife officers eventually came and captured them and moved them out of the neighborhood."

"So Ramos's boy got scared by a little kitty cat. Guess these LAPD dudes aren't as tough as we thought," Denny said with a laugh.

"You telling me you wouldn't have messed your drawers if

you came face-to-face with an apex predator?" I asked him. "If so, you're a damn liar."

Denny tried to give me an incredulous look but then he sighed. "Okay, yeah. But only because I've seen the aftereffects of an attack. Remember that guy in Kernville? Brutal."

"Yeah, I remember you telling me. It was before my time," I said, unable to resist getting another dig in.

"Again with the old man jokes."

"I should quit, really. Watching you scale the side of that mountain just now... I couldn't do it."

"That's right. Because I'm a Marine, dammit. We can do that shit 'til we die."

Then we burst out laughing, because we both knew he'd be in pain later from that stunt.

Kal got up minutes later and made coffee for everyone. He was extra quiet, but he did say Ryan hadn't slept well, and that he'd be up a little later. I took the opportunity to thank him again for all he'd done for Dane. "You two have been great sports, letting us all crash here. Especially since this is supposed to be your honeymoon."

He shrugged and leaned back against the counter. "We're glad to help Dee Dee. I've been where he is, although he's handling things well, considering."

"Do you have any advice? Anything I can do to make things easier for him?"

He thought for a moment. "Don't stand in his way of trying to make things right. I know it's dangerous, and I'd hate for him to not be safe. But I know how important it was for me to find out about my past. I know it's not exactly the same thing, but Ryan didn't like me going off by myself to find out about my past. He knew I had to do it, but he worried about me. " He lifted the corner of his lip. "I gotta say, you took Dane's youthful appearance better than Ryan did when he met my ninety-something-year-old baby sister on FaceTime."

"That would be a shock," I said with a smile. "I couldn't deny it after seeing him at the carnival when I was a kid. That memory stood out to me so vividly. Hey, Kal? What can you tell me about this carnival?"

"It's old. It goes where it's needed, wherever the owner decides to go. Nothing bad happens there, the sun always shines, and the people there look out for each other. It's simple. We work at our job, we're fed, we sleep, we move on. It's hard work, but it's a good place. We bring people happiness and take them away from their worries for a time."

"You were rescued by them like Dane was?"

He nodded. "There's magic there. It heals what ails you. I don't know how else to explain it, but there were a few of us who were found at stops, including Rafe, the ringmaster. Once Nik and Ame picked us up, we were given accommodations and eventually we got better. Do you believe in magic, Walter?"

"I suppose I have to."

He smiled. "That's a good answer."

"Hey, baby." A sleepy Ryan entered the kitchen and went right into Kal's arms.

"Ryan, I want to thank you," I started, but he held up a hand.

"No need. Shit happens and it happens for a reason. This was all part of a plan."

"Well, I'm grateful that you found him. Grateful you brought him here. We're going to get to the bottom of this."

He nodded and took a sip of Kal's coffee, then let his eyes roll back in pure bliss.

"Yeah, well, it worked out for me too. I got myself a guitar player and a teacher. Maybe I'll even hook him in to tour with me, if and when I get that all lined up."

I felt his words like a pit in my stomach. Would Dane want

to go back out on the road and live the life of a touring musician? How would that work?

The more important question, though... how could I go back to being a detective after all this? It almost felt as if my whole career had been careening toward this moment, and now that my life had shifted, I needed to take a hard look at whatever came next.

Would Dane want me around? Would I stay?

"I'm sure he'd appreciate being included." That was as much as I felt I could actually say. I *did* know that Dane was happy playing with Ryan and Kal, that he seemed to appreciate their friendship and acceptance. "And hopefully we'll be out of your hair soon, so you two can spend some alone time together."

Ryan grinned as he sipped his coffee, and his gaze went to Kal's. "Oh, we're enjoying ourselves, don't you worry."

Kal blushed bright red, and he lifted his arms to grab the back of his neck, exposing a great big hickey on the inside of his bicep.

"Thanks for the coffee," I said, and left to give them some privacy. I brought cups of coffee to Denny and tea to Dane, who were still chatting in the living room.

"Thanks, man," Denny said. "What time do you want to go up to Diane's?"

Dane's smile fell. "Right. We need to do that."

Denny looked between us. "I'm going to get cleaned up. Mind if I use the bathroom?"

"Go ahead," I said.

I sat next to Dane and took his hand in mine. I loved being affectionate with him. I was starved for touch whenever I was around him, almost as if *not* touching the man would allow him to disappear once more.

"She's going to be elated to see you," I said. "I promise. When I saw her last, what... three days ago? She told me not to come back on the anniversary of your disappearance, but to come when I'd found someone." I gazed into his eyes, hoping he would get my meaning.

He blinked. "She knows about you? About... men?"

"Yeah. She was sad when I told her that Lisa and I got divorced, and then she was a little confused when I got together with Brady, but she was happy for me."

Dane's eyes got big. "Did she know about me? Did she ever say anything?"

"Not to me. She called you 'sensitive,' but she never said to me that she thought you might be gay. I think moms know, though. Mine wasn't surprised, but she had a tough time with the whole bisexual concept, like I should only be gay or not. Maybe your mom didn't want to speak for you."

He blew out a big breath. "Okay. Then let's do it." He stood and walked toward his bedroom, but then he turned.

"Wait. When you said found someone..." He trailed off.

Make or break time. "I think I have." My voice cracked. I rubbed my sweaty palms on my thighs, waiting for his reaction.

He didn't run, but he speed-walked back to me and straddled my lap, taking my mouth in a desperate and relieved kiss. Maybe he'd been worried too. I held him tight in my arms as our tongues tangled, the tentativeness he'd had before gone.

"Walter," he whispered, pressing our foreheads together. "Are you being serious?"

"I am. Same rules apply, though. If you get to the point you want to go out on your own, I'll understand."

"You know what I want?" He was frowning now. "I want what I've always wanted. Someone who wants *me*, who's *like* me and wants to be with me. Someone waiting for me at home, someone who's happy to see me. Someone who makes the world make sense and wants to keep me safe."

I brushed his hair back from his face and held it there. "I want all of that. I want *you*."

He smiled so brightly, his eyes wet with tears. "Then I think you can tell my mom you found someone."

"Okay, then. Let's go tell her."

Only, when we got to her house, there was no cop out front and no one answered the door. I called and the phone rang unanswered.

"She didn't mention she was going anywhere," I said. "She has, in the past. Called, or had Barbara email me if she was going out of town." I turned to Dane. "She never wanted to miss any news about you."

He smiled but the tremors were back in his hands, though he tried to hide them.

"Maybe try Barbara again?" Denny offered. "I'll call Ramos."

I hit Barbara's contact and waited.

"Oh, Detective Muse. I'm sorry I haven't returned your call."

"It's all right. Is everything okay?"

There was a pause, and I reached for Dane's hand.

"I'm afraid not. I'm at Cedars-Sinai with Diane. She had a stroke. The day after your visit."

I tightened my grip on Dane's hand. "I'm so sorry. How is she?"

Barbara laughed. "Stubborn, actually. The doctors have kept her to continue running tests, but other than her sight being somewhat compromised, she's got mental clarity and full mobility. She should be able to go home in a day or two."

I sighed with relief. "That's great news. Is she allowed to have visitors?"

"She is as long as the visits are short. Shall I tell her you're coming?"

I grinned at Dane. "Yes, I'll be there in a few minutes. And I'm bringing a surprise."

"Oh! Very well. I'll meet you in the waiting room."

I hung up, and both Denny and Dane hurled questions at me.

I held up my hands. "She's okay, but she's at Cedars-Sinai."

"Ramos said his guy stayed all night and no one showed up. He was going to call you this morning."

"All right then. Let's go. I'll explain on the way."

Dane fidgeted with his clothes as we approached the hospital. He was wearing another pair of jeans, these ones flared at the bottom and fit him a little better, and on top he wore a white tunic with long, loose sleeves and an open neck. The flash of skin when he moved had my mouth watering, thinking of all the places I'd kissed him last night. This morning. Whenever that was.

"I wish I had something nicer to wear to see her," Dane said.

"Well, it sounds like she can't see well right now. Barbara said the doctor's hoping that might be temporary, but that Diane is taking it well." I gave him a once-over, loving the picture he made. He was timeless. He could have stepped out of a modeling shoot from the 1970s *or* today. "We'll take you shopping soon."

He tucked his hair behind his ear and smiled at me, and this time he left it there.

We checked in with the front desk and then got into the elevator, Dane's gaze darting everywhere, though he walked with his back straight. *So brave.*

"You know we had a fight the last time I saw her. I was leaving for the last tour with Tess. She was after me to get my own manager. She didn't think Tess's manager was looking out for my best interests. He tended to put my job as Tess's guitar player above my solo career. She told me I shouldn't spend my whole life in Tess's shadow." He shook his head. "I could never tell if she was jealous of my relationship with Tess or if she saw something I didn't see. The last thing I said to her was, 'I know what I'm doing.' I think we can all agree that I did not."

The elevator doors slid open, and I gripped Dane's hand.

"I sure as hell didn't know what *I* was doing at twenty-seven," Denny said. "Did you, Junior?"

"Do I know what I'm doing *now*?"

We both laughed, and it did the trick to loosen Dane up.

I heard a voice call out behind me. "Detective Muse?"

I turned, and Barbara smiled warmly at me—

Until she saw Dane.

"Oh my God. He looks—"

I rushed to Barbara's side as she listed to the right. "Whoa! Careful. I know, it's a shock, but we need to keep this quiet."

She nodded at me but stared at Dane with wide eyes.

A doctor came toward us. "Ms. Dunne? Are you all right?"

I looked to his badge. "Dr. Santos? I'm Detective Walter Muse, my partner, Detective Dennis Hamilton, and this is Dee Dee Miller. We came to see Mrs. Donovan."

The doctor shook our hands, and I put my hand on Dane's lower back to give him a little support.

"How is... Mrs. Donovan?"

The doctor brightened. "She's doing wonderful, considering. Her vision may remain affected, however. I don't know to what extent. It will take time to know. I'm happy to accompany you to her room."

"Thank you," Dane said.

I'd been so wrapped up in this moment with Dane that... thank God for Denny. He was doing his role as protector, surveying the area for any threats. As we made our way to Diane's room, he was checking everyone out and watching our backs. I would be eternally grateful to him for this.

Barbara went in first. "Diane? I brought a special visitor. Are you up for a visit?"

"Oh," she said, tucking her sheet around her. She looked lovely, her white hair fanned out around her, a much healthier glow to her cheeks than I would have expected from an 80-something-year-old woman who'd just had a stroke. But then I noticed that her eyes were directed toward the ceiling and unfocused. "Who did you bring?"

"Hello, Mrs. Donovan, it's Detective Muse." I moved to her side and took her outstretched hand. She turned her face toward my voice.

"Walter! Oh, you dear man. Thank you for coming to see me again so soon."

Barbara said, "I'll be just outside if you need me," and Denny led her out into the hallway.

I turned to Dane, who had tears streaming down his face.

"Well, you told me to come back when I found someone." I pulled Dane forward gently and put his hand in his mother's.

"Mom?"

Twenty-One

D ane Walter's steadying hand at my back was the only thing keeping me from falling to my knees. Seeing my mother in a hospital bed, old and frail, when she couldn't even see me, was breaking my heart.

"Oh, Detective... You found my boy?!" She took in a shaky breath. "Dane? Is it really you?"

She held my hand with both of hers, and I broke at the sight of her gnarled knuckles. Her hands had created so much beauty in this world, had raised me by herself, had made me her whole world...

"It's me, Mom. I'm so sorry!"

She reached up and touched my face, her eyes open and unfocused, and when she touched my hair, she smiled so wide.

"My blond baby. It's been so long! What happened to you, baby?"

"I'm sorry." I couldn't... I cracked wide open. Walter pushed a chair under me just as I collapsed, and I put my face against her hands and cried. How could I have left her for so long? How could I have hurt her like this?

"Mrs. Donovan, Dane has had dissociative amnesia. I found him the day after I came to see you."

Her brow furrowed. "My baby... were you hurt?"

"I'm okay now," Dane whispered.

"Mrs. Donovan, for reasons I'll explain to you in the future, we must keep his true identity a secret for his safety. His memories were triggered by an encounter with a young man, at the place where he's been working this whole time."

"Oh," she said, brightening a little. "You mean your friend Hunter? He was just here, before you came in."

And the bottom dropped out.

"Hunter was here... to see you?" The shakes took over, and I turned to Walter.

"Denny!" he called out the door. "What did Hunter say to you?" Walter asked Mom.

"Oh... he said he'd been your friend. He said he hadn't seen you for a long time and hoped you'd be back soon. It was odd, I don't remember you ever mentioning anyone named Hunter."

"He's not my friend, Mom. He's—"

Walter squeezed my shoulder and shook his head. "We'll talk to him, ma'am. Is there anything else you remember about his visit?"

Her eyes traveled to the ceiling as she thought for a moment. "He said, 'I'll see you again.' Maybe he works here? I heard the wheels of a cart when he left the room."

Walter held up a finger, and he stepped outside the door

with Denny. They whispered to each other, and then Denny hurried down the hall.

"Are you hurting, Mom? Are you in any pain?"

"No, not at all. It was the strangest thing. The morning after Detective Muse came to see me, I woke up and my eyes wouldn't work right. I couldn't see straight ahead at all and the sides were unfocused, and I had a bit of a headache. Barbara called an ambulance and they brought me here. Once the headache was gone, I felt fine, only I still can't see right. The doctor says it's a visual processing issue, that the messages between my eyes and my brain are scrambled. It may or may not last. A bit of a nuisance, but Barbara has assured me we'll make it work. This might be the next phase of my painting. The blind phase." She laughed then, though I couldn't imagine how she could find humor in her situation. Then again, she'd made it through so much, including losing her son. She might see this as yet another trial to endure.

"Mom, I'm here. I'll help you."

"You're such a good boy. But I'm okay, and I have Barbara, plus we'll be hiring a nurse to come in during the day. I would be more upset... but I feel grateful. Grateful I had so much time to create and see the world." Her smile fell. "My only regret was not having you in my life."

"Mom—"

"No, baby. Don't be sad for me. But I want to know more. Are you okay? Were you hurt bad?"

"Yeah, I was hurt." I blew out a breath. I didn't ever want her to know the full extent of what happened to me. "But I'm okay now. Everything's okay now. Walter is helping me, and my new friends Kal and Ryan, they were the ones who found me... I'm going to be okay. I'm home, and I want to take care of you."

"You're here. That's all that matters to me."

We held hands, and I thought, maybe she's right. I'm here now, and that's all I can do.

Walter was out in the hallway with Denny and a couple of uniformed police officers, and the tension coming off them filtered into the room. Barbara was out there as well, leaving Mom and I alone.

"I've missed so many things about you," she said quietly. "But I especially miss your singing. I'm sorry I put so many barriers in the way of you living your dream."

"Mom, you didn't. I was stubborn—"

"Of course you were. You're my son. Would you sing for me?"

I smiled. I recalled the day she'd come home early from one of her trips to surprise me, and I was in the living room singing along to Buffalo Springfield's "Flying on the Ground is Wrong." I'd come home from school, and I was frustrated because a boy I'd been friends with—well, in *his* mind we were friends, but I'd felt a lot more for him—had told me to get lost so he could hang out with the cool kids. Mom had let me buy a few records the last time we'd gone to town, and I'd had Buffalo Springfield on repeat, deconstructing their lyrics and harmonies. I wanted to learn how to play the songs, but I wanted to play them on guitar. I hadn't yet worked up the guts to ask Mom for one. So I stood in our living room in front of the big windows and sang into the afternoon sun.

I sang those words for her now.

She closed her eyes and tapped her fingers on the back of my hand in time with the beat. Walter came in the room. I felt him at my back, but he didn't interrupt me, and by the time I'd finished the song, Mom had fallen asleep with a smile on her face.

"She's so happy," Walter whispered. "There's been a tension in her face all the times I've seen her, but it's gone. Look at her, Dane."

"I put her through so much." If I'd thought I'd been through all of the emotions in the past three days, I'd forgotten I could feel small. So small. I'd caused this woman so much pain. What an awful, awful legacy. A good-for-nothing son who complained about the rules she'd put in place to protect me. "I should have listened to her..."

Walter dropped to a knee, and I wrapped my arms around him.

"You can't help what happened, Dane. But you coming back, you being here now when she needs you most, what a blessing for her. She had no idea she'd ever see you again, and now she has you for the time she has left."

"I almost didn't make it in time," I said to him. "Walter, I almost *didn't* see her again."

He held me so tight, and absorbed my tears and shakes until I was able to breathe again.

"Oh no! I didn't tell her about us."

He pulled back and smiled at me. "We'll have time for that. It's okay."

I laughed. "That might have sent her over the edge. Which would be a bigger shock? That her son, who's been gone for forty years, shows up out of the blue? Or that he's got a boyfriend?"

Walter's eyes flared but his smile grew wider. "Definitely the boyfriend part, especially because he's a pig." He winked at me, and I covered my mouth to keep from waking my mom.

"You're not. You're not like the cops were."

He raised his eyebrows. "How do you know? Maybe I'm a billy-club-wielding asshole."

I snorted. "Who listens to hippie folk music? I doubt it. Oh, but a uniform... do you wear a uniform, Detective Muse?"

"Only when I'm called out for special occasions or if I'm doing extra shifts on patrol."

I started fantasizing about him in tight navy-blue pants, but there were more serious things to worry about right then.

"What happened with Hunter? Was he here?"

Walter's serious expression was back. "Yeah. They've got him on surveillance cameras on this floor and then leaving the hospital before we got here."

"Did you check on the house?"

Walter's eyes narrowed. "Let me call Ryan." He tapped his screen and waited a few beats, his frown growing deeper. Finally it picked up. "Kal? Where's Ryan? He *what*?" Walter's gaze shot to mine. "Okay. Okay, we'll be right there. No, don't leave. Lock the door and don't open it for *anyone* but us or Gene, all right?"

Walter took a deep breath.

"What happened?"

"Ryan mentioned he was waiting for a delivery, I should have warned the officer at the house. Someone showed up, the officer saw the delivery uniform and a box. He called up to the house through the intercom and when Ryan said he was expecting something, the cop let him in the gate."

"Is Ryan okay?"

Walter nodded slowly. "He's okay, but we need to get back there."

I didn't want to leave my mom. "Is she—"

"She's safe here at the hospital. They'll have an officer guarding the door at all times until we catch this guy. He's taking chances—he's going to get caught."

"Walter…" I didn't want to say the words, but enough was enough. "I should use the board again. I can find him."

"Dane, you can't. It takes too much out of you."

"If it means catching him and putting an end to all of this?"

Walter stood and took my hand, leading me from the chair. "I don't like it," he said.

Barbara came in then. "My goodness, Detective Hamilton told me about the man who was here earlier! I'm afraid for Diane."

"We're going to catch him, I swear. Stay here with Diane. If anything happens that makes you feel uncomfortable, call me right away. If the patrol officer leaves for any reason, call me."

She nodded, her eyes wide. "Thank you, Detective. And Dane... I'm so happy you're okay. I know you don't know me, but I've worked for your mother for a long time. You've always been her greatest joy. I hope you'll be able to spend more time with her."

I took her hand. "Of course I will. Thank you for being with her when I couldn't."

Small. So small.

Walter leaned in close to her. "If anyone asks, this is Dee Dee Miller. He's Dane's son. I'll explain everything when Diane is well."

"Thank you, Detective."

We found Denny outside the elevators, and he was on the phone. He pushed us toward the open doors and inside the elevator while he ended his call.

"Clusterfuck of epic proportions. These goddamned LAPD... rookie fucking move."

"What happened, exactly?" Walter asked him. He pulled me against him, and I held on tight.

"It wasn't Holland, but they shouldn't have let *anyone* up to the house. Whoever it was, he got past the fucking patrol officer, and I don't know where the fuck the *rest* of Ramos's guys were. He walks right up, rings the bell, Ryan answers, and he fucking clocks him with a club. Twice! The guy's crying, screaming 'he's making me do it,' starts to drag Ryan out the door but Ryan, thank God, fucking shouts, and Kal comes running. The guy tried to hop the fence, but one of the cops nabbed him when he heard the screaming. They've got him at the station."

"Oh my God, Ryan! Is he okay?"

"Paramedics came, they patched him up. He didn't want to go to the hospital, so they said to monitor him for a concussion. And fucking Ochoa and Brown aren't picking up. There are too many moving parts."

"Walter," I said, tugging on his shirt. "I can find him."

The elevator doors opened and the men put me between them. There were a couple of police cars in the driveway and Denny directed us toward them.

"You have the photo?" he asked the first officer, a woman. She nodded. "Good. Your guy does not leave Mrs. Donovan unattended for any reason, do you understand me?"

"Yes, sir," the officer replied. "Our captain has us here, two more officers on the floor, and one outside her door. He's sent another officer over to the Cross house, as well."

Denny nodded, thanked her, and we made our way back to Walter's truck.

Denny's phone started buzzing as soon as he climbed into the backseat.

"About fucking time! What...? Shit. All right. You hear about Ryan? Yeah... we've got a third guy now. Fuck. Okay. See you back at the house." He hung up. "The halfway house was a bust. Neither Evans nor Holland were there. Evans hasn't shown up for work for four days. Holland missed check-ins the last four days, as well. His parole officer hasn't been able to locate him either—no shit, because he's out slashing and bashing." Denny had several more curse words to get out of his system before he sat back.

Walter was watching him in the rearview. "You gotta talk to this guy who came to the house."

"I will, but right now, I want you two back at the house—"

"Denny—"

"Fuck, just get us back to the house and we can get organized."

The tension level in the truck rose and my shakes started up so bad, I had to sit on my hands. I wasn't about to fall apart now.

"We still doing the interview?" Walter asked Denny.

"Ramos said to still have the reporter come over and interview Dane, so we gotta get back for that. When that shit hits the news, get ready."

"What do you mean?" I asked.

Denny leaned forward. "We need to be prepared for Holland or Evans to make another desperate move. There's also the chance we flush out Evans that way. Everyone's gotta be alert at the house. Moving you to another location would be dangerous... but I'm confident, barring another fucking mountain lion or some shit, no one will get into the house. I don't see them doing a big show of force. We just can't take eyes off you, not even for a second."

I nodded and wrapped my arms around myself.

"You should also be prepared," Walter added, "that other people may reach out to you once you hit the news. Old friends of your 'mom and dad's,'" he said, using finger quotes. "Enemies, people looking to make a buck. We should get you an attorney to be a point of contact. They can also start figuring out your financial situation."

"Okay. Thank you for thinking of everything. I wouldn't even know how to start."

"We gotchoo," Denny said, patting my shoulder.

Walter took my hand in his and lifted it to his mouth. He kissed my knuckles and then held my hand against his thigh as he drove us back up into the canyon.

The street was clogged with activity. Cops were talking to people on the sidewalk and there was a news van parked down the street. Walter had to drive down a few houses to find a place to turn around. When he drove back past, Denny showed his badge out the window and they moved the vehicles blocking the gate so Walter could pull up the driveway to the front of the house.

When we got out of the truck, Denny called over one of the other cops.

"Make sure you get video of every person out front, every license plate number that drives by the house."

"Yes, sir."

Denny and Walter had such different energy, but I had no doubt Walter could be just as take-charge if the situation called for it. Despite the circumstances, I felt safe being back at the house.

When we stepped into the foyer, I heard raised voices. Denny rushed past me, and Walter stepped in front of me.

"Who is it?"

"It's Gene and Dax. Come on, it's okay."

We entered the kitchen, and Denny and Gene were standing with another man who I assumed was Dax, and Denny and Gene were both yelling at Ramos.

"All I'm saying is, how the fuck does your guy let someone come up to the house unescorted?!" Gene shouted.

"You're right, you're right. They'll be on a tighter leash now."

"Damn right," Denny said. "And I'm going to clear every inch of this house. I don't trust that no one got through in the middle of all this circus bullshit." He left and went into the living room, where I heard Kal's voice.

"I want to check on Ryan," I said, and Walter nodded, taking my hand.

We found Kal and Ryan on the couch, talking to another police officer.

"I'm fine, he just sucker punched me. I should have known better. Ouch!"

Kal was trying to hold an ice pack on the side of Ryan's head, but it was obvious he wasn't being a good patient.

"You're going to have a huge bump if we don't keep the ice on," Kal murmured. The crease on his forehead was the most intense I'd seen it yet and his cheeks were splotchy, like mine sometimes got if I was mad or embarrassed.

"Hey, Dee Dee! How's your... how's Diane, man?"

I went and sat next to him, wincing when I saw the bandage on the bone above his temple. "I'm so sorry, Ryan—"

He waved his hand at me. "Don't even worry about it. I'm just getting soft is all. I haven't had to watch my back since last year, so I'm off my game."

"Did he say anything?" Walter asked. "Do you remember anything about him?"

Ryan winced. "Yeah, he said, 'I'm sorry. He's making me.' What do you suppose that means?"

"Maybe we've got a weak link. We need to talk to this guy."

"Ry-an," Kal said, flustered because Ryan kept taking the ice off his head.

He pulled Kal's face in and kissed him, which flustered Kal even more.

"You're impossible."

"I love you too, baby. Can I have a Monster? Oh, and some of those grapes, please, baby? I'll sit still and let you feed them to me."

Kal shot up off the couch and muttered something under his breath.

"Dude," Gene said to Walter as he joined us. "I thought he was going to murder someone with his bare hands when we got here. He had blood all over him and he was standing over Ryan, wouldn't let anyone get near him."

"Isn't it romantic?" Ryan chirped. "Seriously," he lowered his voice so only the four of us could hear. "How's your mom?"

"She's okay. She can't see too good, but she seems to be okay about everything. Otherwise, the doctor said she's perfectly fine and should be able to go home in a couple of days."

"Or straight into protective custody," Gene said. "I don't know, Walter. I'm starting to think we need to get all these people into a safe house until we catch the guy."

"I'm not opposed to that idea," Walter said. "Someplace that's more defendable than this."

"But Walter, if he can't find us, he's going to hurt someone else." That was my biggest fear, more than him coming after me. That I wouldn't stop him and he'd kill again.

Denny and the new guy came in. The new guy who gave Walter a frown when they shook hands. I didn't like the way this guy looked at him. I also didn't know whether I had a right to feel *any* kind of way about it, but I did. I might be the one who needed protecting right now, but for all of his strength and stoicism, Walter had revealed a vulnerable side to me that I felt compelled to protect in whatever way I could, even from someone who was supposed to be his friend.

"I'm Dax, by the way." He stepped closer and shook my hand before shooting Walter another look. "It's nice to meet you."

"Dee Dee, this is Detective Dax Brown."

"Detective," I said, but I didn't like the vibe I was getting off him. He kept staring at me, sizing me up.

We all stood there for a moment, the detectives passing looks between each other I couldn't quite interpret.

"Great," Gene said. "Well, the reporter will be here in a

little bit so we can get this over with. Hey, Dax, you should talk to him, give a statement about what we know so far."

"Which would be more if you guys had told me what the hell was going on down here."

"Dax," Walter said, but Dax held up a hand.

"You're on vacation. I'm not sure I want to hear anything from you right now."

"Excuse me." I felt a jolt go through me as all four pairs of eyes turned on me. "Ask me anything you want," I said to the rude detective. "But don't take out your feelings of inadequacy on Walter."

Walter put a hand on my arm, but I pulled away from him.

Dax shot me a cold gaze.

"Dax, don't," Denny said, taking him by the arm. "That's enough. Let's go check in with Ramos, then I'm gonna take Walter's truck and go down to the police station to talk to this fake delivery guy."

Walter started to speak, but Denny's eyebrows shot up. Walter cursed and handed him his keys without another word. Denny nodded at him in thanks, but there was also that sad look again.

Why did they all get that look when talking to Walter?

Dax went back into the kitchen with Denny to talk to Detective Ramos, who now had a full command center it seemed going on at the small table in there.

Gene shook his head as they walked away. "That little twat needs to watch his mouth."

"Let him get it out of his system," Walter murmured. He turned to me. "Do you have any questions about what to say? Anything we can do to help?"

I blew out a long breath. "Stick to the story, right? Say as little as necessary about my father." It was so weird to say that. "And tell them what I remember about this Hunter guy and the crime scene?"

"Maybe don't go into detail about the crime scene," Gene said. "Just that you saw the victim and then you guys called the police from Ryan's truck. Maybe don't mention Ryan's name, either. That will bring up a whole lot of questions about your connection to him, and I don't want to bring more heat on him and Kal."

"Good. Okay. Do I have time for a smoke?"

Gene smiled. "Yeah. Take your time. I'll let you know when he's here and set up."

I thanked him and headed out back. I needed to muster up every bit of courage to get through this next part. It was one thing to talk to people I knew were on my side, but I didn't know what this reporter was going to ask me.

I was tired of the unknown.

TWENTY-TWO

alter

I'd been fuming since Dax decided to run his mouth, but I was trying to keep it together for Dane's sake. When he decided to take a smoke break, I asked Gene to keep an eye on him and I went in search of the man who I'd trained, who I'd supported through field training, the detective exam process, and, once he was selected—based on my recommendation—his schooling in solving cases.

I didn't know if it was my ego that was bruised, my superego that wanted to go all "respect your elders" on him, or my id that was tired of being held back and wanted to rage against the slight.

None of these were a good reason to confront Dax right now, but I was beyond caring.

When Denny saw me approaching the kitchen, he stood up and his eyes flared the slightest bit.

"Detective Ramos," he said. "Would you excuse us for a moment? Boys?"

Denny led us through the house and into the back bedroom where he and Gene had taken turns crashing the previous night. He ushered us inside and closed the door behind me.

"I don't think we need an audience for this conversation," was all he said in explanation.

I didn't wait for Dax to start in with his whiny bitch attitude again.

"I'd say I want to know where all this animosity is coming from, but I really don't give a shit. I don't deserve it, and frankly, I'm not going to take it from you. I took that call because dispatch forwarded it to me. I didn't want it, I tried to get out of it, but there you have it. The caller specifically requested me. I came down here because the caller said they had information to give, and they mentioned the Donovan case. So I came down here and shit went a little sideways. The lot of you were all for getting me out of town, probably because you, like our captain, seem to think I can't hold myself together and I'm going to go off the rails at any second. Let me tell you, I have *always* supported you, Dax, no matter what, and you have done nothing but question me—"

"You withheld evidence that was vital to my case! Another person died, and you could have helped me. And you didn't come down here and just take a statement, you crossed a line, and in the process you've obstructed justice. I could submit a complaint! I could—"

"You could shut the fuck up. Right now," Denny said, getting nose to nose with Dax and going all drill sergeant on him. "You don't know dick about shit, you little fuck!"

Dax backed down a bit, if only because he knew Denny wasn't quick to anger but when he *did* get pissed, he'd wipe the floor with whoever was in his way.

"You're right about one thing, Dax. I did more than take a statement. I learned the truth about the one case that has held me captive for most of my life. And that truth—that *man*—is more important to me than my career right now, and the moment that became clear to me, I stepped back. I called Cap, I turned the Donovan case over to Denny and Gene, and I'll be *damned* if you're going to come down here and get in my face when I turned over *everything I could* to you, as soon as I could. Everything that was relative to your case. If that isn't good enough for you, then do it. Write me up if it makes you feel better. But I'm not going to let you put that man out there in danger, do you fucking understand me?"

Dax's tanned face had lost some color. His eyes were wide, and as he ran a hand over the bottom half of his face, I noticed a sheen of perspiration on his upper lip.

"Walt, man—"

"I'm sick and tired of everyone treating me like I'm going to go off the rails any second. You know what? I have done my job for twenty-seven years, and I've done it well. I've done everything asked of me, and the one thing I wanted more than anything was to learn the truth about Dane Donovan's disappearance. I wanted to know if my father told the truth or if he was as disturbed as everyone made him out to be. My father *did* tell the truth about what happened that night at Buttonwillow—"

"Junior," Denny said in warning.

"*Everything* my father thought about that case turned out to be true. It's too late for him to find peace in that, but it's not too late for me. I know what happened to Dane, and I'm going to guard that truth for the rest of my life, no matter what it costs me. Even if it costs me my job, my friendship with you, or the respect of my colleagues."

"Junior," Denny said. "You need to get that out of your

fucking head right now. No one here thinks you're going off the rails—"

"Don't think I don't see it in the way you and Gene have been looking at me—"

"Because we don't want you to get *hurt*, dumbass, not because we don't have absolute faith in you and your ability to handle yourself. You're not your father, Walter. And your father, despite what everyone may have said about him over the years and what happened to him, was fighting demons long before he became a police officer. The Donovan case triggered shit he'd tried to keep buried for years. He was a victim of the stigma and problematic beliefs that put a lot of veterans in the ground before their time. You have given him the greatest gift possible by becoming the incredible man that you are, not even including the fact that you solved the case that proved his downfall. He wouldn't want you to do anything more than to grab on to this gift you've been given and hold on with both hands."

And when Denny Hamilton lays that kind of shit on you, you have no choice but to cry like a fucking baby.

Which I did. Which further freaked out Dax.

Denny pulled me into his arms and pounded on my back. I don't know why us menfolk feel the need to hit harder when the feelings are bigger, but there you have it.

I tapped out, and he smacked me one more time, hard enough to make my teeth rattle, before he let me go.

Denny turned on Dax with a deep scowl. "Any more shit you want to—"

"I'm sorry," Dax said. "I don't know what you've been through down here, Walter. I should have asked before I assumed."

I nodded. "Now you know."

"I'm just trying to do my job, the way you taught me. I didn't mean to—"

"It's fine. Now, ask whatever questions you have remaining so I can get back out there and be there for—"

"Dee Dee is going to be interviewed by a local news investigative reporter. He's Dane's son. Dane's dead. That's all you need to know." Denny apparently didn't trust Dax to be brought into the inner circle. And I'd trust his lead.

"Oh. Whoa. Donovan had a kid?"

"With Tess Miller. She was pregnant when Dane disappeared. No one knew about him. She sent him away to live with family before she was killed." My heart was pounding in my chest as Denny laid out the story. Could we convince everyone it was true? It was going to take some magic, to be sure.

"Wow. Okay. And you two..."

"Yes," I hissed. "You got a problem with that?"

"No, Walter. Jesus. Did I ever have a problem with you and Brady?"

I shrugged. "Just because you never said, doesn't mean you never did." And just the fact that he used that as his answer had me on edge. Maybe I'd been too trusting of the kid. It hurt to know that an officer I'd trained, who'd looked up to me and learned everything about the job I could teach him, might have been sitting in judgement of me this whole time.

It hurt, but Dane was the most important thing now.

"Walt—"

"We're done here," I said. I nodded at Denny and walked out of the room. I was glad that was over, but it left me with a tight feeling in my chest. On one hand, I was grateful Denny had my back, but on the other... God, had I really read my friendship with Dax so wrong?

I heard Gene laughing in the foyer, so I made my way to his side.

"Oh good, you're here. Walter, this is Cooper Harris. He used to work with Sam. Coop, this is Detective Walter Muse, my best friend. He's been lead detective on the Donovan case. Well, until recently."

I shook the guy's hand and tried not to stare. Cooper was one of those men who's so damned attractive it's hard to breathe around them, much less speak.

"So nice to meet you," he said, and he flashed his million-dollar smile. He wore a light pink button-down shirt that looked like money. His tailored light gray slacks hugged his perfectly formed hips and thighs as if made just for him. Probably they were. Platinum cufflinks glittered in the afternoon sun and his sleek Italian oxfords had a greenish hue to the shine—they looked like a pair of Berluti's that Brady once tried to buy me—and probably cost as much as I made in a paycheck. He was as put together as if he were about to sit behind the desk on the evening news.

Gene had let me know that Cooper was the highest-paid investigative journalist in Southern California, and he was even doing some work with MSNBC, not to mention being a best-selling author and a recipient of the GLAAD Media Award.

"Gene's told me all about you, and I've done my research on your case. I have so many questions." His face lit up with excitement, but I didn't get the creepy feeling I did with some reporters, who wanted salacious details to back up their macabre bylines. If Gene was friends with him, he had to be good people.

"Nice to meet you," I said, a little nervous about his enthusiasm.

There were three women who stood in the doorway with equipment.

"Is it all right if my crew sets up?"

"Sure," Gene said. "Why don't I bring you in and you can decide which is the best place to do the interview."

As we walked into the great room, I spotted Denny on the back patio with Dane. Both of them were smoking. Man, I was going to have to put my other best friend through detox when this was all over.

Something Denny said made Dane laugh, and I was caught up in the picture he made. A sensitive, creative man who'd survived an attack that would have killed someone with less resilience. His green-eyed gaze could be soft and sweet one moment, and the next, harder than steel as if daring you to question him. His limbs were somewhat willowy, but his strong bones that jutted out at his collar, ankles, and, when we were alone, his hips, showed a sturdiness that could withstand hell's worst trials. I wanted to take him away from all of this. I hoped I could, and soon.

I wanted him to myself.

As if I'd somehow telepathically sent my intent through space, he turned and our gazes locked as he took a hit off his cigarette. The surprise was there in his bright eyes, but then a quirk of his lip and a softening around his eyes was the invitation I'd grown to crave. Knowing that he trusted me, wanted me at his side, wanted *me*...

Denny must have noticed Dane's attention wandering, so he gestured for me to join them outside.

I opened the slider, and Dane's smile grew wider as I moved to his side.

"Everything okay?" he asked. His brows furrowed the slightest bit, as if he could read the residual tension on me.

"It will be." I didn't want to tell him about the bullshit with Dax. Not right now. I needed to cool off.

"So," Denny said, blowing out smoke rings in my direction. "Dee Dee's been telling me about his board."

I raised my eyebrows. "You? And what did you have to say about that, Mr. 'if it ain't science, get it away from me'?"

Dane laughed and put out his cigarette. He tossed it into the garbage, then wrapped his arms around my waist. I loved holding him close to me, my arm draped over his shoulders. He fit so well against my side. I kissed his forehead, and he gave a happy sigh.

"I'll have you know," Denny said, this time exhaling the smoke with a huff, "I happen to be a very open-minded person."

I stared at him with my lips pressed together as he grew increasingly indignant.

"Just because I question things. I mean, no one trusts what the government says about UFOs... and hey, I went along on the twins' ridiculous 21st birthday party on the haunted-as-fuck Queen Mary, didn't I?"

"Right, you're absolutely right. But Staff Sergeant Dennis Hamilton believing in Ouija boards? That might be the end of the world."

He rolled his eyes at me and shook his head. "All I said was that I'd be willing to go in with Dee Dee, you know."

My gaze shot to Dane. "Honey..."

He blinked those big green eyes up at me. "I told Denny that I wanted to see what I could find out about Virgil Evans. If I ask the right question, maybe we can find proof of what he's done, find out how many people he's got involved in this. Answers that can put him away and give peace to the families of the people he's hurt, like you said."

And how was I supposed to argue with that?

"Let's get you through this interview first, all right? And then I want you to eat a real meal. Please?"

He squeezed me tight and presented his lips for a kiss, which I was desperate to give him.

"I'm going to leave you two alone for a minute," Denny said, turning for the house—but then he stopped. "Holy shit."

"What is it?"

Denny was staring at Cooper Harris. He and Gene talked to Kal and Ryan as the crew busied themselves with setting up lights and putting the chairs in the right spot for the best shot.

"Denny?" There was some sort of recognition going on there, but I had no idea how he would have known this guy.

"I'm... I'm going to talk to Ramos, get the story on this fake delivery man. I don't want to be out of earshot. You two go on inside."

He hurried away, shooting another perplexed look over his shoulder at Cooper.

"What was that all about?" Dane asked.

"You know, I have no idea, but I'm going to find out. Later. Right now, I need to know you're okay with this. God, Dane, I want to take you away from all this."

He grinned up at me. "I *want* you to take me away. When this is done and it's safe. Where would we go?" He turned to me and we stood in an embrace.

"Anywhere you wanted to go," I whispered. "I'll do anything."

"Will you stay with me? When this is over? Can we—"

"That's what I want," I said, my heart working overtime. I could barely believe he was real, but now we were talking about a future? It almost hurt to hope for one. "But you don't have to decide now."

"Do you have to go back to Bakersfield?"

I nodded, but then I frowned. "For a bit, yeah. Get my mom through the healing process from her hip replacement surgery. She's normally really independent. We're more like roommates these past couple of years. I moved back in with her to save some money after Brady and I split. It's been nice, but that's because we know it's not permanent. Then I gotta decide what I'm going to do about my job."

"And after that?" he asked, pulling me tighter against him. "Would you come back to me? Here?"

I smiled. "Where would we live?"

He shrugged. "We could find a place in the canyon, or in Hollywood. Or maybe, I don't know, go someplace totally different."

"Uh-huh, and what would we do? Busk on the streets? I do have to work, you know."

He wrinkled his nose. "We don't have to worry about that right now. What would you *want* to do?"

"I'd want to take care of you," I said, because honestly, that's all I wanted to do. I pushed his hair back out of his face and pressed a kiss to his nose. "I'd want to cook for you, hold you at night, keep you safe. Let you have the life that you were robbed of. So, the question is, what do *you* want to do?"

"I only know how to make music, to write. That's what I would do, because I can't *not* do it. I don't know if there's a place for me or what I do in this time, but I'd want to try."

I pressed my forehead to his. "Then I'd help you do it."

"And my mom. I'd want to take care of her."

"We could introduce our moms. Take care of both of them."

His eyes brightened. "We could have our own place. I could work, and you could cook dinner for me when I got home, and then we could sit together on the couch and watch... what do people watch now?"

"Whatever they want. Or we could just sit and look into each other's eyes. That'd be perfection."

"I told you, you're a poet, Walter."

"You're the poet," I corrected. "You're the magic one. Now kiss me before we have to go back to reality so I can hang on to this feeling a little longer."

"Reality will be what we make it. Soon," he whispered against my lips, and then he kissed me, a whimper escaping from his throat. "Soon. We'll lie naked under the stars and be grateful for everything that happened to bring us together. We'll make love, we'll make a life, and we'll take care of each other."

I pulled him in tight and pressed my face against his neck, running my mustache over his sensitive skin until he started to laugh.

"I want that mustache."

And I wanted to give him everything.

I prayed I'd have the time.

I took him by the hand and led him into the living room.

"How do I look?" Dane asked me. "I didn't even think about being on camera."

"Still gorgeous. Younger than me," I said, brushing his hair off his shoulder. "You're ageless, just like Brad Pitt."

"Who's that?"

Oh, we had so much ground to cover. I would love every minute of it. "He's considered one of the most attractive male actors of our generation. He's in his late fifties, but you'd never guess."

He frowned at me. "You don't seem like you're almost fifty, though, Walter. I picture fifty and I think of old men with hats and suspenders going to church or something, and ladies with curler-set hair wearing polyester and pearls."

"Things are a lot different now. You'll see. You ready for this?"

"Let's get this over with."

"Dee Dee," I said, keeping hold of his hand as I led him over to the area where they'd set up chairs for the interview. "This is Cooper Harris."

Cooper turned that megawatt smile on Dane, who blinked a few times as he slowly held out his hand.

"It is such a pleasure to meet you," Cooper said, his voice

full of awe. "I'm sorry it's under such circumstances, but I'm delighted."

"Thanks, me too."

"Won't you have a seat? You are such a handsome man. So like your father. You've got that lovely shade of golden-blond hair that he had, and those seafoam-green eyes. Your mother was a stunning woman, but you certainly favor your father. I've done a whole series of shows about the Laurel Canyon scene, and their stories were two of the most compelling and tragic of them all."

Dane sat and pulled me down beside him, not letting go of my hand. "You probably know more than I do," he said with a small smile. He would have to be careful with Cooper. The man seemed to be hyper-aware of everything. I was just as nervous as he was.

"Well, let's start with the most important question. You shared with the detectives that you've been living and working with a traveling carnival, and that you found the carnival when you were out looking for clues about your father?"

"Yes. My aunt and uncle, they raised me, and they wouldn't talk about him much. I only knew he'd disappeared before I was born."

Cooper's eyes lit up. "Your family didn't believe he ventured off of his own volition then?"

"No," Dane said firmly. "He would never have left, especially if he knew about me."

Cooper nodded and gazed at Dane thoughtfully. Watching a seasoned reporter like Cooper wasn't a whole lot different than a good detective doing an interrogation. "Well, he's certainly been missed, as has your mother. Now, may I ask, do you take after them musically?"

Dane shrugged a shoulder. "I write and play music."

"Wonderful. And you spent the last twenty years with the carnival?"

"I did. I liked the travel, the work was good."

"I'd love to know more about this carnival," Cooper said, but Dane frowned.

"There's not a lot to tell. It's old, been around for a long time."

Cooper nodded at him, his eyes narrowed in thought. Then he tilted his head and the look was gone. "So, Dee Dee. What brought you to Kern County in the early morning hours of December fifteenth?"

This was the part I was worried about. Dane kicked up his chin and exhaled through his nose, his green eyes locked on Cooper's.

"I went to meet up with friends. It had been a strange day. I'd had a weird interaction with a guy at my carnival booth, and I decided to leave. I let my boss know I needed some time off, he was fine with it, so I hooked up with my friend and his husband. They were heading to LA to record some music, so I figured I'd tag along. But then we stopped at the rest area in Buttonwillow, and there was a guy standing over... well..."

Dane couldn't seem to be able to say the words "dead" or "body". Cooper had been filled in on the details and thankfully didn't push.

"And you believe you saw the same man who was at your carnival?"

"Yes. He has very distinctive teeth. There were other links to me at the crime scene, but I don't know if I'm supposed to talk about it." He looked to me, and I smiled at him, giving his hand a squeeze.

Cooper looked thoughtfully at Dane, as if he was deciding where next to go with this interview. Then he turned on me.

"Detective Muse, I'm sure this has been a shock to you. You've been the lead detective on the Donovan case since your father left the Kern County Sheriff's Department?"

"I have been," I said, hoping this guy didn't ask questions

about my father. I was doing the best I could to hold it together under the circumstances. "And yes. To have the answers now after forty years is a blessing. We still don't have a firm suspect for Dane's abduction, but we're closer to the truth now."

"And were you surprised to find out that Dane Donovan had a son?"

I smiled at Dane. "Very. I'm disappointed that I don't have answers about what ultimately happened to him. But I'm grateful to have met Dee Dee."

Dane smiled back, and the twinkle in those green eyes let me know that he was enjoying seeing me on the spot.

"My understanding is that you've stepped back from the case?"

"I have. Detectives Ochoa and Hamilton will be taking over for me."

Cooper's small smile faded. "You mean Detective Dennis Hamilton?"

I nodded. "Yes. He and Detective Ochoa came down to help out when it appeared that the suspect from the Buttonwillow attack had a connection to Dee Dee."

"And is he... Detective Hamilton... is he still here?" He reached up a hand to smooth down his perfect hair. His eyes darted around, as if Denny would crawl out of a shadow at any minute. What a strange reaction.

I frowned. "Yeah, he's around."

Cooper exhaled. "Good... that's good." He cleared his throat and then seemed to recover. He smiled at the two of us, looking down at our clasped hands. "We'll keep this part off the record—I'll edit it out—but it seems as though the two of you have become close?"

Dane looked at me with his eyebrows raised. "Detective Muse—Walter—found me during a dark time, and he's supported me through all of this."

"I'm just glad I could."

What went unsaid was that this connection between us had taken us both by surprise. I still wasn't sure what it all meant. I'd always been a practical guy, even when it came to love, but this? Practical wasn't going to cut it. I needed to think beyond my normal Walter Muse City Limits. And pray I got it right if I was going to keep Dane in my life.

Twenty-Three

Dane

Walter sat beside me through the interview, frowning most of the time. I wasn't really sure how a story on the news was going to help us, but the man had been nice about it.

"Thank you so much for your time, Mr. Miller. Detective."

We shook hands with him, and then he told his crew they were finished. Gene came over to talk to Cooper as his crew took down the camera and lights.

"You okay here for a minute? I want to go find Denny and see what the guy who attacked Ryan had to say."

"I'm fine."

He squeezed my hand and took off for the kitchen.

Kal and Ryan hadn't been around for a while. I figured they were in their room, since Ryan probably needed to rest after his interaction. I thought I'd take a peek and see if they needed anything, but as I passed the doorway to my room, I saw the board sitting on the bed.

I hadn't left it there.

But I'd been thinking about it, hadn't I? That I could use the board and put an end to this.

I stood next to the bed and stared down at it, the shakes coming on strong. How could I help? What could I ask that would bring this insanity to a halt?

"How did it go with the reporter?"

I spun around to find Kal in the doorway. His gaze landed on the board.

"It went fine. I—"

"I'll use it with you. I'm not afraid. Let's see what we can find out."

I nodded at him, knowing Kal would be the perfect person to use the board with. He understood the magic of the carnival, and he and I were... connected somehow.

"Kal, I don't want you to be upset by what happens. I know it was hard for Walter and Ryan."

"I know what it's like to see disturbing things. I'm not afraid of the board. I'm afraid of these men coming back and hurting Ryan or any of you again. This has to stop. I will help you. We can do what the police cannot."

Kal stepped in and closed the door behind him, then he sat on the floor, his long legs crossed.

I guess we were doing this.

I placed the board between us on the floor.

"What should we ask?" I asked Kal, rubbing my hands together.

"What do we need to know to end this situation?"

We stared at each other for several beats.

"That's actually the perfect question," I finally said. We both placed our fingers on the planchette, and I took a deep breath. "What do we need to know to end this situation?"

Almost immediately my vision darkened, and I felt the sensation of being sucked down a tunnel.

"I am here, Dee Dee. I won't let go."

I felt stronger with Kal beside me, holding my hand. It was as if he was sharing whatever essence he'd brought with him from the carnival. We couldn't have spent time in that place and not absorbed some of its magic and power. Certainly my experiences with the board had grown more vivid and intense during my time there.

The darkness was broken by the illumination of one light-bulb after another flicking on along a cinderblock hallway, the same one I'd seen with Walter.

"Virgil is here." I wasn't sure if I'd spoken aloud or if Kal and I were somehow psychically linked, but suddenly Kal's face was there.

I felt him squeeze my hand, and I was grateful for the connection.

A voice... someone humming... came from the darkness at the end of the hallway and suddenly the last bulbs lit up, revealing an open doorway. The bald man stood just inside, looking into a dark pit.

"I wondered when you'd find me."

We moved closer to him, and then he turned around.

This time I saw his face, and I recognized him instantly.

"Welcome, Dane, to your final resting place. Or at least, the place where I plan to watch your life bleed out."

How could he see me? No one else I'd seen in these visions could see me.

"When you spend as long as I did in prison, you learn all kinds of things about yourself. You develop certain skills to protect yourself, or, in my case, to find pleasure. I had no way of drawing blood from others when I was locked in a cinderblock cell, so I learned how to make others do it for me. Eventually, creating a psychic link with others became as easy as breathing. And at my age, with my debilitating physical limitations, I learned to take great pleasure in watching my sentinels carry out my work. You've met Hunter. He's been my greatest pupil, so eager to do what I ask of him. But there are others... and as long as I live, they will do my bidding."

One word kept echoing through my mind. *Why?*

"I've always loved the sight of blood. As a young man, I waited patiently for the scenes in movies where they'd show bloodshed. Others might scream or flee in fright, but I became... *excited*. And then it wasn't enough to *see* it. I needed to *cause* it. Believe me, I'm well aware of the psychological implications, and I freely admit that I'm the textbook example of a subject with paraphilia.

"By the time I met you, I hadn't yet graduated to humans, but that night at Buttonwillow... *ohhh*. I'd been working the late shift when I saw your van pull into the parking lot. I thought mistakenly that Tess would be with you. She was my obsession, my hope for some sort of normalcy in my life. She was to be my salvation. With her, I could have a wife, a happy home... but you were always in the damn way. I saw my opportunity to remove an obstacle that night, and to finally spill the blood of a human. I *delighted* in spilling yours. It was perfect, *you* were perfect—until that cop showed up. I was able to hide you before he came back, but then that fucking carny appeared out of nowhere and stole you from me!"

"So you killed others." Kal loomed next to me with that forehead crinkle of his cutting into his flesh between heavy brows. How could he speak? I'd never been able to speak or even move during one of these visions. This was alarming. I didn't like this at all. Kal shouldn't be talking to him. This was wrong!

"To sate my thirst, yes. But when I was finally allowed to see Tess, she was useless to me. I knew better than to strike in my social circle, but I couldn't help myself. I couldn't bear to watch her waste away, pining for another man, even if it was her queer best friend. I could have made her happy, given her a child. But *no*. She was lifeless before I even drew my blade."

The shadows across his face morphed into a hazy gray, and it dawned on me... that's why I hadn't remembered his face. Perhaps in addition to his ability to create a psychic link, he'd learned to mask himself.

"Oh, did you want to see her, Dane? She's here, along with all the others. They're waiting for you."

He gestured with his hand, and a moment before we were sucked out of the vision, the view before us shifted from him to...

Bones.

Piles of them.

So many bodies.

And in the foreground, I saw the bones of a hand reaching out, and her silver bracelets, one of which had our initials engraved together. A gift for her thirtieth birthday from her best friend. She never took it off.

I screamed as the blackness pulled me away.

"Dee Dee, it's okay, you're safe!"

Kal tried to calm me even as the door flew open and people poured into the room, reaching for me.

"Paper! Paper and *pen now*!

My heart beat so hard it bruised my ribs, my throat felt as if it had been shredded by glass, but the words were there.

"Here."

It was Gene, I think. I didn't take the time to worry about who was there or what they were seeing. I began to write as fast as my hand could move.

Deep in a hillside
  Forgotten by most

A man resides
As death's morbid host
His chamber houses
His myriad trophies
They lie in repose
Full of macabre stories
Of anger and fear,
Betrayal and violence
Their voices and spirits
So long have been silenced
The morbid host
And his insatiable need
Their life's essence
Taken by his greed
But there is a light
He didn't account for
A shining survivor
To settle the score
He spotted the numbers
Written on the door
Caltrans Maintenance
H-two-one-eight-five-four
The morbid host
His vessel is weak
Though his sentinels
Still hear him speak
They grow weary
Of their terrible task
They hope for a sign
For mercy they'll ask
Only the hunter
Wishes for peace
And with one last task
He'll find his release

The end grows near
The showdown is soon
In the hidden chamber
By the light of the moon
It's time to reveal
This terrible truth
to unleash vengeance
where evil has roots
To defeat this monster
You have all you need
To bring them justice
and allow them to be freed

"He's going over—Walter," Gene cried out.

I dropped the pen and felt darkness pulling me under, but this wasn't like the tunnel, and this one smelled like honey.

"Walter," I sighed as his strong arms caught me.

I heard someone ripping the paper out of the notebook as Walter lifted me and set me down on the bed.

"Someone get Caltrans on the phone. We need to find this place."

"What's going on here?" Was that Cooper? He was still here?

"Kal? What can you tell us?"

"Is he okay?"

Walter's voice was so close to my ear, the gentle rumbling of his speech against my cheek. "It's taking more out of him every time."

"I'm okay," I tried to say, but he shushed me. I couldn't open my eyes, and I felt sleep pulling me under.

"It was Virgil Evans. He has her there. Tess. Her bracelet."

"Sleep, honey. Rest now. It's okay."

Twenty-Four

Denny and Kal whispered to each other by the door as I lay Dane on the bed and covered him.

"What did you see?" I asked him. The tall man was shaking, his face paler than I'd ever seen it.

"He was... underground, part of the building was finished, like cement, and the rest was old and shaped like a cistern, a water collection container, but it wasn't wet. A pile of bones, some still with remains attached. He wanted us to see it, but I don't know if he knew about the code on the door, the one that Dee Dee saw. Do you think it will help?"

"Fuck yeah, it will," Denny said. "The Caltrans part alone will help us. We'll find this guy. Did you see any weapons?"

"No. He talked to us, though. He knew we were there. It wasn't like Ryan described it, like watching from afar."

"No, and when I went in, we were just watching. I wonder what changed?"

"He said he learned how to make a psychic link with people when he was in prison. That he could make people do things for him. I spoke to him, I remember that, but Dee Dee couldn't speak. He seemed shocked that the man could see us at all. He intends to spill Dee Dee's blood, somehow. And he wants it done *there*."

"That's not going to happen," I said. "Denny, we've gotta find him."

"I'm on it."

He left the room, and Kal reached for me. "He's so strong, Walter. Dee Dee. The deep sleep is how his body recovers. I don't think he knows that, but this isn't harming him, his use of the board. He's connected to it, but it does not harm him. I know you worry, but he's stronger than even *he* knows. I could feel it as he faced his would-be killer. He was not afraid."

I didn't know how to respond to that, but I shook his hand. "Thank you for going with him, for being there for him."

Kal nodded. "He and I are linked by the magic of the carnival. I don't think I realized that until I touched the planchette with him. I know Ryan told you that we made a promise to help another Traveler, but I think it's more than that."

I felt such gratitude toward him and Ryan. If they hadn't stopped for him in the desert, if they would have left him to walk... if Holland would have found him? Alone? I never would have found the answers, I never would have found him... never would have felt the profound depths of emotion he'd awakened in me.

"You've gained a lifetime of gratitude from me."

He smiled and patted my shoulder before taking his leave.

I exhaled and sucked in a huge breath, realizing I'd been

in such a panic when I found Dane and Kal with the board that I'd been near to hyperventilating. I checked on Dane one last time before leaving him to rest. He was breathing so soundly, not twitching like he had after the last time. He was even snoring softly. I hoped what Kal said was right, that he wasn't being harmed by the use of the board. Maybe the visions weren't harming him, but the stress of constantly being in danger would take a toll. We had to end this threat. Now.

I stepped out of the room and into another heated discussion.

"You can't expect me to not have questions after what I just saw, Gene."

Gene hung his head as he stood before Cooper, and he rubbed his face. The exhaustion was getting to all of us. I'd probably slept the best of all of them in the past forty-eight hours, and that wasn't saying much.

"It's fucking complicated, Cooper, and not from a police perspective. Hey," Gene said as I joined them. "How is he?"

I shook my head. "I don't even know. Resting, at least." But the determination on my face must have snapped Gene out of his tiredness. I started to say we needed to fucking go get this guy, but two things: Cooper was there, and I wasn't leaving Dane. I couldn't.

"What happened in that room?" Cooper repeated his question. "Does this have to do with the carnival?"

"What the fuck do you know about it?" Denny asked as he joined us.

Cooper's eyes went wide as he took in Denny's fierce countenance. "I... I've heard some things. It's one of those journalistic myths, like, one of those stories you'd expect to find in the *Inquirer* so most people ignore it, but it's been circulating since my grandfather was in the business. I only brought it up because Mr. Miller mentioned it..."

We all gave him our full attention, but Denny took a step closer, menacingly.

"What. The Fuck. Do you know about it?"

"*Nothing.* Nothing concrete, anyway. There are stories about this carnival that travels around, that there have been people who were never seen again after attending, or people who attended and had bizarre experiences that changed their lives. I've never been able to find anything to corroborate the stories, but I've heard enough to not be able to ignore it."

"We can't talk about it, Coop," Gene said. "It's not our story to tell, and we've got an obligation to protect these men."

"I'm not asking because I want to hurt anyone." His big blue eyes were round. "Gene, you know me. I don't hurt people intentionally."

"But you're a reporter," Denny said. "Your work hurts people whether you intend it or not."

"Investigative reporter, Detective Hamilton. And my intention is to do all I can to *prevent* harm." He looked between us and took a step back. Somehow this exchange between him and Denny seemed to have another level. Had they met before? "And that's what I want to do here. Don't tell me anything, that's fine. But how can I help?"

We all looked at each other, and then back at him.

"You *could* help," Denny said, his voice less gruff, but I wouldn't call it softer. "You could get this fucking guy's face all over the news and help us catch him. You could forget what you saw in that bedroom and anything that has to do with the fucking carnival. That's what you can do to help."

"Done. My crew is already working on the edits in the van. Do you want to see it before we put it out?"

"Please," Gene said softly. "And probably Detective Ramos should see it too, out of courtesy."

Cooper nodded. "Fine. I heard you mention Caltrans too. I've got contacts over there if that would be helpful."

We looked at each other again. It was always tricky accepting help from the media because it was usually tit for tat.

When we didn't answer, he rolled his eyes and stomped his foot a little. "Come on, Gene! Sam is my best friend. I'm not going to screw you guys over. I just... want to help. That man seems to have been through a lot, and there have already been too many people dead. Let me help you."

"Okay," Gene said. "Don't make me regret this. You take advantage of this and put a wedge between me and my wife, and I will—"

"I won't, Gene, I swear. You can trust me."

Denny cursed, and again I wondered what the fuck was going on between these two.

"Can you work with Walter and Denny, please? I'm going to talk to Ramos. As soon as we get a location, we'll mount up."

"Sure," Cooper said. "Whatever I can do."

Denny frowned and walked out back, probably jonesing for a cigarette now that he'd fallen off the wagon.

"Yeah, okay," I said, ignoring my best friend's surprisingly bitter attitude. I didn't have time to grill him right now about this shit.

"Oh, another thing. Let me give Gene the number of my manager, Arthur Frye." He pulled out his phone and sent a text to Gene. "After everything Mr. Miller has been through, he's going to need someone to help him navigate his situation. Arthur's an attorney as well as a talent manager. He can suggest someone to handle all the requests you're going to get for more interviews. National news outlets are going to be hounding you as soon as this breaks, as well as print, radio..."

"Thank you," I said, getting the info from Gene on my phone right away. "Appreciate it."

This was exactly what Dane would need once we got through this immediate threat. Someone to help him navigate the travails of his "father's and mother's" legacies, and whatever financial pieces were left for him.

"I'll be back," Gene said. He frowned in the direction of Denny before heading into the kitchen.

"Great, now, what information did you need from Caltrans?"

"A location. We've found a site that may be connected to our suspect, but all we have is a code."

Cooper nodded a couple of times, then he reached into his shoulder bag and brought out a laptop. He carried it over to the couch and set it on the coffee table. He logged in and tapped with lightning-fast speed.

"Okay, I've got an internal map of all Caltrans properties in the state. What's the code?"

"Do I want to know how you have this?"

He shrugged, not looking up. "I did a story on Caltrans last year after questions arose about their budget and the lack of maintenance at a lot of the facilities. Unsafe working conditions, blah blah. The code?"

I still had Dane's poem in my hands, and I read him the line with the numbers.

"That number doesn't match anything on this map. Hmm. Okay, let me play with this."

"I'm going to check on…" I caught myself before I said "Dane".

"Sure." Cooper didn't look up as I left.

I peeked into Dane's room and noticed he'd rolled onto his back, but otherwise he was still out. I wished I could curl up beside him and hold him, but I felt like we were getting close—

"Found it," Cooper shouted from the couch. Dane flinched but didn't wake up, so I eased the door closed and hurried back to the reporter. Gene and Ramos met me there.

"I think I have the connection. I located this Angeles Crest Scenic Byway Roadside inventory, and here's the map. So, the byway is off Highway 2 from Cañada. There's a Caltrans maintenance station there, but check this out. This bit of the Angeles forest was mined for gold. I found a listing for a mine from 1854. What if that number is related to the mine? It's literally underneath the Caltrans maintenance station—which is out of use now, by the way."

"Jesus," Ramos said. "That's not far off the two-ten. Evans worked that whole area. Let's go check it out."

"Let me call Dax," Gene said. "He can meet us there. Where's Denny—"

"I'll stay here," he said as he returned to the room from the patio, glancing at me. "If Dee Dee remembers anything else when he wakes up, we can let you know."

I felt better knowing that Denny was staying. I didn't trust Dane's safety to anyone else, and who knew how many "sentinels" this guy had out there.

"Thank you," Cooper said. "I'll send Gene the final clip as soon as it's ready."

I shook his hand. "Thanks for your help."

Cooper nodded and then gave Denny a lingering look before he left.

Gene and Ramos headed out, promising to keep us updated, but as soon as the door shut, Denny turned to me.

"I've got an idea, and it's fucked up—but hear me out. That fake delivery man? Ramos would only say he was one of the residents from the halfway house, and that he knew Evans and Holland." He looked around the corner. "I'm glad he's gone, because when I went outside, I called and got a buddy who knows someone at LAPD to get me the transcripts of the interview. This fucking guy, he was *crying*, said Evans was in his head, making him crazy. That he wanted to be locked up to get away from him, wanted to be 'free'. They have him on fucking suicide watch at the jail, man. He was crying about how Evans was going to bleed him and throw him in a pile of bones."

"That's... Kal described it as a pile of bones underground. That has to be the place where they're going..."

"I'm texting Gene and Dax. I don't trust Ramos, since he didn't fucking tell us that shit. Walter, man, we've got to make a move here. If we stay in this house—"

"I know," I said. He was right. But here, we could control the environment. The minute we left, Dane would be vulnerable. I was about to say more when my phone started buzzing in my pocket, at the same time someone pounded on the front door.

"What the fuck?" Denny said, moving to check it.

I pulled out my phone... *Mom?*

Denny checked the peephole before opening the door. "What is it?"

I accepted the call. "Hey, Mom? Hang on a second." I paused to hear what the officer at the door had to say.

"Sir, dispatch called, there's apparently a gas leak reported on this street. We've got to evacuate you all."

"Walter? Is everything okay?"

I stood from the couch and put the phone back to my ear. "Is everything okay, Mom?"

"Oh, yes, I wanted to say thank you for the flowers—"

"You better fucking check this out before we leave this house and become sitting ducks. Verify this with PG and fucking E right now, goddammit." Denny returned to my side as the officer spoke into his radio.

It seemed we would be leaving the house regardless. This

felt too coincidental. And my mother's words just registered. Flowers?

"Did you say flowers, Mom?"

"I'm sorry, did I interrupt? I just wanted to say thank you for this beautiful bouquet."

I put the phone on speaker and held it out to Denny. "Did you see who brought the flowers, Mom?"

Denny's eyes flared, and he dialed his phone, and I heard him ask for our captain.

"No, Kathleen answered the door."

"Mom, where are the flowers now?"

"They're in the kitchen with Kathleen. She's putting them in water."

"Mom, listen to me carefully. Tell her to leave them on the counter. Have her lock the doors, and I want you to get my gun out of the safe. Denny's calling for an officer to come out to the house. *Do not* open the door until Denny calls you with the officer's name."

She was silent for a moment, and then I heard her exhale into the phone. "Okay," she said, her voice deeper now, deadly serious instead of the lighthearted tone she'd started with. "Do you want me to stay on the phone with you?"

We'd been through these instructions hundreds of times with Dad. What to do if there was a threat, what protocol to follow. It had been a long time since I'd even considered we might have to use it.

"I do. I'm sorry, Mom. I'm going to have an officer take you into protective custody until I can get there."

"Whatever you think is best, Walter. Are you safe?"

"I am. I love you."

Denny hung up his phone. "Mrs. Muse? It's Denny. It will be an Officer Santos arriving in less than ten minutes."

"Thank you, Dennis," she said, and then I heard her tell

Kathleen to please grab her medications and the duffle in the bottom of her closet.

"I'm so sorry, Mom. I'm going to be there as soon as I can, okay?"

"I'll be fine, dear. Be safe."

"I will. Mom?" I took the phone off speaker, stepped out onto the patio, and shut the door. I had to tell her, as I knew it would mean as much to her as it had me.

"Yes, son?"

"I found him."

She was quiet for a few beats, and I heard Kathleen talking in the background.

"Dane Donovan?" Mom's voice was barely above a whisper. "Oh, Walter..."

"I know. I can't tell you everything now, but I will. He's alive and... really something." I took a moment to savor the satisfaction of solving the most important case of my life, despite the fact I couldn't go on record with my findings. "Mom? I'm sorry I didn't send you flowers, but there's a chance the delivery is connected with his case. Did you happen to see the card?"

"I did. It said, 'I'll see you again. Buttonwillow.' I thought it was a strange way for you to sign it. If I would have been thinking a little clearer, I would have called you before accepting them. You don't send flowers, you bring them to me. I'm sorry."

"You couldn't have known, Mom. It's okay."

"Is he okay? Dane?"

"He will be," I said. "I have a lot to tell you, but I'm with him now. You'll be meeting him soon."

"Oh," she said, surprised. "Walter, Kathleen is at the door. Officer Santos is here, along with Captain Barnett. I'll ask that they keep you posted."

"I love you, Mom. Be safe."

We hung up, and my heart was pounding, but I had to think straight.

I jumped when the door slid open behind me, and someone grabbed my arm. I turned to find Dane clutching my forearm.

Dane's eyes widened. "I'm sorry. I've got to stop sneaking up on you."

I put my hand over his and started to assure him I looked forward to getting used to it, but then Denny jogged up behind him.

"Fuck this piece of shit," Denny said as he returned from checking with the officer at the door. "We've got to evacuate. Somehow the fucker managed to cause a gas leak."

"I'll grab Ryan and Kal," Denny said. "No time to pack up, we gotta go."

"Walter, the board."

It had helped us up to this point. Evans and Holland seemed to be everywhere, and he somehow knew how to get to each of us. Mom's card said, "I'll see you again. Buttonwillow."

I turned to Dane. "Let's grab the board."

I followed him down the hall to his room.

"Is your mom okay?" he asked as he picked up the board and planchette. He slipped his old boots on and rubbed at his eyes. "How long did I sleep?"

"Not long enough. Mom's okay, she's in protective custody, but we've got to go. We're out of time here."

He held up the board. "We'll find him."

"He's going to be at Buttonwillow." I wasn't the magic one in this scenario, but I knew it was true. Holland wanted a showdown.

Dane took my hand and I unholstered my pistol as we left the safety of the house together.

"Hey," an out-of-breath Ryan said as he and Kal met us

outside the front door. He pulled out the keys to lock it up. "We can help—"

"We need to get you two somewhere safe," Denny said. "I'm going to have the officers here take you into protective custody."

Ryan and Kal looked at each other, and Ryan gave Kal a sad smile. "I don't know what we could do for him now," he said. "I'm sorry, Dane."

Kal turned to me, and that crease formed on his forehead. "Keep him safe, Detective," Kal said.

"He'll be in touch when it's safe. I'm sorry—"

"Don't be. Just take care of him."

I nodded and pulled Dane against me. "I will."

I threw my keys to Denny when we reached my truck and I opened the back door. Dane looked at me in surprise.

"Let's find him."

Dane's determined expression sent shards of fear into my heart.

Make or break time.

Please don't let it be break.

Twenty-Five

D^{ane}

"But Walter," I said. "He saw me last time. If I use the board to find him, won't he know we're coming?"

Walter held my hand in both of his as Denny started the drive down Laurel Canyon.

"I think we may need to take that chance. I want to know what he's got planned, and maybe with the board we can see that. Hey, Den, you needed to go the other way—"

"I know, I know, fuck! There's no place to turn around."

"By the Canyon Store, you can turn around... right there, turn left—"

Denny cursed as he took a sharp turn, but he missed the driveway and passed the store.

"Stop!"

He slammed on the brakes at my command, and we

stopped right in front of the two old ladies with their stand. And like me, they looked the same as they had always looked.

"Shit, pull over, Denny," Walter said. "That's them? Where you got the board?"

As soon as Denny was at the curb, I was out the door with the board, Walter hot on my heels.

The old women sat in their camp chairs in the late afternoon light, sunglasses on, heads down almost as if they were napping. Their wild curly gray hair blew gently in the breeze. Music played from under their table on a tinny radio, Carly Simon, I believed. The table was covered with crystals of all shapes and sizes in bowls with little cardboard signs saying what they were and how much. There were also piles of handmade hair pins, candles, some jars filled with questionable substances, and a... Magic 8 Ball toy?

They didn't look up as I approached.

"Excuse me, this is going to sound strange, but—"

"No returns or exchanges." They didn't even move so I wasn't sure they'd actually spoken.

"No, I don't... I have questions."

No response.

"I bought this board from you years ago, and I need to know... can I make sure that what I see, can't see me?"

Neither of the women moved nor spoke. The traffic went by and the breeze blew my hair off of my face for a moment, and then my surroundings seemed to fade away, go still.

The women's voices echoed in unison around me, but they still didn't move.

"You are in control of the board. It will do what you need it to do. You must be clear in your intentions. It will show you what's true. You're limited by your limitations. The possibilities are endless, in spite of you."

They'd spoken in rhymes, like I heard the words when I used the board. Were they connected to it? Was I connected to it on another level? Was that what this was all about? A link on another dimension where truth was spoken only in rhymes? The board and I were linked, and I knew that it didn't just belong to me, since Ryan had said his friend had it at one time. But then, how did Evans link with me when I used the board? And what did they mean by my limitations?

"How do I keep others *out* when I'm *in*? I don't want to put anyone in danger, and I need to stop these killers."

"Make of your question all that you desire. Be ever thoughtful and in control of your ire. Picture your intent as taut as a wire. Remain steadfast or the end will be dire. As pure as ice and hot as fire, love is the power behind all you aspire. Trust in the truth and never the liar, and you will avoid the funeral pyre."

I felt a weight in my palm, and I looked down. I swore the women hadn't moved, but in my hand were two large, rough stones.

"Obsidian will keep your heart and mind clear, to bring you balance and keep away fear. Quartz for clarity both far and near, together the stones protect all you hold dear."

I closed my hand and felt heat emanating from the stones. It took my breath away for just a moment—

The breeze blew my hair off my cheek.

"You gonna pay for that?"

I shook my head to clear my vision, and Walter stood beside me, pulling out his wallet.

"How much?" he asked them.

"Twenty bucks."

Walter looked between the women and fished a bill out of his wallet.

"For a couple of rocks?" Denny muttered.

"You, take this." One of the women moved for the first time that I could see and she plopped the black plastic ball in Denny's hand, catching him by surprise.

"That's more your speed," the other woman said, and they both cackled. They fell silent as quickly as they'd moved, and we were left staring at them, which had me wondering if it was possible we'd just imagined this whole scenario.

When they said nothing else, Walter gave a gentle tug on the back of my shirt. He gestured for us to move toward the truck. I walked with him, glancing at Denny, who was examining his ball—

"It's a Magic 8 Ball. What the fuck do I need with a damn kids' toy?"

I chuckled and turned to look back—but then I stopped in my tracks.

"Walter!"

He turned as he got to the truck.

The women were gone. There was no sign anything at all had been on that stretch of sidewalk. But as the wind died down for a moment, I heard their tinny radio, just as I had on that afternoon all those years ago.

"Oh, fuck this shit," Denny said. "I'm out of here."

Denny darted over to the truck, hopped in, tossed the Magic 8 Ball into the backseat, started the engine and barely waited for Walter to shut the door after us before he sped away, squealing the tires as he pulled into traffic going up Laurel Canyon.

"Are you all right?" Walter asked me.

I brushed my hair back behind my ear with a shaky hand. "I don't know. You just saw that, right?"

Walter nodded.

"Did you hear them speak?"

He frowned. "But their mouths didn't move. It was like, in my head. Wait, the words. Here." He tapped on his smart rectangle phone thing, then handed it to me with a blank screen and a flashing line. "Here," he said, tapping the screen, and an image resembling a typewriter keyboard appeared.

I'd ask questions later.

I took the device from him and did my best to type without too many mistakes. I tried to do as she'd ordered, and focused on the heat from the stones, now in my pocket, and attempted to find clarity. I focused on my breathing, on the ticking sounds of each tap my fingers made.

"Yeah, that's what I heard, too." Walter had been watching over my shoulder as I typed. He placed a hand on my back and squeezed my shoulder. "Does it make sense to you?"

"Sort of? I guess it's just that I need to consider every possibility when asking my question, including who I bring into focus, who I allow access to my thoughts, to what I see and hear. I can't just ask a question. I need to be aware of all the elements involved." I turned to him and moved the board in between us on the backseat. "I want you to go in with me, Walter. But help me to make this as specific as possible. What do we need to know? Who do we go after first? What if they're together? How will we... I don't know, Walter! Help me."

"Hey, it's okay." He cupped my jaw with his hand, and I saw the words from the women. *Love is the power behind all you aspire.* Walter was the love, and the power would come from trusting in him. He would stand beside me, and together, we could put a stop to this nightmare.

I smiled and leaned forward, pressing my lips to his. It seemed to catch him by surprise, and then he sighed softly, kissing me back with an intensity that matched mine. I refused to let the intrusive thoughts in. *This could be the last time I kiss him. We might not both make it out of this. I could lose him too.*

I would trust him. I would trust in my own power.

"Got a message from Dax," Denny said, breaking through our moment. "They've met up near the Highway 2 spot and they're mobilizing to go in. He's got unmarked units at Buttonwillow in case either of them show up there."

Walter smoothed my hair back and kissed me once more. "Are you ready?"

I nodded and let go of his hands. I took a deep breath and tried to remember that state I was in when the women spoke to me. *Shut everything out except for Walter.*

"What I seek is for our eyes only. No prying eyes shall fall upon us. Take us to the current location of Hunter Holland. Show us what he's planning to do. Show us his weakness. Show us how to stop him." I locked eyes with Walter. "Anything else?"

Walter thought for a moment. "Show us how he's traveling so if he slips away, we can catch him."

I sucked in a deep breath, we both placed our hands on the planchette, I focused on my intention, and then I breathed out.

"Show us."

We were once more sucked into the darkness, but it wasn't pitch, it was dusk. A series of images flashed before my eyes: cornfields, eucalyptus trees, cinderblock buildings. I could hear the rumbling of big rig motors, the whoosh of cars flying by, and the leaves of the trees rustling in the wind. The flushing of toilets? But it was different, unlike the Buttonwillow rest stop.

And then he was there, in the shadows of the dying light, smiling, his teeth slick with saliva. He gripped the hair of a man I felt I should know, but there was so much blood.

"I'm ready. It's almost time. I can't wait to be with you. I'm ready. I'm *ready ready ready.* I'm ready." Red and blue lights splashed across his face, and he laughed, throwing his head back in the throes of madness.

Questions. I had so many questions for him. I wanted to know why? Where was Evans? What was their endgame?

The words came, but they were short.

· · ·

Two cannot be got
One shall go free
Choose the spot
End the spree

"No no no," I heard myself saying as the blackness took over and I was slammed back against the seat. "No, it wasn't enough, no!"

I grabbed Walter's phone and typed the words in and then slammed my fist against my knee. "I'm sorry, I thought—"

"Honey, no, that was great. He's there, Denny, he's at Buttonwillow, but the northbound side this time. Tell CHP and Fern County officers to approach with caution, he's got a hostage."

Denny called someone on the phone and started to fire directions at them, and Walter took my face in his hands.

"Did you recognize the man he had?"

I shook my head. "I feel like I should—"

"Yeah, me too."

I felt my throat tighten and I swallowed back fear. "We have to save him, whoever he is!"

"We'll do everything we can. Tell me, do you know if what we saw has happened already, or if it's *going* to happen?"

"I..." I didn't know. I hadn't thought to ask that. "I don't know, Walter, I don't know how the time works."

I hadn't asked that of the ladies. I hadn't accounted for time.

"How much further?"

"Thirty minutes," Denny said from the front seat. He was driving so fast, everything was passing us by at a blur. "They've got SWAT mobilizing to go to the northbound side. When we get there, Dane, you need to stay in the truck—"

"I want him with an officer," Walter said. "I don't want you unprotected for one second."

I couldn't protest. I wasn't going to be helpful.

I poured over the words and the images I'd seen as we drove through the twisty mountain road and then down into the valley. It seemed that the more focused I was with the board, the less I'd seen that was helpful. I was still trying to gather meaning when a car went flying past us on the shoulder, and Walter shouted.

"Watch it, Den—"

My gaze followed the sedan as it clipped the car in front of us, which swerved into the right lane and hit the front of a big rig that began to jackknife right into our path.

"Sonofabitch." Denny expertly applied the brakes and was able to go around the semi and onto the shoulder to pass the accident. "Walt, call it in."

"On it." Walter used his phone to call emergency personnel to come to the accident site.

"Shit, that motherfucker had been following us for a while. This was no accident."

Sure enough, another car came flying up on the left side of Walter's truck, and the man inside stared us down.

"Step on it, D."

But before Denny could get away from the guy, the exit for the rest area came up on the right. He tried to pull off the road onto the ramp, but the car sideswiped us and Denny ran off the asphalt. A row of pilons appeared in front of the truck, and Denny swerved to miss them. He got control of the truck just in time to crash into a cyclone fence. A huge white ballon exploded in front of Denny, Walter threw out an arm to catch me, and I screamed as I threw my arms up to protect my face, afraid I'd hit the seatback in front of me.

"D?" Walter said, then he turned to check me over. "You hurt?"

I didn't know, honestly. I must have nodded. Walter unhooked both of our seat belts and pulled his gun out.

"*Fuck*. I'm okay," Denny said, fighting to get the car balloon out of his face. He pulled his weapon and turned around. "Get down on the floor, Dane," he said, and then he was out of the truck, his weapon in front of him.

"Stay down," Walter said, before he, too, climbed out. I did as he asked. My ears were ringing, and I was having a hard time hearing anything. This was all wrong. There was nothing about this—

A shot rang out, Denny and Walter started yelling, then more shots were fired. I heard sirens, shouting, and more gunfire so loud, it sounded like it was next to my head. A shot hit the back window, then the metal bed of the truck.

Then it stopped. It was silent outside. I wanted to go to Walter, be sure he was okay. Yet, I didn't want to move.

The board was on the floor in front of me.

What is my intention?

To end this.

"Take me to him."

Twenty-Six

From my vantage point, I couldn't see a damn thing. I stood crouched behind the rear driver's-side quarter panel of my truck in the fading light, and I couldn't see or hear Denny. I knew I'd hit at least one of the gunmen, but who the hell knew how many more guys were out here? There were at least two drivers, as one had caused the accident and the other had driven us off the road.

I heard the unmistakable sound of a magazine ejecting and a slide pulling back.

"Den," I whispered—and a bullet went whizzing by my cheek, so close I felt a sting. We were sitting ducks out here. I made for the front of the truck and peeked around the side to see Denny was reloading. I called out to him a little louder, and his head whipped around.

"I'll cover you. Get him out of here."

"To where? We're out in the open."

"Into the fucking field. Move!"

Denny stood up and used the hood of the truck as cover and he laid down a few shots as I ran back around to grab Dane from the truck. I opened the back door—

No.

"Move it, Muse!"

"He's gone!"

I pulled the blanket off the floor, and no, he was gone. So was the board. He couldn't have opened the other back door without Denny knowing. No one could have snuck up in front of him and taken Dane.

Holy shit. Had Dane been... *transported* with the board? Was it possible?

Another bullet pinged off the top of the truck door, narrowly missing my head.

Think. What had I seen in the vision? I'd known we needed to go to the northbound rest area and not the south-bound one, where all of the previous activity had taken place. I'd seen the buildings of the old rest area. It hadn't had a makeover in a long time, unlike some of the others. The trees, the cornfield.

Two squad cars pulled in and pinned down the shooters, giving Denny a window to move. He would be in the clear.

"Den, I'm going after him." I spotted an opening in the chain-link fence separating the rest area property from the next-door farm. The dense corn would be tough to navigate, but Holland couldn't be too far.

"Shit, you're bleeding," Denny said, reaching for my cheek. "You got grazed."

"I'm fine. I'm going—"

"Hang on. I've got no way to communicate with these patrolmen. I'm coming with you." He pulled out his phone and hit the voice-text button. "Detectives Muse and Hamilton are headed into the corn-field after the suspect." He gave our descriptions as we crawled through the hole in the fence and then proceeded to get beat to shit by cornstalks.

"How the fuck did he get out of the truck?" Denny groused, and then cussed as a cornstalk hit him in the forehead.

"I don't know, but you would have seen if someone grabbed him, right?"

"Yeah," Denny said, shaking his head. He grabbed my arm and pulled me down, holding a finger to his lips.

At first, all I could hear was my heart pounding in my ears... but then I heard it.

Laughter.

It made my hair stand on end. Denny's eyes were wide as he slowly cast his gaze toward the north end of the property.

"The trees," I said, seeing the tops of the eucalyptus in the distance. We took off at as much of a run as we could, between the fence and the stalks. I saw the blue and red lights of the patrol cars that were blocking the exit reflecting off of the buildings. We were going in the right direction.

"*Stop!*"

That was Dane.

More laughter.

We stopped at the sound and began to creep forward, hoping to make less of a disturbance in the stalks.

"You came. I hoped we'd have this time together. He wanted me to bring you to him, to take your life in front of him, but I want you for myself. This is *my* triumph, not his, and I won't have him in my head trying to control me anymore. I wanted to make *you* bleed, but he wasn't going to let me have you, so now I ain't gonna do his dirty work no more. I found you, that's what he wanted. I had my taste of blood. I won—*do you hear me, old man?*"

We broke through the stalks to find Dane standing before

Hunter Holland, pleading with him to stop as the madman screamed at the sky. Holland held a bloodied victim by the scruff of his collar, and in the other hand was a huge cleaver pressed against the victim's throat. Hunter caught sight of us, and his smile widened impossibly.

"Drop your weapon." Denny's commanding voice boomed out, and the two of us moved forward with our weapons to flank him.

"Oh, man. We're out of time, Mr. Troubadour. I hoped to take my time with you."

He looked down at the bloody man at his feet. Then he looked up at Denny. "The pretty man was a nice surprise. He got here a while ago, was taking pictures of the place when I moseyed on up and introduced him to my knives. We had some fun. I'm sorry I wasn't able to watch *your* pain as I spilled this one's blood, Detective." He jerked the collar of the man he'd wounded, and the man moaned. "This'll have to be enough. Sorry we didn't get to share more time, Dee Dee. I'll see you again. Next time around." He laughed, those teeth barely fitting in his mouth.

"Drop it!"

Holland raised the cleaver, and even as Denny and I both opened fire, he slid the sharp blade across his own throat, opening a bloody maw in the same shape as his gruesome mouth above.

He dropped the wounded man, who let out a grunt, and then he fell to his knees. Blood gushed from his throat, and he continued to smile in Dane's direction as the life bled out of his eyes.

"I'm... free," he spoke in a garbled whisper.

He fell face down and blood continued to pool around him.

Denny moved forward and kicked the cleaver away as I darted to Dane's side.

"How... are you hurt?"

Dane turned on me, and his face was ghost white. "I wanted it to stop."

I pulled him into my arms, but he didn't grab me back. He held the board in one hand and the planchette in the other and his frame remained stiff, trembling.

I cupped his jaw with my hands. "Honey, talk to me. Are you hurt?"

He shook his head. "I came here... it brought me here."

"Walter! Get an ambulance! Oh God!"

Denny's voice was just short of hysterical. I turned to find him cradling the wounded man in his grip.

And then I noticed the shoes. The Italian loafers were scuffed and marred with dark stains. The clothes were cut to pieces and covered in crimson splashes. His hair, which had been perfectly coiffed this afternoon, was matted with blood.

I used my phone to call it in as I pulled Dane in close, hiding his view of the carnage before us.

"It's that reporter, isn't it? I was too late, Walter. I didn't stop him in time, and he hurt that nice man."

Dane buried his face in my shirt, and all I could do was hold him as I identified myself, gave our coordinates, and agreed to stay on the phone until an ambulance could make its way through the blockage on the highway.

"He doesn't have time. He needs Life Flight. I don't care what you have to do, the victim is losing blood rapidly, he's been—Thank you."

Denny was speaking to Cooper and holding him to his chest. Tears ran down his face. "Walter, I need help," he called to me softly.

"Dane, honey, please. Turn away. Don't look at him, okay?"

"I'm okay," he whispered. "Let me help."

The fiercely calm expression on his face startled me, but I

didn't have time to worry about his change of demeanor. I led him over to Denny and ripped off my sweater and then my t-shirt, tearing it into bandages so we could try to stop the bleeding. Dane took direction and we ripped at Cooper's pants to find the cuts. Dane took off his sweatshirt and used it to press against a deep cut on Cooper's inner thigh.

"Denny," Cooper moaned, and then his body went limp.

"Where's that fucking helicopter!"

Within moments, light appeared in the sky before the sound hit us, and soon it was landing in the parking lot of the rest area.

"Stay here," I said to Dane. "I'll direct them over here."

He nodded, and I ran toward the lot, my brain filled with questions. What was Cooper doing here? And why was Denny fawning over him like a lover? My best friend was crying over a man I had no idea he even knew.

I waved my arms, shivering now that the adrenaline was wearing off. It was nighttime, December, and damned cold. I had a split second to worry about Dane before two paramedics with a stretcher and kits came jogging my way.

"Victim is male, mid-thirties, multiple lacerations, significant blood loss."

"Got it, boss," the EMT said. They set their items down when we reached Cooper and Dane moved out of the way.

Denny wouldn't let go.

"Sir, we've got this," the lead EMT said.

Denny kept rocking Cooper.

"Hey," I said, kneeling next to him. "You gotta let them take over, Den. Come on."

Denny turned his head slowly, and the haunted expression on his face took my breath away.

"I can't leave him like this." His broken, cracked voice was the worst thing I'd ever heard from my best friend.

"Den, come on. We can meet them at the hospital."

Den's wide eyes were desperate, but he loosened his grip. He eased Cooper's limp body into the hands of the EMTs and he knelt behind them, watching their every move.

"His blood type is A negative. It's rare. Call ahead to make sure they have enough."

How the fuck did Denny know Cooper's blood type?

"Thank you," he said to them. He took my extended hand and let me pull him up.

"Den, man," I said, placing my hands on his shoulders. "You okay?"

He planted his hands on his hips, blew out a long breath, and nodded. "I'll tell you. But not now."

"Whatever you need, man. I'm here."

Denny nodded, but he wouldn't make eye contact.

"Walter."

I turned to Dane.

His face was afire with the setting sun. The breeze blew his hair back off his shoulders. The fear was gone, and in its place that dogged determination to do what he'd set out to do.

"We can get to Virgil. We can find him."

Denny and I exchanged looks.

"Dane, the others went after him. They'll catch him."

Denny pulled out his phone and started scrolling through the group text. "No word."

"How did you get out of the truck?" I asked him, afraid to hear the truth.

"It's like she said. I'm only limited by my limitations. The ones in my head."

"What happened, Dane?"

I was beyond the mental capacity to figure out riddles and bone-deep exhausted. I didn't want to lose patience with him, despite the fact that he was acting bizarre, but this had to stop.

"I told the board to take me to him." He gazed at me with those green eyes and instead of fear and wariness, like I'd been seeing ever since I'd met him, he seemed... supernaturally charged. Shadows fell on his face, giving him an otherworldly appearance, and his eyes nearly glowed. There was no tremble in his hands. No quiver to his chin.

"Dane," I pleaded. "We picked our spot. We stopped him —well, he stopped himself. Dax and Gene will get Evans if he's there. If not, at least the immediate threat has passed. You did what you set out to do." I wanted him to let it go now, let the police handle Virgil, but I could tell from the set of his jaw that he'd made up his mind.

"We just saw how much power he has. If he's psychically linked to Hunter, and all the others who helped him, he'll send someone else after me."

"How far are you going to take this?" I was ready to beg. "If you go to him, he wins. You don't know what you're walking into."

He smiled, but it was with sadness, not joy. Not the loving way he'd looked at me earlier when we'd talked about where we hoped we would go together when this was all over. He was about to slip from my grasp—and I had no way to convince him not to let go.

Kal's words echoed in my head. *Don't stand in his way of trying to make things right.*

But how was I supposed to let him go into danger?

"I'm sorry, Walter. I have to." He held the board in front of him with one hand, placed the planchette on top, closed his eyes...

And he was gone.

"Dane!" It felt as though a cold hand had reached into my chest and ripped my heart out the moment he disappeared. I'd promised him I wouldn't let go, but he hadn't given me a choice, not even a split second to react.

"What the *fuck*? Walter, what just happened?"

"It's the board. He went after Evans."

I stared at the empty spot where he'd stood seconds before. Denny shoved me.

"Then fucking go after him! I got this. I'm going to get one of the patrol officers to take me to the hospital. You go after him, and dammit, don't lose him."

"Denny—"

He tossed me the keys. "Go! He thinks he's got this, but he needs you."

"You sure you're—"

"Fucking. Go!"

He took off at sprint toward the parking lot, and I did the same toward my truck, my chest tight the whole time.

My hesitation may have cost me the most important person in my life, and I didn't think I would recover if I lost him.

Then there would be two Muse men destroyed by Dane Donovan.

Twenty-Seven

Dane

The trip gave me a rush. I had no way to describe it except maybe the feeling of sitting in the way back of a station wagon facing backward when the driver floored the engine and the car lurched forward. I pictured it more, though, like being sucked through space, like the scene in *Star Wars* when they made the jump to light speed.

That thought made my heart hurt.

Walter's face had been so full of anguish, and I hated that I'd put it there. I didn't want that to be the last time I saw him, but I'd been clear with him. I needed to do this. I had to stop Hunter Holland from hurting people, and when we discovered his tie to Virgil Evans, I knew I couldn't rest until Evans himself was unable to kill anyone ever again.

This time the board had brought me to that dark tunnel built of cinder blocks and the lights were on, illuminating my path, but the end of the hallway was dark, just as I'd seen it in my visions before.

The sound of humming echoed down the hall, and then Evans was humming that creepy song.

"I'll see you again, whenever spring breaks again…" He sang with an eerie, rapid tremolo like the old-timey singers from the thirties and forties were known for. The words to the song were meant to be nostalgic and loving, but coming from Evans, they were twisted and sinister. He sang of regrets, destiny, and fate and love, but I knew the man had no idea what love was. He'd confused love with obsession and possession all those years ago, when he'd been Tess's stalker. He had no clue what it meant to put someone else's needs above his own. He was a narcissist, and I would stop him. Somehow.

Although, in my haste to leave Walter in hopes of protecting him, I hadn't quite thought far enough ahead.

How did I plan to stop this man? Would I kill him with my own hands? I had no weapon, I only had the board, and though Evans was an old man, I wasn't a killer.

And now it was too late.

At the end of the hall, I'd find the pile of bones and Virgil Evans. I'd walked right into his hands, just like Walter feared I would. I could use the board to escape, but that wouldn't put this nightmare to rest.

I only hoped the police were close by, that they'd actually found the right place.

"I'm so happy you're here."

The bald man stood in the doorway, but this time I saw his face.

The Virgil Evans I recalled from Tess's house had been a small, weaselly kind of man, but this man was frail. Old. One could easily underestimate him, but I wouldn't.

I knew better.

"Come in, come in. We have much to discuss."

"The only thing we have to discuss is that this is over. You're done hurting people." This was the first time I had spoken to him face-to-face since that show in Phoenix. Not even when the man had taken a knife to my skin, the memory of which was still fresh in my mind, had I possessed the ability to speak to him.

"Oh, but this is only the beginning. You've arrived, and *with* your arrival, I now have the tools to take me to the next level of my journey. Don't you want to know what's next?"

"What's next is that the police are coming to arrest you, and you'll go back to prison, this time for good."

"It's funny you think that walls can contain me. You of all people should know that my reach goes beyond boundaries... as does yours. I saw through Hunter's eyes what you can do. I'm impressed."

"Hunter is dead."

"Mmm. Sad. But you won't be surprised to discover that the men I tend to have access to are already a little unhinged. They don't make for the most reliable sentinels."

I stepped into the room and tried to ignore the smell of rot and mildew, and the fact that there was a waist-high pile of bones behind him. There was a dim light filtering in through a hole in the roof above us. I wondered how far underground we were, and what the original purpose of this place was. Off to the left and right, there were arches that led into additional tunnels with what looked like tracks leading into them, like maybe for carts. There was no telling how many tunnels there were in all, or how far they went. The construction seemed too new to be a mine, but perhaps only this part had been constructed and the rest was older mine shafts? That would make the ground unstable.

I was quickly adding ways I would hate to die to my list. Trapped underground was now at the top.

"What do you want from me? You already took forty years

of my life—nearly *took* my life. You sent Hunter after me to torment me. What else?"

He smiled and clasped his hands in front of him. "What I desire is an ever-evolving outcome. I could spend eternity with you and not find enough ways to make you suffer, Donovan. But right now? You possess knowledge that I'm in desperate need of."

"What is it?"

"I want what you had—the carnival. You know the night I had my fun with you, I was interrupted. I'd wanted to watch the life fade from your eyes. That's always my favorite part, that and the terror. And the blood, of course. But I had to hide when that damned deputy showed up. Walter Muse, Senior. Your lover's father. He ruined *everything*, and I'm glad he suffered for all the pain he's caused me. Both of them, actually. See, while I was hiding from Muse Senior, a glowing light appeared, and I watched it descend from the sky. Suddenly there was a huge collection of tents that hadn't been there before. A man in overalls came out of the light and walked straight up to you. He picked you up, then turned to glare at me, shaking his head. Before I could do anything, he carried you into the circle of tents and out of sight."

He had to be talking about Pokey. I remembered the strange man telling me everything would be all right as he lay me down on what would be my bed for the next several weeks —well, forty years, actually.

"I tried to follow but no matter how long I walked, I never reached the tents. It was like an optical illusion. It seemed like it was just over the next hump, and then I'd get there and it'd be like I hadn't moved. I followed you until the sun came up, and then I had to go back to where I'd hidden my work truck or I might've been found out."

"What do you want me to say? Too bad you weren't able to finish what you started?"

He laughed. "No. What I want *you* to do... is take me there."

I balked. "To the carnival? No way. Even if I knew where to find it, there's no way I'd take you there, and if I did, Mr. Ame wouldn't let you in. He don't let bad people in."

"I know. That's why I sent Hunter to find you. He was curious, but he hadn't intentionally spilled blood yet, despite his bullshit prison sentence. I spent *years—decades—*looking for any information I could find. I had to settle for vague stories about that carnival. There was no trace of it in any records anywhere. I found a few articles in the looney papers about people running off to join a carnival and then coming back years later as if no time had passed. One man said he'd had a limp when he went in and when he left, he could walk fine. Another said there was a calliope there that sounded so perfect, it could cure whatever ailed you."

He knew about Kal? Were there others who had left and talked? I'd told only Walter, and Denny and Gene knew some parts of the story. If enough people talked about their experiences, it would put the carnival at risk.

"I knew it had to be the same carnival that took you," he continued. I tried to look around for a weapon, any way to stop him, but he seemed content to keep his distance from me. While he spoke, he walked around the backside of the pile of bones, as if to keep his deeds between us, keep my focus on them rather than whatever he might be planning to do.

"I tried so hard to find it, but I knew that someone like me with a... colorful past... well, I wouldn't be allowed in. So, I used my unique talents to suss out which of my prison pals, and then my cohabitants at the halfway house, had a fairly clean slate. Do you know that Hunter had never done any intentional physical harm to another human being? He'd been in the military, and after he was discharged for psychiatric concerns, he wound up in a bar fight, but he never even threw a punch. Happened to be with the wrong people in the wrong place. He did his stint and then they sent him to our little happy home to help him re-engage with society. I think that was how they put it. Instead, he became my roommate, and boy, did I ever have fun with him. I played around in his dreams for months before I knew just what I needed to do to make him pliable. I simply needed to lead him to *you*. I told him you had a story to tell through your talking board... oh yes, I knew all about that. Plucked it right out of Tess's head one night after she'd passed out. She really let herself go after you disappeared."

Hearing him say awful things about Tess made me burn, but I couldn't react. That was what he wanted to happen.

"I told him if he found you, you'd show him how he could use his special gifts. All he had to do was touch the board with you. You led him right to his dream come true. All he needed was to see the possibilities."

"And now he's dead, and so are more innocent people."

Virgil shrugged. "And you came here to stop me."

"The police know where you are. They're on their way."

He looked up at the ceiling and his eyes trailed over the support beams. "They may be, but they can't stop me."

"What do you want?" I had to stall him somehow. I didn't know how long it would take the police to find us down here. I didn't know if they were on the grounds. I really should have planned things out better, but after seeing what Hunter had done to Cooper, I couldn't take anymore chances. Time was running out.

"I want you to take me to the carnival, Dane. It's a simple request."

"But you can't go in," I said. "What good will it do you?"

He smiled and laughed with his lips closed. "You let me worry about that. I saw what you can do now with your board, you're very strong. You get me there, and I promise anything that Mr. Ame throws up to keep me out will be useless."

This power I'd been given, whether it was solely from the board or if, like I'd thought before, Kal and I came away from the carnival with something extra, I couldn't allow Evans to manipulate me for his purposes.

But what if it only *appeared* that I was being manipulated?

Make of your question all that you desire.

What if I only *appeared* to take him to the carnival?

Be ever thoughtful and in control of your ire.

What if I acted as if I were under duress...

Picture your intent as taut as a wire.

But in my mind, I held the truth?

Remain steadfast or the end will be dire.

Could I fool him?

As pure as ice and hot as fire,

Love is the power behind all you aspire.

I pictured Walter in my mind. I had to stop Evans or we'd never have that life we imagined together, and that was unacceptable.

You can do this. You can stop him and save yourself.

"If you choose not to take me there, well... I'm in need of some new sentinels. How brilliant would it be to recruit from the Kern County Sheriff's Department?

Trust in the truth and never the liar,

My truth. I would stop him. I would trust in Walter or his friends finding me. I couldn't believe in his lies.

and you will avoid the funeral pyre.

I would not burn. This man, this horribly violent, sick man would no longer hurt another soul.

I sat down on the dirt floor, never taking my eyes off him. "Then let's go."

His eyes flared with excitement, but I could tell he didn't totally buy my cooperation.

He came around the bone pile, slowly, and as I watched him, I caught sight of Tess's bracelets.

My breath caught but I couldn't react, couldn't show my pain. This predator would pick up on it.

"So glad you see things my way. It would be awful to have to harm an innocent officer of the law. Ha!" He laughed out loud. "I'm sure there are many people who don't believe cops are innocent. I've certainly run across my share that could be encouraged to look the other way." He winked as he lowered himself awkwardly, stiffly to the floor. He grunted with pain and it showed on his face.

"Sorry," I said. "I bet you'd prefer a chair and a table."

He glared at me, seemingly unhappy that I saw his weakness. This close, I could really see that age hadn't been kind to him. I was a small man, but he seemed downright frail. He was in his seventies now. Who knew how many ailments he had?

I set the board on the ground between us and placed my hands on the planchette.

I am in control of what is seen.

I will hone my intent and prevent harm.

I will stop him from hurting another soul.

I will save me.

"Let's see the carnival," he said with a smirk.

He reached out with shaky, gnarled hands and placed them on the planchette.

I nodded. "Here we go."

I could immediately tell the difference. The pull wasn't quite as strong, but he wouldn't know that. The sky was dark around us, but the night was clear. Stars in the sky were so bright, likely because there was no light pollution out here, wherever here was.

I walked toward the dim light in front of us, which grew brighter as we approached.

"It's just how I remember it," Evans said. "It's so quaint, so enticing!"

We moved closer and the carnival didn't move away, as he'd said it had before. I concentrated all my focus on every detail a person would see on their walk up to the place. I may not have gotten around much when I was there, but I remembered what the front gates looked like.

A man appeared at the gate wearing a top hat and a red coat. Rafe. He removed his hat and bowed toward me.

"You've returned to us," he said, because I wanted him to say it. "Who's your companion?"

"Rafe, this is Virgil Evans. He's interested in joining the carnival."

Rafe raised his eyebrow, just as I'd seen him do the few times I'd interacted with him and acted a fool.

"Is that so? Well, Mr. Evans. What would you bring to the carnival?"

Virgil opened his mouth to speak, but he was in awe. He had a childlike look of wonder on his wrinkly, gaunt face. He smoothed back his hair and tried to smile.

"Well, sir, I'm a maintenance man. I can fix many things."

I felt hands on my back and lips close to my ear. "Don't let go of him." I recognized Gene's voice, and I nearly breathed a sigh of relief. "We're checking the room for explosives. We just need a minute."

"That's wonderful." I recalled Rafe saying that to me when I told him I could write poems. "We just might have a space for you."

"Thank you so much, I appreciate—"

Evans reached a hand toward Rafe and let go of the planchette.

The carnival was gone—and we were back in Evans's den of sin.

"Don't move! Put your hands on your head."

I looked to my left, and there was Dax with his gun trained on Evans.

Evans grinned menacingly and slowly fastened his hands behind his head.

"You're a fool if you think you can stop me." He turned his beady eyes on me, and his sick smile made my skin stretch tight over my bones. Every scar I had burned, as if hot pokers branded me.

I collapsed to the side and tried to curl into a ball, anything to make the pain stop.

"Dee Dee," Gene yelled, but then I saw Dax drop his hands and start moving toward the wall. His gait was stumbly, his gun was down at his side. He stared at something with his head cocked to the side.

Gene shouted, "Dax! No!"

Dax reached up and pulled a lever.

Evans cackled and let his head fall backward, dropping his hands. Then he smiled at me once more. "Boom."

The explosion deafened me, and I was pelted with stones and rocks. The ceiling began to crumble and drop to the floor as I was yanked to my feet.

Gene screamed in my face. *"Run!"*

He pushed me down the hallway, and I ran as fast as my legs could carry me, but I had no idea where I was going.

I turned to look back and the lights were flickering, but I made out Gene dragging a limp Dax beside him. The walls of the hallway were beginning to crack. They were never going to make it.

I darted back toward them and ignored Gene's orders as I wrapped Dax's other arm over my shoulder. The hallway wasn't quite wide enough for us to all fit three wide, so I took the lead.

"Up ahead, turn left at the end!"

I turned left and nearly ran into the metal rungs that led up and out.

"Go, Dane, I've got him." Gene bent and threw Dax over his shoulder. I climbed as fast as I could, but the metal rungs were starting to come loose from the cracking concrete. Once I got to the top, I was coughing from the dust, but I turned and reached down for Dax.

"Here, let me grab him," I said. I got a hold of his jacket and yanked with all of my strength, pulling him on top of me and out of the hole so Gene could get out.

"*Dane!*"

Walter was there, lifting me from the ground as I continued to cough. Two other cops in what looked like military uniforms lifted Gene and Dax and carried them away from the hole we'd climbed out of as the tunnel collapsed. The ground rumbled as we sped away, and as I looked over Walter's shoulder, I watched as the ground imploded as far as I could see.

Walter set me down and pulled me against him.

"Thank God," he whispered against my hair. "Thank God, honey. I thought—"

"I'm sorry," I said. "I—"

"Not now," he said. "Just let me hold you."

"Is Dax okay?"

We both turned to see paramedics working on him. He was moving, coughing, and gesturing wildly with his hands. The paramedics forced him onto a gurney and threatened to strap him down if he kept fighting them. Gene took his hand and spoke quietly to him, which calmed him down.

The men who carried Gene and Dax out of the way of danger stood with us, staring in shock at the ground, which now consisted of ravines and caverns.

"He had some fucking powerful charges down there."

"Yeah, but with this old mine, it could have gone at any time."

"There goes our crime scene."

"Did you get him?" I asked. "Evans?"

The men looked at each other and back at me. "Only you three made it out. There's a chance he made it into one of the other tunnels, but there's no way to tell. We've got to get a crew out here to make sure this place is safe before we can search."

I sighed, exhaustion and despair running through me. "What if I didn't stop him?"

"I highly doubt he made it out of there, old man like that. We're going to go report back to our lieutenant. You need anything, we'll be at the mobile command center."

"Thanks," Walter said to them as they walked away.

Gene stepped back from the gurney as the men loaded Dax into the back of an ambulance. He shook his head when they offered to look at him and walked over to us, then put his arm around Walter.

"You okay?" he asked me.

"Yeah. You?"

He nodded and swore. "What the fuck was he doing, wandering around like that? It was like he was in some kind of daze."

"I think Evans was controlling him, like he had the others," I said quietly, so only Walter and Gene could hear. "He warned me he would use cops as sentinels if I didn't help him."

"You know, I got a bad headache when I went in that room. I wonder if he was trying to use it on me?" Gene rubbed at the side of his head.

Walter squeezed his shoulder and sighed. "Guess you were too thickheaded."

Gene swore, and we all laughed, a good hearty one to shake off some of the dread that had been weighing us down.

"Where's Denny?" Gene asked.

Walter frowned. "He went with Cooper to the hospital."

Gene's eyes widened. "Cooper? Oh shit. Did he get hurt? He asked me for details about the Buttonwillow crime scene, said he wanted to get shots for his report. I told him not to go out there until we caught this guy."

Walter kept his arm around me but he put a hand on Gene's shoulder again. "I'm sorry, Gene. Hunter got to him."

Gene let out a heavy breath and stepped away. He bent forward and put his hands on his knees. Walter left my side to go to him.

"I'm so sorry, Gene," I said. "I didn't get there in time."

Gene held up a hand to me and shook his head.

"He was hurt bad, but he was alive when they flew him to the hospital."

Gene stood and ran a hand over his face.

"Denny went with him," Walter said. "He... how well do those two know each other?" His voice went up in question at the end.

Gene frowned at him. "What do you mean? They might have met at one of Sam's fundraisers. Why?"

Walter shook his head. "There is definitely more to the story than that. Denny was... he was distraught. He... I've never seen him so upset."

"Shit. Let me call Sam. She'll want to go. Cooper's one of her best friends. She'll want to be there."

"All right." Walter said. "What do you need from me?"

Gene looked between the two of us and smiled. "I think the two of you could use some real rest. Here," he said, removing a set of keys from his ring. He handed them to Walter. "Go stay at our place in Manhattan Beach. I'll check on your mom, too, but you two need to rest."

"Thanks, man," Walter said. "You need his statement?"

"I'll get it. Get out of here."

The two hugged tightly and held each other for several beats. I was so glad Walter had such good friends, and I considered his friends lucky to have *him*.

I only hoped I would be lucky enough to keep him.

Gene surprised me and grabbed me for a hug too, pounding on my back hard enough to make me stumble. "Take care of this guy, okay? He's important."

I grinned at Walter. "I will if he lets me."

Walter's expression was unreadable, but he put his arm around me and walked me over to his truck. He opened the door for me, but he didn't speak as I climbed in, nor when he closed it behind me.

My stomach fluttered as I watched him walk around the truck, but then it clenched.

Would he forgive me for leaving him? Would he understand?

He climbed into the driver's side and closed the door, taking a deep breath before he put the key in the ignition.

"Walter?"

He didn't look at me but he took his hand off the wheel.

"I'm sorry," I finally said, when he didn't speak.

He nodded and put the truck in reverse. He looked over his shoulder as he backed up, and then he put the truck in drive. Finally, he turned my way.

"Give me the drive. Then I'll be over it."

What else could I do?

I gave him a quick smile and then turned to look at the window. I didn't want to cry in front of him, and I feared if I looked at him again, I would.

· · ·

I woke as he put the truck in park. It was full dark and we were stopped in the driveway of a three-story town house with modern-style architecture. I had no idea how long we'd been driving. I had no idea what day it was, what time, where we were...

All I knew was that everything I wanted was sitting beside me, and I had no clue whether he—

"I love you, Dane. It nearly killed me when you disappeared, but I understand why you did it. Just... please. Don't do that again."

I dared to breathe.

"I won't. I'm so sorry."

He still wouldn't look at me. He nodded and opened his door.

"Wait for me," he said, when I reached for the handle.

That walk around the front of the truck took forever, and in that time, I recalled something my mother told me once.

"Remember, when you take someone special out on a date, it's important that you walk around the front of the car to open their door for them. If you walk around the back... well, it indicates that you don't think highly of them."

I had no idea where she got such an idea, but as Walter opened the door for me and stood watching me, I knew. I knew he thought very highly of me, that he'd been there for me through a horrible ordeal, and I hoped he'd continue to be there.

I turned my body to step out of the truck, and he didn't back up. When I slid down from the cab, our bodies came in contact. He stared at me with mixed emotions, and for a moment I worried—

He moved so fast, pulling me into a bone-crushing embrace, and he held me so tightly I couldn't breathe. With his face buried in my hair, he spoke close to my ear.

"Let me take care of you? Let me love you?"

His voice sounded unsure, for possibly the first time since I'd met him.

I didn't hesitate.

"Only if you let me take care of you. I love you, Walter. Please... please say you can forgive me."

He pulled back and held my face in his hands. "Already did."

He led me inside the sparsely decorated home, which looked like it was made up for a magazine spread. We climbed two sets of stairs and straight into a bedroom on the top floor with a spacious bathroom.

"Tell me if at any point you need me to stop."

"Don't stop," I whispered.

He took my clothes off me, took off all of his, and dropped everything on the floor. We went into the large shower and stood holding each other for several minutes under the hot spray. When I swayed on my feet, he smiled. "Let me wash you."

He gently scrubbed every inch of my body, and he kissed every one of my scars. He washed my hair, used conditioner, and then rinsed me off. He sat me on the bench before taking a quick shower himself, and when he was finished, all I could do was stare at this beautiful man and wonder how I'd been so lucky that he was the one to find me.

If Hunter had never come to the carnival, would I have ever left? If I hadn't gone after him, would Walter have ever seen me? If Ryan hadn't called the tip line, would we ever have met?

"Come here," he said, and I did. I would follow him anywhere. He pulled out two giant, fluffy white towels and wrapped me in one as he'd done the morning I'd jumped in the pool, when I'd been naked before him. At that moment, he'd looked on me with admiration and not disgust at my scars. Now, he took care with me as if I were a beloved treasure.

As he stood before me, drying the ends of my hair, I reached up and gently touched his cheek.

"Does it hurt?"

He shook his head. "Nah."

I chuckled softly. "You match me now."

He glanced in the mirror and shrugged. "Scars add character, that's what my father used to say."

He finished drying me off and walked me into the bedroom.

"Do you need—"

"You," I said, grabbing his hand, not letting him finish asking me if I wanted space. "I need you."

I'd been alone in my space for too long. I wanted him.

I lifted the covers and lay on my back, spread my legs, and held my arms out to him.

He hesitated only a moment before he covered me with his strong body. I wrapped my arms and legs around him and held on tight. I could almost breathe a sigh of relief, but there was still a nagging fear.

What if Evans managed to get away?

And my board. I'd left it behind. There was no way for me to look for him.

"Hey," Walter said, interrupting my thoughts before they spiraled into a tunnel of doom. He brushed my hair back from my face and kissed my forehead. "It's going to be okay. They're going to search the area in the coming weeks and the detectives will track down everyone who's been associated with Evans. We won't stop until we've put an end to this. In the meantime, I'll make sure you, your mom and Barbara, Ryan and Kal, are all protected until we have definitive proof that Evans is dead or we catch him."

I nodded, tracing his lips with my finger. "And where will you be in all this?"

He cocked his head to the side and kissed my fingertip. "With you. As much as I can be."

"Your job?"

He nodded. "For now. I want to see this case through, and then... we can decide."

"We?" I said, a smile forming, when I'd been worried that I might not have much to smile about again.

Walter smiled, too. "Yeah, we. If we're going to be together, you have a say in what I do. Whether I retire now or in two years, and what I do with the rest of my life. I *want* you to have a say. Of course, that means meeting my kids and my ex, and my mom. We'd have to decide between Bakersfield and LA for a home base..."

"Is that really a decision? I mean, I know I've been gone for forty years—"

Walter laughed and pressed his forehead to mine. "I'll go anywhere with you."

"Good. Because I want you. Please," I pleaded, my voice shaky. "Make me yours, Walter. I want it."

He sucked in a breath, and then moaned as he kissed me deeply. He pulled at my shoulders and rutted against me, his hard cock leaking as he moved.

"Honey, are you sure? We haven't... I don't want to hurt you."

"You won't. Please, Walter. Take me out of my head. I just want to feel you, feel *us*."

He was panting now, and he stopped moving for a minute. "Hang on."

He climbed from the bed, and I watched him walk into the bathroom.

"What is this place?" I asked, my nerves making me a little restless.

He came out with a small zipper bag. "Sam and Gene used to live here, when they worked in LA. When they moved to Bakersfield, they decided to keep it and use it as a vacation home. The beach is only a block away. They rent it out sometimes to help cover the costs, but after I saved Gene from the business end of a carving knife, his wife said it's mine whenever I want it. She kind of loves me." He set the bag down on the nightstand and stood motionless for a moment. I took the opportunity to run my fingers over his cock.

It jumped at my touch, and he moaned, his hips flexing.

"We don't have to..."

"I know what to expect. I may not have done it, but I know what happens." I loved that he was concerned, but I knew what I was getting myself into, and I was ready to get into it with him.

"I'll be careful," he said as he slid back into bed with me. He reached for the bag and took out a bottle of what I assumed was lubricant. "Roll onto your stomach," he said quietly.

I did as he asked, and I turned my head to watch him. His normally so-alert eyes, wide and piercing, were heavy-lidded, his lips pursed out and swollen from our kisses. He poured some lube in his hand, and then he leaned over me. He licked and sucked at my shoulder, my earlobes, my neck as he spread the cool liquid in my crease, gently rubbing circles with his finger over my sensitive hole. He'd touched me like this before, and he'd touched inside me, but now he added another finger, stretching me as he kissed along my shoulder blades and licked up my spine, causing me to arch into the bed.

My erection throbbed and the friction against the soft sheets felt so good, I couldn't help but buck my hips—back to meet his hand, forward into the mattress.

My body was alight with sensations. I couldn't decide what felt best as it was all so, so good. When he nuzzled the globes of my ass and licked around where his fingers were working me open, I was so distracted I barely felt him add a third finger. I felt so full, so hot, and I loved it all.

I pushed against his hand, feeling those fingers deeper and deeper inside of me, loving the burn and the pressure, but I wanted more.

"Fuck me, Walter. Please!"

"God, you say that and this is going to be over too quickly."

"Fuck me? Walter? Please? Which one?"

He covered his erection with a condom and smeared more lube on himself.

"All of it. Fuck, Dane. I can't take it. Roll over."

I did as he asked, surprised that he didn't want me from behind. He pushed my legs up and draped them over his shoulders.

"This okay? You'll tell me if—"

"Walter, *pleaaaase*." I chuckled. Here I was, begging for him.

He smiled and ran his hands up the backs of my thighs and under my ass. "You're so beautiful, Dane." He pressed his cock against me and eased in so slowly, barely moving. I sucked in a breath, expecting it to hurt, but he'd done such a good job preparing me, I merely felt full. *So* full. So full I thought I might split in two, but it was so *good*.

He'd push forward the slightest bit, then rest, then moan as he pushed in more. His eyes were squeezed shut and he was panting hard, his muscles straining because he was being so careful.

"It's good, it's good, Walter, it's good. Please—*ahhhh*." He bent me in half and slid the rest of the way in, his pelvis slapping against my ass at his thrust. Every bit of it was incredible. I expected him to begin moving faster, but he merely slid most of the way out and then shoved back in slow at first, then with a snap of his hips, thrusting against me, hitting so deep inside it brushed against that spot that turned me inside out.

I groaned and linked my fingers behind his neck, pulling him in to kiss me. I held on as his thrusts became so strong, he pushed me up the bed until my head hit the headboard. He was lost in his passion, but he managed to lift up my head, pull his knees up next to my hips, and then he was pounding into me with small strokes that took my breath completely away.

I shuddered as I held on and welcomed the liquid heat that traveled down my spine, into my groin, and then erupted from my cock without even a stroke.

"Walter, I'm coming, I'm... *coming*!"

He growled and pumped hard a few more times until he froze and pulled me down hard on his cock. He gripped me tight, pressed to his chest, as his heart thundered, his skin drenched in sweat. He panted for a long time before he loosened his hold. He pulled out and grabbed a tissue from the nightstand and took off the condom.

"Be right back," he said as he went into the bathroom, still breathing hard.

I let my legs down finally and stretched my arms over my head, feeling blissfully worked out. I let my eyes drift closed and thought, *Yes, this is Heaven. Right here.*

Walter came back in carrying his phone, frowning as he typed.

"Is everything okay?" *No, please not more bad news...*

"Your mom and Barbara are back home and there's a patrol car out front. My mom is going to stay with her sister in Santa Barbara for a while. Cooper is in stable condition and is resting comfortably in the hospital, with Denny refusing to leave his side. Sam says she can't wait to meet you. Ryan and Kal decided to go spend some time at their place up north to shake off the stress of this week. My kids are mad I'm at the beach without them and want to know when they get to meet my new boyfriend."

He set his phone down on the table next to the bed and gave me a shy grin.

"Do any of those require us to take action at this very moment?" I asked him, patting the bed beside me.

He grinned and stretched out next to me, resting his head in his hand. "Not a one."

I sighed. "Good, because that was incredible and as soon as you're ready, I want to do it again."

Walter barked out a laugh and flopped onto his back. "Wow, I can see I'm going to have to up my fitness regimen if I'm going to keep up with you."

"I'm the old man, remember?" I teased.

He turned and used his finger to lift my chin so he could kiss me in that sweet way of his, with those plump red lips and the gentle scratch of his mustache.

"No. You're a young man with a lot of time to make up for. I promise I'll take care of you. Always."

"I'm going to hold you to that," I said as I rolled on top of him and kissed him as if I really had gone forty years without kissing to make up for. There were so many things I wanted to do with Walter, and I was grateful for this opportunity to try them all.

Before we went to sleep, Walter opened the drapes on the large windows that surrounded the room on three sides. The moon was full and we had a clear panoramic view of the sky.

"You'll appreciate it in the morning," he said, kissing me once more before turning out the lights. "Let's get some rest. Then we can figure out our next move."

"I don't care what we do, as long as I get to wake up beside you tomorrow and the day after and the day after."

He pulled me against his chest, wrapping his arm around my shoulders. He kissed my forehead and then sighed as he lay his head on the pillows.

"And all the days after."

Epilogue

D ane

Six Months Later...

I gripped the steering wheel tight, my knuckles white and my scars stretched almost to the painful point. Walter had been so good about helping me ease into the twenty-first century—at least during the days we had been able to carve out together—and he'd decided a month ago that it was time for me to learn how to drive.

Driving had proven to be the first thing we didn't do gracefully together. At least, I didn't. He was a wonderful teacher, but I was a pretty terrible student. Once my finances had been settled, he'd asked me what kind of car I wanted. That's how he informed me that I needed to learn to drive.

It turned out I certainly *had* been paid royalties all this time, and they amounted to a hefty enough sum that not only was I able to buy myself an electric spaceship car that Walter said would be good for me, but also a lovely home for the two of us across the road from my mother in Laurel Canyon, so I could spend time with her. Her vision had mostly recovered, and she had a little more pep in her step each day, thank goodness. We had certainly made up for lost time.

The house was spacious enough for Walter's kids to each have a room of their own when they came to visit. I'd met them over the holidays, and soon the three of us were ganging up on Walter in the most loving of ways. Our place also had an in-law unit for Walter's mother to live in, whenever she was ready to move to LA, which she said would be never, but Walter wanted to be sure we had a place for her. In the meantime, it was perfect for when Ryan and Kal visited, which they would be doing for an extended period as we went into rehearsals in a week for my first time on tour since nineteen seventy-nine, only this time, instead of folk music, I would be playing hard rock and heavy metal with Ryan. I looked forward to the challenge. After everything I'd been through, the angrier music helped me begin the healing process.

We were currently on our way to Santa Barbara to attend Stacia's graduation from college and it was my first test driving long-distance on the interstate. I wasn't thrilled, but I had an appointment to take my behind-the-wheel test in a month, so Walter wanted me to practice. A lot.

"I would have loved for us to take the scenic route on Highway 101, but we have a stop to make," Walter'd said that afternoon as we loaded into the car.

"Oh yeah, where's that?"

"An old associate of my father's," was all he'd said.

I'd agreed, of course. As much healing as I'd had to do,

solving my case meant Walter could finally grieve for his father. He and I each had a therapist, and when it was appointment time, we'd head to rooms at opposite ends of our house and talk to people through a fancy typewriter screen.

Look, some things I still hadn't fully grasped, and though I was learning to use a computer and a smartphone, I liked my names for them better.

"Can you tell me about the person we're going to see?" I asked him as the car began to climb into the Grapevine in the late afternoon light. I wanted to focus on something else rather than the last time we'd driven through here... on our way to find Hunter Holland at the Buttonwillow Rest Area. I didn't think I could ever stop and use one of those again, so I wanted Walter to talk to me.

"Her name is Charlene. He, uh, he consulted with her on some of his cases."

"Consulted... like how?"

I glanced over and caught Walter smoothing down his mustache as he looked out the window.

"She helped him with missing persons cases."

He didn't seem to want to add any more. "All right. How about, is everything set up for Stacia's graduation party tomorrow?"

"It is! I've rented enough rooms for all of us and booked a reception room at the Best Western in Goleta. Sam took care of the catering for me. Everyone will meet us at the hotel after the ceremony tomorrow, since they only give out four tickets to each of the grads."

"Got it." I knew Lisa and Steffan would be meeting us at the ceremony, and I was grateful that it had been Lisa's idea that I come with Walter. She'd been so welcoming to me when we'd met. It was odd, we'd all had Christmas dinner together at Walter's mother's house in Bakersfield, and it hadn't been weird.

"How you doing? Remember to watch your speed once we hit the turns."

"Got it," I repeated, not wanting to give him a bratty retort like I'd been known to do. It was true, driving would give me freedom when Walter wasn't with me, but I didn't think I'd ever love it.

He'd used his paid time off the first week or so after we'd found Hunter and Virgil, until we had a chance to breathe and start making plans. Unfortunately, he'd had to go back to Bakersfield sooner than anticipated, because Denny had gone AWOL—and then abruptly put in his retirement papers without a word to anyone, not even the guys. They were all worried about him, even more worried than they'd been about Walter.

It seems Denny was being uncharacteristically silent in their group chat, and all they knew was that he'd taken the reporter, Cooper Harris, out of the hospital and they'd gone off somewhere together. That was pretty much all he'd say. That he loved his friends, and he'd let them know what was going on as soon as he could.

The sheriff's department was struggling without two of their detectives, so Walter had to go back. Dax hadn't been hurt seriously, but he'd been very confused about what happened below ground. Gene confided in Walter that he wasn't sure he wanted to tell Dax what he'd done. Walter worked three twelve-hour shifts per week, sometimes more, to support his friends and department, and then he'd drive home to LA to be with me the other days.

I stayed busy, though. I met with Arthur Frye, the manager and attorney Cooper had referred me to, and he helped me sort out my "parents'" affairs. Tess had made "Dane" her sole beneficiary before they'd gone on that last tour, without telling me, of course. Everything had gone into a trust because Dane hadn't been declared dead, and her royalties kept accruing. Between her money and mine, which my mother had kept for me, Arthur had a lot to sort out. Thankfully the billfold came in handy whenever I'd needed to provide documents. He'd helped us with the purchase of the house and had his financial planner help me plan for my future, as well as put money away for Walter's kids, which had made Walter very emotional.

"Okay, you're going to be taking the exit after next, so use your blinker and start to move over."

I had to fight to control my desire to make a snarky comment. Driving still made me nervous, but the hand shakes had gone—mostly—and I was perfectly capable of remembering to turn on my damn blinker. But when I looked over at him and opened my mouth to speak, he was smiling at me so lovingly he just made my damn heart melt. *Jerk*.

"Okay, watch your speed," he said as I took the exit ramp, "and when you get to the end, you're going to make a left."

"Wait... why are there signs here that say rest area, Walter?"

"Oh, shit. I forgot. No, I promise we're not going to the rest area. Charlene lives on some property adjacent to the Jehovah's Witness Church, go around behind the rest area and... yeah, turn there on Houser Road."

Boy, he was lucky I trusted him with my life. My heart, too. He'd taken such good care with me, had been so patient. This driving shit was my problem.

We pulled onto a dirt road and drove through a dusty plain toward the hill until we stopped in front of a small house that was hidden quite well from the road by brush and trees. I turned off the car and exhaled. "How'd I do?"

He leaned over and kissed me. "Great, as usual. Practice will make you more confident when you take the test."

I couldn't help it—I groaned, which made him crack up.

"Don't worry, honey. As soon as you pass your driver's

test, I'm going to take you to the department's defensive driving course. Then you'll *really* learn to drive."

"Are you going to take me to firing range, too?"

His smile faltered a bit and he nodded, clearing his throat. "I'd like to. I think you'd feel more comfortable. I would too. Stacia and Steffan went when they were teenagers and it helped them feel better having guns in the house."

"Okay," I said with an exaggerated sigh. "Besides, if this music gig doesn't pan out, I'll have to have some sort of skills for when you retire. Maybe I'll go into law enforcement."

I laughed as he groaned and knocked his head back against the headrest a few times. I'd teased him a lot about what I might do for a job. He'd hated the idea of me having to work at all, but he knew I wasn't the kind of guy to sit around and be pampered. We'd have plenty of money to sustain us, but there was no way I'd stop making music, however that looked. I'd already filled up three notebooks with song lyrics and had bought myself a whole studio full of instruments, which currently filled our living room.

Walter suggested we either convert the garage to a studio or build something on the hillside below our house eventually, but he also said he loved to listen to me play, loved to come home and cook dinner while I played old and new songs for hours. We had a TV, but we barely had it on, although he'd made sure I saw *Speed* and *Roadhouse,* so I knew what he'd been talking about when he mentioned those movies. I loved every minute of them, and when the latter was over, I told him it was *definitely* time to not be nice.

The front door of the house opened and three big dogs came running out to the electric spaceship.

I hesitated before opening the door, but Walter was out of his and down on one knee as the dogs ran up and nearly tackled him. He hugged all three of them as they licked his face and ears excitedly. I hadn't been around dogs much, but watching Walter with them had me thinking... maybe I'd get him a puppy for his birthday? I'd have to consult with the kids.

The kids. It was weird, they were only technically a few years younger than me, but their lives were so different than mine had been at their age. Where they had me bested with book knowledge, they'd had very little life experience. I looked forward to spending more time with them, and I hoped that they could fully accept me as their father's companion.

A stocky woman leaning heavily on a cane came to the front door. She wore a gray ARMY t-shirt and an old pair of Levi's. Her silver hair was cropped short like Walter's. She called for the dogs to return to her as Walter came around and opened my door.

"They're big lover boys. I didn't think to ask if dogs bothered you."

I took his hand and climbed out, glad I'd tied my hair back as it was quite windy up here. And hot.

"Not if they're loving all over you."

He took my hand and gave me the kind of smile that let me know he was proud to have me on his arm.

Man, was I in love with him. And he with me.

"Charlene, I want you to meet—"

"It's about time you found him." She turned around to go back in the house, muttering under her breath while Walter laughed.

"Come on! It only took me twenty years!" He closed the door behind us and then guided me to follow her into her small kitchen. She lowered herself into a chair at a round table barely big enough for three, and she gestured for me to take the seat in front of her. The kitchen looked like the one in my mom's place back when I was a kid. There was none of the fancy gadgets Walter had brought when he moved his things into our home.

"Thank you for seeing us," Walter said. "This is D—"

"I know who he is. Tell, me, Dane Donovan the Troubadour, do you miss your talking board?"

I opened my mouth to speak... but then her words hit me. *How?*

"Honey, Charlene is a psychic. My father worked with her. He brought me to see her before I became a police officer, and I've worked with her since becoming a detective myself. What was it you told me that first visit, Charlene?"

She sighed as though she couldn't be bothered. "One hunt will take you a particularly long time, but you shall reap rewards both personal and professional. Don't give up. Don't be deterred, no matter the cost, blah blah blah. Well, I see you found who you were looking for."

"I did," Walter said, squeezing my shoulder as he sat in the chair beside me. "And I brought him to see you because—"

"You have questions," she said, directed at me.

"I... how do you know about my board?"

"I know all kinds of things. Your board is safe. It'll be around when it's time. You don't need it now, do you?"

Well, no, I hadn't needed it. The police had found several of Virgil's associates, and all had admitted to helping him under duress during the time he'd been at the halfway house. The FBI had taken over recovering the remains from the collapse of his hiding place, and while they hadn't found *him* yet, they were confident he hadn't made it out of the explosion.

I'd tried to put it out of my mind as much as possible. I'd talked with my therapist about it, and she encouraged me to focus on the things I could control, like moving forward with my life and writing music, which was coming to me like breathing. Effortless.

"I don't think so."

She nodded with a grunt. "Guess you'll be wanting to know about your friend, then. Tessalyn Miller?"

Tears stung my eyes. "Tess? You know about her?"

Charlene held out her hand. "Let me see."

I put my mostly steady hand in hers and she sucked in a breath. "You poor dear," she said, tracing my scars with her fingertips. "You were lucky. Errante Ame can certainly bring people back from the brink of death, but even with his enormous power, there are things he cannot do, I'm afraid."

"You know about the *carnival*?"

"Shhh. Tessalyn first." She closed her eyes, her face went lax, and she placed her palm over mine. Her hands were rough, as though she did a lot of work with them, but her touch was... comforting. She lifted her head and let it rest back with her chin in the air. "She sings in another dimension. She's happy with her child who never made it to this plane. A miscarriage after your disappearance. His name is Dee Dee. She tells him about you. She's young again, and at peace, once more surrounded by the friends she couldn't save in this life, but who now thrive with her presence."

"Another plane? You mean, like Heaven?"

"Eh," Charlene said, coming back to her grumpy countenance. "Not like the Christians believe. It's another existence. It's different for everyone. She was one of the good ones, though, and continues to bring light to those around her."

I wiped at my eyes with my other hand, and then Walter handed me a tissue, though he took care not to touch me.

"Thank you. I want her to be happy."

"She is. Pain and ugliness can't touch her now. She's in a better place. As for Errante Ame, there's nothing I can tell you that you don't already know, whether you recall it or not. Everything happens for a reason."

"I believe you." How could I not after everything that had happened?

She nodded at me then turned her gaze on Walter. "He's proud of you. I don't even have to reach out to him. He's always with you."

Walter's jaw ticked but that was the only reaction he showed, though I knew he was unsettled.

"He was right all along. I hate that he had to carry that burden for so long, that he..."

"He's ready to let go now. He's proud of you, and he's ready to move on. You should say goodbye."

Walter nodded and dropped his head. I heard him take in a shaky breath, and I wanted to touch him, but Charlene hadn't let go of my hand.

"It's all right, son," she said to him. "He's happy about this, too. Says you're where you're supposed to be, with who you are meant to be with. He says he loves the kids and he's proud of the father you became, no thanks to him."

"Stop," Walter said with a laugh as he wiped at his own tears. "Enough."

She smiled for the first time. "Gotcha." She put her other hand over his—and then her smile was gone. Her grip tightened almost to a painful pressure and her eyes shut. I could see them moving rapidly behind her eyelids. "Just as Dane was assisted upon his arrival, so will the two of you be required to help fellow Travelers. Will you do as you are asked?"

"Yes," Walter said without hesitation. He didn't seem as surprised by Charlene's change of demeanor as I was.

"Of course," I whispered. "Anything."

"And you both will encounter obstacles in your future. Trust each other and your friends and you shall persevere. Once the two of you are wed, your bond will be even stronger, and you will be able to withstand anything that threatens you and yours."

I gasped. I'd wondered if Walter would want to get

married again. I knew he'd had a mixed experience with it before, and I hadn't wanted to rush things—

"How soon should we take care of that?"

She relaxed and patted our hands before letting go, her trance seemingly over. "You have a little time. Talk about it. You'll be taking on each other's challenges, but then you've already done that for each other, so a little time ain't gonna make much difference. Sooner, later, it's up to you, but if it's done before shit hits the fan, you'll be stronger together."

Walter turned to me. "I'd planned on proposing; I just didn't want to rush you."

I put my hands to my face, happy tears blurring my vision. "Oh, Walter. I wasn't sure you'd want to. It's what *I* want. Whenever you're ready."

He took my hand in his and brought it up to kiss. Then he turned to Charlene. "Do you mind?"

She shrugged. "Already got the altar set up out back. Figured this might happen." She pushed herself up out of her chair with the help of her cane, and she hobbled slowly toward a sliding glass door. "Let me just light the candles."

As soon as she shut the door behind her, Walter squeezed my hand.

"Honey, we don't have to if you're not ready—"

"I'm ready whenever you are."

Walter blew out a breath and he smiled. Relieved.

"It won't be legal yet. We'll need to get a license to make it official, but it will be official to me. I love you, Dane. I want to spend the rest of our lives together."

"I want that, too. I want you, Walter."

He moved from the chair to take a knee and smiled up at me. "Dane Donovan, will you follow me out into the backyard of this creepy old house and make a covenant at her woo-woo altar before all of the universe that we'll belong to each other from here on out?"

"I thought you'd never ask. I'll follow you anywhere."

So once more I found myself beside a desert highway, but this one was hotter than Hades as the sun began to set beyond the hilltop. I found myself walking a path into the unknown, but this time I wasn't alone. This time I was beside the man who I knew would be there for me the rest of my days, however many I'd been given after stepping through the years and into a nightmare. We'd made it out the other side stronger, and I knew we would face whatever life threw at us together.

Charlene's altar was surrounded by twisted vines and stones. She said a few words we could barely make out over the winds howling along the side of the mountain. She had us drink from a silver cup, something that I knew most likely contained mind-altering substances, though Walter trusted her enough that I doubted we were in any danger. I didn't care, as long as we got to the part where she pronounced us husbands and I got to kiss him.

She held up a silver ring, said some words, and then somehow pulled the ring into two rings. She handed them to us, and we turned to face each other. I swear mine was too big when Walter slid it on my finger, but it seemed to shrink down and hug my flesh with just enough room that I didn't panic. I don't even remember what vows we made beyond loving each other for all time.

"Walter and Dane, you will move together through life from this moment on as one, no matter the distance between you, no matter what passes, and when it is time, you shall leave this plane as one. Uphold your vows to each other and to the covenant you've made to your fellow Travelers, and may peace be with you the rest of your days." Her face and voice had taken on a serene vibe throughout the short ceremony, but then she hunched over with her cane supporting her, and she coughed.

"You can kiss now."

I barked out a laugh, and Walter pulled me into his arms, pressing the sweetest kiss to my lips. I wrapped my arms around his neck and deepened the contact, desperate to show him I meant everything I'd agreed to. My heart pounded out of control with the weight of what we'd just done, although it didn't feel impulsive. It was merely the next step in our magical journey together.

When we came up for air, Charlene was already at the backdoor, leaning on her cane as she pushed the slider open.

"Thank you so much," I called out to her. "This was perfect."

She turned and nodded. "Uh-huh. When you get back to Laurel Canyon, tell those old bitties I said to stay out of trouble."

I heard her cackle as she slid the door closed behind her.

"Does she mean—"

Walter frowned and nodded. "This gives new meaning to 'we're all connected.'"

I blew out a breath and then smiled so wide my face hurt, which I figured would be my state for a while. "I can't believe we just did this."

"Believe it," Walter said. "I promise, this wasn't an ambush. I hadn't planned this at all, but to be honest, it's been on my mind."

"Mine, too," I said. "I guess she knows best?"

"I guess so. Look, we can have a wedding, we can have a party with our friends, whatever you want."

"Whatever *you* want, Walter. I got what I wanted." I pressed up on my toes and kissed him once more. "But I think you'd better drive the rest of the way. I'm not going to be able to stop looking at my ring."

He chuckled and wrapped me in his arms, picked me up, and swung me around as he kissed me once more.

"Good, because I can get us there faster, and I'm ready for our honeymoon."

We ran to the car and we waved to Charlene, who was standing at the front door to see us off. Walter held the door for me to get in on the passenger side, a habit he hadn't given up once I was safe, and then he jogged around the front of the spaceship and climbed in. He paused before pushing the button to start it.

"I love you, Dane. Thank you for saving me."

"We saved each other. I love you too. Now, drive like the wind. I want to make love to my husband."

"Your wish is my command."

Stay Tuned for More...

If you enjoyed *You Can Save Me: Carnival of Mysteries*, don't miss *You Can Do Magic* from Season One of the shared world series, and stay tuned for book three!

From the author of Foreword Indies Finalist *Summer of Hush* and BookLife Prize Quarterfinalist *Brains and Brawn* comes a contemporary gay romance with a side of time travel and magic. WINNER of the Paranormal Romance Guild's Reviewers Choice Award and FINALIST in The North Texas Romance Writers' Carolyn contest.

Musical prodigy Kallos Alexandrou has played his calliope for countless visitors at Errante Ame's Carnival of Mysteries, but his one-year residency has come to an end. Scars from a terrible tragedy in his past are the only explanation he has for his loss of speech and memory, but it's time to move on, so when a music festival sets up next to the carnival, Mr. Ame sends him off with identification, a bottomless billfold, and a set of new clothes. Outside the carnival's perimeter, Kal finds himself in an unfamiliar world surrounded by strange instruments and vibrant people like nothing he's ever seen.

Ryan Wells is the troubled and celebrated lead singer of the metal band Backdrop Silhouette. He's brought more than his share of baggage on the last cross-country Warped Tour, including harsh restrictions placed on him by his parole officer and the band's label, but it's the treatment from his band-mates that have him feeling unsettled. After a tough morning, he spots a strange young man playing carnival music on a keyboard backstage, and the sound takes him back to a partic-ularly vulnerable time in his youth. Intrigued, Ryan asks the young man's name, but he flees only to appear later as a replacement stagehand for the tour.

An invitation from the band Hush to ride on their bus gives Ryan and Kal a welcome distraction. They find the cama-raderie and support they've both been craving...as well as a little magic and a fresh new romance. But personal secrets and the music business make relationships difficult to maintain, and when the tour ends, Ryan and Kal will have to make a choice: move forward together on an uncertain path, or let fear keep them from trusting that sometimes you really *can* have everything you desire.

You Can Do Magic is part of the multi-author Carnival of Mysteries Series. Each book stands alone, but each one includes at least one visit to Errante Ame's Carnival of Myster-ies, a magical, multiverse traveling show full of unusual acts, games, and rides. The Carnival changes to suit the world it's on, so each visit is unique and special. This book contains a Depression-era calliaphone, a Ouija board with a purpose, and tour bus hijinks that will warm your heart and make you gigglesnort. Reading Summer of Hush and Brains and Brawn before this book will give you the full Warped Tour experience, but *You Can Do Magic* can be read as a standalone as well as the other books in the shared universe. Recommended 18+

Carnival of Mysteries and Up Next...

Once more we bid you Welcome, Travelers, to Errante Ame's Carnival of Mysteries! Join us for another round of fantastic, space-and-time spanning tales by a talented group of some of the best authors to be found in M/M romance. Whether you enjoy mystery, action, danger, or just sweet romance, there is something for everyone at the Carnival!

Rook's Time -- Kim Fielding
The Wrong Familiar -- Megan Derr
The Villain Who Wasn't -- Liv Rancourt
Blue Lightning -- BL Maxwell
Magic Escaping -- Kaje Harper
Light in the Darkness -- Eden Winters
You Can Save Me -- RL Merrill
Go for the Climate -- Ander C. Lark
Flames of the Arcane -- Nicole Dennis
Airs Above the Ground -- Rachel Langella
Midnight on the Midway -- Morgan Brice
Dust Bowl Magic -- Zam Maxfield
Dragonspark -- Elizabeth Silver

And coming next from R.L. Merrill... Ro joins the Road to Rocktoberfest 2024 crew with Feuds and Interludes! *Check out the blurb and pre-order today!*

From the award-winning author of *Hurricane Reese, Summer of Hush,* and *You Can Do Magic* comes a new rock star romance series inspired by legendary rock 'n' roll love affairs. *Feuds and Interludes* is a rivals-to-lovers, hurt/comfort love story complete with adorable septuagenarian lovebirds and beloved characters from Merrill's previous rock-inspired series.

Boone Collins and Shane Butler are two of rock music's brightest stars today. Their grandfathers founded a powerhouse rock supergroup that ruled the airwaves in the late 1970s, and the grandsons grew up in their shadows to become frontmen of their own successful bands. The epic rivalry between Boone and Shane is notorious, and it's about to blow up.

When Shane's grandfather Bruce inducts his deceased bandmate into the Rock Music Hall of Fame, he admits to the world that he wrote the band's biggest hit about his best friend's widow—Boone's grandmother Vera Jean. The two want to rekindle their relationship, and their grandsons are determined to keep them apart. Only, working together for a common goal reveals surprising similarities between the rock stars as well as a chemistry they cannot ignore. Shane sees behind Boone's glittery facade to the secrets he hides from his bandmates, and Boone is there to pick up the pieces when Shane's professional world implodes. Together, they plot a musical collaboration to celebrate their grandfathers' accomplishments instead of fighting—a star-studded tribute at the storied Rocktoberfest event in the Nevada desert—but will being in the spotlight prove to be too much for their fledgling romance to handle?

Feuds and Interludes is part of the multi-author Road to

Rocktoberfest 2024 series. Each book can be read as a stand-alone, but why not read them all and see what antics our bands get into next? Hot rockstars and the men who love them, what more could you ask for. Kick back, load up your kindle, and enjoy the men of Rocktoberfest!

ACKNOWLEDGMENTS

I know I bullied Ari McKay into doing a second season of Carnival of Mysteries, but I'm so glad she acquiesced! I'm so excited about this book as well as the books of my fellow carneys! A lot of history, folklore, and musical lore went into the writing of this book. Be sure to check out the blog tour posts through Other Worlds Ink for those stories, which will also be shared on my socials.

Thank you to Kim Fielding for her support in getting through what turned out to be a total wackadoo year of writing. Between her and my editor Kelli Collins, this book has had a lot of feedback and I hope it accomplishes everything I hoped it would! And a shoutout to my pal Jen Graybeal for being there when I was ready to chuck it all out the window. Thank you for always getting me unstuck! And to Amy Lane, Cari Zee, and BL Maxwell, thank you for reminding me this isn't my first rodeo and I actually can get a book finished!

Thanks to Allison for her trusty proofreading skills!

Thanks to Gloria and the folks at The Paranormal Romance Guild for helping out with our cover reveals for season two! And Dianne at Lyrical Lines, WOW have you outdone yourself! Thanks for bringing Dane to life! Huge thanks to Mark and Scott at OWI for all of your support in getting the word out and to Gay Romance Reviews for your patience.

To my pals at the Bay Area Queer Writers Association, my SBC crew, and the Kiss and Tell Salon, thanks for making space for me! I love you all.

And to my family...I love you all to the moon and back. Thanks for supporting me. I swear I'll get to all the things...

About the Author

Whether she's writing contemporary romance featuring quirky and relatable characters or diving deep into the paranormal and supernatural to give readers a shiver, R.L. Merrill loves creating compelling, diverse, and inclusive stories that will stay with readers long after. Winner of the Kathryn Hayes "When Sparks Fly" Best Contemporary award for *Hurricane Reese*, Paranormal Romance Guild's Best Rockstar Romance for *You Can Do Magic*, and Daphne DuMaurier finalist for *Connection*, Ro spends every spare moment improving her writing craft and striving to find that perfect balance between real-life and happily ever after. You can find her connecting with readers on social media, advocating for America's youth, cruising around town with Great Dane Velma, cuddling with twin black cat familiars Frankenstein and Dracula, or head-banging at a rock show near her home in the San Francisco Bay Area! Stay Tuned for more...

Newsletter: www.rlmerrillauthor.com
 Facebook: www.facebook.com/rlmerrillauthor
 Instagram: www.instagram.com/rlmerrillauthor
 TikTok: www.tiktok.com/rlmerrillauthor1342
 BookBub: www.bookbub.com/profile/r-l-merrill

ALSO BY R.L. MERRILL

Haunted Series: (Contemporary Romance)

Haunted

Fated

Bated

Jaded – (Coming Soon)

Minded Series: (Paranormal Spinoff of Haunted Series)

Minded

Blossomed

Father F'in' Christmas

A Peculiar Prom Night

Magic and Mayhem Universe: (Funny Paranormal Romance in the universe created by Robyn Peterman)

Shifted

Ghoul Me Once

Gator Me Twice

Magic and Mayhem/Shifted Collection

Fang Me Three Times

Fangtastic Four

Five Fanger Witch Punch

Hollywood Rock 'n' Romance Trilogy: (Contemporary Romance)

Teacher

Teacher: Act Two

Teacher: The Final Act

Contemporary Romance Series:

The Rock Season

Road Trip

You Fell First

The Heart Knows (Re-Releasing Soon)

A Match Made in Spain

LGBTQ Romance

Pinups and Puppies (Originally in Love Is All Vol. 2)

I Want, More – Bolder Breed Studios #1 (Originally in Love Is All Vol. 3)

Love and Pride – Bolder Breed Studios #2 (Originally in Love Is All Vol. 4)

Everything's Better With You: An MM Sports Romance

All I Wanna Do — Bolder Breed Studios #3 (Email Ro for your copy)

Under His Sheets: Accidentally Undercover – Out April 9, 2024

Feuds and Interludes: Road To Rocktoberfest 2024 - November 2024

The Banes of Lake's Crossing (Historical Horror Romance)

The Fourth Man (The Banes of Lake's Crossing) (Historical Horror Romance)

The Redemption of Nathaniel Bane

The Absolution of Jonah Bane

The Gifted Series: (Supernatural Suspense/Paranormal Romance)

Healer

Connection

Protector

Sundowners (M/M Paranormal Romance

Sundowners Book One

Sundowners Book Two (Coming Soon)

Forces of Nature Series: (Gay Contemporary Romance)

Hurricane Reese

Typhoon Toby

Earthquake Ethan

Summer of Hush Series: (Gay Contemporary Romance)

Summer of Hush

Brains and Brawn

You Can Do Magic: Carnival Of Mysteries (A Summer of Hush Tie-In)

You Can Save Me: Carnival of Mysteries (Season Two, Book Two)

Anthologies:

Thanksgiving Day Parade From Hell (Worst Holiday Ever) (Gay Contemporary Romance

Valentine's Day From Hell (Worst Valentine's Day Ever) (Gay Contemporary Romance)

Salty and Sweet (Summer Fair) (Lesbian Contemporary Romance)

The Fourth Man (The Banes of Lake's Crossing) (Historical Horror Romance)

A Piece of Him (Gone With The Dead) (Horror)

Breaking Bread—Dark Divinations from HorrorAddicts.net Press (Horror)

Exchange (Renewal) (Science Fiction)

Tap-Tap-Tap (Impact) (Horror)

Human Sacrifice (Innovation) (Horror)

The Sitter (Clarity) (Horror)

Joy Is A Phone Call Away – A More Perfect Union (Lesbian Contemporary Romance)

The House Must Fall – Haunts and Hellions from HorrorAddicts.net Press – May 2021 (Horror)

A Kept Woman – BAQWA Presents: Horror Show 2021(Lesbian Horror Romance)

Gods of Rock 'n' Roll (Free on Wattpad)

How Bittersweet is Karma? Free on Wattpad)

Let Me Stand Next To Your Fire (Queer Cheer)

Midnight in the Renaissance Elevator

Holiday Romance

A Peace Offering (Re-release)

Love and Pride – Bolder Breed Studios #2

Once Upon A Holiday Story 2024 (Coming Soon)

Audiobooks

The Rock Season (Kiss App)

Brains and Brawn (Kiss App)

Teacher (Kiss App)

Hurricane Reese (Kiss App)

A Match Made in Spain (Audible)

Healer: Gifted Book One (Audible)

Under His Sheets (Audible Coming Soon)

Non-Fiction

Horror Addicts Guide To Life Volume 2 - Edited by Emerian Rich

Death's Garden Revisited - Edited by Loren Rhoads (Out Fall 2022)

www.ingramcontent.com/pod-product-compliance
Lightning Source LLC
Chambersburg PA
CBHW051433190726
48289CB00001B/166